CON
AT
ALEXANDRIA

THE
BEACON
AT
ALEXANDRIA

✛✛✛

GILLIAN
BRADSHAW

SOHO

Published by
Soho Press, Inc.
853 Broadway
New York NY 10003

Library of Congress Cataloging-in-Publication Data

Bradshaw, Gillian, date
The beacon at Alexandria.
1. Rome—History—Empire, 284–476—Fiction. I. Title.
PS3552.R235B4   1986   813'.54   86-3017
ISBN 1-56947-010-3

Printed in the United States of America

A BIT OF HISTORY

IN THE YEAR A.D. 293, the emperor Diocletian looked at the state of his empire and found it desperate. Staggering out of a half-century of civil war, pressed by foreign enemies along the whole of the northern and the eastern frontier, torn still by civil rebellion, plagued by rampant inflation, administrative corruption, and a crumbling tax base, the Roman Empire was on the brink of collapse. Diocletian pulled it back. After vigorous campaigns against foreign and domestic enemies, he instituted a number of administrative reforms which caused the empire's citizens to refer to their age as the Diocletian Era for the next century and more. But the empire he created bore little resemblance to that formed by Caesar Augustus.

Chief among Diocletian's reforms was the division of the empire into two halves: the Greek East and the Latin West. Each of these had its own emperor, who took the title of Augustus and had his own civil and military staff. The "college" of emperors in theory acted as one. (In practice they not infrequently killed each other, but that is not to the point.) The number of provinces was increased (Britain, for example, became four provinces), and provinces were grouped in dioceses (nothing to do with the church). Thus the province "Asia" became a section of the coast of Asia Minor, and was in the diocese of Asiana. Civilian provincial governors were joined by regional military commanders who bore the title of "comes" or "dux" — commonly rendered here as "count" and "duke," though this is a bit misleading because the offices were not hereditary.

Diocletian's eventual successor, Constantine, further altered the face of the empire by instituting more administrative and financial reforms, by founding a new capital for the East (which he named, with typical self-effacement, Constantinople), and by favoring the (comparatively) new religion of Christianity, which Diocletian had tried to stamp out. Christianity moved within a generation from being the faith of a persecuted minority to being the official faith of the Roman world. The shock to the church was enormous, caused an immediate outbreak of heresies, and left scars that persist to our own day. But the new faith caught on. Constantine was baptized on his deathbed, and his three sons (Constans, Constantine II, and Constantius) were all Christians. Their successor, Julian the Apostate, attempted to reinstate paganism, but met with only limited success before his early death during a campaign against the Persians.

Following the death of Julian, the army elected Jovian (another Christian) as emperor; when he died shortly thereafter, in February 364, Valentinian, a Christian army officer from Pannonia, was chosen. Valentinian took command of the Western Empire, leaving his brother Valens to rule the East.

The historical events that form the background for this novel took place between 371 and 378: I have somewhat distorted the chronology, and slipped in a couple of extra years. I apologize to the purists for this liberty, but I can't say I find it significant. The historical background may be tolerably accurate, and many of the characters are based on real people, but the central events and characters of this novel are my own invention. I wrote it for fun, and in the hope that others would enjoy it.

I apologize also for the chaotic spelling of proper names. The old tradition was to transliterate Greek names into Latin spellings; the new tradition is to put at least some of them into English spellings. I have followed the new tradition, except where there is some chance that the name will be familiar to my readers. My motive for doing this is not pure pedantry. I doubt that the general reader can tell a transliterated Greek name from a native Latin one, and I thought that this must obscure the considerable cultural diversity that marked the later Roman Empire. But the situation is complicated by the fact that in the late empire, there were plenty of prominent individuals with names neither Greek nor Latin but Persian or Gothic or Alamannic or Syriac or even Judeo-Christian, and it is very hard to know what to do with them. I'm afraid that I gave up on system and simply chose the form of name I liked most.

Finally, a word of special pleading. Scholars of the period will not need me to tell them of the debt I owe the historian Ammianus Marcellinus: it shouts itself from all the most accurate bits of this piece of fiction. Unfortunately, nonscholars are unlikely even to have heard of this writer. The last English translation printed was, as far as I can work out, C. D. Yonge's in 1862. This is shocking treatment for a writer generally acknowledged as one of the finest historians of antiquity, who is not only honest, intelligent, and comprehensive but vivid and forceful, elegant and witty as well. Ammianus, like the period he describes, deserves more attention.

I

EPHESUS

THE BIRD HAD DIED. It lay on its side in the bottom of the wicker basket, its eyes glazed and shrunken in its head. Its feathers still felt warm when I touched them. But it was a warm day.

I'd found the bird at the bottom of the garden wall. It had a broken wing, and sat under the wall with its beak agape, panting. It didn't stir itself much even when I picked it up. I guessed that some boy in the street beyond the wall had thrown a stone at it.

I splinted its wing very carefully, extending it first and then wrapping it crosswise with linen over wool, compressing the material a little over the head of the joint, as Hippocrates recommends. Hippocrates says that people should have a light diet while recovering from a fracture, and can be dosed with hellebore; but I didn't have any hellebore, and anyway I didn't know the correct dose for a bird. So I gave it a drink of water and fed it some bread and milk. I put it in a basket, together with some more water, in the loft of the stable, where the hay was kept, and gave Philoxenos, the groom, a present so that he wouldn't tell anyone about it. My nurse, Maia, didn't like me playing doctor, particularly to common field birds and animals. "You are a young lady, Charis," she would say. "You are the daughter of the clarsisimist Theodoros of Ephesus, and I expect you to behave like it!" She meant *clarissimus*. That's a Latin title; I think it means something like "very brilliant," which is a silly sort of thing to call a man like my father, who was really only interested in horse racing and Homer. But it only meant that he was of consular rank and important in the province. Maia never could say any Latin word properly, not even titles, and she loved titles. "My master is His Excellency Theodoros of Ephesus," she would tell the people in the market, "clarsisimist and consular. He was governor of Syria and of Galatia and held the rank of consul at Constantinople — and you

3

want to overcharge *me* for a yard of dirty woolens? Off with you!"

Behaving like the daughter of Theodoros of Ephesus meant wearing long dresses with purple stripes on the hem and gold embroidery on the cloak, and never, ever getting them dirty; having my hair curled and piled up to make it look fashionable, and trying to keep it that way; looking at the floor if a strange man was present; and keeping my mouth shut. It also meant not playing doctor. But I was allowed to read Hippocrates. Well, to be more exact, no one objected when I read Hippocrates. Maia couldn't read, and thought it ladylike to read anything; my father never knew or cared what I read, so long as I knew my Homer; and Ischyras, my tutor, loved Hippocrates. Not that he was interested in medicine. "Pure Ionic!" he would exclaim delightedly when we read some passage about vomiting. "It's as good as Herodotos: voh-meet-ing! Such lovely long vowels, so musical!" He never seemed to notice what was being said, only the style it was being said in. Once I suggested that we read some Galen, and he was shocked. "Galen! That Alexandrian quack! Why, he writes almost in the common speech, like a tradesman, not a scholar. No, no, my dear, let us leave science to tradesmen. We shall read something elevated, something in a beautiful style." I could have pointed out that Hippocrates had written in the common speech of his day, and that it was just luck that this happened to be a beautiful Ionic dialect rather than our own Koine. But I considered myself lucky to be reading him at all, and kept my mouth shut. So we read Hippocrates, bless his beautiful Ionic vowels, and I played doctor on the sly, with injured songbirds and lapdogs, and tried to keep my dresses clean. My brother, Thorion, kept promising to copy some Galen for me in the Celsian Library, but he never did.

I had brought another dish of bread and milk for my thrush. I'd have to feed it to the guard dog now: taking it back into the house would lead to too many questions. I was very sad that the bird had died. Death is sad, even the death of a bird, and I wished I hadn't tormented the poor creature with my splinting first. But I couldn't have known that it would die. And why had it died? It had seemed to be perking up when I had left it.

I picked the bird up and examined it. There was no swelling in the wing, so I hadn't got the dressing too tight. Unless birds don't swell the way people do. Most likely, though, the stone that broke the bird's wing had damaged it inside as well. There was a little dried blood around the bird's nose. It hadn't moved its bowels, so I couldn't tell anything from that. I'd know what was wrong if I did a dissection.

4

But I'd need some good sharp knives for that, somewhere to work where I was sure not to be interrupted, and something to cover my dress with. In other words, I needed the help of my brother.

I put the dead thrush back in the basket and climbed down the ladder from the loft. No one was in the stable, except the horses. I took my cloak off and picked all the straw off it, then put it on again and walked out into the yard. Philoxenos was there, exercising a pair of my father's racehorses on a lead rein. He nodded when I came out. "Fed your pet, then, young mistress?" he asked.

I shook my head. "It died."

"Phew," he said sympathetically. Philoxenos liked animals; horses in particular, but animals in general. He knew a lot about them too, together with all sorts of remedies for hoof galls and sprained joints. He saw nothing odd about splinting a field bird's wing. But he was a practical man. "Do you want it cooked?" he asked me. "Nice braised with honey, thrushes are. My wife could do it for you."

"No, thank you. Not yet, anyway. Could you please not touch it until this evening?"

He smiled and nodded. He assumed that I was just squeamish about eating a bird I'd made a pet of. I didn't want to tell him that I meant to dissect it: he'd see no point in that, and he always got very annoyed when his masters behaved unreasonably.

The horses had stopped their trotting and were standing with their heads down, nuzzling the gravel for stray wisps of hay to eat. Philoxenos turned his attention back to them; he cracked his whip and shook the lead rein. They started off — in different directions. Philoxenos swore at them and pulled them together again, coaxing and easing the reins until they trotted together in a circle. I went on toward the house.

Our house was by the northeast edge of Ephesus, where the land rises in the hill called Mount Pion. It actually straddled the city wall, which ran through the back garden. We had a gate set into the wall, so that we could go through it to the stables outside. Thinking back on it now, all these years later with the world changed, it seems extraordinary: a private gentleman knocking a gate into the city wall so that he wouldn't have to go through the streets to see his racehorses. What if the city came under siege? Even at the time, the city council and the army dukes who stayed in Ephesus didn't like our postern, but whenever they mentioned it to my father he just smiled and said he couldn't keep his horses properly if he couldn't reach them from his house. "And really, Your Excellency," he would add, if it was a duke, "what's the use of Ephesus having a wall anyway? There's not going to be a war *here*, is there, eh? And even if there were, with *you* in charge, the enemy would never come anywhere *near* the city. No, no, you leave my little gate alone!"

The house was at the end of its street. It had a marble front, but otherwise didn't look very impressive — viewed from the street. But from the back it sprawled magnificently down the hillside. I stood in the postern for a moment, looking at it. It was a bright, sunny spring day. Behind me the hillside was green and hot, and the sky was still the intense moist blue of spring, not yet faded with the summer heat. The horses, two matched black mares, circled the gravel yard behind me, in step now, their coats shining in the light, their hooves crunching the stones, with Philoxenos crooning at them. The gateway was dark and cool, the stone damp to the touch. Ahead of me the kitchen garden and the whitewashed plaster and red tile roofs of the back of the house seemed to shine: deep green, vivid white, blood red. Rising beyond them was the dome that hung over the central part of the house, painted a light green, like a bird's egg suspended against the blue sky. It was a whim of my grandfather's to build a house with a domed banquet room, like a palace; my grandfather had inflated ideas of his own importance. But it was a beautiful house. It had five courtyards, two colonnaded, three with fountains; it had a separate bathhouse and a separate bakery; it had nearly a hundred rooms, with tiled floors and painted walls, hypocausts to keep it warm in winter and gardens to help cool it in the summer.

It was not an old house. My great-grandfather had acquired the fortune that founded it. He was the owner of a fair-sized farm in the valley eastward, and he profiteered in the sale of its produce during the civil wars, then succeeded in backing the right emperor, proved himself an exceptionally competent administrator, and profiteered further from imperial appointments. My grandfather finished the house and consolidated the fortune: more farms were added to the first, with vineyards and olive groves, wheatfields and orchards, but particularly stud farms to breed racehorses. He left my father one of the largest estates in the province. So my father now passed as a man of established and noble lineage. Well, three generations of wealth is more than the emperors themselves can claim. The father of Their Sacred Majesties, Our Lords the Augusti Valens and Valentinian, was a common soldier from Pannonia.

I went into the house and looked for my brother Thorion.

Thorion was really called Theodoros, like our father, but when he

6

had been five and called me Charition, "little Charis," in a superior fashion, I had called him Thorion back; I was too small then to say Theodorion. He was seventeen, more than a year older than I, and he was supposed to be grown up, while I was still considered a child. Boys are allowed more freedom than girls anyway. When we were both small we used to play together, spying on the household slaves and stealing from the kitchen. When we had to study, I helped Thorion out with his reading — he was never very good at books, though he'd inherited our grandfather's sense about money. So when he finished school and was given his own room and an allowance and three slaves and his own carriage, it was as though the privileges were given to me too. That was how I saw it, anyway, and Thorion, after some protests, usually agreed.

I found Thorion in the Blue Court, studying Latin. The Blue Court was called that because of the fountain in it, which was covered with blue tiles and a mosaic of dolphins; it also had a plane tree to sit under, and it was light and cool in the hottest weather. Thorion was sitting on the ground beside the fountain, scowling at his tablet and chewing on his stylus. He'd taken his cloak off and his green tunic was halfway up his thighs: if Maia saw him, she'd be furious. "Theodoros son of Theodoros!" I exclaimed, imitating her. "Look at you, a nobleman of an ancient line, sitting on the ground in your tunic like a peasant, and chewing your stylus! I'm —"

Thorion threw his tablet at me. I caught it. "Shut up and help me," he said. "What's the plural of *magister militum?*"

"*Magistri militum,*" I said, after thinking for a moment.

"Not *milita?*"

"No. They're already plural, aren't they? Master of arms, masters of arms?"

"Don't ask me," said Thorion. He hated Latin. Our old tutor Ischyras hated it too. "That the world should come to this!" he'd lament. "A Hellene of noble family, studying a barbarian language!" But the law uses Latin, and if you want to get anywhere in the imperial administration, you have to know it. Thorion wanted to get somewhere in the administration. "Father does nothing but spend money," he would say in disgust. "Horse racing and magistracies! I'm going to court to *earn* some. You can get thirty pounds in gold just for recommending somebody as a notary!" He talked Father into arranging lessons for him with the local professor of Latin and law, and dragged me into learning it too, to explain it to him. "You're good at book-learning," he told me.

7

"Have you copied that Galen for me?" I asked him. I knew he hadn't, but I'd be in a better position to get his help with the dissection when he admitted it.

He bit his stylus and jerked his head back: no. That was another peasant habit Maia detested. But Thorion had a lot of peasant in him. He was already big for his age, very wide across the shoulders, with big hands, and his teeth were crooked. His hair was as black as mine, but his curled naturally, while mine had to be fixed with curling irons all the time — unfair. He was said to look exactly like our grandfather. I took after our mother: tall, thin, and bony, with big eyes. "She was such a *lady!*" all the house slaves said. "So delicate, so polite!" But she had died of childbed fever the week after giving birth to me, so I couldn't judge of this. I'd rather take after Grandfather.

"Can I use your room for a bit?" I asked. "And your knives?"

Thorion scowled. "Did it die?" he asked. He knew about the thrush, of course; I'd shown it to him after I splinted the wing, and he'd been impressed by the splint, though really he thought that thrushes were better braised with honey.

"I wouldn't be asking for knives if it were alive, would I?"

"I don't know. You could have found something dead."

"Well, I didn't. I want to see why the thrush died."

Thorion scowled again. "What's the point of that? I can understand wanting to make an animal better, but cutting it up after it's dead . . ."

Thorion and I had had this argument before, but I sighed and repeated my usual points. "If I understand why it died, I'll be in a better position to help next time."

"What next time? The bird's dead!"

"The next bird. Or the next animal."

"Or the next person? Would you chop people up to see why they died?"

"The surgeons in the school of medicine at Alexandria do that. It helps them to treat diseases if they know how the body works. Galen did that."

"I won't copy that bit of Galen, then," said Thorion. "And what the doctors in Alexandria do isn't the point, Charition. You're not a doctor."

"I can study medicine if I want, though."

"You shouldn't. It's not proper for a woman. For a lady."

"Sitting on the ground studying Latin isn't gentlemanly. But you do it."

"That's different. I'm a man. I can do what I want."

I snorted. "Well, when I'm a grown woman, and married, I'll be able to do what I want. And I'll be the doctor for my own household. It'll save my husband money."

"What man would want to marry a doctor?" asked Thorion, but without conviction. Saving money was always a powerful argument for him. "You'll have to do as your husband says," he added halfheartedly.

"Can I use your room, Thorion, please?" I asked. "I'll clean up when I've finished, I promise."

"I wish you could use your own room."

"I wish I *had* my own room. But you know Maia will spot what I've been up to, even if I do it while she's out. But you won't find a trace of it, Thorion, I promise."

"Oh, very well," said Thorion. "The knives are in the case in the middle of the clothes chest." He scratched moodily at the plaster between two tiles of the fountain.

"Thank you," I said. I went over, handed him his tablet, and kissed him. "I knew you'd help."

He grunted and said, "Be careful. I'm afraid that someone will catch you at it and accuse you of black magic. Or worse, accuse *me* of black magic."

"Is anyone likely to come in?" I asked. There'd been a scare in Ephesus over black magic recently: a charioteer at the racecourse had been found to have worked curses against three of his rivals, including one of my father's drivers. My father's man became sick, and didn't recover till a crucified toad was discovered and removed from the hypocaust under his bedroom. I'd been very surprised at this: personally, I'd thought the man was suffering from an enteritic fever. But charioteers are always working magic. My father's man always looked very knowing when the subject was mentioned, though he wouldn't talk about it, and it was said that he had himself killed several rivals either by magic or by poisoning. Certainly anyone found in our house mutilating the body of a small animal would be accused instantly, even if she was the daughter of the house.

Thorion shrugged. "Father's got some visitor, someone important, I think. All the slaves are rushing about fetching things for his staff. No, I suppose my room's safe for you. But bolt the door, will you?"

I nodded and ran back through the house. The slaves were busy; I had to scramble out of the way of two of the houseboys who were carrying a table down one of the corridors, and when I went through the kitchens, half the household seemed to be there, discussing the visitor and what to do with his staff. Perhaps it wasn't such a good time for a dissection. On the other hand, it was likely that no one would go near Thorion's room at such a time. And I ought to do the dissection quickly, while the body was still fresh. Then I could pluck it and give it to Philoxenos to cook, and he'd just think I'd been helpful.

When I got back to the stableyard, Philoxenos had put the mares in their stalls and was rubbing them down. He didn't even notice when I went up to the hayloft and picked up the thrush. I put the bird in the belt purse Father had given me. It was a good-sized leather purse, this, and besides being of a useful size, it had a set of cosmetic tools in it. My father had given it to me at the last festival, when two of our chariots won in the races; I'd told him that it was the best present I'd ever been given, and I meant it. The cosmetic tools — the tweezers, the little probes used for applying eyeliner, the little razor on its stem — doubled perfectly as surgical instruments. All I lacked were the larger knives. The only nuisance was occasionally having to use my tools for cosmetics.

I climbed back down the ladder, picked the straw off myself again, checked my hair, and went back into the house. There was less bustle now: the visitor and his staff had been catered for, and the house could relax. I wondered idly who it was: someone important, judging from the stir. But my father had lots of important friends, and they visited frequently and discussed who was entering what in the next festival's races, so I wasn't more than idly curious.

I was in the corridor where both Thorion and I had rooms, when the door of the room I shared with my nurse opened and Maia came out. "There you are!" she exclaimed triumphantly. "Where have you been this last hour? I've been looking for you."

Damn. "I was down at the stables," I said truthfully. "I was watching Philoxenos work. Then I helped Thorion with his Latin."

"Helped Thorion indeed! It's most improper for you to be looking at his old Latin, stupid barbarian tongue as it is. You have straw in your hair; what were you doing, lying in the straw to watch the horses? Most improper!" She pulled the "straw" out; it was a piece of chaff that only she would have spotted.

Maia's real name was Elpis, "Hope." She was a devout Christian and fond of her name. But all children call their nursemaids Maia, and I could never think of her as anything else. She was a thin, bony woman, with arms like leather bands and straight red hair, now graying. Her father had been a Scythian barbarian, captured in some war, and her mother was the domestic slave of an Ephesian merchant; her ideas about propriety were her own. She was fond of telling me the story of how Father had bought her and she had come to our house. "There was my husband, dead of the pneumonia," she'd say. "And there was my little baby boy, just a month old, dead too, and there I was, sitting in the kitchen and weeping my eyes out, and who comes in but my master and your most noble father? 'There she is,' says my old master, and I sat up and tried to pull myself together, for it isn't proper to go weeping and wailing in front of people, especially gentlemen. Then I see that your most generous father is in mourning too, all dressed in black. 'Her child died just two days ago,' says my old master, 'but that was the fever; it's been very bad, very bad' — and the dear Lord knows it was bad that summer. 'Elpis was a good mother,' says my master, 'and a good servant too, and I'd not part with her lightly, but because I so esteem Your Excellency, I will sell her to you.' And your most illustrious father looks at me and says, 'Well then, Elpis, I need a nursemaid for my daughter; can you care for a young lady properly? She's just a week old; she's been passed about among the house slaves, but she needs someone to look after her properly, someone to attend to her alone, for she's lost her mother. My dear wife's dead.' So I said — I don't know what, that I'd do my best, and your excellent father bought me for sixty *solidi*. 'Money's no object,' he said. And I packed up my things and went back with him, in his own carriage. Well, what was there to keep me where I was? Though I did wonder what would become of me. And when I saw this great house, like an imperial palace, and all the slaves — hundreds, it seemed to me — phew, I was frightened. But your father himself brought me to our room, and when we got there, there was old Melissa walking you back and forth, and you screaming your little head off: nobody'd enough milk for you, had they? But it was as though you were mourning your mother's death. Tiny little thing you were, my dear, all bones, and red as a cherry. My heart went out to you. I always wanted a little daughter. I went straight over and took you from Melissa and sat down and nursed you, and when you settled down and clung to me with your little fingers, bless you, I knew I was home."

In time Maia had become Thorion's nurse as well (the previous

11

one drank too much, and Father retired her to the farm, where it didn't matter). She had considerable power in the household, because of her position as guardian of her master's children, and because of her native acuteness — for she was a sharp-eyed, sharp-minded woman who missed nothing. A less honest woman might have tried to amass a fortune by selling her influence or by petty theft; a more frivolous woman might have tried for the position of my father's concubine; but Maia adored propriety; she reveled in it. The sight of Thorion and me, scrubbed and curled and sporting our purple-striped cloaks, made her cluck her tongue in an ecstasy of pride. She liked to go to church with us and sit between us at the front, where everyone could see us. (Our family had been Christian, but not devout, since my grandfather was young. Grandfather converted because he saw that Christians got preferment at court; he died of rage when the emperor Julian assumed the purple and preferred pagans instead.) The possibility of showing us off before important, titled visitors made her sharp eyes dance with delight. For our part, of course, Thorion and I cringed whenever she had that light in her eyes. She had it now.

"You must put on another dress, my love," Maia told me, bright-eyed with pleasure. "Your most noble father has a visitor, a very distinguished visitor, and he wants to present you and Lord Theodoros to him." (Since Thorion had come of age she always called him Lord Theodoros; in the marketplace she even added "His Excellency" and "the most noble" and so on — though I'm sure she still thought of him as Thorion, really.)

I wondered what I could do about my thrush. With any luck, Maia wouldn't look in the purse. Should I give up my attempt at a dissection? That was probably the wisest thing. I could drop the body in one of the courtyards, if I couldn't get it back to the stables: a dead bird isn't that suspicious in a courtyard. I wished the visitor in Hell, whoever he was, and let Maia pull me into our room and choose a new dress for me, and rearrange my hair, and give me a better pair of earrings. "There!" she said. "The loveliest young lady in Ephesus!" And she held out a mirror for me to admire myself in.

I never admired the effect as much as she did. A thin, big-eyed face, elaborate black curls, and gold and pearl earrings — the earrings more impressive than the face, really. I never really felt that the girl I saw in mirrors, the demurely proper, overdressed doll, was *me*. I was fifteen, just in the middle of puberty, and the changes in my body seemed to make it even less mine. I could see myself at age twenty, married to some gentleman, doctoring his household, but I could never visualize myself getting married. I knew it would happen, but it would happen to the girl in the mirror, not to me. I would have to wait a bit longer before I lived my own life.

I nodded and smiled at Maia, and she put down the mirror and clapped her hands together. "Well," she said contentedly, "I'll bring you in to see the gentlemen."

"The gentlemen" were in the Charioteer Room. This was my father's favorite room for receiving visitors. It was on the first courtyard, which was colonnaded and had a fountain in it. Coming from the street, one walked around the colonnade to reach the room, thus getting an impression of the size and richness of the house before greeting its master. The room was called after its floor mosaic, which showed a four-horse chariot in full career, its driver garlanded with laurels. Officially it was a picture of Achilles, but it looked very like my father's champion driver, Daniel, and his best team, of bays. Father was very pleased with it; he had commissioned it himself — one of the few times when he had altered the design of my grandfather's house.

The room was large, well lit by its windows on the court. Its walls were decorated with patterns of trees and birds and hung with embroidered curtains; it had some paintings in it as well, mostly of horses. It had four couches, a large table for wine and some smaller ones for cups and bowls, and a brazier to warm the water to mix with the wine.

Maia and I came not through the courtyard but through the corridor from the back of the house. There were soldiers outside the door of the Charioteer Room, huge men in trousers, boots, and military cloaks. They had swords, and when Maia reached for the door, one of them put his hand on his sword and told her to stop. "What do you think you're doing?" he asked with a sneer.

Maia pulled herself up. She assumed, as I did, that the visitor must be a count or master of arms, and that his bodyguard was being overzealous — as indeed soldiers often are, contemptuous as they are of civilians, especially Asians, whom they despise as soft. "Mind your tongue," Maia told the soldier. "This is the lady Charis, daughter of the most excellent Lord Theodoros; His Eminence has sent for her, to present her to your master." She stressed the word *master*: she and I were going to go see the gentlemen, and not stand about chatting with subordinates.

The soldier sneered again, and stared at me. I was not used to such stares — hostile, curious, assessing. I felt a slight coldness suddenly, a feeling of shock. I pulled my cloak up and held it over my face. I was for once glad of the maidenly modesty that meant I did not have to meet the stare but could look away and try to think. Something was wrong. Bodyguards might be insolent, but they would not stare that way at a nobleman's young daughter unless something had happened to the nobleman.

"Present her to my master," said the soldier sardonically. "Well, well, very generous of your master, you old bitch. The governor likes presents like that." For a moment Maia was too shocked to do anything; then she pulled her thin shoulders back and looked ready to spit on the soldier and tell him that she would see him whipped for his insolence. But he laughed and moved away from the door. "Go on then," he told her.

She gave him a furious look and opened the door, stood aside to usher me in, then gave him another look before going in and closing the door. I knew she was resolving to complain of him as soon as she got the chance.

She didn't get the chance. It was plain as soon as we came into the room that something was indeed wrong. My father was standing in the middle of the room, on top of the chariot mosaic, and he was wringing his hands. Thorion was already there; he was standing by one of the windows, looking upset. Next to him were our tutor Ischyras and Johannes the steward, and they looked equally distressed. Everyone else in the room was a stranger to me; half of them were soldiers of some sort, the rest had the look of court officials. Through the open windows I could see that the courtyard was full of more soldiers and officials.

"But why?" wailed my father, without glancing at Maia and me. He addressed his question to a large man who was sitting on the best couch, drinking some of my father's wine.

"Because your name is Theodoros," said the man. "If you are innocent, you have nothing to fear. But justice must be served; there must be an investigation. The charges are extremely serious."

This man was wearing the purple-striped cloak of the senatorial rank. The cloak itself was green brocade, very richly woven in a leaf pattern, and his green tunic was long, almost to his feet: the dress of a man of rank. He was about my father's age, tall, stout, with a florid complexion. His chin was shadowy with stubble, but his hair was unusually fair, almost white, and he had blue eyes. He spoke with an accent I had never heard before, a sort of nasal slurring, and sometimes hesitated before his words, as though Greek was not his native tongue. He wore around his neck a chain laden with official signets.

"But . . ." said my father, and had to stop because the word came out in an undignified squeak. The stranger watched him with amusement. Normally Father looked well bred, refined, lankily graceful — he was a tall man, very thin, with brown hair going bald on top and large hands. But now he looked a pathetic clown. His Adam's apple stuck out as he swallowed several times, trying to control his voice. He was wearing his best cloak, of white and gold with its own purple stripe, but in his agitation it had slipped over one sharp shoulder and hitched up on the opposite side, showing his thin, hairy shanks under his blue tunic. His hands were shaking; realizing this, he pressed them together and again began to wring them. I had not realized that distress could make a man ridiculous.

"But I have done nothing to deserve such suspicions!" my father protested at last. "No one has been more loyal to Their Sacred Majesties than I have! I have fulfilled all my duties as a citizen and a loyal subject; I have been magistrate of Ephesus five times in the last eight years; I have paid for I don't know how many races; I've contributed money to the repair of the public baths and the aqueduct and the dredging of the harbor; I've —"

"You have done a great deal to win the affections of your fellow citizens," the stranger put in smoothly. "But His Sacred Majesty, our illustrious and most illustrious lord, Valens the Augustus" — and he rolled the emperor's titles off his tongue with relish, as though chewing a sweetmeat — "is curious to know why you have done this."

My father stood still, opening and closing his mouth like a fish. His expenditure on magistracies and horse racing had always been his great defense when anyone questioned him about, say, our postern. He had never conceived that anyone might interpret it as a deliberate and calculated bid for popularity. He was popular, of course. Few other gentlemen in Ephesus were eager to take the position of municipal magistrate, entailing as it did the vast cost of maintaining the public baths and entertaining the public with chariot races on feast days, and they were pleased that my father relieved them of the necessity. The public, of course, drank his health freely and cheered him whenever he appeared : the most excellent Theodoros, master of the races! They were as keen on racing as my father was.

"I . . . I am just a public-spirited citizen," said Father pathetically, "seeking the good of my city. And I like racing."

"Perhaps." The other sat up on his couch, putting down the wine. "Perhaps. We shall see. What did you do when the pretender Procopius attempted to claim the imperial purple?"

"I? What could I do? I stayed in my house like an honest man."

This was true as far as it went, which wasn't very far. He'd sympathized with the pretender, who had been a man of the noblest lineage — my father fancied himself an aristocrat. When Procopius had gained control of the province, my father had in fact debated with his friends whether they should go up to court and offer the pretender their best wishes. But they had decided to see which way the wind blew, first — a fortunate decision, since Procopius had been defeated by the emperor Valens a few months later.

"Indeed? You did not drink the pretender's health and swear that he, a cousin of the emperor Constantius, would make a finer emperor than the son of a Pannonian peasant?"

"No! No, of course not." My father swallowed again. Perhaps he had, I thought. But surely the emperor wouldn't accuse a man of treason on the strength of that alone? Most wealthy men in the eastern provinces of the empire had done just the same. And the whole issue was a dead horse now: no use flogging it.

But the stranger had not finished. "You were a friend of Euserios, the former governor of this province," he stated. Not "His Excellency Lord Euserios," not "the most distinguished clarissimus Euserios." Euserios was plainly in trouble.

"Yes. That is, I knew him. Of course, Your Excellency, I knew him; he resided here in Ephesus two years ago: how could I, as an ex-governor and a leading citizen of the metropolis, not know him? But I have not seen him since then, Your Excellency; we were not particularly friendly."

"You have corresponded with him."

"No! Nothing to speak of, anyway, just letters of recommendation for a few young men who wanted a place on his staff. I hope he has done nothing wrong; I am sure he meant no ill . . ." My father stopped, sweating. I could just remember Euserios, a plump, cheerful man and a competent governor, toasting my father's latest triumph at the hippodrome.

"He is dead," the other returned. "Strangled. After torture."

My father went white. He sat down heavily on the nearest couch. Maia hurried from my side, caught up a wine cup and gave my father something to drink, pulled his cloak straight, fanned him. I felt sick.

I had not felt particularly frightened before this. I knew that the stranger was being unpleasant and that my father was upset, but I believed that nothing would happen: not to my father, not to Theodoros of Ephesus, master of the races. But if it could happen to Euserios, it could happen to anyone. Tortured. Ordinarily, people of Euserios' rank could not be tortured. For the law that protected them to be suspended meant that there must be a real and very large conspiracy against the emperor. And the cruelty of Their Sacred Majesties was legendary. Every trace of treason would be pursued with the utmost severity.

"You also knew my predecessor Eutropios," said the stranger. Eutropios had been the previous year's governor, so this must be the current one. The soldier had spoken literally, referring to him as "the governor." What was his name? Festinus, I remembered. A Latin, a westerner from the unimaginably distant province of Gaul. There had been considerable gossip about him: "An absolute *nobody*," Maia had told Ischyras in disgust. "Scarcely more distinguished than I am myself as to family; but he was lucky enough to go to school with powerful friends, and now he's left the West and come here, the plague."

My father jumped. "Yes. Yes, but how could I *not* know the governor of Asia? When he lives here in Ephesus? I hope Eutropios —"

"He is under suspicion," Festinus said; he seemed displeased that it was only suspicion. "But Euserios was in the thick of it." He stood up and poured himself some more wine. "This is excellent," he said, sipping it and taking his seat again. "You are to be congratulated on your vineyards."

My father gave him an anguished look; Festinus smiled. Maia fanned my father some more, not looking at the governor, and Festinus indicated her with a nod of his head. "Who's the slave? When did she come in?"

My father took a gulp of the wine Maia had offered him. "She's the nurse of my children," he said. "My daughter, Charis; my son, Theodoros." He indicated us with a limp hand. Festinus looked at each of us carefully, smiling. His teeth were very white in his reddened face.

"Your Excellency," said Thorion boldly, "my father is no traitor."

"I hope not," said Festinus. "Did this slave, and the young lady, go out after coming in?"

"No, Your Excellency," Maia said, bowing her head and still not looking at Festinus. Her tone was very respectful, but the voice scarcely seemed hers. "We came in just now; no one has been out. I believe your guards would not let them by if they tried."

The governor nodded. "Good. No one has been told to hide anything." He nodded again to one of the other officials. "Tell them to start searching the house." He looked back at my father. "Give him all the keys."

"Johannes," said my father to his steward, in a broken voice. "You have the keys; go with this gentleman and do as he says."

"Your private keys as well," insisted Festinus.

My father stared at him wretchedly, then very slowly pulled from his tunic the thong that held the keys to his storechest and writing desk. He stared at them for a moment. Johannes the steward came over and held out his hand for them, looking as miserable about it as Father himself. Father dropped them into his outstretched palm. Johannes went over to the official the governor had indicated.

The official bowed to Father and Festinus, nodded to some of the soldiers, and went out into the courtyard. The crowd there began to disperse, going off to ransack the place for evidence of treachery. When they had finished that, I realized, they would torture the slaves. Then, if any evidence turned up, or if any of the household said anything, true or false, while on the rack, they would torture my father, execute him if he confessed — and he would confess anything under torture — and confiscate his estates. I felt myself starting to shake; I pulled my cloak over my head and chewed on the edge of it. Thorion came over and put his arm around me. He whispered into my ear what must have seemed like words of comfort; what he actually said was "What did you do with the bird?"

That stopped my panic. If the men found the mutilated corpse of a small bird in Thorion's room, he would certainly be accused of black magic, and black magic and treason go together like salt and vinegar. I patted the leather cosmetics purse at my belt and Thorion gave a faint gasp of relief. "This is all nonsense," he told me, a bit louder, not minding if Festinus heard this. "They won't find anything, and they'll go away again. You can't convict a man of treason because he knew one of the traitors socially two years ago."

Festinus did hear it; he glanced over at us and smiled again. "Ah, but there's more to it than that," he said. He seemed to be enjoying this. He took another sip of wine. My father stirred himself and looked at him. "I said the reason was that your name was Theodoros," Festinus went on, looking at Father again. "The conspiracy which Heaven

18

has mercifully uncovered would have made a Theodoros emperor."

"I know nothing about it," said Father.

"The conspirators weren't thinking of you," Festinus admitted. "They wished to give the purple to Theodoros the Notary. But another Theodoros might have been meant. The oracle wasn't clear." Everyone stared at him and he took another sip of wine. He *was* enjoying it. I had no idea, then, who Theodoros the Notary was: I found out later that he was a wealthy nobleman of far greater distinction than my poor father. But what riveted everyone was the mention of an oracle. All the ancient oracles were silent, either, as the church maintained, because the coming of Christ had robbed them of their power, or, as the pagans claimed, because the Christians interfered with them and because the weakness of the priesthood meant they had become unreliable.

"A few months ago," Festinus said in a leisurely fashion, "it happened that a couple of poisoners and magicians, Palladios and Heliodoros by name, were brought into court on an insignificant charge. To save themselves the torture, they promised to inform the court of a far more serious matter which they knew of — professionally. For it seems that Fidustius, Pergamios, and Irenaios, all courtiers and noblemen of great distinction" — he looked ironically at my father —"had by secret and detestable arts learned the name of the man who will succeed our most glorious and beloved Lord Valens."

Festinus surveyed us all again with his cool blue eyes. I stopped chewing on my cloak and stared back, thanking Heaven and good luck that I still had the bird's body. They were unlikely to search me personally; it should be safe. But any evidence of magic now, and we'd all be strangled. I worried suddenly about my father's champion charioteer. Well, at least he was a free man, not a slave, and had his own house in the town, thank God. They might search him, they might find God knows what; but they couldn't prove that we knew anything.

"Fidustius happened to be at court in Antioch when this happened," Festinus went on. "He was tortured, and revealed all he knew. With the aid of two *nobly born* magicians" — again the ironic smile, this time directed at Thorion and me — "the conspirators had constructed an oracle like the oracles of old. They built a tripod like the Delphic tripod, and stood it upon a round dish made of diverse metals, around the rim of which were engraved the letters of the alphabet. Then, after various pagan and unholy rites, they fastened a ring to the tripod by a thread of fine linen, which they set swinging.

This ring stopped over one or another of the letters, which the conspirators wrote down, and so it responded to their questions. And it answered in verses, Delphic hexameters like the oracles of old. It said that the next emperor would be a man accomplished in every part" — he smiled at my father, then dismissed him with a shrug — "and that his name would be . . . it spelled out THEOD —, at which one of the conspirators cried, 'Theodoros the Notary!' whom these depraved men had already decided upon as the best candidate for the purple. So they did not question it further on the succession, but instead asked about their own fates. And it prophesied, and prophesied truly, that for this work of inquiring into the mysteries of Fate they would all perish most miserably."

He smiled once more, then swilled his wine about his cup and drank it. "Fidustius also confessed that your friend Euserios brought this news to Theodoros the Notary. Theodoros was sent for from Constantinople; he at first denied everything, then admitted knowledge of the oracle, but said that he had responded to Euserios by saying that if God would have him emperor, they might trust to God and the workings of Fate to achieve it. Euserios, under bloody torture, said the same, but Theodoros was eventually convicted by a letter written in his own hand. There was in fact an attempt to assassinate His Sacred Majesty, before this evil plot came to light, but no one had known what lay behind it. Heaven itself protected Our Sacred Lord Valens, and turned the sword of his attacker." Festinus set his cup down. "But now that that pretender is dead, His Sacred Majesty is troubled. Was the oracle mistaken, or only the conspirators? Could another Theodoros have been meant? Inquiries are proceeding. I, for my part, since our most religious and discerning emperor has entrusted to me the governorship of this province, am determined to carry them out with the utmost rigor. And when I find a Theodoros — a rich nobleman who had little love for our most beneficent Augustus when he was challenged by a usurper; a man who was a friend to some who were involved in this conspiracy; a man who has set out to win the support of his fellow citizens, expending on this task thousands of *solidi* in gold — when I find such a man, then I am suspicious."

Father looked at him miserably. He seemed crushed, as though he were already facing the rack. "I have done nothing," he whispered, "nothing."

Festinus laughed. "I can believe it, now that I see you. Well, well: if you have done nothing, you have nothing to fear."

Hippocrates says that a doctor must observe his patients carefully and miss nothing if he is to make a good diagnosis of their illnesses. I had been training myself in observation; I observed Festinus now, despite my fear. He meant it when he said that he believed my father had done nothing. In fact, he probably had believed that all along. This whole drama was being performed for some other reason. Perhaps to show the emperor his zeal in rooting out enemies. He was a stranger to the East, without friends: he did not have to worry about how others would treat him when his governorship was over with. He wouldn't be received by anyone anyway, unless he were sure of the emperor's favor; he was, as Maia said, nobody as to family. So to get and keep the emperor's attention was all-important to him.

But when I saw him laugh, I knew that he liked to humiliate men who, like my father, thought of themselves as aristocrats. Here he was, the son of nobody, and yet he could threaten a wealthy senator with the rack and watch him tremble. Yes, he enjoyed it.

"Theodoros is a common name," Thorion said angrily. "There must be hundreds of powerful men by that name in the East alone. Is the emperor going to accuse all of them? And under what legal procedure?" Thorion always got angry when he was afraid, angry and belligerent.

Festinus sneered at him tolerantly. You are very young, said his look, and don't understand these things. "We will investigate anyone who incurs our suspicion on these very serious charges," he said formally.

The door from the corridor opened, and the official in charge of the search came in, dragging Johannes, who was weeping. After him came two of the soldiers. I was watching Festinus, and I saw him go rigid, his mouth opening with genuine surprise at what he saw. Only then did I take my eyes off him.

The soldiers were carrying a large cloth of purple silk. It was embroidered with golden bees, and the edges were hemmed with golden fringes. They spread it out on the floor, over the mosaic of the chariot. It glowed rich and vivid over the colored tiles: imperial purple. Only emperors were allowed the purple; for another man to own such a robe was a capital crime.

"It was in his private clothes chest," said the official. "None of the slaves admit to having seen it before, and all deny any knowledge of it."

"No!" protested Father. He jumped up, knocking the couch over, then fell onto his knees. "No, it's not what you think; I can explain!"

"You will explain everything, be sure of that," Festinus said grimly. He too was on his feet, staring at the purple. "I congratulate you, Theodoros. I believed you were as weak-spirited and foolish as you pretended; I thought you were innocent. So, so: you were plotting with Euserios after all. Is Eutropios in on it? Who else? Confess your accomplices!"

"But I'm not . . . that is, it wasn't for me . . ."

"Who is it for, then? Who? We will have the truth out of you; we will *dig* it out. We can put you on the rack, despite your riches; we can *claw* the truth from you! It's no use keeping silent now!"

I had been shocked almost to fainting when I saw the purple. I could not believe that my father had such a thing. If I had not seen the surprise on Festinus' face, I would have thought that he had had it planted. But it was my father's. Even the governor's present fury showed that. He was not just angry, but vindictive: he had been fooled. No more formal talk about "incurring suspicion" and Heaven's favor to His Sacred Majesty.

My father knelt on the floor, scrabbling at the edge of the robe with his fingers, too terrified to speak. I was still too horrified to cry. But the shape of the purple cloth suddenly recalled something else, something I had seen recently. In the stables. And I realized (and the rush of relief as I realized brought on the tears) that the purple was not a robe but a hanging to drape over a chariot.

"It's for a chariot," I said aloud.

Everyone stared at me as though I'd gone out of my mind. All those nobles and officials, staring at a fifteen-year-old girl.

"Can't you see it's for a chariot?" I said. I ran over and picked the cloth up, draped it so that the front fell over the arm of one of the couches, the fringes hanging down over the back and sides. "You couldn't wear that for a robe," I told Festinus. He towered over me, very close, frowning.

"Who'd want a purple robe for a chariot?" he demanded, but a trifle uncertainly.

"Father would." I had not known that he had wanted such a thing, but now that I understood what the cloth was, I could fill in the rest of its purpose. "He had it made for the games this summer. He's magistrate. He wanted to put a statue of our lord the Augustus in the winning chariot and parade it through the city. He didn't tell the slaves because he wanted to surprise everyone with a new spectacle, and if you tell the slaves it's all over the market before the day's out. Everyone expects him to do something different every time he's magistrate, and he likes to surprise them. But he told me and Thorion all about it — didn't he, Thorion?"

He had told Thorion nothing of the sort, I knew. He was well aware what Thorion thought of all his magistracies and horse races. But he would have told a few others — Daniel the charioteer, and Philoxenos, and perhaps one or two of his friends. I hoped it was true about the statue: I put that in because I didn't think he'd be foolhardy enough to parade his winning chariot (and he'd been sure that the winning chariot would be his, or he wouldn't have bothered with purple) without some public excuse. If it was true, he'd have had to arrange with some others on the town council to move the emperor's statue from the marketplace to the hippodrome and have it ready to put in the chariot. So he'd have other witnesses.

"That's right," said Thorion. He was not good at book-learning, but he was far from stupid, my brother. "It's been such a long time since the Augustus actually visited Ephesus that Father thought it would do the city good if he refreshed the citizens' loyalty with a representation of His Majesty. He told us all about it."

"Yes, yes!" said Father, straightening up, though still on his knees. "And I told Philoxenos, my groom, and their excellencies Pythion and Aristeides, councilors of this town: they were to undertake to move the statue of our most religious emperor to the hippodrome for the festivities. It would have been as though the emperor watched over our festival from afar. And when the races were ended, the winning chariot would approach the emperor's statue, and attendants would hang it with purple and then stand the statue before the charioteer. He would drive it through the streets into the marketplace, receiving the acclamations of all the city." Father was recovering himself. He spoke with some of his old fluency, picturing what he undoubtedly saw — his chariot, driven by Daniel, parading through the streets full of cheering crowds.

Festinus stared at him, then at the purple hanging on the couch. Once I had pointed out what the cloth was, it was hard to imagine it as anything other than a chariot frontal. If my father had been less panic-stricken, he could have pointed it out himself. Though perhaps no one would have believed him while he was threatened with the rack.

"Go fetch the groom," Festinus ordered his men, still staring at Father. "Take him off and ask him, under torture, whether this is true. And arrest that charioteer — what's his name?"

Father winced. "Daniel."

"Arrest him, and ask him about the purple cloth found in Theodoros' possession. Give him a taste of the rack — not too much, he's not charged with anything. And check this story with those councilors."

The officials nodded, bowed, and went out. Festinus bared his teeth at Father — the return of the amused smile. "A chariot frontal. Well.'" He laughed, throwing back his head, then stopped abruptly. "How did you get the purple?"

Father climbed slowly to his feet, stared at Festinus, then sat down on the couch. "I wrote letters to the factory at Tyre, telling the officials there what I wanted it for, and it was given to me in the usual way. They should have the letters, or at least remember about them. I paid thirty *solidi* for it."

Another soldier came into the room and saluted. "We have finished the search, Your Excellency."

"Good. Any letters, any evidence of sorcery?"

"We're taking the letters back, sir, to go through them at leisure, but nothing stands out. There's a book on astrology."

"What?"

The soldier consulted a note. "It's called *Phenomena*, Excellency. It's by a sorcerer called Aratos."

Festinus snorted with disgust. "You idiot. Everyone owns that book; it's a classic poem. Nothing else?"

"Nothing, Your Excellency," said the soldier, disappointed.

"Then tell your men to take a few of the slaves for questioning and go," said Festinus. "And don't be too rough on the slaves; it appears that Theodoros is probably innocent, after all." He bared his teeth at Father again, then glanced round the room. "We will need to question a few more of your slaves, most excellent Theodoros," he said, polite now. "Your steward, your private secretary, one or two others . . ." He glanced round again, and his eyes fell on Maia, who was standing behind Father and fanning him. It happened that she was looking at Festinus, not at the floor, and no one could have mistaken the look of hatred on her face. Festinus smiled. "And that woman there."

Maia said nothing. One of the soldiers came over and tied her hands, and she did not resist. Johannes the steward began sobbing again. He was an old man; he'd been steward for my grandfather. He had a lot of money stashed away somewhere, and Father was always saying that he'd free Johannes and let him retire and give the management of the house to Johannes' son. Well, he might have to do it now.

Father cleared his throat. "You . . . you won't do anything *extreme* to them, excellent Festinus?"

Another baring of teeth. "Nothing that they won't recover from in three days' time. You won't need to claim compensation on them — unless we discover anything. If not, we will return them to you tomorrow."

"Maia," I said.

She looked up at me, her sharp face haggard, and she managed to smile. "Never mind, my dear," she said. "I'll be all right."

Festinus and his party left, taking with them all my father's correspondence, all his accounts, the purple cloth, and Maia, Johannes, Philoxenos, two stableboys, three housemaids, and my father's secretary, Georgos. I would have wept for Philoxenos and Johannes and the others, only I couldn't think of any of them but Maia.

From the front of the house we had a view over the whole of Ephesus, down the street past the theater into the marketplace and on to the blue of the harbor. I watched from one of the windows as the party wound down the street. Some of the soldiers went first, then the governor in his litter, then the officials on foot, followed by the rest of the soldiers with the slaves. Maia was walking very straight and proud, but she looked tiny among all the others. I wondered if the soldier who'd been rude to her was the one next to her. I wondered what they'd do to her. They always torture slaves when they question them; they say that otherwise they won't get the truth. I don't know how they expect to get truth by torturing people.

I went back to my room. I'd shared it with Maia since she came to the house: there was her bed beside mine, and her little clothes chest beside my big one. I sat down on her bed and cried, then curled up on the bed and cried harder, holding the dented impression of her body there as I wanted to hold her. She'd always comforted me when I was hurt. Now she would be the one to suffer, and no one would comfort her. I wished that I had clung to her and cried — but what would have been the point? She'd been trying very hard to keep her dignity, and no one else would have paid any attention to me.

After a little while I noticed that I was sitting on a lump of something. It was my leather cosmetics purse — or, to be more accurate, it was the thrush.

I sat up, stopped crying, and took the bird out. It was cold now, and going stiff; its eyes seemed still more shrunken. What would happen if I did mutilate the body? If I prayed to Hekate, Tisiphone, and the Evil One, and worked at it with hate and the right words, would Festinus the governor crumple up and die? I tried to picture him dying of some painful disease, his fat red face beaded with sweat, his eyes glazed and bloody. But the picture didn't comfort me at all; his pain wouldn't stop Maia's.

In the oath of Hippocrates a doctor promises to use his art to heal the sick, and to abstain from harming anyone. I supposed that this should extend to using other arts to harm anyone. Anyhow, I didn't know how to work black magic.

I got up, washed my face, then went and dropped the bird in the First Court, beside the fountain.

When I went back to the room, Thorion was there, sitting on Maia's bed and holding her favorite icon, a picture of Mary the God-bearer and her Son which ordinarily stood in a niche by the window. He'd been crying too. I sat down beside him and we hugged each other.

"Festinus won't dare hurt her badly," Thorion said after a minute. "He knows that Father's not guilty. He's done this out of sheer love of evil."

He too was thinking only of Maia. It was odd: we were always laughing at Maia, making fun of her love of propriety, cringing before her urge to show off — we never said anything about loving her. But she was our mother, much more than that "perfect lady" who had disappeared after I was born, and there was no one on earth we loved more.

"It was clever spotting that chariot frontal," Thorion said after another minute. "Had Father told you about it? I thought not."

"He'd have managed to explain it eventually," I said.

"They wouldn't have trusted it, *eventually*," said Thorion. "He had to say it right away. He should have explained it before they found it. I wish he were stronger. *I* wouldn't have let that bastard get away with it." His hands twisted into fists as he said this, and he scowled at the icon. "That jumped-up nobody from Gaul! He's only here because he went to school with the prefect Maximinus! I'd like to flog him like the slave he is!"

There was nothing I could say to that.

The following afternoon Festinus sent a messenger to say we could have our slaves back. Father at once sent two carriages to fetch them. They had all been racked — tied on their backs along a post with lead weights fastened to their arms and legs. They had also been beaten with rods; one of the housemaids had been repeatedly raped. Philoxenos, who had been questioned hardest, had been torn on the chest and thighs with the implement they call the fork, and couldn't stand. Father had all of them put to bed and sent for his own doctor to attend to them.

While the doctor was attending to the others (he looked after Philoxenos first), I did what I could to make Maia comfortable. Thorion and I helped her out of the carriage, and she staggered along to our room with each of us holding one of her arms. She hugged us both when she saw us, but winced when we hugged her back. Some muscles had been torn on the rack, and the joints of her shoulders were swollen. The marks of the rod were all over her arms and across her chest, and one long bloody slash lay across her face.

"That needs to be washed with warm water," I told her. "And bandaged with white cerate. Would you like some hot compresses for your poor shoulders?"

Maia smiled at me, leaning back on her bed. "My little doctor," she said. "Well, for once I don't mind you playing Hippocrates. I would like some hot compresses. Later on I would like a bath, but just now . . . just now I don't want to move.'"

I went down to the kitchens and got some hot compresses; the house slaves were warming up a lot of them on top of the stove, getting them ready for all the slaves who had been tortured. I took three for Maia and wrapped them in a blanket to keep them warm. They were made from barley mixed with vinegar and sewn up in little leather bags; these stay hot for a long time, and are very soothing for sore joints. I put one on each of Maia's shoulders and one under her back, wrapped in a piece of cloth so it wouldn't be too hot for her.

"Festinus will regret this," Thorion said.

Maia snorted. "Don't waste your time on him, my dear! He isn't worth your attention." She thought for a moment, then added, "And our Lord Christ said that we must forgive our enemies and pray for those who injure us."

"How can you forgive an evil man who hasn't repented in the least? He's pleased about what he's done to our house, pleased that he frightened the master and tortured the slaves!"

"Well," said Maia practically, "as a Christian nobleman, you can at least not seek revenge. It isn't proper for you to talk in that barbarian fashion. And Festinus is a nobody, and doesn't deserve a gentleman's hatred."

"Maia," I said, "I love you." Only she could have coupled pure Christian forgiveness with such snobbery.

Of course Festinus had discovered nothing except that Father was very fond of chariot racing, and that the purple cloth was exactly what he had said it was. The slaves who had been tortured were all back on their feet within three days, even Philoxenos, though the housemaid who had been raped kept having nightmares and woke up screaming several times a night. In the end Father sent her out to one of the farms to keep house there, hoping that the quiet of the countryside would settle her nerves again. He did free Johannes, and he talked about freeing Philoxenos, but didn't. Philoxenos was worth too much. Because of Father's enthusiasm for racing, Philoxenos was one of the more important slaves in our household. He'd been born into the family, the son of my grandfather's chief groom, and he bossed all the stable lads and gardeners about. People sometimes think that if you're the child of a wealthy father, you just snap your fingers and point at what you want your slaves to do, and they go do it. But slaves run a house just as much as their owners do, and a prudent master has to treat them reasonably. Father would have liked to free Philoxenos, but didn't feel wealthy enough. He always said that we weren't that wealthy, not by the standards they use in the West. He owned just over two hundred slaves, and most of them lived on his estates and worked the land; only forty were in our house in town at any one time. It would cost him a lot to buy a groom as good as Philoxenos, if he could manage it at all, and he'd still feel obliged to spend more to set Philoxenos up in business. Philoxenos was eager to strike up on his own; he wanted to breed and train horses in the country. In the end Father gave him a brood mare instead, to contribute to this stud farm. I didn't think that was much compensation for the torture Philoxenos had endured because of his master's vanity, but Philoxenos was pleased with it.

Father's chariot driver, Daniel, had been tortured as well, but not badly. We were lucky that there had been the earlier scare over sorcery in Ephesus: Festinus' men found no evidence of black magic in Daniel's house. I was fairly sure that this was because Daniel had hidden his books and tablets somewhere else, but he played the unfamiliar role of outraged innocent with some relish, and Father had to give him a lot of money to soothe his feelings.

But we escaped lightly. All over the East men were being put to death for having so much as heard of the conspiracy, and nowhere more so than in Ephesus under Festinus. The philosopher Maximus, who had been the emperor Julian's most trusted adviser, was beheaded in the hippodrome before the races because he had heard the oracular verses about Valens' successor. So instead of my father's surprise parade, we had Festinus' surprise execution. Festinus had the poor man marched into the middle of the ring, then stood up in his place of honor and made a speech about the wickedness of disloyalty. Maximus had no chance to say anything. He stood there, bareheaded in the hot sun, wearing only a brown tunic, looking old and ill. The city had been proud of him, and was horrified. When Festinus finished speaking, his guards threw Maximus to his knees, and the executioner brought down the sword. His blood splashed widely over the ground, and many took it to be an omen.

If so, it was an accurate one. All summer people were being accused, dragged into court, tortured, and executed on the flimsiest grounds. One merchant had his business papers confiscated on a charge of peculation. Among these was discovered a horoscope cast for one Valens. The merchant said that this was his brother, who had died several years before; he offered to get proof of this assertion from the astrologer who had cast the horoscope and from people who had known his brother. He wasn't given any chance to do so, but was sent off to the rack and the executioner's sword. There was a silly old woman who used to try to cure fevers with a charm (as every doctor knows, an unreliable method): she was accused of witchcraft and executed after she cured a slave of Festinus', with Festinus' own knowledge. And these cases were only a few of many.

And Festinus was rewarded for his loyalty to His Sacred Majesty, the most religious Augustus, our Lord Valens. In the autumn it became known that his term of office would be extended for another year, and he was given a hundred-year lease on some crown lands in the Cayster Valley, which had formerly been managed by one of his victims. Such lands are much sought after, because they are untaxed. And it was good land, too, rich and level.

To celebrate his gains in wealth and position, Festinus gave a party to which he invited all the important men in Ephesus, including Father and Thorion. Everyone was too afraid of him to refuse. So Thorion put on his best cloak and tunic, let Maia brush his hair and pin his cloak — he'd got it crooked, she said — and set off, scowling. I wasn't going, of course. I'd had my sixteenth birthday in late spring, but girls aren't considered to be of age until they're married, and don't go out to dinner parties.

If Thorion was scowling when he set out that afternoon, he looked like thunder when he came back that night. I heard the group come in and ran out into the First Court to see. Father just looked limp, and went straight to his room; Thorion came up to my room and told Maia and me all about it.

"He thinks he's a gentleman now!" Thorion said bitterly. "A gentleman and a landowner; he was talking of settling in Ephesus, when he's done at court, and becoming a citizen!"

"He's nothing but a peasant," said Maia. She was sitting on her chair by the window, spinning. It was dark, and we'd lit the lamps: the little room looked rich and warm. The white walls glowed golden in the lamplight; Maia's icons smiled tenderly from the wall; Maia's spindle whirred softly in her hands. From outside came the sound of the crickets singing and the rustle of trees in the courtyard. I'd been getting ready for bed when Thorion came in, and I sat on the bed in my tunic, hugging my knees; my cloak was folded up on top of the clothes chest, waiting to be cleaned. (It was white and green, with the inevitable purple stripe. Why does it have to be white for young girls? It's impossible to keep anything white clean, and now I had some bloodstains on it from watching Philoxenos geld some of the young stallions.) Despite the angry summer, I felt that everything was back to normal at home. I didn't want to think about Festinus, so I didn't say anything — though I might have pointed out that we were hardly the ones to talk about peasants scrambling into noble homes and titles.

"He's a common thief!" said Thorion. "He was wearing a cloak with a purple stripe as wide as my hand" — he held out his big peasant hand, fingers outspread — "and he had a purple stripe down the tablecloth. I thought it looked familiar somehow, and about halfway through the first course I realized why. It was *our* purple, that cost *us* thirty *solidi*, which Festinus confiscated and never gave back!"

"The dirty robber!" said Maia, shocked. "Did he say anything about it?"

"No. I think he'd forgotten where it came from, he was so busy congratulating himself." He paused to catch his breath, then went on in a peculiarly even tone. "And he talked about you, Charition."

"About me?" I asked, shocked in turn. Thorion nodded, looking more thunderous than ever. Maia gave a hiss of disapproval, and looked at me uneasily.

"He asked Father, 'How's your pretty daughter?' " said Thorion. "And when Father said that you were very well, Festinus told everyone there that you were a very pretty girl, and modest; and he said that when Father was under suspicion — just like that, 'when His Excellency Theodoros was under suspicion' — you'd kept your head and pointed out proofs of innocence that everyone else was too excited to think of. And he asked Father your name; he said he'd forgotten it."

"A modest young virgin's name is no concern of his!" Maia exclaimed indignantly. "It's enough for him to know her as His Excellency Theodoros' daughter. Really! You didn't talk to the governor at all when he was here, did you, Charis?"

"Just what you heard," I said. "What he remembered. I'm surprised that Festinus remembered; I think even Father's forgotten."

"He remembered that you were pretty," said Thorion. He pulled at his lip, a bad habit that Maia hated. "I could have hit him! Lying there on his couch, talking about how pretty you were and how Father had been under suspicion, and leering at us all! By God and his saints! And we've got to see him again next week!"

Maia was frowning. She didn't even say anything to Thorion about pulling his lip. "He invited you back?"

"No. He made it clear to Father that he'd like an invitation here, so Father had to give it to him."

"Thorion," said Maia, and I knew she was really worried: she only used Thorion's nickname when she forgot herself. "Your most noble father must invite a lot of other people to this dinner party. Men. Distinguished bachelors — your law teacher, perhaps? At any rate, no women."

Thorion looked at her grimly. "So you think there's something to the way he talked about Charis?"

Maia pressed her lips together and rolled her spindle. "I know nothing about it," she said after a minute. "But people will talk: it's most improper, to ask a young girl's name at a dinner party. And I

31

think it would be better if Charis stayed out of that brute's way. If there are no women at the party, there'll be no reason for her to meet him."

Whereas if Festinus came alone, I'd be expected to be at my father's table.

"You can't think that means anything," I said. I felt very uncomfortable, knowing that Festinus had talked about me. "Isn't he married?"

"Widowed," said Maia, who always knew such things. "And if he intends to settle in Ephesus, he'll need a new wife — preferably a young Ephesian noblewoman. So I don't want you to catch his eye."

I felt shaken. "But I'm too young, aren't I? And Father wouldn't —"

Thorion looked at me glumly. "Pythion's daughter is only a few months older than you, and she's going to be married this spring. And you know, Charition, you are rather pretty. I could kick that Festinus' teeth in!" he added savagely.

"But Father wouldn't —"

"Father wouldn't want to displease Festinus. He's afraid of him. Maia's right: you must keep out of the brute's way. I'll ask Father to invite a lot of other men, and you can stay in your room. And if Festinus mentions you, we can all go on about how young and silly you are. That should put a stop to any ideas he might have."

But Father had already invited his friend Pythion with his wife, and he insisted that no other guests were needed. "He said that Festinus particularly asked for an informal occasion, when they could talk freely," Thorion told me next day. "I said I was worried about the way Festinus had talked about you, and he said that that didn't mean anything, it was just a way to show a fatherly interest in our household. He thinks Festinus is trying to make peace, and wants to be agreeable now that we're neighbors. I said that as far as I was concerned, the best neighborliness I want from Festinus is a stone wall between him and us."

But Father was master of the house, not Thorion. And with a party of mixed company, I'd be expected to be there.

I felt hot and uncomfortable on the day of this dinner party. I hadn't seen Festinus, except from a distance, since the day he made his accusations. I was afraid of him, the more so because I could not understand him. I felt fairly sure that he had acted as he had, to us and to the rest, out of a desire to impress the emperor and out of a lust to display his power over men of rank. But the cruelty that had tortured Maia and Philoxenos and the rest, and that had killed so many others — that I did not understand. His motives seemed mysterious, irrational, scarcely human. I could not really believe he had any interest in me, not even as an eligible Ephesian noblewoman. But of course he knew nothing about *me*: he had seen the painted doll in the mirror.

I had lessons that day, but it was only Euripides; we'd finished Hippocrates for the time being. Ischyras was not as fond of Euripides as he was of other writers: the style was insufficiently elevated. Neither of us paid proper attention to the tragedy, and in the end I was allowed to go early. I went down to the stables. Philoxenos was letting me look after a mare with an infected hoof; I was treating the injury with hot compresses and with regular washing with boiled water and a cleansing solution of vinegar and cedar oil, and it seemed to be working. I also had a sick rabbit, but I didn't know what was wrong with her, except that she seemed to be getting worse.

Maia came and fetched me in the middle of the afternoon. I was down on my knees in the straw, cleaning the mare's hoof, with my cloak hung over the stable door. I finished swabbing the hoof out, using a length of linen tied round one of my cosmetic applicators, then sat back on my heels and examined the pus on the cloth. Pale and not too foul-smelling: good. I looked around and saw Maia standing there watching me. "Oh," I said.

Maia didn't throw up her hands and exclaim in horror, as she ordinarily did. "It's a pity you can't appear like that tonight," she said instead. "That would put Festinus off you: you look like a stableboy! But I can't have my master's daughter going to a party like that. Come along!"

"Just let me finish bandaging this hoof first," I pleaded, and Maia actually smiled and nodded. I bandaged the hoof up, patted the mare, and we went back into the house. Bath, hair-curling, perfuming, face-painting, dressing — what a waste of time a young lady's life is! In the end I had another look at "the loveliest young lady in Ephesus," and she seemed stupider and more unlike me than ever. For once Maia didn't seem too pleased with her either.

Because it was a small, informal party, the dinner was held not in the domed banquet hall but in the Charioteer Room. A rack of lamps burning sweet oil scented with myrrh was set up against each of the side walls, and the floor and citron-wood table were scattered with roses. The light bathed the rich hangings, the silver dinner service; it added depth to the pictures on the wall, and the chariot on the floor

33

seemed almost to move. Everything in the room spoke of wealth and culture, and when the slaves showed Festinus in, he looked at it appreciatively. There were four couches round the table: one for Father, one for Pythion and his wife, one for Thorion and me, and one for Festinus. Father, as the host, had the highest place, with Festinus on his right and Pythion on his left; Thorion and I shared the bottom couch.

Festinus had brought Father a present, a Corinthian-ware goblet painted with a chariot. Father expressed his delight with it, and we all reclined in our places. Festinus kept looking at me, but I kept my eyes modestly on the floor, and Thorion made sure that he took the place facing the governor, so Festinus couldn't in fact see much but my hair. The slaves brought in the first courses: boiled eggs, leeks in wine and fish sauce, sweet-and-sour pea soup. And they filled the green glass drinking cups with honeyed white wine, chill from the underground cellars.

"Excellent," said Festinus, waving his hand at the lot. "That's the thing I like about Asia: people here understand how to live. In Rome they either glut themselves on overcooked rarities and make themselves sick drinking, or they live like peasants on bread and water. No moderation, and no taste." He went on in this vein right through the first courses, praising Ephesus and all its ways, and Father and Pythion began to lose their nervousness and resume their usual air of gracious complacency. Only Thorion retained his suspicious scowl. I kept my eyes down.

During the second courses (grilled red mullet with asafetida, Parthian-style chicken, and sow's wombs in dill sauce) the talk turned to literature. Festinus, as honored guest, called for the slaves to start serving the wine for the main course; Father had had an amphora of prime Chian opened. Festinus asked the slaves to mix it so it contained only a third water. This was stronger than we usually drank it, and soon Father was laughing loudly and expounding Homer.

"You're quite a scholar, most learned Theodoros," Festinus told him. "What of your excellent children? I am sure a wise man would not let his children grow up ignorant, and I always admire education in the young. It is an adornment superior to gold, as the poets say."

"Oh, indeed," said Father. "I have paid great attention to my children's education. I hired a very clever tutor for them, Ischyras of Amida: he can write the purest Attic dialect, and is well read in all the classics. And I fancy that my children have not been slow learners. And my son Theodoros is now studying the laws and Latin, with a view to making a career at court."

"A wise choice, young man," said Festinus approvingly. Thorion muttered indistinctly and stared into his wine cup. "And your daughter?" Festinus went on. "Some say it is not worthwhile, educating women, but I have always found a literate woman to be an ornament to her house."

"Oh, Ischyras has given the same attention to Charis as to Theodoros," said Father. "That is the way we do things in the East. I would never bring up a daughter ignorant of Homer."

"Splendid! Perhaps she would favor us by reciting something? Many of the great Roman noblemen always have poetry recited during their banquets, and I think the custom a fine one."

"We have that custom here too," said Father, the wine glowing in his cheeks. "Charis! Stand up, my dear, and recite something!"

I stood up, reluctantly. I hadn't drunk much wine, and the slaves hadn't kept refilling my glass as they had the men's. Everyone stared at me; Pythion's wife gave me an encouraging smile. Festinus bared his teeth, and for a moment all my lessons went out of my head. I had passages memorized, of course: everyone has to memorize bits of Homer and the tragedies. All I could think of now was "Sing Goddess of the Wrath," which a four-year-old knows by heart — that, and a bit from Hippocrates about the treatment of wounds. Then the Euripides I'd read that morning jumped into my head, and I quoted that. It was from *The Trojan Women*, the final chorus, when the women lament their dead and the destruction of their city before the Greek men drag them off into slavery: "A wing of smoke fades into the air, is gone: there is no more Troy. Leave, then, with heavy feet; below in the harbor, the Greek ships wait."

About halfway through it I realized that it was not a very tactful thing to quote. Everyone was looking at me very strangely, and Father was worried again. Pillaging cities, though no one would admit it, was something everyone associated with Festinus; and it was at least suggested that Festinus meant to carry me off. Well, it was too late to stop now.

I finished and sat down. "That was lovely, dear," said Pythion's wife. She was a nice woman.

"We were reading it this morning," I said, to allay the strange looks. I stared at the floor.

Thorion nudged me; I looked up to find that he was grinning. "You've left him no doubt what you think of him," he whispered happily. "God and his saints, look at him trying to change the subject!"

Festinus did in fact change the subject to the theater, and there was talk about that through the rest of the fish and meat courses. Then Father suggested that we rise and walk about the gardens before the sweets and apples, and everyone agreed. After all that wine, they wanted to use the latrines.

I went to latrines in the women's side of the house, then went and sat in the First Court, waiting for Thorion. I was sitting there beside the fountain when Festinus came in, alone. He saw me at once, so there was no use trying to hide. I folded my hands in my lap and sat still.

"Lady Charis," said Festinus, and he came over. He stood looking down at me for a moment; I looked at the ground. He gave a grunt and sat down beside me, close enough for me to feel the heat of his body and smell the wine on his breath. "What did you mean by quoting that bit of Euripides?" he asked.

I tried to ease away from him. "Nothing, Your Excellency," I said. It was, I thought (thinking like Maia), most improper for a man to speak privately to his host's unmarried daughter. "I read it with my tutor Ischyras this morning, and it was all I could think of on the spur of the moment."

He laughed, moving closer to me; he put one heavy hand on my shoulder. "Is that all?" he asked. "You don't like me, do you?"

I didn't look at him. It was on the tip of my tongue to shout, "You had my nursemaid and some of my friends tortured!" but he was still governor; he could have them tortured again, if he was ruthless enough. "Your Excellency, I am a young girl, too young to have opinions, and I do not know Your Illustriousness."

He laughed and put his arm around my shoulders. I sat still, pressing my hands together, as Father had, to stop them shaking. "I'm not an illustriousness," he said. "Not yet, anyway." He put his other hand against my chin and pulled my head around so that I had to look at him. The light from the lamps in the Charioteer Room spilled out into the court and lit his face; the crickets were singing, and the fountain made a quiet gurgling noise. His face, I thought detachedly, showed the burst veins that are caused by too much drinking, a coarsening that would no doubt grow worse through the years. He ought to take a drier diet, and eat more bread.

"I may be an illustriousness one of these days," he told me, licking his fleshy lips. "I have the emperor's favor; he knows that I'm zealous in his service. Fifteen years ago I was nobody in particular, now I'm *spectabilis*, governor of Asia with proconsular rank, friend of His Sacred Majesty. You hate me because my father was an auctioneer, don't you?"

"No," I said. "I didn't even know that."

The hand that had been around my shoulders thrust itself down the front of my tunic. I gasped, and he pushed his mouth over mine. I couldn't breathe. He fumbled with my breasts, pinched hard. I couldn't cry out, his tongue was in my mouth. I tried to lock my teeth together, and he thrust his fingers into the side of my jaw, holding my mouth open. I shoved my elbow into his ribs and kicked him, and he pulled his head away and laughed. There was sweat on his face. His hands stayed where they were. "That's to teach you not to lie," he told me. "You do hate me; I can tell that. You really are very beautiful, with those big dark eyes. 'Vitas inuleo me similis,' Charis —you are like a deer." He laughed again. "Yes, I think I will speak to your father about you. How your little heart is pounding!"

All I could think of to say was "You're hurting me. Let me go!"

He took his hand out of my tunic. I jumped up, trying not to cry; I was badly shaken. No one had ever touched me before, and I'd never wanted anyone to do so, even in a dream. All that belonged to the other Charis, the lovely young lady in the mirror. "I want nothing to do with you," I told Festinus. My voice sounded surprisingly even: it was not the young lady's voice, it was mine. But his hands had not been on the mirror; they had hurt *me*. "It's nothing to do with who your father was. I hate cruelty, and you love it. You had better speak to someone else's father."

He bared his teeth and laughed again, so I walked out and went back to my room. Maia was there, sewing; she looked up in surprise when I came in. "The dinner's not finished yet?" she said.

"No," I told her, and burst into tears.

When Thorion came in about half an hour later, Maia and I were sitting on her bed, with Maia still rocking and crooning to me as though I were a little child. I'd stopped crying but I had the hiccups.

Thorion stood in the doorway for a minute, looking angry. Maia nodded at him to come in, and he did so, slamming the door. "By Artemis the Great!" he said. "Why did you run off? Why didn't you go straight to Father and tell him you won't have the brute?"

"Thorion!" said Maia. "You let her be! And if you must swear, don't swear by those pagan devils!"

I wiped my nose. "I had to get away from him," I told Thorion.

37

"There was no one else around, and he . . ." I couldn't finish the sentence: the little scene was too painful, too shameful, and my emotions were still in turmoil.

Thorion seemed suddenly to take in the tears, and looked shocked. "What did he do? If he's . . . I'll *kill* him!"

"Oh, it wasn't that," I said, getting better control of myself. "He put his hand down my tunic and he kissed me, that's all."

Thorion looked thunderous. "You have a bruise on your face."

"He had to stop me from biting him."

For some reason he looked relieved at this. "May he perish most miserably and go to Hell," he prayed, and came over and sat down beside me. He put his arm around my shoulders and hugged. "But I wish you'd gone straight in and said that he assaulted you. He told Father that he'd 'expressed his admiration for your beauty' — those are his exact words — and you were overcome with shyness and maidenly modesty and ran off. And so he expressed the same admiration to Father, and repeated that he meant to settle in Ephesus, and said that since he'd seen you for himself and knew that you were modest and well educated and nobly born as well as beautiful, he wished to marry you, if this was agreeable to Father."

I said nothing. It was what I had thought he might do.

"What did your father say?" asked Maia in a low voice.

"That this was too important a matter to discuss at a dinner party, and that they should meet soon to talk it over properly. Then I said that Charis was too young to marry anyone, and that she was half-promised to someone else — well, I had to say something. But the brute just laughed at me. Father told me that I was being insolent to my elders — he was afraid of what I might say next — and told me to go. But if you'd come in, Charition, and said that the governor had assaulted you in your own house, he'd have had to take no for an answer."

"Would he?" I asked bitterly. "He might have had to accept less dowry, but he can take what he wants from Father, and he knows it. Father is still afraid of him."

"Couldn't you have said something to *him?*"

"I told him that I wanted nothing to do with him. But he liked that. Thorion, he *wants* me to hate him. He wants to . . . to triumph over me. Over Ephesus and its rulers."

"He enjoys inflicting pain," Maia said quietly. "Yes." Her arm tightened around my waist. "Who did you think we could say she was promised to?" she asked Thorion.

He shrugged helplessly. "I thought maybe Palladios, Demetrios' son. Or my friend Kyrillos."

Maia thought them over. "Palladios is young and a gentleman," she said after a moment. "I don't think it's been arranged for him to marry anyone else yet, either. And his father would be pleased to spite Festinus. Yes, he'd do. But Kyrillos?"

Kyrillos was a young man Thorion had met at his Latin teacher's; he was the son of a small landowner, a man more or less like our own great-grandfather, neither powerful nor wealthy.

"He's very clever," Thorion said defensively. "And he thinks the world of you, Charition. I think he'd be willing to run off with you, if all else fails."

I was a bit surprised at this. I'd met Kyrillos a few times, when Thorion had asked him to dinner, but we hadn't spoken much. But I knew that Thorion had told him that I helped with the study of Latin law, and perhaps this had impressed Kyrillos. He was impressed by anyone who could conjugate properly. Not that he was bad at it himself; he was considerably better than Thorion, and enjoyed the law. I wouldn't mind marrying him, particularly if I could take Maia with me. I didn't know Palladios at all, but at least he wasn't a torturer — and he was young and fairly good-looking. "Very well," I said. "It might work. Festinus might not believe it if we suddenly say that I've been engaged to someone else all along, but he won't be able to do anything about it. And I'm not going to marry him, not under any circumstances. All we need to do is convince Father to help."

We waited for the dinner party to end and the guests to go home. You could hear people in the First Court from my room, and we listened to Father saying goodbye. "Until tomorrow!" Festinus said in his loud voice with its now familiar nasal slurring. We couldn't hear Father's reply.

When the guests were gone, we went, all three of us, to see Father. We found him sitting in the Charioteer Room, where the slaves were clearing up the remains of the dinner; he looked exhausted and unhappy.

"Father," said Thorion, "we need to talk to you."

"Oh, my dears," said Father, "not now, please: it's late."

"Now," said Thorion. "If we're to get ourselves out of this marriage, we have to arrange something at once."

Father made a noise between a snort and a sigh. "Get out of it? What makes you think we could or even should get out of it?"

I realized, as I looked at my father reclining there on his couch, that I knew him no better than did the household slaves, and he knew me not at all. I could just remember him coming into my room when I was tiny and playing with me, but since I had begun to become myself, never. I had seen him at meals sometimes; he had occasionally asked me about my lessons, and praised me for reciting this or that, but we had never touched on what interested me. In serious conversations no one asked me anything, and I behaved myself and said nothing. To him as much as to Festinus I was simply the young lady, the daughter of the house, quiet, pretty, obedient. And easily disposed of. I began to feel very cold.

"You can't mean to let that brute marry Charis!" said Thorion.

"Sst!" Father glanced at the slaves, who had stopped clearing up and were standing by the wall, trying to keep out of the way.

"No! Festinus is a brute, and an enemy of our house, and I don't care who knows that I think so!"

"My dear son!" said Father. "You must speak of powerful men with respect! It is true that His Excellency the governor is of low birth, but so are many men who today hold the highest ranks; so indeed was our own grandfather. The most esteemed Lord Festinus has acquired wealth and power through his own merit, and he is well thought of by our most religious Lord Valens the Augustus. Moreover, he is now our neighbor. I see no reason why our houses should not be united by a marriage. True, I had other plans for my daughter before — but this marriage will be an advantage to both of us. He will gain in respectability, and we will benefit from his protection and his influence."

"So a man can come marching in here with a troop of soldiers," Thorion said, "he can threaten your life; he can drag off your slaves and torture them; he can assault your daughter in your own house: that's all fine by you! You'll give him your daughter in marriage just to make everything all right. Christ the Eternally Begotten!"

"He didn't *assault* Charis," said Father testily.

"Yes he did," I said. I turned my face so that he could see the bruise.

Father looked uncomfortable for a moment, then shrugged. "Well, he's a passionate man. He'll settle down; he's already settled down a great deal since he first came here. And he was much struck by you, my dear; he spoke of your eyes and quoted some Latin poetry. I didn't know the Latins wrote poetry."

"Father," I said, "he didn't assault me out of lust. He likes to hurt and humiliate people; he likes the power of it. He's done nothing else since he came to Ephesus. I will not marry him."

Father looked still more uncomfortable. Maia went over to him and prostrated herself, face down on the shining mosaic. She was wearing her work clothes, a plain blue linen tunic and blue cloak, and Father was in his white-and-gold brocade, but they didn't look like king and suppliant. Father looked too unsure of himself, too ashamed of himself, for that. Maia rose onto her knees, and clasped his knees with her hands. "Please, master," she said. "It's true, what my Charition says. That man . . ." She stopped; to my horror I realized that she was crying. Crying for me, from fear of what Festinus would do. "That man is one of those who enjoy cruelty. When . . . when I was put to the question, he came down to the torture chamber himself and took the rod in his own hand. He was the one who did this." She touched the mark on her face, now a fine white line. "And he hit me . . . elsewhere, too. It gave him pleasure, sir. Please, my lord. Next to the Divine, sir, I have always reverenced you, but I have loved Charition as though she were my own. You must not give her to that devil, sir. No, send to the most noble Demetrios: tell him what has happened, and ask his help in arranging a marriage between Charis and his son Palladios. We can pass it off as a long-standing agreement. Even Festinus couldn't take exception to that."

"But I've already told him that Charis isn't promised to anyone!" said Father, now looking really distressed.

Thorion groaned.

"Well, he asked me," Father protested.

"Tell him you lied," said Thorion. "Tell him that you meant to call off the marriage to Palladios, but that Demetrios is unwilling to do so. Or tell him that she was secretly engaged to someone — to my friend Kyrillos. Tell him anything, but get out of it! Nothing's been arranged yet, there's still time!"

"I will not lie," said Father, annoyed. "It is not fitting to a gentleman." He looked at Maia, who was still clutching his knees. "I'm sorry," he told her. "I'm very sorry to hear what you say. But after all, he won't dare to mistreat his own wife, a woman of noble birth. He's very rich, and likely to get richer; he'll be able to afford a separate household for Charis. She won't need to see him too often, I hope, if she dislikes him. And I'll include you and a few others from our house in her dowry, so she'll have her friends about her. And the match will be an advantage to our house." Maia stared at him in anguish.

"You're sacrificing Charis so that you can benefit!" shouted Thorion, now going quite white with anger. "You . . . Agamemnon! It's all to get influence and have enough money to spend on your damn horse races! You spineless —"

"You must not speak to me like that!" shouted Father. "Have you no respect for your own father?"

"How can I?"

"Barbarian! Pagan!" Father threw Maia's hands off his knees, and she fell back onto her heels, staring at him miserably. "Don't the Scriptures say —"

"Father," I interrupted. If Thorion went on, he would make it impossible for Father to back down. "Father, I will not marry Festinus."

He stopped shouting. "What do you mean by that?"

"What I said," I told him, again surprised that my voice stayed level. "I will not consent. You'll have to tie me up and gag me to get me to go through with it."

"My dear!" said Father. "Don't let all this talk frighten you. Leave decisions like this to responsible men. A young girl doesn't know enough to be able to judge what's good for her."

I shook my head. "It's my life at stake. I ought to be able to judge what would ruin it."

"My dear!" Father still looked exasperated rather than seriously angry. "Of course it's natural that you should be afraid. He is a frightening man, and all girls are afraid to marry and, um, part from their families. But it will be for the best. You will be mistress of a house, have your own slaves to order about and your own money to dispose of in whatever way you fancy. Lots of lovely dresses, and your own carriage, eh? And the wife of an important man has a lot of power; other women will come running to you, asking you to help their husbands and giving you presents. You can go anywhere you like — dinner parties, the theater. Don't let Theodoros frighten you."

He was speaking as though to a stupid child. But I'd never shown him that I was anything else. I had always gone along with his and the world's expectations of how a young lady should behave, thinking that if I did what others wanted, they would be more likely to let me do what I wanted. But instead they had concluded that I had no wants but theirs.

"Festinus is cruel," I said to him, still sounding calm, though my heart felt shriveled up inside. "He has injured my friends, and he will hurt me as much as he can. I know that. I would be a fool to go into such a marriage with my eyes wide open. I will not marry him. If you can't think of anything else to tell him, you can tell him that."

"I am not going to tell him any such thing!" said Father. "Who is master in this house, eh? Me, or a pack of slaves and children? Go to bed, all of you, immediately! And let me hear better sense, more respectfully expressed, when I see you tomorrow."

Thorion opened his mouth and Father shouted, "Silence! I'm tired of you telling me how I should spend my money and how I should dispose of my own daughter! Who pays your allowance, eh? Who pays for your clothes and your tutors and your drinking parties? Behave, or I'll stop the lot!"

Thorion looked ready to start shouting again, so I took his arm. It was plain that we'd get nowhere, certainly not as long as Father was in his present mood. Perhaps we'd have done better to wait until morning, when he was less tired and when the wine fumes had left his head. Perhaps we might yet do better then. But I doubted it.

"Goodnight, Father," I said, and I pulled Thorion out after me. Maia followed, covering her face with a corner of her cloak to hide her grief.

⌐⌐⌐

Father did not change his mind in the morning. Instead he set off to make the arrangements with Festinus, and refused to talk to any of us. We watched from the guest room window as his litter proceeded down the street, a gilded canopy heading toward the marketplace and the governor's palace. It was a beautiful day, and the gilt on the litter glittered cheerfully against the red roof tiles below; the harbor was a deep, rich blue, checked with orange and yellow sails. Everything seemed to smile on Father's errand. Maia turned away from the window and sat down on the empty clothes chest, folding her hands. For the first time I could remember, she actually looked like a slave.

"He doesn't care what that brute does to you," said Thorion.

I shook my head. "He's frightened of Festinus." I'd thought it over carefully during the night. "He wants to make himself secure, and the best way to do that is to make an alliance. And he's probably talked himself into believing that we're exaggerating, and that it will all be all right really."

"We'll have to go on with the secret engagement plan," Thorion said after a moment. "It will be harder if Father genuinely forbids it. But I can promise to make it up to Kyrillos after Father dies."

"It's a bit hard on Kyrillos, don't you think?" I said. "Seduction is a crime, you know. He'd have to flee Ephesus with me, and he'd have to give up his career and all his prospects. He'd be abandoning his family, and it would hurt them." Thorion scowled. "And I don't like the idea of you sitting there waiting for Father to die," I added. "He's not really a bad father. He isn't happy about this, either. But he's just . . . just a coward. He can't help it."

And, I added privately, Kyrillos was unlikely even to agree to such a mad scheme. He might think the world of me, but I knew that he was ambitious. It was much more likely that he'd tell Thorion that he didn't want me, which would be the end of their friendship, and get us nowhere.

Thorion bit his lip, then jerked his head back. "What do you think we should do, then? Charition, we don't have anyone to smuggle you to; anywhere you went, Festinus could find you in no time. It's all very well to say that you don't consent, but you don't have any rights in the matter; you're supposed to do as Father says."

"I have another idea," I said, and stopped. I'd lain awake all night, thinking of the other idea. It had seemed to me that I'd spent enough time pretending that I was the girl in the mirror, waiting for my own life to begin. Perhaps, I thought, it was fortunate that Festinus had proposed to marry me. If it had been almost anyone else, I would have meekly obeyed my father. And once married, would my life have started, as I planned? Or would my husband have discouraged me or forbidden me to play doctor, and made me play virtuous wife instead? He wouldn't have had to use force. I was used to pretending, I saw that now — used to taking the easy way and letting people think I was what they wanted me to be. And if I was busy enough pretending, I might have no time for being. So perhaps I would have waited out my life, marrying, bearing children, growing old, never again speaking in my own voice or thinking my own thoughts, and in the end, perhaps, becoming indeed the thing I pretended to be.

As it was, I had been forced to be bold.

Thorion and Maia looked at me, both with the same mixture of puzzlement and hope. Maia's eyes were red; she had cried herself to sleep beside me in bed, stroking my hair and calling me her baby.

"I want to go to Alexandria," I said. "And study to be a doctor."

"You can't do that," said Thorion in disgust, the hope replaced by irritation. "Women can't study medicine."

44

"I'll pretend to be a man."

"You don't look it. And what would you do in the public lavatories, piss in a corner with your tunic down? Nobody does that. And you couldn't go to the public baths, or exercise in the gymnasiums, or . . . anything. No one would ever believe you!"

"I'll pretend to be a eunuch. Eunuchs have to be modest: I bet they do piss in the corner, with their tunics down, and don't show themselves naked anywhere. And everyone says they look girlish when they're young." All the eunuchs I'd seen in Ephesus were middle-aged, and didn't look particularly girlish. But they didn't look like properly mannish men either.

"What would a eunuch be doing studying medicine in Alexandria? He could be at the court, earning money. A retired chamberlain gets a thousand *solidi* a year! To say nothing of what he makes in taking bribes!"

"Maybe I might not like being an emperor's chamberlains and taking bribes. And anyway, all the chamberlains are slaves. A freeborn eunuch might want to study medicine, if only because everyone hates the chamberlains so much."

"Eunuchs aren't freeborn. Who'd do that of their own free will?" Thorion put a hand protectively over his genitals. "And it's illegal, too. The eunuchs are all Persians or Abasgi from Colchis, slaves imported into the empire to be things like chamberlains and private secretaries."

"Oh stop that!" I said. "You know perfectly well that some eunuchs are freeborn, the ones who are captured by the Persians. Well, say I'm a eunuch from somewhere in the east . . . from Amida. The Persians captured it, remember? Ischyras told us all about it; it was his home. So I'm from a respectable Amidan family; I was captured by the Persians and castrated when I was little, and then redeemed by you and, say, Ischyras. Now I want to learn a useful trade, so you and Ischyras are sending me to Alexandria to study medicine because I have no inclination toward administration. That all makes sense, doesn't it?"

Maia began to cry again. I went over and put my arms round her. "Please don't," I said.

"But I wanted to see you married!" said Maia miserably. "Married to some fine young gentleman who'd treat you kindly. I thought I could go with you to his house and help you run the household and nurse your children. To see you forced into such an unnatural pretense, calling yourself a eunuch, living in a foreign city — you might die there, you might be discovered and punished, you might be raped." She tried to dry her eyes. "Anything might happen to you. And I built my life on you; what will happen to me?"

"Don't," I said. "You built your life out of yourself. It's no good building it on other people; anything can happen to them. That's as true here in Ephesus as it is in Alexandria. And you don't need to think I'd go away forever. If I wait a few years, Festinus may be out of the way, and I can come back."

Thorion shook his head. "Maia's right. The life you're proposing is unnatural. Always pretending to be a man, living in a foreign city under another name, without any money to speak of — you couldn't stand it."

"Thorion, Maia," I said, "please. It's what I want. You know that. I'd rather be a doctor than anything. You know I've wanted it for years."

"I don't know why you want it," Thorion protested. "Digging about in people's bodies, looking at shit and vomit and urine, analyzing pustules, doing dissections — it's a filthy business, the sort of thing ordinarily left to slaves. It's no job for any person of quality, let alone a girl."

"The art of healing is the noblest of the arts," I protested, quoting Hippocrates. Then I tried hard to explain what I had never before explained, even to myself. "There is nothing that causes more misery than disease. It kills more people, more painfully, than even Festinus does. Think of our mother, Thorion, or your husband and your own baby, Maia. Oh, I know that there's little that even the best doctor can do — but a little is still something. In ten or fifteen or twenty years' time, if I can look back and say, 'That person, and that, and that, would have died but for me; that one would have been crippled for life; that baby would have been lost at birth — if I can say that, how can I be unhappy? And as for its being a slavish sort of job, I can't see that at all. To understand the workings of our own bodies, and of nature, is the purest philosophy; and to heal is almost divine!"

"Oh, Charition!" said Thorion with a groan. "I don't understand you. How could I possibly let you do a thing like that?"

"Would you prefer me to marry Festinus?"

Thorion said nothing. He stared out the window for a moment, looking toward the governor's palace, then slammed his fist angrily into the window frame. He sucked his knuckles, glaring at the bright rooftops.

Maia had been watching me hard; at last she reached out and

46

touched my hand. "You are right," she said slowly. "You know your-self what is good and would make you happy, and you are right to seek it."

I hugged her, deeply moved; Thorion turned his eyes from the palace and stared in surprise. After a moment he shrugged, came over, and hugged both of us. "I suppose anything would be better than marrying Festinus," he said. "And I can't think of any other way out. But I'll make him pay for this. I'll miss you, Charition."

"It needn't be forever," I said again. "In a few years, if Father or Festinus dies, or if Festinus marries someone else in some other city, I can come back. You can tell everyone that you had me hidden in some private house in the country, and arrange for me to marry whomever you like — Kyrillos, if he's still around."

They both looked happier at this prospect.

"So you'll help me?" I asked. This was crucial: I'd never get out of the city on my own, and I'd need letters of recommendation to get an apprenticeship in Alexandria.

"There was never any question of that, was there?" Thorion pulled on his lip. "Now, how on earth are we going to get you to Alexan-dria?"

The obvious, and indeed the only, way to get to Alexandria is by ship. But it was already nearing the end of September, and few ships will brave the treacherous winter seas between mid-October and the end of March. Thorion went down to the harbor and inquired of the shipmasters; he found one who was planning to sail the following week, and after that there was nothing until the spring. He didn't much like the look of the one that was to sail, though. "Mixed cargo of wine and dyed cloth from Asia and slaves from the north," he told me. "The master didn't look above trying to add to his cargo during the voyage. He could sell a eunuch for more than a hundred *solidi*, and he might be tempted to take the risk of being found out."

However, we didn't have to risk the slave ship. Father negotiated a marriage contract with Festinus that put the date of the wedding back to May. Festinus had wanted a quick marriage, but Father had ar-gued that I was still young, the proposal was sudden, and time was needed to prepare my trousseau. Before February, he said, was impossible, and after that it was Lent, an inappropriate and unlucky time for a wedding. Easter, fortunately, was late that year, so the beginning of May was settled on. That gave us plenty of time.

Everyone was very kind to me that winter, kind enough that I felt guilty about running off. Festinus visited occasionally, but not indecently often, and I was not obliged to do more than nod my head at him and sit in the background looking modest; he did not try to talk to me privately again, and I avoided speaking to him at all, successfully enough that the revulsion I felt for him grew somewhat blunted. Perhaps, I thought sometimes, lying awake in bed at night, perhaps I should go through with the marriage. If I did disappear before the wedding, Festinus would make trouble. I didn't think he could actually accuse Father of anything, only a year after acquitting him, but he was still a powerful man. He could block Thorion's career, and make legal trouble for Father. Moreover, Father was so much afraid of the governor that he might have Maia and the other slaves beaten or tortured to make them tell where I was.

On the other hand, Father meant to give me Maia and a few others as part of my dowry, and life wouldn't be any easier for them in Festinus' house than it would be for me; on the whole I thought they'd be better off with Father. He was a gentle man, and hated to hurt anyone. He was afraid of what he was doing now, and gave me various embarrassing presents, offering them with a clumsy jocularity that didn't hide his nervousness. He also spent a great deal of money on clothes and carriages for me to use when I was married. Thorion spent the winter pressing for Father to make arrangements for his career — he wanted to have it all settled before we made Festinus our enemy. These arrangements proved expensive, and Father had to sell some land. I felt very sorry that all this preparation and worry was for nothing, but I didn't say anything more about the wedding. I might have doubts sometimes, but already I was burning to be in Alexandria. Thorion did make a few more attempts to talk Father into canceling the wedding, but Father insisted that it was too late now, and anyway, Festinus had "settled down" a great deal, and wouldn't hurt his own wife.

Everyone's sudden kindness meant that I was able to read a few more medical texts. Ischyras agreed to abandon Euripides and read Nikandros' poem on drugs. I felt rather ashamed whenever I looked at my tutor: I had now firmly decided to bring his name into my plans, but I had no intention of bringing in the man himself. I worried that my escape might one day cause him trouble, but I comforted myself with the assurance that if it ever came to that, I could always confess that he knew nothing about it.

I also finally read Galen that winter. Maia took her savings down to the marketplace and bought me a copy of his work on anatomy. It was the most beautiful book I had ever seen: a great heavy codex, not a scroll, and on parchment, not papyrus. It had beautiful illustrations in red and black ink, and was written out in a tiny but perfectly clear book hand, with explanatory glosses in the margins. It must have cost a fortune. I told Maia that I must pay her back, but she refused to let me.

Another of the slaves who was very kind to me was Philoxenos; he too had had experience of Festinus. He looked grieved whenever he saw me, and I almost told him not to worry, I wasn't going to marry the governor. He promised me the first foal his brood mare produced, and told me to call him if I ever needed help, which was an astonishingly generous and courageous, if very rash, thing to say. And he gave me his own carefully written-out remedies for various equine diseases, clumsily printed over a parchment cookery book, but all of it good sense and of real value.

We knew that we had to exercise considerable care in making our preparations. Anyone whom we involved might be tortured and severely punished if they were found out. It was quite certain that Thorion would be suspected of concealing me somewhere, but the worst Thorion had to fear was having his allowance cut off, and Festinus' enmity. Thorion resolved to leave Ephesus to avoid the latter. He wanted to get an office at court and a proper law degree, and he could get both in Constantinople. Father wrote letters to all his old friends who were at the capital, and eventually paid eighty *solidi* to get Thorion a junior position, with light duties (doing taxes), in the office of the praetorian prefect; the arrangements to study law were much cheaper and easier, since they involved only fees and not bribes.

We began making our serious preparations after Christmas, and finished by the middle of Lent. By that time the shipmasters were thinking of moving their vessels: it was clear spring weather, mild with a light breeze predominantly from the northeast — perfect winds for Alexandria. Thorion found a ship that would leave in the middle of April. It was called the *Halcyon*; it was a fairly large ship, and it was to take a cargo of timber and assorted luxury goods but had room for a few passengers as well. The master was well known in Ephesus, but not Ephesian; he was thought to be honest, but wouldn't know enough about the city to guess who I was, and Thorion's name meant little to him. Thorion booked me a passage and paid half the fare in advance; I would pay the rest when we docked in Alexandria.

Alexandria! The city of the old kings, the city of scholars, the city that was once the greatest in all the world and is still the greatest in the East, for all the glory of Constantinople. A doctor can produce no better recommendation than to declare "I studied in Alexandria." And I would go there: I, Charis daughter of Theodoros, would read in the great library, and study in the famous Museum where Herophilos and Erasistratos and Nikandros and Galen himself had studied! I stopped worrying about what would happen to my family in Ephesus, and I dreamed of Alexandria. I pictured the *Halcyon* sailing into the great harbor, and saw the city rising, white and glowing, out of the sea, lit by the fires of its famous lighthouse, the Pharos which was one of the wonders of the world — but all of Alexandria was wonderful. I was ashamed of myself, particularly when I looked at Maia, but I couldn't wait to go.

Maia wanted to come with me. "You'll need someone to look after you," she pointed out. "Everyone who's anyone has at least one slave. And, my dear, you don't know how to do anything for yourself. But you'll need someone you can trust. Why, if you counted on buying someone when you reached Alexandria, what would happen? Whoever you bought would find out within a week that you were a girl, and then he could blackmail you into whatever he wanted! No, I'll go with you."

But I refused to take her. I told her that I was worried about her health on the sea voyage, and in fact her joints often pained her since she had been tortured, and I thought ships and cheap lodgings would do her no good. I told her that I didn't want her classed as a runaway and myself called a thief: she was legally my father's property. "I want to see you when I come back," I told her. "I'd never forgive myself if you took sick and died while following me about."

But there was more to it than that. Maia still hated the notion of my disguise. I didn't want to pain her by enjoying it too much. She loved propriety, belonging to a great house, serving a fine lady. What would happen if I took her to a great city where I would live as a poor student, lodging in some tenement, working late, jostling the crowds? She would be miserable, thinking always of what we had been, hating the present. And I would be miserable if she was, I knew that. And could I trust her? I knew I could rely on her loyalty, but could I trust her not to hint to neighbors and shop owners that there was more to us than would appear and that she could, if she would, tell them . . . she would not tell them. But she would want them to guess. And if I was to make my disguise succeed, I needed to have no one guessing, no one even suspecting. I must change the way I walked, the way I sat — no more lowered eyes and folded hands — the way I spoke. That would be the hardest, I thought: to remember to use the masculine form of adjectives to describe myself; otherwise, every little phrase like "I'm hungry" would give me away. It would be better, I thought, to have no slave at all, and pay someone to do my cleaning and cooking for me. Maia could go to Constantinople with Thorion.

The day before the *Halcyon* was to sail, Thorion had my traveling chest sent down to the ship and stowed on board. He had hidden it in a cave on Mount Pion, outside the walls, and it was an easy matter to load it onto a donkey and bring it into the city, then get a porter to take it onto the ship. I'd already packed my books into it. That left only the change of clothing — and my mother's jewels. These were my property, and I was counting on selling them to support myself while I studied, but I would have to do so in Alexandria, where the gems would not be recognized.

I was very much afraid that night that something would happen: that Festinus would appear and demand to marry me on the spot; that the ship would sink in a sudden storm; that Father would command that I be somewhere next day. I couldn't sleep, and lay awake staring at the moonlight on the wall, realizing that I might never see this room again. When the moonlight fell on Maia's bed I saw that she was awake and staring at me, so I got up and climbed into her bed. "I'll miss you so much, Maia," I whispered to her, and she hugged me. I think after a couple of hours we both slept a little.

I had a lesson with Ischyras that morning, and I suffered it grimly, so inattentive that my tutor asked me whether I was feeling well. I said I had a headache. The *Halcyon* was not to sail until the evening tide; if I left the house after lunch, I wouldn't be missed until suppertime, when it would be too late. But when lunch came I could scarcely eat. Father was there for the meal, and he also asked if I was ill. I again spoke of a headache.

"You look quite pale, my dear," said Father. "Do you want to lie down? Shall I call a doctor?"

"Oh no, no!" I said, stirring myself and trying to smile. "It's not that bad. I think I'll go for a walk in the garden: that ought to help it."

Finally able to leave the table, I went up to my room and fetched the case that held my mother's jewels. I slipped it into my cosmetics pouch and then looked around. The last time, I thought. I took a deep breath and left the room.

Through the First Court, through the Blue Court, past the bathhouse, through the kitchen garden to the postern. Past the stables and into the fields. Philoxenos and the stableboys were grooming some horses in the yard; they waved to me, and I waved back. The fields were green with the wet spring grass, dotted with red poppies. I picked up my skirts and ran, not looking back. Nobody had asked where I was going, and nobody would wonder, until I didn't come back.

Thorion had told me how to find the cave. It was on the northeast side of the hill, near the place where they say some martyrs were walled up during the reign of the emperor Decius. There was a cleft in the rock, and there Maia was sitting, waiting for me. When I ran up she stood and kissed me, then pulled me into the cave. It was not large — there was about room for the two of us to stand, with a crevice at the back where Thorion had hidden the traveling chest and where he had left a smaller clothes chest with the men's clothing he'd bought for me. We'd thought at first I'd be able to wear some of his, but even the things he'd outgrown were too wide across the shoulders, and too richly made for a student doctor. So he'd bought some things secondhand in the marketplace: two linen tunics and one woolen one, all in heavy, hard-wearing weaves and cut respectably long, below the knee, though they were plain and undecorated. There were also a good woolen traveling cloak, a hat, a pair of sandals, and some boots. Most of these were already on the ship, but not the tunic, cloak, hat, and boots.

"First your hair," said Maia when I went over to the clothes chest. So I sat down in the shadowy cleft and Maia got out the shears. From that cave on the hilltop I could see for miles. The river valley was all green with new corn, the roads raw red earth. I could see the Temple of Artemis shining white and gold a mile away, the white paving of the Sacred Way leading up to it. I wondered if Egypt was as beautiful as Asia. I supposed that it too was flat, mostly. It was river plain as well. Maia's shears snipped steadily, hair fell down my back, and my head felt lighter. Goodbye, you artificial and unwanted curls. No more time wasted on hair styling. I knew that Maia had dreaded this — I suspected that she was crying over my long black curls — but I tried not to look at her.

Maia had brought a pitcher of water, and I washed my face and rubbed the last of the curls out of my hair. We'd stopped plucking my eyebrows a month before. My ears were pierced, of course, but it's not unknown for boys to have pierced ears; it certainly wouldn't be out of place in a eunuch redeemed from the Persians. Maia had also brought one of those corsets that women sometimes wear if they are going to be driven somewhere, or if they just don't want to look fat, and she helped me put this on. My breasts were small anyway, thank Heaven; with the corset they wouldn't show at all. I put on the tunic: it was the woolen one, and it was dyed a pale blue, faded almost gray. I started to tie it around my waist, but Maia stopped me, shaking her head, and fastened it around my hips, to disguise my shape. It felt very strange to wear a short tunic, to feel the air against my legs. The cloak was good quality, warm and solid, but plain blue: no pattern, and no purple stripe. Maia handed it to me, and I put it over my head. I eased it over and pulled it sideways like a shawl, trying to avoid disturbing the curls that were no longer there. Must remember not to do that. Maia shook her head again, took the cloak off, and pinned it at my right shoulder, draping it straight back and across, the way men wear it.

Thorion came in while Maia was tying the boots on for me. He stood outside the cave, staring at us; I waited for Maia to finish, then stood up and went out into the light so he could see properly. "Well?" I asked.

He gave me a very peculiar look, then flung his arms round me. "Oh, Charition," he said breathlessly. "I don't want you to go."

"Don't I look right?" I asked.

Thorion shook his head. I realized that he was crying. I felt awful.

"Maia," I said. She was crying too. She handed me a mirror.

A thin, long, narrow face, with a long nose and a wide, thin-lipped mouth; large, intelligent eyes, quizzical and detached; straight dark hair falling over the straight brows. For the first time in my life, I looked in the mirror and saw myself. Not a doll dressed by somebody else; myself. I smiled, and the face smiled back. Not a boy's face, not properly a girl's. Goodbye, Charis, I thought. Hello, Chariton of Amida and Ephesus, a eunuch and a student of the art of healing.

"It's perfect," I said.

"You don't look like *you* at all," groaned Thorion. "I'll kill that Festinus."

"He'll probably die of apoplexy," I said. "He has a choleric disposition and he drinks too much." I smiled at Thorion. "I'll be all right."

Maia shook her head. Carefully she gathered up my discarded clothes — the long white and yellow tunic, and the long white and green cloak with its purple stripe. She folded them and put them in the little clothes chest. "It's sandalwood," she told me. "They should still be here when you come back." She picked up a lock of my hair and stroked it, then put it on top of the clothes. Thorion shoved the chest back into the crevice and pulled some rocks down over it so that it wouldn't show. Maia tidied up the shears and the pitcher of water. "Let us pray for your swift return," she said.

We joined hands, standing cramped in the cave, and Maia prayed. My head felt light and empty, and her words meant nothing. A swift return? Not too swift. Chariton, I felt, had a more interesting life before him than Charis did.

We went back out into the sunlight and walked together around the side of the hill. Ephesus lay at our feet. The green dome of our own banqueting hall stood out nearby, the red sands of the hippodrome to its left. Below us to our right was the theater, with the white paved Harbor Street, fringed with colorful shop hangings, running from it to the sea. Ships were tied up at the docks, and we could see the bustle about one of the vessels, a large ship with orange and yellow sails. The *Halcyon*. The water of the harbor showed brown and muddy from this height, but beyond it the sea shimmered with light, dissolving into the sun.

"Well," said Thorion, and swallowed. "Farewell."

"Farewell." I hugged him, and then Maia. "I will write. I'll have to wait a little while, but I can write when you're in Constantinople."

They each hugged me back, Maia letting go of me very reluctantly, and then I started down the hill. I would go in by the main gate and so down to the harbor; Thorion and Maia would go back through the postern and try to establish that they'd been in all afternoon. I walked on a hundred paces and then looked back, but they had already turned, and all I saw was their backs walking slowly home. I looked at the orange-sailed ship in the harbor. "The Greek ships wait," I thought. But no, that was wrong; what I wanted was another chorus from another play:

    . . . on the wide surge
    The halyards wing out the sails to the wind
    by the prow of the swift ship.
    Flashing like couriers I'd go
    where sunshine comes afire.

Because I was going not to slavery but to freedom.

II

✠✠✠✠✠✠✠✠✠✠✠✠✠✠✠✠

ALEXANDRIA

THE HALCYON ARRIVED in Alexandria on the first of May. We'd had a smooth voyage, sailing by way of Cyprus but not stopping anywhere apart from that until we saw the light of the Pharos ahead of us. The ship's master sailed all that night, with the beacon of the lighthouse before the bow, and I stayed up as well, too excited to sleep. In the morning we saw the smoke rising thick and black as the fire was extinguished. The tower itself stood out on a promontory, white and tall, decorated with bronze statues of sea gods and dolphins; the mirrors on its summit were blinding in the early sunlight. Beyond it, across the vivid blue of the sea, lay the city: a jumble of red tiled roofs, domes and gardens, walled and gated and magnificently huge. From a hill in the middle came a glint of gold where the light caught some gilded monument; it looked like the catch of a treasure chest.

Alexandria has two harbors, divided by the Pharos promontory: the Eastern, or Great, Harbor, and the harbor called Eunostos, "of happy return." As we approached I expected to go into the Great Harbor, which was embraced by the Pharos and a smaller lighthouse and which was ringed by splendid stone fortifications, palaces, and gardens. But instead the ship turned right, into the Eunostos Harbor. This was much less impressive: the buildings ringing it were warehouses and dockyards; fishing boats were drawn up on the beaches, stinking of offal. Beyond the docks were streets of narrow houses, very tall, all built of a dirty gray brick. I found out afterward that all the merchant shipping used this harbor; the Great Harbor was reserved for the government.

While the *Halcyon* was waiting to dock, I asked the shipmaster where the Museum was, and he laughed. "Under three feet of earth," he told me. "It was destroyed in the old wars, or in some rebellion. Nobody's ever rebuilt it." I learned later that it had been in the

Broucheion quarter, which was once the best part of the city: it had held the imperial palaces, some of the temples, the Museum, and the library. All was gone now; a field of willow herb and acanthus covered the broken stones, and children chased rats over the ruins. What was left of the library was now at the Temple of Serapis in the Rhakotis quarter, which led to the Eunostos Harbor. The city wall had been rebuilt, and rebuilt around a smaller city after the wars. The Delta quarter, which used to be a Jewish city within the city, was gone altogether. The only new buildings were the churches.

When the *Halcyon* docked, the master gave me some advice. "Leave your valuables at a bank," he said. "Isisdoros son of Heron is reliable, and won't ask too much in interest; you'll find him at the second warehouse on your left as you leave the harbor. The city is full of pickpockets and thieves, so never carry much money around. Stay out of back streets, especially in the Rhakotis quarter. The Egyptians don't like foreigners, particularly eunuchs. What's your religion? Yes, you said Christian, but are you Arian or Nicene?"

I said I was a moderate homoiousian, neither Arian nor Nicene; but I didn't know much about theology. The dispute has to do with the nature of Christ: the Arians say that he was created by the Father, while the Nicenes say that he is "coessential" with the Father, a term that other Christians dislike. Arianism is favored by the emperors but not by the bishops, who've never accepted it in any synod, and Grandfather thought it a bit risky.

"Well, then, say that you're Nicene," said the master of the *Halcyon*. "It's better to be a Manichee than an Arian here. The people are all madly in love with their archbishop, and he's an arch-Nicene and has been exiled five times because of it. Arians aren't popular. Stay away from the public baths: pretty boys aren't safe in this city."

"I'm older than I look," I protested.

"Very well, but it's looks that count with those buggers! You seem a pleasant young man, for a eunuch; I'd be sad to hear that you came to grief. Good luck, and look after yourself!"

The city was not what I expected. Leaving the ship, I walked through the narrow streets of the Rhakotis quarter, frowned over by the dingy narrow-fronted houses and two churches, the old small one of Theonas and the new big one of the popular archbishop, Athanasios. I found the banker the shipmaster had recommended and left my jewels with him, then started out to find the scholars at the Temple of Serapis. A ship canal connects the harbor with Lake Mareotis, and I walked beside it up to the Canopic Way, avoiding the back streets as I'd been advised. The people looked very foreign — darker than people in Asia. "Honey-colored," the census always puts it. Some of them were speaking in another language, not Greek. Coptic, I supposed. These were the Egyptians, who didn't like foreigners. It seemed very strange.

The Canopic Way was more like the Alexandria I had imagined: a great street wide enough to drive four chariots along abreast, and teeming with people, with loaded donkeys and camels, and with cats — animals that are rare outside of Egypt but very common in it. On either side ran a double colonnade of shops, which the Alexandrians call the Tetrapylon. Street criers were hawking candied citron, dates, fresh hot cumin bread, sausages, and sesame cakes. I passed shops selling wine from all over the empire, selling woolen and linen clothes and yarns dyed unfamiliar bright colors, selling magic charms, selling books, selling glass, selling gold from Nubia and pearls from Britain, selling carved furniture and terra-cotta images of a hundred different gods. Beggers pleaded for alms. I passed a young eunuch in a Phrygian hat, sitting in front of a bronze begging bowl and singing a hymn to the goddess Kybele in a reedy voice; he glanced at me, then looked away again without interest. A tall bearded man in a black cloak stood on a wall, preaching Stoic philosophy to a few attentive pupils. On the other side of the road a hairy peasant in a homespun tunic was preaching some variety of Gnosticism; "The world was made by the Devil!" he shouted (he had to shout to be heard at all). People were all shouting as they bargained, and jostling each other, singing, swearing. I passed a shop full of caged birds, piping away like a chorus of bacchanals. There was a succession of smells: of honey, of dung, of unwashed flesh, of perfumes, of fresh bread, of sewage, of spices. Everywhere there was sound and color and life, and it stunned me.

Even as a stranger, though, I could tell that the city was not what it had been. When I reached the central square, where the Canopic Way crosses the other great thoroughfare, the Soma Street, I saw the first of many ruins. The mausoleum of the great Alexander, the son of Philip of Macedon, the man who conquered the world: a ring of broken columns and a bit of wall. The embalmed body was gone, and so, of course, were the golden coffin and the treasure that had surrounded it. Well, the empire he had founded went long before his tomb did, so I don't suppose he can complain. I turned right on the Soma Street and went up toward the Temple of Serapis, where the fragments of the library and the Museum were still preserved.

The Temple stands on an artificial hill in the southwest part of the city, near the stadium. It wasn't hard to find it: as soon as I left Soma Square I saw it floating over the roofs of the nearby houses. The gilded column I had noticed from the ship stood in its grounds. The turning from the Soma Street was clearly marked with a white marble slab, engraved with the image of the god, set into the road. I followed this Sacred Way to the Temple: it wound up the face of the artificial hill, flanked by date palms and bushes of purple cistus flowers. The Temple complex itself was walled off from the rest of the city, but the gate was open and unguarded; I went through into a paved court-yard. It was now nearly noon, and the sun glared painfully bright from the white paving. Among more date palms a fountain played, cool and sweet. Beyond stood the Temple, its columns painted and gilded, its façade decorated with images of Serapis, Isis, and their son Harpokrates, chief among the old gods of the Egyptians.

I didn't go into the Temple; as a Christian, I had no business there. But it was surrounded by buildings — lecture halls, residences, the library, cloisters and gardens — and most of these were owned by what the Alexandrians still call the Museum. I had some letters of reference that Thorion and I had drafted, addressed to some of the leading doctors of the medical faculty, and I looked for someone to give them to.

I wandered into one of the larger and more public-seeming an-nexes. It was a library, the walls lined with book racks. A thin, dark Alexandrian was sitting at a desk in the middle of the room. He had a bronze writing case slung around his neck, together with an official-looking signet, and he was writing carefully on a sheet of papyrus; he had to be a scribe, an official. Nervously I went up and asked if I might arrange to see the most esteemed Adamantios (he was the head of the medical faculty).

"What do you want him for?" the scribe demanded irritably, put-ting his pen down and glaring at me. Then he gave me a second look, noticing my appearance and smooth face, and his mouth set in distaste. I grew to know that look well: it was the one that followed the decision that I was probably a eunuch. I hadn't realized how much eunuchs arc hated. Everyone blames them for all the ills of the empire, saying that they are just imported slaves but they have the emperor's ear and won't let honest men get to him. Greedy and corrupt half-men, they call them — they want a bribe for telling you the time of day. It didn't matter that I wasn't an imperial chamber-lain; I was hated as though I were, and sneered at for my lack of virility, as though I might have chosen to castrate myself simply to take bribes.

I explained, a bit nervously, what I wanted to see Adamantios about. The scribe snorted, sneered a bit, but directed me to an office off one of the library courts. It was a small, dark room with stone walls, pleasantly cool. A writing desk stood by one wall, with a bookcase next to it. There was nobody there, so I sat down and waited.

After about an hour a tall, dark man in a fringed cloak and a small hat came in, talking loudly to two well-dressed attendants. I stood respectfully, and he asked me what I wanted.

"Esteemed sir," I said, "I am Chariton, a eunuch from Ephesus, and I am waiting to speak with the most excellent Adamantios. I wish to apply to train in medicine here."

"I'm Adamantios," said the man, looking at me suspiciously. "Have I heard of you? I don't recall the name . . ."

"I have some letters," I said eagerly, and offered them to him. He took them and glanced through them, frowning down his nose.

"Why didn't your patron arrange something in advance?" he asked me. "We are very busy this season, very busy. And I wouldn't have thought that you were, um, *suitable* material for a doctor. It is not a luxurious life, you know. I would have thought that an, um, eunuch was better off in an *administrative* post."

"I don't mind hard work," I told him. "And I am very eager to learn the art of healing. I have the money to pay for my teaching."

"We-ell . . ." said Adamantios. He shuffled through the letters and handed them back to me. "You are of course free to try any of the doctors associated with the Museum. You will need someone to take you on as an assistant. Then you can attend any of the lectures, for payment of a fee to the teacher, of course. It is up to you to find a master, really."

"I thought perhaps Your Prudence . . . that is, I thought you might know of someone who wanted an assistant."

"Oh." He contemplated me for a moment, then shook his head. "No, I can't think of anyone. Can you, Timias?" he said, turning to one of his companions.

The companion laughed. "Not an assistant like that!"

Adamantios gave a smug smile. "No, I can't think of anyone. You are of course free to ask around. Is that all?"

I spent my first week in the city lodging in a flea-ridden tenement near the ship canal and knocking on doors near the Temple of Serapis, being laughed at while I trudged from one to the other. My letters of recommendation, so carefully prepared, were useless. Such letters should be sent before the person they recommend arrives; they should not be thrust at their recipients by an unknown eunuch in shabby clothes. Nobody trusted me: either I wouldn't work hard enough, or I was probably unreliable, and I was probably a runaway slave. My scheme, which had seemed so good in Ephesus, looked half-baked and impossible in Alexandria. I wasn't prepared for the refusals, the sneers, the distaste and outright hatred that met me, and I was quite wretched.

It was also assumed that I was on the lookout for more virile men, since eunuchs are a luxury-loving species. I lost track of the number of times I was approached with offers of money, of how many groping hands I eluded. I was still inexperienced enough to be shaken by this, though it was easier than it had been with Festinus. These people didn't know who I was. If they'd succeeded in groping, they would have had a surprise. But no one seemed to suspect that I was anything other than what I claimed to be. At first I was nervous, prepared to answer accusations, but eventually I grew used to it. People rely so much on clothing, on all the signs of one's sex and rank one gives them in dressing. I could almost have dispensed with the corset; short hair and a short tunic made all the difference. People looked at me and thought "girlish boy — a eunuch?" rather than "dressed-up girl." Of course I'd had the sea voyage to accustom myself to the change in sex before I plunged into the city; I no longer found it such an effort to refer to myself as masculine, and it had been surprisingly easy to drop all the manners of a noble maiden. But I still had endless difficulty. It was hard, trying to remember that I was a man, trying to put on my own clothes and tie them properly, walking on foot about a strange great city when before I'd always had a litter or carriage to ride in. My feet hurt. I couldn't wash properly, either: there wasn't enough privacy at the inn. I lived on cheap bread rolls bought from corner vendors. I didn't have much money, as I had not yet been able to sell any of the jewels. The banker wouldn't change them, so I took them to an expensive shop on the Canopic Way, but the owner pretended to believe that they were glass, and when I insisted that they were my mother's, and real, he said that I had stolen them and threatened to tell the magistrates. I walked out with them, then spent a miserable day wondering whether he would carry out his threat. He didn't, but I was afraid to try somewhere else. If I'd been more familiar with the city, I'd have realized that he was simply trying to drive the price down. Alexandrians are aggressive people, irritable, and collectively turbulent, violent, and dangerous.

After ten days I was wondering whether I should go back to Ephesus and marry Festinus. I looked around at some of the Alexandrian doctors who weren't affiliated with the Museum; most of them were superstitious quacks, the sort of men who tell their patients to roll in the mud, run three times round the temple invoking the god, and then go swim in the ship canal — a course that will kill all but the healthiest. But then I met Philon.

It was a chance meeting, in the library of the Temple. I was recovering from my latest rejection by reading Krateuas' *Herbal* when a middle-aged man with a beard came up and asked if he could see it, "when you've finished with it, esteemed sir." It was pleasant to be called "esteemed sir" after the sneering, so I put the book down.

"I was just looking at it," I told him. "If you want to check a reference, sir, go ahead."

He smiled. I had been in the city long enough now to recognize that the beard and the fringed shawl and the little cap were signs that the man was Jewish; he had brown hair, and was lighter than the usual honey color. He was tall, and wide across the shoulders in a way that reminded me of Thorion. "Thank you, sir," he said, and looked up a reference to a prescription for some gynecological disorder, then shook his head. "Won't work," he said. "Still, we can but try."

"A patient?" I asked, and he smiled again.

"What else? And there's little enough I can do for the poor woman. Opium, that's all. Relieve the pain. A cure — that's in the hands of God."

" 'Life is short and the art long,' " I quoted. " 'Opportunity, elusive; experience, deceptive; judgment, difficult.' "

" 'But not only must the doctor do his duty, but patient and attendants do their part as well, if there is to be a cure,' " he finished for me. "Ah, Hippocrates! You are a student here, sir?"

"No," I said shortly. Then, because he reminded me a little of Thorion: "I'd like to be. But no one seems to want me. I'm a eunuch, and I haven't proper recommendations."

He gave a little grunt — still more like Thorion! — and surveyed me. "Where are you from? If I may ask. Your accent is Asian."

"Ephesus," I said. "That is, Ephesus and Amida." And I outlined my little story about the Persians, and "my cousin Ischyras" redeeming me, and Thorion sending me off to learn medicine.

"You have been unlucky," he said, in reference to the supposed massacre of my family and my castration. "And your patron should have taken more care, and arranged where you should study before you arrived. But why medicine? I would have thought —"

"That a eunuch would do better at court, taking bribes? I *want* to study medicine. I don't care about money, but I care about healing. It is the noblest of the arts, and I have wanted to study it all my life." I spoke with some intensity: the past week had made me defensive.

"Ah," he said. "May I perhaps see your letters of recommendation?"

I had them, of course, and I showed them to him. He read them through ("This Theodoros — he's not the one who was executed? No, no, of course not . . ."), then asked me some medical questions, mostly drawn from standard texts like the Hippocratic works and Galen.

"You are very well read for such a young man," he said at last. "And you speak with an educated accent — you know the classics as well as medical writers? Yes? I am surprised no one has taken you as a pupil. I myself . . ." He stopped, looking uncertain; then he seemed to nerve himself and took the plunge. "I myself greatly need an assistant. My nephew was to have studied with me, but he died of a fever last year. Of course you would have to arrange to attend lectures as well, but I am affiliated with the school here . . ." He coughed, cleared his throat. "Of course, I am not such an educated man; I was brought up on the Law, not on Homer and the classics — but I know Hippocrates. I know him better than the Torah, God forgive me! If you do not mind studying with a Jew who can quote no more than "Sing Goddess of the Wrath," you are most welcome to study with me . . ." He trailed off a bit uncertainly.

"If you know Hippocrates," I said, "you can throw Homer in the Great Harbor. But I am a Christian — you don't mind?"

"Oh, no, no!" he said, smiling again. "It would in fact be very useful."

So, both of us perhaps wondering what we were letting ourselves in for, we went to Adamantios. He greeted Philon warmly, and when he heard what he'd come for looked surprised, then amused; he shook hands with me and congratulated me in a condescending fashion. Philon would take me on as his assistant, and agreed to teach me the art; I was free to attend lectures by other doctors, on payment of a fee; and when I felt ready I would be examined by the professors of medicine at the Museum. I agreed to pay Philon ten *solidi* as soon as I was able to sell my jewels, and we shook hands on the bargain.

Then I went back to my lodgings and worried. I knew nothing at all about Philon. I had been in the city just long enough to know that the Egyptians hated the Jews, and that the intellectuals of the Museum, who were mostly pagan, distrusted them, and ignored them as much as they could. That might go far toward explaining my ignorance — but what if the man was dishonest, or just incompetent? And Adamantios was Jewish too, and everybody had heard of him — though it was true that he was upper-class, and better read in Homer than in the Law. Anyone can quote Hippocrates. Well, I told myself, I can go to lectures now, and I can get other opinions. I should be able to learn something even if Philon can't teach me.

But that just started me worrying about the lecturers and, worse, about the other students. I had seen them around, checking books in the library, arguing by the fountain in front of the Temple, examining herbs in the Temple gardens. They were all young men, about my own age or older, and they all acted as though they knew every secret of nature already. They would certainly know more than I did. And I suspected that they despised me already. It shouldn't matter, I told myself, trying to still the fear. Here I am in Alexandria, and tomorrow I'm going to start my study of the art of healing. Even if I am ignorant, even if I'm not good at it, it's still what I've wanted all my life. A dream come true.

It did make me feel better. I got out my copy of Galen and went through it again, wondering at everything there was to learn.

✜✜✜

I met Philon the next morning at the Temple, as we'd arranged. He looked a bit unsure of me as well, but he greeted me politely and we started off on his rounds.

Philon's patients were mostly Jewish, but there were a scattering of lower-class Greeks and Egyptians. We worked our way around a series of narrow houses and tenements, some of them tacked onto the back of small shops, in the southeast quarter of the city. There was a carpenter recovering from a fever; a scribe's little daughter with earache; a bathhouse attendant's wife with a broken collarbone. "No one of any distinction, I'm afraid," Philon told me, smiling. "I am not a fashionable doctor. But I'm not an expensive one either!" He introduced me to the patients carefully, and asked me to make notes in his casebook, which allowed me to see what each patient had suffered and what Philon had done for him. He was gentle and careful, used a great variety of drugs with discretion, and avoided bleedings and purgatives. He took time with each patient, answering questions and explaining what he was doing.

The fourth or fifth patient we visited that morning was a coppersmith's wife who was recovering from childbirth. The lintel of the house was covered with laurel branches and cinquefoil as a charm against the evil eye, and a magic charm was pinned to the door beside the Jewish scroll of the Law. Philon looked at the charm and frowned unhappily. "I know that one," he muttered, and shook his head. He knocked on the door.

The house slave, a shriveled old woman, let us in, and even before Philon had put his foot across the threshold she was telling him that "the mistress is worse, much worse, and the baby's ill too, poor thing; it's gone yellow."

"That often happens a day or two after the birth," said Philon resolutely, and went to examine the patient.

The house smelled of incense, and under the incense was a peculiar acrid smell — burnt hair and some plant, I decided. The mistress was lying in bed, unhealthily flushed. She had a magic charm around her neck, and a knife under her pillow, to ward off devils.

Philon smiled, introduced me, and examined the patient. He cleaned her up with a solution of vinegar and myrrh, and gave her a drink of opium and dittany in wine. He looked at the baby, who was a bit yellow, and sound asleep with a magic charm around her neck. He pulled it off, then picked up the one the woman wore as well. "This one's no good," he told her with a cheerful air. "It's a pagan thing, no good for a Jew. You shouldn't trust in a thing like this, but in the Law. Jewish devils won't pay any attention to it. Do you think the demon Lilith minds what Isis says, eh? What you want, my good woman, is a scroll of the Law. Tie it to your stomach with strips of new linen, and get your husband to sing the psalms while you burn incense. The eighteenth psalm is good. I know the fellow who made this for you: he thinks you can appease every devil by giving it blood. But that only makes them greedy, and they keep coming back for more. You listen to him, and you and the baby will both die. You do as I say and don't let him in here again, and just see how quickly you get better. Don't worry about your daughter, either: a mild jaundice like that is common. Nurse her often, and perhaps give her some boiled water to drink as well, and the yellowness will leave her quickly if you say the right prayers and burn the incense."

The woman looked happier for the visit, and nodded. Philon went out, taking the magic charms with him. He tore the other charm off the door and threw them all into the public sewer, "where they belong," he said angrily. "And I wish their maker was with them." Then he looked rueful at my surprise. "One of our Alexandrian sorcerers," he explained. "We have a lot of them. This one specializes in childbed fevers. Did you smell anything?"

"Burnt hair and . . . something else."

"The hair was the woman's, and the something else was papyrus written on with the woman's blood. It's the first part of the charm. If it doesn't work, he cuts fingers off the baby, to appease the devil that threatens the child's life. He has no idea of hygiene, though; those cuts of his usually go septic, and the child ends up a cripple, if it lives. He likes burning things, too. The people he's killed!" Philon sighed. "Well, the Egyptians are addicted to magic, and have passed the taste to some Jews. But I hope our patient will leave it alone now."

"What was it that you told her to do?"

He smiled still more ruefully. "A thing that disgraces me as a Hippocratic. But she wants magic; Hippocratic medicine can promise so little. Leave it to the wisdom of the body, we say: your body will recover if it can. But meanwhile she is in pain and frightened. A sorcerer comes up and says, 'I can cure you,' and it's more than the doctor promised, so she listens. Well, I gave her a charm to keep her happy, and if it calms her mind, that in itself will be helpful."

He started off to the next house, and I followed him slowly, thinking hard. It was all very different from the Hippocratic texts I had read. Philon glanced back, then stopped to let me catch up.

"Practice is different from theory," I observed, apologizing for my slowness.

He grinned. "Why, esteemed Chariton, you have already learned something that half the doctors at the Temple don't seem to know."

I smiled back, and asked, "Do you have a theory you work by, at all?"

He stopped smiling and shrugged. "Not really. I'm not a Galenist or a systematic or an allopath — they have more theories up at the Temple than a dog has fleas, and I can't remember them all, and certainly can't teach them to you. But I can practice. Some of them will tell you that to come up to a patient without a theory of disease, with a knife in one hand and a drug in the other, is like stabbing in the dark. But in my view, none of the theories is quite right, and a man has to practice in the dark as best he can. Only he has to be aware that he is in the dark, and be careful. I try to treat the symptoms, make the patient comfortable, and help the body in what it seems to be trying to do. I can teach you some things that work, but no great mysteries."

"That sounds like Hippocrates."

"Hippocrates knew less than Galen, but he understood more. Or so I think." The grin was back. "We must hurry: I have another patient waiting."

After working with Philon for a week, I was glad that the more prestigious physicians had turned me down, for I could not have found a better master. He was my ideal of a true Hippocratic: scientific, detached, methodically observant — and selfless, generous, and kind. The poorer patients he treated out of charity, not taking a penny from anyone who couldn't afford it. He did it, he said, "for the love of God," and since most of the patients he accepted on this basis were Egyptian Christians or pagans who traditionally despised the Jews, his generosity was astonishing. He was also a good teacher: he liked explaining things and took time with me, and he was pleased when I asked a searching question. He seemed happier with me too, and dropped his earlier, rather diffident manner; he called me Chariton instead of "esteemed sir," and occasionally let slip sarcastic comments or jokes about his patients ("That one wants to be praised for spitting well"; "Never mind her symptoms — she only said that because of your bright eyes, my lad!"). He suggested that I lodge somewhere closer to his own house, so that I wouldn't have the long walk from the harbor to meet him every morning.

I asked if he knew of anywhere without fleas. "Somewhere where I could take a bath," I told him. "I can't use the public ones here, and I feel like a monk from the outer desert."

Philon laughed, and then looked shy. "We have a room in my house," he said. "It's small, on the third floor, and rather plain, but if you like . . ."

"You wouldn't mind? That is, your wife wouldn't mind taking in a foreigner, a Christian and a eunuch?"

"Oh no, no! She's a good woman — as the psalmist says, 'worth more than rubies.' I've told her about you; she wants to meet you anyway."

So that afternoon Philon took me to his home and introduced me to his family: his wife, who had the exotic Jewish name of Deborah; his fourteen-year-old daughter, who had the more ordinary Greek one of Theophila; and his two slaves, Harpokration and Apollonia. The slaves were both pagans; I discovered that this is fairly common among the Jews, whose Law requires them to free any Jewish slave after seven years. Philon had a son as well, but this young man was off studying the Jewish Law in Tiberias. Philon announced to them all that I was to lodge with them. They looked somewhat taken aback but did not protest, and Harpokration, a stout middle-aged man who was an Isis-worshiper, was sent to help me fetch my things.

Philon's house was near the new city wall, to the south of the Canopic Way. It was a narrow house, no more than two rooms wide, though it was three stories tall. My room was on the third floor, under the roof, and the window looked out on the house next door. So I stared through it at a wall of yellow-gray brick; if I twisted my head I could see into the neighbor's window. When I first moved in she closed the shutters against me, but after a few weeks, and after I offered her a prescription for varicose veins, she just left the window open and her swollen veins on view, and occasionally swapped gossip, laughing at my modesty because I persisted in closing my shutters to her.

Lake Mareotis has an inlet that runs up toward the Gate of the Sun, and the Canopic Canal, which joins the lake to the Nile, runs into this. On hot, still days the stink of mud and harbor sewage was overpowering. Hippocrates says that stagnant water is very bad for health, and that those who drink it develop dropsy and diseases of the stomach. People in this quarter didn't actually drink the water from the canal, and the lake water is brackish and undrinkable, but they still seemed to come down with fevers and infections more often than people living in other parts of the city. All in all, the house was quite different from Father's house in Ephesus.

Still, it was in what was otherwise quite a pleasant corner of Alexandria. The old park dedicated to the god Pan was only a few blocks away, and there was a public fountain just on the corner with the Canopic Way. And I liked the house, and the family, very much. I paid Philon four *solidi* for rent for the year; this covered the water Apollonia fetched for me from the public fountain, and a brazier to heat the room in the winter, and even having my clothes washed with the rest of the household linen. I paid another two *solidi* toward buying food, and took most of my meals with the family.

By this time I had plenty of money, as Philon had also found someone to buy some of my jewelry — an old Jewish merchant who lived in what was left of the Delta quarter. He made no pretense of thinking that the stones were glass, but asked me instead why, if they had been my mother's, I wanted to sell them. "I can have no wife and no daughter to wear them," I told him. "I thought my mother wouldn't mind if I used them to pay for my education." The old man nodded and muttered, and offered a price so good that I was almost ashamed to take it. And in fact I only sold a pair of earrings. They were of pearls and sapphires, and the old man paid me sixty-eight *solidi* for them — enough for me to live on for years, the way I was living in Alexandria.

It seemed to me that I'd done nothing all my life until I came to Alexandria, almost that I hadn't existed before. I missed the comforts of home only at first, then soon forgot them in my happiness. I hadn't believed it possible to be so happy. Every morning I woke up and thought, I'm in Alexandria! And it was as though my whole body began to sing.

I would get up before dawn — everyone does that in Egypt in the summer, because it's so hot. I would wash by the early gray light that slid through the shutters, standing over a basin and splashing tepid water over myself while from the street below came the sound of carts and camel trains taking goods to the market, and of women shouting to each other as they fetched the day's water from the public fountains. The slave Apollonia did that for our house; I'd usually meet her in the kitchen when I came downstairs. We'd wish each other a good day, and I'd take a roll of cumin bread from the kitchen and eat it on my way to the Temple. It would still be gray pre-dawn when I went out the door of Philon's house, but the streets would be crowded. Respectable men and women hurried to work; schoolboys pelted down the street shouting to one another, or walked quietly beside one of their family's slaves, escorted like little gentlemen to the day's dose of Homer. On the Canopic Way the shops were opening: bakers piled fragrant loaves of fresh bread, baked during the cool of the night, on long tables before their shops; butchers set out young goats, legs tied, and wicker cages full of chickens onto the pavements; barbers whetted their razors and looked for customers; peasants from the countryside settled themselves by the side of the road, spreading the fresh fruit or green herbs that they'd brought to sell and calling to the passers-by in nasal, singsong voices. The covered litters and sedan chairs of the wealthy sailed above the heads of the common throng like ships on a rough sea. It was hard to remember that I had been accustomed to ride in one of those. I'd jostle my way down Soma Square, where birds sang in the ruins, and then pause to look back: if I timed it right, I'd see the red dawn flooding down the wide Canopic Way from the Gate of the Sun, sculpting the masses of the public buildings in heavy light, outlining figures of people and animals sharp and clear like figures in a painting. When I reached the Temple, the sun would have climbed up over the flat green delta, and from the gateway I could look down at the whole great city, a jewel-bright mass of color around the glittering sea.

I'd spend the early part of the morning at the Temple, listening to lectures and debating with the other medical students. There were about a hundred of these, and they came from all over the Eastern Empire, though I suppose most of them were Alexandrians. During the first couple of weeks I kept quiet in discussions, still awed by their appearance of knowledge. For their part, both students and lecturers tended to sneer at me. It was clear they saw me as a pampered Asian eunuch who only fancied himself a doctor, and expected me soon to give up and go home, particularly as Philon was known to work "like a slave." But at the beginning of June one of the students, a very talkative young Antiochene, made a public comment in which he confused the techniques of setting dislocations with those for muscle strains. No one else said anything about it, so I rather hesitantly suggested that my esteemed acquaintance had made an error, and quoted Hippocrates. My esteemed acquaintance looked confused, the other students laughed, and the lecturer looked surprised and applauded me. I realized that none of the other students had read the work in question. I could feel as free to talk as any of them, and didn't need to keep quiet for fear of making a fool of myself. After that I began to make comments and ask questions more and more often, and the others began to take me seriously. Some of them liked me even less for being a rival instead of a joke, but others began to watch me with some respect. "And what would Hippocrates have said about it?" Adamantios would ask his classes; and he looked at me expectantly as he asked.

Late in the morning I'd go back down into the city to meet Philon. We usually met at Soma Square, by a plinth carved with a dolphin. A grin and a word of greeting, and then I'd take his medical bag and we'd set off to see his patients, discussing medicine as we went. Sometimes the patients fed us lunch; sometimes we bought some wine and bread or fruit to eat from a shop or street vendor. Philon worked through the afternoon, even during the hot noontime hours when most people sleep: he said people often felt worst then. And he liked to spend his evenings at home with his family; we were always back home before sunset. We'd have a simple meal in the main room of the house, with its yellow tile floor and worn oak table, talking about medicine, the patients, or the gossip of the neighborhood. Then, after supper, Philon and his family would sit down to say prayers and read from their Law, and (after the first few weeks) I'd go up to my room and read medical texts or prepare medicines for Philon to use next day.

I did find this life exhausting at first. For several weeks I was unable to do anything in the evening except go up to my room, bolt the door, and collapse on the bed. I suppose that Adamantios and the sneerers at the Temple were right: it was hard work, and someone who was unaccustomed to hard work was ill advised to do it. Only it didn't seem like work. To spend the whole day, from dawn till night, on nothing but the art of healing — that was perfection and joy, not work. The feeling of weariness passed as I got used to my new life, but not the happiness. I hadn't realized before just how confined my old life had been. I hadn't been able to walk down the street by myself, or spend my own money, or even choose simple things like what I would read or wear or eat for lunch. It had all been arranged for me. And now the taste of freedom was delicious.

The summer seemed to last years, I learned so much, changed so much. It began to seem natural to refer to myself as a man, and I lost the last of my maidenly modesty in the lecture rooms at the Temple. I bought and read books furiously. Some of them were on the different theories of medicine, but on the whole these were not very helpful. One writer would say that disease is an imbalance in the proportions of the four humors of the body, and that these are blood, phlegm, black bile, and yellow bile; another writer would agree as to the nature of disease but disagree about what the four humors are; yet another would disagree altogether, and say that diseases are caused by a disproportion between eating and excretion. None of this is any help when you are actually faced with a real patient, sweating and white with a real disease. I agreed with Philon, that practice is truer than theories, and I concentrated on learning to practice.

I studied herbs, and asked questions about them; it was in the field of drugs that I felt most ignorant, since I knew nothing about them, and one of my responsibilities as Philon's assistant was to prepare medicines — though that job was certainly easier in Alexandria than in most places. I did study the herbs in the Temple gardens as well, but the ones we used we bought in the marketplace, already boxed and bottled, so we had no need to wait for the right season, or collect the sap, or boil down the juice, or wander up into the mountains looking for the right kind of root. We just mixed the preparations with the required amount of wine, vinegar, or oil, and tried to estimate the right dose for the patient. Gentian and hemlock, melanthion and myrrh, crocus and cassia, opium, Greek cyclamen, oil of cedar — in Alexandria you could buy any herb in the herbal. And most of them were drugs that Hippocrates had never heard of. We do know more about the body and about nature than he did. But, as Philon said, he understood more than he knew. His method, and his inquiring attitude of mind, I found far more impressive than the doctrinaire statements of some later writers. And the question "What would Hippocrates have done?" was always worth asking. I certainly became notorious for asking it. My fellows at the Temple began to laugh at me every time I repeated it, but they stopped sneering altogether, and they asked my opinion.

In early August, Adamantios did a dissection of a human subject. This was uncommon, even in Alexandria, where there is a tradition of such investigations. The authorities always suspect dissections of being sorcerous — though as to that, magical practices that would have brought the death penalty in Ephesus were done openly in Egypt, so I don't know why they make such a fuss about medical dissections. The Hippocratic tradition has always been opposed to magic. But the authorities do sometimes make a fuss, and it's hard to find a subject, and so dissections are not as frequent as one could wish. Whenever one of the Museum professors did manage to arrange one, the students all tried frantically to get a place near the table to watch. Adamantios had five student assistants of his own, and they naturally got the best places, but the next-best places caused considerable intrigue and elbowing among the rest of us. I ended up at the back near the wall, where I could see nothing whatever. But before Adamantios used his knife he looked around at his audience and noticed me. "Chariton," he called, "can you see from there?"

I admitted that I couldn't.

"Come to the front, then," Adamantios said. "You're still new here, and haven't seen one of these before. And you'll be able to make better use of what you see than most of this lot."

"Most of this lot" groaned — some looked genuinely angry — but they made way for me. I scarcely dared to breathe. I felt I had never been paid a higher compliment. I edged my way to the front and watched as though my life depended on it. When Adamantios put his knife into the body (it was an elderly woman's; I think she'd been a friend's slave) I felt a bit sick, but I soon forgot to be. The human body is a riddle, a mystery and a miracle, and I was fascinated. Adamantios worked slowly, lecturing, asking and answering questions as he went. The stomach and digestive tract, the liver, the diaphragm, the lungs, the heart . . .

At this point one of Adamantios' students, the young Antiochene, fainted. Adamantios put down his knife, looking exasperated, then came round the table and shooed the other students off. "Let him breathe!" he told us. He pulled the young man into a sitting position, checked that his throat was clear, then put his head between his knees. After a moment there was a groan and the head came up again.

"It's very hot and crowded in here," Adamantios said tactfully. "Why don't you go sit by the fountain until you feel better?"

The Antiochene — his name, I remembered, was Theogenes — blinked, looked ashamed, picked himself up, and went outside. Adamantios went back round the table and went on with the dissection.

I had to leave before Adamantios was completely finished; I had to meet Philon before lunch. When I crossed the Temple yard, Theogenes was still sitting by the fountain, peering moodily into its depths. When he heard my feet hurrying over the paving of the court, otherwise empty in the noonday heat, he looked up, then shouted, "Hai! Chariton! Have they finished?"

"Almost," I answered, pausing. "He was just taking general questions when I left."

"I made a fool of myself, didn't I?" said Theogenes, and grinned. He had a pleasant smile, all white teeth and good humor. He was a tall, thin young man, with thick, curling black hair and brown eyes; he moved his hands a lot when he talked, and he smiled often. "It was the first one of those I've been to — but it was your first as well, wasn't it? And I've heard about things like that since I was so high, so I don't have any excuse. Didn't you feel sick at all?"

"I did at first," I admitted. "But I wouldn't worry about it; it was very hot in there, and everyone was breathing down your neck."

"Weren't they just! You'd think it was a chariot race, the way everyone was straining to see. 'Go, Greens! Chop from the small intestine to the stomach!' "

"Go, Blues! Up the aorta to the lungs!" I returned, grinning back. Father usually ran his teams under the blue colors, and I was used to cheering for them.

"Never!" Theogenes replied. "Did they find out why she died?"

I shook my head. "There was nothing obviously wrong."

"Poor old woman! Could you maybe tell me what they did find? I'll treat you to lunch."

I was surprised, and very pleased at the offer. Even the students who had become polite hadn't spoken to me outside discussions. Nonetheless, I had to turn it down. "I'm sorry, I can't. My master will be waiting for me — I'm late already. Some other time?"

"He makes you work in the afternoon?"

"He always works in the afternoons. He has a lot of patients, and he likes to spend the evenings with his family."

Theogenes let out a whistle. "It's a hot afternoon for working! Well, maybe tomorrow evening then — no, tomorrow the Sabbath starts."

"You're Jewish too?"

"Yes. My father's a second cousin of Adamantios. But you're not Jewish, are you?"

"Oh, no. I'm a Christian. But my master's Jewish, so I keep the Sabbath."

Theogenes laughed. "Your master sounds a character!"

"He's one of the best doctors in the city," I replied sharply.

Theogenes looked a bit surprised. "I only meant that it's unusual for a Jewish doctor to have one lone Christian assistant keeping the Sabbath. Particularly . . ." He looked embarrassed and stopped.

"Particularly if the assistant is a eunuch?"

"Well, yes. No offense. Look, Chariton, I'd like to get your view of the dissection. Some of the others and I like to meet at Kallias' tavern by the Castellum the evening after the Sabbath, to talk about things. You want to come then?"

"Oh!" I said, and stared stupidly at Theogenes. For the first time in weeks I felt shy, clumsy. I had been able to ignore the sneerers because I hadn't been asking anything from them, and because I was spending most of my time with Philon anyway. Now Theogenes was offering some kind of comradeship, and I didn't know what to say. Young ladies don't frequent taverns. But I wasn't a young lady, so why not? "Certainly," I said, smiling nervously now. "Thank you."

He grinned again. "Right, then. It's a big tavern, with a sign shaped like a horse's head; you can't miss it. See you there!"

I arrived at Soma Square so late that I missed Philon and had to chase after him from patient to patient till I found him. But when I explained why I was delayed, he was pleased.

"I asked Adamantios to give you a fair trial, for my sake," he told me. "We studied under the same master, so he agreed. But he wouldn't have asked you to the front unless he'd decided you showed promise. I thought he'd come round."

I felt as though I'd conquered the world.

That evening when we came back, I enthusiastically told the household about Theogenes' invitation, and all about the dissection. They were used to discussions of such things at the dinner table, and it didn't affect anyone's appetite.

"Wonderful!" Deborah said, smiling tolerantly. "Does your patron know how well you've settled in here?"

I was shocked into silence for a moment. The shock came from the realization that I'd scarcely thought of home for weeks. I muttered something or other in response — that I meant to write soon — and returned to a description of the dissected liver. But when I got back to my room, I worried. I'd put off writing to Thorion, uncertain whether he would be at Ephesus or in Constantinople; I couldn't risk the letter going astray and arriving at Father's house. I heard something of the news from Asia in the marketplace — Alexandria gets the news from all over the world. My disappearance a month before the wedding had caused a huge scandal. Festinus was said to be outraged; I imagined that Father was petrified with fear. If he knew where I was, he'd send someone to take me home at once, and once home, I'd be forced back into my outworn maidenly modesty, and perhaps even into the marriage. Where I'd been would be hushed up.

But I had to write to Thorion and Maia. They must be worried by now. Only, what could I say to them? "I went to a dissection today; one of the other students has invited me to a tavern to discuss it. Yesterday my master let me lance and stitch up a carpenter's abscessed finger"? They'd be horrified. I felt suddenly frightened. A huge gap had opened between what I had been and what I was, and I didn't know what they would think of it.

I went over to the table and poured myself a drink of water from the pitcher there, then sat down. There was a book out on the table, one of Herophilos' anatomical tracts. I picked it up and looked at it idly, then something in it seemed relevant to the dissection and I began to read in earnest, forgetting, for the time being, my family and the looming necessity of a letter.

Two evenings later I went to meet Theogenes and the others at the tavern. The building was, as I'd been promised, impossible to miss.

It firmly faced the public square opposite the supplementary barracks of the Castellum, and besides the large gilded horse-head sign, a garishly painted frieze of bacchanals decorated its porch, which was full of amphorae of wine. I stood outside in the warm bright evening, almost sick with nervousness. From inside came the sound of voices, not many and not loud, since it was still early. It wasn't a disreputable tavern anyway, but that didn't matter. Here I was, the well-brought-up daughter of a man of consular rank, about to go into a public tavern — and beyond that I was terrified of what the others would think of me, whether they'd be angry that Theogenes had invited me. I almost turned around and went home; only the thought of having to explain myself to Philon and his family stopped me. Well, I told myself, if they think you're a conceited, overconfident eunuch, they're wrong; and whatever they think, it can't hurt you. I straightened my shoulders and went in.

Inside there was a large main room, lit by a number of polished brass hanging lamps and filled with tables. I was still standing by the door looking about when Theogenes called my name, and I saw him and some half-dozen others sitting at the far end. I hurried over and Theogenes introduced the others breezily: I'd seen all of them at the Temple, and knew most of their names already. They were not, as I had expected, all Jews like Theogenes, but a complete mixture: Jewish, pagan, and Christian, students of several different doctors, and natives of several different cities. Most of them smiled and nodded to me as they were introduced, looking curious; one or two looked a bit sour, but no one remarked on my being there. Theogenes made room for me on the bench and I sat down.

"Another cup for our friend, and some more wine, dear!" Theogenes said to the serving girl, and looked after her a moment as she trotted obediently off to fetch them. "She's pretty!" he added, to no one in particular. Then, turning back to me: "We have one rule in our discussions here, Chariton: no talk about religion. Anyone who brings up a religious argument has to pay for the wine. Other than that, we split costs and please ourselves, though we talk medicine most of the time. Can you tell me what you made of that dissection? I've had a completely different description from everyone I've asked."

And he got a different description from everyone present. I forgot to be nervous, the discussion was so interesting. By the time we'd finished with the dissection (and I'd had a couple of cups of wine), I felt that I was among friends, and leaned back against the wall, relaxed and comfortable.

"Your Hippocrates says that the vessels that carry a woman's seed into her womb are the same as the ones that go to the penis in a man, and that they come from the head through the kidneys," one of the other students told me as we were winding up. "I couldn't see anything like that."

"You didn't know what to look for," Theogenes told him in a lofty tone.

"You didn't see anything at all," his friend responded. "You were out in the courtyard."

"I'm not sure there was anything to see," I said, a bit reluctantly. "I think maybe Hippocrates got that one wrong."

"What!" exclaimed Theogenes, grinning. "The immortal Hippocrates made a mistake?"

"Well, he never did any dissections, did he?" I replied, smiling. "They had even more trouble about them in his day than we do in ours. He made the best guess he could without cutting anyone open."

"Hippocrates also said that in a man the vessels go through the testicles," the other student went on, a bit hesitantly but as though Theogenes hadn't spoken. "And that that's why eunuchs can't have children, because the passage is destroyed when the testicles are removed." He looked at me curiously. An awkward silence fell, and everyone stared at me. Theogenes looked embarrassed. "How did they do it to you?" my questioner demanded. "Did it hurt much?"

I felt isolated again, and quite sober. "I don't remember," I said after a moment. "I was very young when it was done."

My questioner looked down. "Sorry," he said. "I was just curious." I knew he was thinking of all the unpleasant things he'd ever heard about eunuchs.

"You were brought up in Ephesus, weren't you?" one of the others asked, in the uncomfortable silence. It could have been a casual question, but somehow it sounded probing, suspicious. "Why did you come to Alexandria?"

But an Alexandrian pagan named Nikias came to my rescue before I had to answer that. "You didn't need to ask whether he was Asian," he said in a tone of forced lightness. He was one of the ones who'd looked sour when I arrived, and he watched me now with a glint of malice on his smooth plump face. "A more perfect Asian lisp I have never heard in my life. 'Hippocrateeth seth that' — no, I can't do it."

On the face of it the words were an innocent joke, but I could feel the undertone of dislike, as I'd felt the test in the earlier question. My face went hot, and I began to get angry. After all, I'd been invited here, and I was as good a student as any of them. They had no business asking me embarrassing questions and making fun of me. I looked round at the faces in the lamplight, all watching me to see what I'd do. Theogenes still looked embarrassed, as though he alone had the grace to be ashamed of his friends' bad manners. That checked my anger, and I forced a smile.

"My accent's the worst you've heard?" I said. "You've obviously never been to Ephesus. You should hear some of my fa— . . . my patron's friends. 'My *dear* and *motht* ethteemed Nikiath, the horthe that you were mentioning is *thuch* a *treathure*; I'd run her in a *moment*, only she jutht *happenth* to be in foal at the minute; really, my dear fellow, I've no *nothion* how she managed it!' " The voice was one Thorion and I had amused ourselves with since we were small, and its original was in fact old Pythion, but you didn't have to know him to find it funny. The tension broke, and the other students roared with laughter.

"By my head, that's good," said Theogenes. "Did your patron run horses, then?"

"In Ephesus they called him master of the races. Maybe you've heard of him — the clarissimus Theodoros."

Theogenes shook his head, but one of the others, a Sidonian, immediately exclaimed that he'd seen some of my father's horses win a race in Tyre, and the whole conversation shifted to chariot racing and the favorite drivers at the local hippodrome. When the group broke up and went home, the others wished me good health with all the warmth of old friends. I responded in the same tone. I had enjoyed the evening as a whole, and I felt that I'd passed some difficult test. But I also resolved to be careful with the others, and never drink too much in their company. I would need to keep my wits about me when I talked to them.

✠✠✠

I put off writing to Thorion for another month. But when September had begun, I knew I had to write something, anything, to let him and Maia know that I was safe, before the winter came and it became impossible to send letters. I knew too that Thorion would certainly be in Constantinople by then. So one clear, warm evening I sat down in my room, took out a sheet of papyrus and some pens, and wrote "Chariton of Ephesus to his patron Theodoros, son of Theodoros of Ephesus. Very many greetings." Then I sat and stared at the papyrus for a few minutes. Through the window I could see my neighbor sweeping her room; she waved to me and I waved back. I had to be careful what I said. I would send the letter on a grain ship, and it was not unknown for the sailors to open correspondence to amuse themselves during their voyage. I chewed the end of my pen. Maia would have deplored the habit. "You get plenty to eat at your proper meals!" she'd say. "You don't need to go gnawing at reed pens like a mouse!"

The thought made me smile. Dear, proper, worrying Maia; dear Thorion, scowling with concern. I dashed off the rest of the letter.

I wished to write to Your Excellency beforehand, but was in doubt whether you would yet be in Constantinople. I hope you are well, and that no tiresome persons have troubled you with their enmity. For my part, I am very happy here in Alexandria, and cannot think of any greater contentment than to live as I live now. The doctors of the Museum think well of me, and say I am making great progress in my studies. I am assistant to one Philon, a Jew affiliated with the Museum, and I lodge at his house, near the Gate of the Sun. He is a skilled and kind master, and I owe much to him. Greet Maia for me. Accept, dear Theodoros, my great esteem. I remain your obedient servant.

It wasn't much of a letter. But if I sent this, he would know that I was safe and happy and be able to write back to me. And to say more, to describe to him how I was living, would be simply to show him the gap that had opened between us, something I was afraid to do. So I folded the sheet over, sealed it, and addressed it to His Excellency Lord Theodoros son of Theodoros, at the office of the praetorian prefect. That should reach him.

I got up, poured myself a drink of water, then went downstairs, carrying the letter. It was the evening before the Sabbath, and the rest of the household was downstairs setting out candles. Philon observed the Jewish laws carefully, as I'd told Theogenes, and the Sabbath was kept by everyone in the house, even the pagan slaves, though they and I did not go to the ceremonies. Philon was not one of the missionary Jews one sometimes meets preaching in the marketplace, and he never tried to convince me to take part in any Jewish rites —

though from what I could see, the Jewish ceremonies weren't so very different from the Christian ones with which I was familiar. Jews read the Scriptures in the same translation and sang the psalms to some of the same tunes. Their synagogues were covered with paintings and mosaics depicting many of the same scenes I knew from church, and they prayed in the same style. Of course, the Alexandrian Jews are a race apart. Many of the educated ones are Platonists, as are many of the educated Christians. Like Adamantios, they are well read in the pagan classics, and they interpret their Scriptures allegorically. Philon was of another type, of some stricter Jewish sect which didn't like pagan literature or pagan philosophy. But he seemed rather embarrassed about it, and certainly never tried to impose it on anyone else.

Deborah smiled at me. "Going out?"

"I have a letter to my patron; I'm going down to the harbor to post it," I told her. "Is there anything you want me to fetch along the way?"

"Could you buy some olives and some fresh cheese?" she asked. "That will save us wanting on the Sabbath. I'll give you the money for it — here. Thank you."

I looked at Philon. He pulled at his lip. "There's that preparation for old Serapion . . ."

"Olives, fresh cheese, bryony, and opium," I said. "A good Sabbath to you, then."

The Eunostos Harbor was on the other side of the city from the Gate of the Sun. But I was used to long walks now, and used the time to think about medical problems. The streets were crowded again; the cool dusk brought people out to buy or sell or just to stroll about gossiping and looking at the world. Whores of all prices were looking for customers. The common girls stood in the porticoes and smiled, pulling up their thin linen tunics to show off their legs and inviting passing men to come have a drink with them; occasionally an expensive courtesan dressed in fine silk rode past in a gilded sedan chair, looking scornfully at her poorer sisters. I picked up an admirer as well, a nervous old man in a garish orange tunic who followed me from Soma Square down to the end of the Tetrapylon and then ran after me to offer me an alabaster flask of frankincense if I'd come home with him. "You're a beautiful boy," he told me, making sheep's eyes. "I'll be good to you."

"No thank you," I told him. "I'm a eunuch and a medical student."

"But I don't mind that!" he said, laying hold of my arm.

"I'm not available," I told him firmly, and jerked my arm away.

He looked woebegone, and I smiled, nodded politely, and set off toward the harbor at a brisk walk. He followed me a bit further, then gave up; I saw him heading back to Soma Square to look for someone else. I remembered how shaken I'd been by similar offers four months and a lifetime before, and smiled again.

When I arrived at the Eunostos Harbor, the Pharos was just being lit. The dock workers had finished the afternoon's work and were heading noisily for the taverns or for home; the round-bellied merchant ships creaked against the docks, rising and falling with the small waves. I found a grain transport that was due to leave for Constantinople on the next day, and I gave my letter to the master, promising him that Thorion would reward him for his trouble in delivering it. Then I came back along the Canopic Way. It was dark by then. The porticoes of the Tetrapylon were all lit, shining with lamps and glittering with merchandise: I had no trouble finding the cheese and olives. The shop I usually visited for drugs was off the Soma Street, not far from the square. It was a narrow, dark little shop, its front covered with crumbling plaster, with nothing to show what it sold; Philon had pointed it out to me. Inside, the walls were covered with shelves full of lime-wood boxes of dried herbs and brass jars of eye ointments, glowing in the light of a single lamp. It smelled of myrrh, aloe, cassia, the strong aromatics drowning the scent of the less pleasant herbs. The shopkeeper was preparing something in the back room when I entered; I rapped on the counter and he came in, recognized me with a grin, and provided the opium and bryony without too much bargaining. I set off home.

It was darker near the Gate of the Sun; the shopkeepers here had locked up and gone home. I walked more quickly, keeping the road between me and the wastelands of the Broucheion quarter. My feet seemed already to know the way to Philon's door; it was odd how I felt at home there. When I came up to it I heard the family singing, welcoming the Sabbath, and I stopped to listen. It was such a glad song, ringing out into the dark, full of the warmth of the house, the happiness of the family.

They stopped singing, and Philon said the blessing. Then I heard him ask Harpokration whether I was back yet. "I hope he didn't have any trouble finding the bryony," he said.

"He shouldn't walk about at night," said Deborah. "It's not safe, particularly for a foreigner and a eunuch. And to post a letter to his patron! Not much of a patron, letting him come here with nothing arranged in advance and no money. I wonder what the truth of that story is."

I'd been about to knock and announce myself, but this comment stopped me short. How suspicious did my story sound to them? Had they guessed anything? I stood where I was, the blood beating in my ears, my hand still raised to knock on the door.

"You're worried about him?" Philon asked in an amused tone. "Such a change in a few short months! You used to be worried that he'd corrupt and deprave Theophila."

It was the first I'd heard of that. Deborah had concealed her feelings well: she had never treated me with anything but courtesy and consideration.

"Don't tease," she told her husband. "That was only at first. He's a sweet boy, and the only thing Theophila could learn from him is some good manners. You can tell he's from a noble house, he's so polite — and *he* wouldn't chew with his mouth open, Theophilion dear, *do* mind yourself! I do find it strange, though, that he was sent here with nothing arranged in advance, and obliged to sell his ancestral jewels to stay alive. Something in that house must have gone wrong. That, or his patron's treated him shockingly."

I drew myself further into the archway of the door and listened. I felt that I had to know what they suspected, so that I could take steps to guard myself. The street was dark and empty, the wood of the door rough against my cheek; gold light seeped through a crack in it.

"I think there's more to it than he's saying," Philon said thoughtfully. "He's a very bright lad, and very well educated: can quote Homer by the yard. It's my guess that his patron didn't want him to come here."

"Do you think he's really a slave?" asked Deborah. "That he's run off?"

"Nooo. That's what Adamantios thinks, but I'm inclined to disagree. Chariton doesn't act like a slave — I don't think he knows how to do so much as sweep a floor. But I don't think his patron wrote those letters. I asked about Theodoros of Ephesus. He's a wealthy man of consular rank, and all the family's money comes from imperial service. There's a son at court now, another Theodoros. He probably doesn't think of medicine as a career at all, and didn't want his client to take it up when a more lucrative career was available."

"So why would he come here against his patron's wishes?" That was Theophila. "I feel sorry for him. It's horrible what the Persians did to him. And he's so good-looking."

Philon laughed. "And what do Chariton's looks have to do with it?"

"Oh, nothing. I just feel sorry for him, particularly if his patron won't help him, and he's been so unlucky already. And I don't see why he came here, if he could be supported at court and get very rich."

" 'The first requirement for the study of healing,' " Philon said, quoting our common master Hippocrates, " 'is a natural disposition to it.' And that is certainly something our Chariton has. Even if he did run away, he was quite right to do so: a gift like that shouldn't be wasted. He'll make a great doctor. But I heard something else about this Theodoros."

There was a pause; I imagined Philon waiting expectantly for the rest of his family to ask him what. I waited too, holding my breath.

"What?" demanded Theophila, as expected, and giggled.

"It seems he has a daughter," said Philon, "a very beautiful girl, with every expectation of a great dowry. The governor of Asia wanted to marry her. You're too young to remember when Gallus ruled here, Theophilion, but you must have heard stories. Well, this Festinus is much the same sort, only instead of being noble he is of very low birth, and the family of Theodoros was extremely reluctant to marry the girl to the brute."

"Poor lady!" said Theophila. "So what happened?"

"She disappeared a month before her wedding. That was last April, just before Chariton turned up here in Alexandria. There was a scandal about it through the whole province in Asia. The girl's father claims to have no idea where she went; the governor is furious, but has to believe him."

I held my breath. The conclusion about myself seemed inevitable. I wondered fleetingly if Philon would still let me study with him. I thought perhaps not, not if he was certain of my sex. I wondered what he meant to do about it.

"You think Chariton had something to do with the girl's disappearance?" asked Deborah.

"Mmm. He says he's the cousin of her tutor. They say that her brother was involved in the disappearance, but to spirit off a young noblewoman, you need more than one person involved in the plot. My guess is that Chariton made some arrangements for her, or is suspected of having done so, and was sent to Alexandria to get him out of the governor's way — perhaps by the brother, the younger Theodoros, and not the father. It would explain the suddenness of his arrival here, and the lack of money. I wonder which Theodoros he wrote that letter to? He wouldn't be able to send it to Ephesus this time of year; my guess is it went to his friend, the younger man, in Constantinople."

They say that eavesdroppers never hear anything good of themselves, but I could prove that false. I had to stand on the step a moment longer, trying to contain my joy. How could they not suspect the truth? Was it just that I *was* good at medicine, that the truth was too outrageous for them to guess at? It didn't matter: I was safe.

I knocked on the door, and Harpokration opened it and let me in. "Greetings!" I told the family. "Olives, fresh cheese, white bryony, and opium. And here's your change."

"Have you eaten?" asked Deborah. "Then sit down, have something. You look happy."

"I am," I told them. "I was just thinking how much this city has become my home. Thanks to you."

✠ ✠ ✠

That autumn I discovered why Philon had thought a Christian assistant would be particularly useful. We began to get a lot of quartan fevers, dropsies, and enteritic fevers among our patients, and particularly among those of the lower classes. A person with a reasonably large family, or even a slave in a good household, stands a good chance of recovering from these. But poor men or women falling ill often had no one to nurse or even feed them; they tried to keep on working, wore themselves out, and died unless they could be got into a hospital.

The big hospitals of Alexandria were charitable establishments controlled by the popular archbishop, Athanasios. They were provided at the expense of the church, and in them many desperately ill people were nursed and fed until they either recovered or died. As such they were worthy and admirable institutions. But they gave Philon no end of trouble. The problem was that the attendants at these hospitals were nearly all monks. I hadn't encountered monks before I came to Alexandria — there aren't any in Asia. I'd heard them mentioned, but as dirty, stupid peasants, men who'd run away from their lands to avoid having to pay taxes. The Egyptians, however, greatly admired the monks — they admire all ascetics, pagan or Christian. After meeting a few, I had to admit that they weren't just lazy tax evaders. They were the stuff that made the martyrs: passionately devout, single-minded, selfless, recklessly and patiently nursing the victims of the most contagious and dangerous diseases. But they were also dirty, illiterate, ignorant, and, worst of all, fanatical. They didn't like taking patients on the recommendation of a Jewish doctor.

I tried to explain the situation to Theogenes and the others one night at the tavern.

"First we had this poor old water vendor," I said, "with a very nasty enteritic fever, and his only living relative was a daughter in some village right up the Nile. Philon and I went down to the hospital by the church of St. Mark and tried to get the monks to agree to take the man. We met one monk at the gate, and Philon began to explain the situation, and everything seemed to be fine. Then another monk came out of the hospital, recognized Philon, and started shouting at him. He said we'd come to spy on them and were looking for some way to betray them to the authorities, just the way our ancestors betrayed the Christ and handed monks over to the governors to die in the arena, and so on and on. And he said we were idolators, and worshiped 'the Great Beast in Constantinople, the king of the heretics.' It took me a moment to understand that he really meant the emperor. I'd never heard anyone speak so recklessly in my life."

"They always say things like that," Theogenes said. "So what did your master do?"

"Smiled and said that he'd come to see if they could take another sick old man, and why didn't they leave ancestors out of it. I was astonished. But eventually the monk calmed down, and they took our patient just as though no one had ever said anything unusual."

"Was the patient Jewish?" asked Nikias, the pagan.

"Of course not. The Jews look after their own. No, he was a Christian. The problem was just that Philon was Jewish. So once we had the old man installed, Philon said that I should do all the visiting and that next time I could talk to the monks. He thought they'd be less suspicious of a Christian."

"Lucky you!" Theogenes said, grinning. "Were they? Or are you considered to have been corrupted by Jewish influence?"

"I'm considered corrupt anyway. They don't like eunuchs much more than they do Jews. We had an old woman with a quartan fever whom we wanted to get into the hospital today, and I had to be almost as persistent as Philon was. Did you know that I am a luxury-loving and venal minister of the imperial idol?" I took a sip of my wine.

"Very luxury-loving you look," Theogenes observed. "Were you wearing that cloak? Or do you have one without five different stains on it?"

"I was wearing this cloak, stains and all. I did point out to them that it was hardly 'scarlet and fine linen.' And I did point out that the pleasures of the flesh are closed to me. And there's a eunuch in the Gospels, bless him, an excellent man who was converted by the apostle Philip, and his example carried some weight. And I said I was a devout Nicene Christian and a passionate admirer of His Holiness Archbishop Athanasios, and I hinted that I'd come to Alexandria because of that, and implied that I was working night and day to convert my virtuous master to the True Way. And finally the monks became friendly, took my patient, and offered in advance to look after any others I want to send them."

"You mean you can reason with them?" Theogenes demanded in mock astonishment. "I've always thought they were like wild beasts. I'd never go anywhere near one of the hospitals."

"You don't have to, do you?" I responded. "Does Adamantios have *any* poor patients?"

There was a general snort of laughter at the idea of the head of the medical faculty of the Museum of Alexandria treating poor patients.

"He's taken a few cases out of charity," Theogenes said, defending his master. "But he puts them in his own household and has his slaves nurse them."

"It doesn't make any difference. You don't *need* to talk to monks. You would if you had to."

Theogenes made a face. "I hope I never have to. My great-grandfather was murdered here by men like that. It was the reason my family moved to Antioch."

"What do you mean by 'men like that'? There weren't any monks in your great-grandfather's time. Christianity wasn't even legal."

"By ignorant Egyptian peasants, then."

"That's not the same thing at all."

"*They* sound like they think it is."

"It's a good thing you don't have to deal with them," put in another student, Kallisthenes the Sidonian. "You'd be sure to lose your temper, and there'd be a riot."

Theogenes grinned and laughed, but the Alexandrians who were with us frowned.

"You foreigners don't know anything about riots," said Nikias. "The next time there's a riot the monks will be in the middle of it, and there won't be anything to laugh at."

We stopped smiling. "What do you mean by that?" asked Kallisthenes.

"Why do you think those monks are so worried about being betrayed?" Nikias demanded impatiently. "They remember what happened the last few times the archbishop was exiled. Or didn't you hear about that, up in Sidon? There were floggings, rackings, execution after execution, and it still didn't stop the rioting. The emperor and some of the court bishops tried to put some foreign bishops on the throne of St. Mark, and the Christians here, particularly the monks, wouldn't have them. The last time it went on for four months and cut off the grain shipments to Constantinople, so the emperor yielded and let the archbishop come back. But everyone knows that as soon as His Holiness Athanasios dies, the whole thing will start up again. The court sympathizes with the Arian faction, and the Christians here are mostly Nicene. And more than that, the sacred offices don't want any other bishop to become as powerful as Bishop Athanasios. Naturally the monks are suspicious of Jews and eunuchs; they're suspicious of anyone they think must be loyal to the emperor and an enemy to them."

"Is Athanasios likely to die soon?" Kallisthenes asked nervously.

Nikias made a rude noise and poured himself some more wine. "I don't know. He's an old man. He doesn't believe in doctors, or doesn't trust them. He could die any time. On the other hand, he's a disciple of Anthony the Hermit, and that old man lived to be over a hundred."

"How many Christians are there in Alexandria?" asked Theogenes thoughtfully.

"The gods know!" Nikias exclaimed contemptuously. "Half the city are Galileans of some kind, though they're not all as tidily orthodox Nicenes as His Holiness would like to believe. But it's not just Alexandrians you have to think about. The archbishop is the metropolitan for the whole diocese, not just the city and not even just this province. And he's popular everywhere. As a matter of fact, even here in Alexandria you won't find many people of any religion who'd back the authorities and oppose him. Whatever happens when he dies, the Christians won't pick another bishop like him."

"But I thought he was an absolute nobody!" protested Kallisthenes, who was a Neoplatonist of good family. "They say that he even preaches in Coptic sometimes, that he's not even properly Greek!"

"He's not," Nikias admitted. "But he's Alexandrian. And if I had a dispute at law myself, I'd take it to the episcopal court instead of to the governor. You don't have to pay a fortune in bribes there, it takes much less time than the provincial court, you won't be beaten by some guardsman, and the archbishop is incorruptible. And Athanasios and his monks and nuns look after the rabble — there are the hospitals, the charities that give dowries to poor girls and cheap clothes to the poor and food to the beggars. Well, the rabble is grateful. Whenever there's as much as a rumor that his Holiness is ill, everything around here gets tense. You'll see. There's bound to be a riot within the year."

"What's the archbishop like?" I asked as everyone digested this notion.

"You're the Christian!" said Nikias. "Haven't you been to the cathedral to listen to him?"

I shook my head. "I'm already keeping the Sabbath with my master. I can't afford another day off every week. I've been to the church of St. Mark once or twice when lectures weren't too early, but that's it. You've never seen him?"

Nikias looked a bit sheepish. "I've been to hear him a couple of times," he admitted. "He knows how to speak. I don't think he wants any more rioting — but he's old. There'll be a riot by the spring, I'd be willing to bet on it."

But there were no riots that autumn, and none that winter. The Alexandrian winter is cold and clammy. The ships stay in harbor, lashed to the docks or pulled up on the beach to keep them safe from the storms. Mists rise off Lake Mareotis and mix with the smoke of the city's countless braziers: Alexandria lies continually in the dank haze. Our patients came down with fevers, now centering more on the lungs than on the stomach. There were pneumonias, pleurisies, and innumerable colds to keep us busy, plus the usual broken limbs and difficult births. But no riots.

Late in January Philon let me take charge of one of his patients. He had allowed this a few times before, but the others had suffered only mild illnesses or minor injuries. This time the man was gravely ill. He was in fact the old merchant who had paid such a handsome price for my mother's earrings; his name was Timon, and he was a widower with a son and two daughters. He had a fever and a hard, dry cough, and he'd had them for some time before his son called in Philon.

Philon made the initial examination, and looked fairly grim when he had finished. "You should have called me sooner," he told the old man.

Old Timon spread his hands helplessly. "I didn't want to miss work. You know me."

Philon snorted, gave him some wine with iris root, then took the son out into the entrance hall, where the patient couldn't hear. "Your father has a pneumonia," he said. "I don't like the sound or the look of his chest; the infection is fairly severe already." He hesitated, looking at the other man sadly, then asked, "Has he complained of pain when he breathes?"

The man nodded, looking nervous and unhappy. "That was why I called you. He kept swearing he'd be better after a couple days' rest."

Philon sighed and shook his head. "I would guess that he was just afraid of hearing bad news from me. I'm sorry, but I don't think he'll live."

I was shocked and dismayed. I liked old Timon. "You don't think steam —?" I began, then stopped. The son looked at me eagerly, seeing some hope; Philon looked at me assessingly.

"What were you suggesting?" he asked.

"Steam, hot compresses, hyoscyamus and iris root, and plenty of fluids," I said. "The way you treated Flavius' daughter."

"She was a lot younger. And the disease wasn't so far advanced," said Philon. Then he sighed, scratching his beard. "It is the correct course of treatment, though." He dropped his hand and looked at me again. "Very well. Why don't you take charge of it then, Chariton? If you and your father don't mind," he added, turning to Timon's son.

They didn't mind. The son was aware that I had more hope for his father than Philon did, and old Timon, when we went back into the sickroom, said he was pleased I was progressing so well at my studies. I was at once thrilled and terrified. I hoped that Philon was mistaken; I swore privately to spare nothing in my efforts to cure the old man.

I started him on the treatment at once, and bought a new casebook so that I could note down Timon's symptoms and keep a record of the ways I tried to cure him. At first everything seemed to go fairly well. The steam and hot compresses eased much of the pain the old man felt in his chest, and the dry cough became wet and productive. He slept better, though the fever did not go down, and he even took some barley broth and kept it down. His family, who were all very fond of him, followed my instructions eagerly. His two daughters both left their husbands for the duration of his illness, and took turns getting up in the middle of the night to change the hot compresses for his chest and boil more water to soften the air he breathed with steam. I visited every morning before lectures, every afternoon, and in the evening as well, and after three days I thought he might be improving.

Then the fever went up and the cough became harder again; the pain came back, worse than ever. He couldn't bear for me to tap his chest to check how the infection had spread. "If you could just give me something to let me sleep . . ." Timon asked, almost apologetically. He had to whisper because it hurt too much to breathe deeply. I was afraid to give him opium in case it suppressed the cough, but in the end I did. He slept, but grew weaker, laboring over each shallow breath.

The family didn't blame me; in fact, they were so sympathetic they made me ashamed, and they listened to all my suggestions as though I were an oracle. They never questioned Philon's decision to give me the case. I did. I consulted Philon, dragged him back to see Timon, and finally asked him flatly if he thought I was doing something wrong. He shook his head. "I would tell you if I thought what you were doing was wrong," he said, and apart from that he made no comment on the case.

I ransacked the Museum library, looking for suggestions that might be helpful; I discussed pneumonias with all my fellow students and most of the lecturers as well. I worried desperately whether I should bleed my patient, whether I should give him purgatives, whether I should try surgery or cautery. My instincts, what theories I had, and my experience all suggested that anything dramatic would kill him, but it was almost unbearable to go on with the same old remedies when they plainly weren't working anymore. In the end I tried bleeding him, from the elbow but only lightly, to see if it produced any improvement. He said that it relieved the pain a little, but it did not help him any that I could see, so I didn't repeat the experiment. He was very weak by then, and I didn't think he could afford to lose much blood.

One afternoon, a week after I took the case, Timon called his children together and whispered his blessing to them, and then crossed his hands and prepared himself to die. "You don't need to trouble yourself anymore, young man," he told me in a croaking whisper when I arrived that evening with some new exotic herb that an obscure authority had promised was all-powerful.

"Just try this in some honeywater, sir," I coaxed. "I found an author who swears it is effective in cases like yours."

The old man looked at me, exhausted but still not angry. " 'Man born of woman is of few days, and full of trouble,' " he whispered slowly. "No, my friend, I've tried enough. No one can put off dying forever."

I stood there with the herb in my hand, looking at the old man, and then I started to cry. I couldn't help it. I'd stayed up with him half the previous night, he was my first real patient, I genuinely liked him, and he was going to die. Timon looked mildly surprised. "You did everything you could," he told me gently. "I'll try your herb, to please you. May I have something more to ease the pain as well?"

I gave him the herb and some opium, but he couldn't drink much of it. His children clustered round the bed all night, and I sat against the wall, feeling helpless. He died quietly an hour before dawn, when the city was just waking to another day.

I trudged home through the morning crowds, and arrived to find Philon and his family having breakfast. "He's dead," I told them.

Philon gave a groan of sympathy and told me to sit down. I sat, and began to cry again. "You shouldn't have given me the case," I told him, sniffing.

Philon shook his head. "No one could have managed it better."

"Oh, by Artemis the Great! *Somebody* could have; *somebody* could have cured him."

Philon shook his head again. "Timon had an infection through the whole of the left lobe of his lung, and he had the beginnings of pleurisy. I have never seen a patient in that condition survive. I wouldn't say that it never has happened, but it's rare, and I think when it happens it's owing as much to chance as to any method of treatment. I hoped that you might have more luck with him than I would; you were eager to try and full of ideas; and I'd given up already. But no one could have honestly promised to cure him. Medicine has limits. Even the pagans say that Asklepios was punished by the gods when he tried to cure death." I sniffed, and Philon put his hand on my shoulder. "Go to bed," he said gently. "You need rest, and we have more patients to see this afternoon."

Timon's family did not blame me for the death; they paid me generously for my futile efforts and invited me to the wake, where they introduced me to their friends as "the nice young student of Philon's who tried so hard to cure Father." I felt very low for some weeks. However, Philon continued putting me in charge of patients he thought I'd do well with, and between study and work I was too busy to brood over my failure.

The Alexandrian spring came slowly. The swallows never left in the winter, so I didn't watch for their return. The earth didn't become green; that happens late in the summer, after the Nile floods. But the air grew steadily warmer, the sky became paler, and the fogs and choking smoke clouds of the winter faded away. The days lengthened; frogs croaked in the marshes by Lake Mareotis; the fig trees and vines in the gardens put out sticky green buds. I began to forget that I had ever been a girl called Charis, that I had ever lived differently from the way I was living now, that I had ever been ignorant of things like the correct dosage of hellebore or the writings of Erasistratos.

One evening in March I took the splints off a child's arm. I had set the bone myself — it had been a bad fracture, compound of both bones in the lower arm. I had known when I set it that unless I did it perfectly, the child could be crippled for life. I held my breath when I cut the arm free. The little girl moved her wrist as I told her to, held the freed arm beside the other, smiled as I smiled, then danced about the floor, waving both arms in the air and crowing with delight. I could have crowed too. Strength, wholeness, life: healing. And I had done it, conspired with nature to produce it. Medicine may have its limits, I thought, but it's a lot better than nothing.

And it was only then that I realized that I would never go back to Ephesus or marry one of Thorion's friends. I wanted to live all my life in Alexandria and practice the art of healing.

✠✠✠

A month later, a year after I had left Ephesus, I received my first letter from Thorion. Deborah handed it to me one evening when Philon and I got back from our rounds; she told me that a sailor had delivered it during the day. I paid her back for what she'd given him and sat down at the table in the main room to read it. My heart was

95

in my throat when I broke the seal; I felt as nervous as though Thorion were standing in the room, about to quarrel with me about the way I'd been living.

But of course Thorion knew nothing except what I had told him in my own letter. His reply was a long one: he had apparently started it in the autumn after receiving my letter, then continued at intervals all winter until the ships sailed in the spring and he could post it. He was full of talk about the capital, about his studies and his friends. He was in good health, but no longer at the office of the praetorian prefect. Festinus and the prefect, Modestus, were "thick as thieves," and he'd been ousted from his job shortly after getting there; however, he now had another job, in the office of one of the provincial assessors, and hopes of promotion. "When I've been promoted I'll have enough money to keep a household, and you can come join me," he wrote. "But it's no good until then." Festinus had been outraged "by my sister's disappearance," as Thorion tactfully put it, and although he had now gone off to govern Paphlagonia, Ephesus was still uncomfortable for anyone in our family, and Constantinople would be just as bad if I showed up again now. Father had had to sell more land and even some of his racehorses to pay for losses the governor had inflicted on him, "but the assessorship is the natural path to the governorship, and I can make up the losses as soon as I'm a governor myself." Maia was fine, and with Thorion in Constantinople, but her joints still pained her. She told me to look after myself, and hoped that I had not had to sell too much of my mother's jewelry, and that I was eating well, and that I had not been converted to Judaism.

At that I smiled; then I looked up and saw Philon and Deborah watching me with intense curiosity. "Good news?" Philon asked.

I'd been reading under my breath, but hadn't needed to: the letter gave nothing away. I put it down, angled so that Philon could see the superscription and confirm, if he liked, his suspicions. "Just advice from my old nurse," I told him, "not to spend too much money. What's a good remedy for rheumatism that I could send her?"

I replied to the letter within the week, sending the remedy and telling Thorion a little about the city and the Museum. But I could say nothing about my own life, and certainly couldn't mention my resolve never to go back. There was no need to trouble them yet, I told myself. Thorion had said that I couldn't join them until he had enough money to maintain an independent household — and anything might have happened by then.

A few days later I was escorting Theophila about the marketplace when we met Theogenes.

I escorted Theophila about fairly often. As an unmarried girl she was not allowed out on her own, and I had considerable sympathy for her. So if there was time before supper we'd walk down to the market, or out to the park. She was a nice girl, though not at all interested in medicine. In fact, she made a much better young lady than I ever had: she liked weaving, sewing, and clothing; she loved small children and was good with them; she enjoyed gossiping with a few friends, and she liked to flirt decorously with young men. She wanted me to tell her all about "the way rich people live," and was disappointed that it was so unremarkable, though she was much impressed by a description of my father's house. For her part, she told me what was happening in the neighborhood, and once or twice, rather shyly, tried to convert me.

On this occasion we'd walked all the way down to the Tetrapylon, where she bought some saffron-dyed linen for a new tunic. On the way back I wanted to stop and buy some drugs, and it was at the druggist's that we met Theogenes.

Though I saw quite a lot of him, at the Temple and at the tavern, I'd never invited Theogenes home. I felt slightly awkward about inviting someone to what was Philon's house, not mine, and besides that, a bit embarrassed that the house wasn't more impressive. I knew that most of the doctors at the Temple looked down on Philon because he didn't earn much or have important patients: they thought it was because he was incompetent. I made sure that I always gave him the credit he was due, and my friends knew better than to sneer at him, but nonetheless I didn't want them to see the house. I knew that Theogenes rented a set of rooms in the Broucheion quarter and had two slaves to look after him, and I was ashamed to show him my bare little room.

However, when we entered the little shop off Soma Square, there he was, leaning on the counter and bargaining over some hyoscyamus. "Chariton!" he exclaimed when I came in, and immediately pulled me into the bargaining. "Wouldn't you say this stuff had lost its potency?"

"Indisputably," I agreed solemnly, and Theogenes launched back into his argument with the druggist, who was entirely unimpressed by this second opinion.

When Theogenes had finally struck a bargain and paused for breath, he noticed Theophila, who was standing beside the door holding her cloak over the lower part of her face and clutching her package of saffron linen. He always noticed pretty girls, and he looked at her appreciatively, then realized that she must be with me. "Why, Chariton!" he said, grinning. "You're the last person I'd expect to find in the company of a charming young lady!"

I smiled. "This is my master Philon's daughter, Theophila. Theophila, this is Theogenes of Antioch."

Theophila looked modestly at the floor. "Chariton's told me about you," she murmured.

"All lies!" Theogenes exclaimed at once, and Theophila giggled.

I took my turn bargaining with the druggist; Theogenes talked to Theophila. By the time I'd collected my own package of drugs, Theophila was saying, "I'm sure you'd be welcome at home; Father's told Chariton lots of times that he'd like to meet you."

"I've told Chariton lots of times that I'd like to meet your father," returned Theogenes truthfully. "But he never will fix a time."

"I've never been sure when would be convenient for Philon," I lied.

"Now would be fine," Theophila said at once, again looking modestly at the floor, then gazing up through her eyelashes. She was enjoying herself.

So Theogenes came back, was introduced to Philon, and stayed for supper. He did not sneer at the house, and we had a three-sided argument about the works of Galen during the meal, followed by a two-sided (I sat and listened) argument about the Jewish Law, which Philon won without effort. Theogenes was enormously impressed. "You reason like a scholar," he told Philon.

"I studied in Tiberias," Philon replied, and Theogenes was even more impressed. When he left, Philon invited him to come back for dinner "anytime," and Theogenes thanked him warmly.

"Your master's a remarkable man," he told me the next day. We were in the Temple herb garden after a lecture on plants, and Theogenes pulled me into the shade of the Lebanese cedar that stood in the middle of the garden, so as to have a proper talk out of the sun. It was pleasantly cool in the shade, a little artificial stream ran gurgling under the tree roots, and the flowers were in bloom.

"I won't deny it," I replied. "It's what I've been saying since I met him."

"Yes, but do you realize how extraordinary he is? To have studied the Law in Tiberias and medicine in Alexandria? The two greatest subjects a man can study, at the two greatest centers of learning? But you're a Christian; I suppose Tiberias and the Law don't mean much to you."

"True, I'm afraid. I hadn't even realized that Tiberias was such an eminent place. Philon's son is there now. He's been studying your Law for a couple of years."

"That's not surprising; scholarship tends to run in families. I wonder if the son will go on and do medicine as well. How old is he?"

"About our age, I think. Three years older than Theophila, anyway."

Theogenes smiled, his eyes lighting up. "She's fifteen, then? She's a very pretty girl, isn't she? Is she engaged to anyone?"

I laughed. "Have you ever met a girl you didn't think 'very pretty'? No, she's not engaged to anyone yet. There's a problem over the dowry."

He sighed. "There would be. Why don't they have more money? I would have thought a learned man like Philon could earn plenty, and you and he certainly work hard enough."

"We don't earn much because we don't treat people who have much money. It's as simple as that. Philon isn't poor, but he'll never be rich either, and that's his own choice."

Theogenes thought about it for a moment, staring at the green of the garden, the white and purple of the irises, the pink cyclamen. "I don't think I'll ever rise to a height like that," he confessed. "When I pass my examination, I intend to make money."

I laughed. "You sound just like my br— . . . like my patron. 'I intend to go to court and earn money!' "

"Did he want *you* to go to court and earn money?" Theogenes asked quickly, looking up from the flowers into my face, openly curious.

I looked away, reluctant to lie to him. "He didn't want me to study medicine," I said after a minute.

"So you have risen to that height."

"Oh, it's not the same for me as it must have been for Philon. It's not hard to give up being rich when you've never been in want and are sure you never will be. And what would I want more money for? Everything I ever wanted, I already have."

"Not *everything!*"

"Everything I ever thought about."

"You must have thought about it much less than I have. Me, I want a good house in the middle of Antioch, with my own slaves to care for it, and my own garden — just like my father has. And I'd like a job like his — state physician would suit me fine. And I'd like some sweet, pretty little wife in the house, to look after it and to welcome me home every evening, and I'd like two or three children running to the door. You need money for all that." He stared at the garden thoughtfully for another moment, then heaved a pebble into the stream. "And I need to study harder. When are you supposed to pick cyclamen?"

Theogenes invited himself to dinner at Philon's every few weeks throughout the summer, usually appearing with a flask of wine or some scented oil or flowers, and staying late to argue medicine or the Law. Everyone liked him. Theophila asked me all about him, and flirted with him exquisitely — but she did that with any young man.

And still, all that summer, there were no riots. A few fights at the docks, a skirmish around the hippodrome after a chariot race, but no riots. At Kallias' tavern we laughed at Nikias for his predictions, but he only shrugged.

"The archbishop is in good health. And they say he's praying for peace at the end of all his sermons," he told us. "His followers must have taken it to heart. And the authorities are going to wait until he dies before they do anything. But just wait until he falls ill!" And he changed the subject to some miraculous cure reported from the Temple of Asklepios on Kos. He was always full of miraculous cures worked by Asklepios. Since his other major topic of conversation was reports of his own prowess with whores, I no longer took seriously anything he said, and decided that all this talk about rioting and civil war when the archbishop died was just intended to scare us.

One day in the middle of the autumn, Philon asked me some rather pointed questions about Theogenes. We were eating a late lunch in the Paneion, the park sacred to the old god Pan. It was another of the city's artificial hills, overgrown with cedar trees, date palms, cistus, and roses, and we were sitting in the shade by a bank of fragrant thyme, eating cumin bread, new cheese, and peaches. We were between patients; I had just come from visiting one of the cases I was managing more or less on my own, and had met Philon at the Paneion gates. After a discussion of medical matters, I remembered that Theogenes had asked whether he could come to dinner the following evening, and I told Philon this.

"Again?" said Philon, smiling. Then he stopped smiling, and gave a slight frown. "It's the second time in a week. He isn't . . . that is — has he talked to you much about Theophila?"

"A bit." I wasn't really paying attention; my mind was still on my patient, who had some growth inside her that was killing her slowly. I'd given her some opium to drink in wine when the pain was bad, but I was wondering whether there wasn't something more we could do for her, whether we ought to risk surgery.

"What has he said?"

"The usual sort of thing. She's pretty, she's charming, she's sweet. He thinks most girls are sweet."

"Oh." Philon sat silent for a minute, frowning down the hill. "Well, perhaps it means nothing. Only she seems fond of him, and he has been coming frequently of late." He sighed, and took a bite of bread. "I suppose I shouldn't give it much thought," he said through the mouthful; then he swallowed. "But I find I'm like any other father, wanting a good match for my daughter. I'd like her to be well-off — more comfortable than her mother has been. I've made my family pay for my way of practicing. She doesn't have much of a dowry saved up for her, and that matters so much. A son you can just give a good education and then leave to his merits, but a daughter needs money to marry on. It would be very good luck for us if Theogenes had fallen in love with her." He sighed. "Well, he's a pleasant young man, and interesting company even if he's not in love with her, and he's welcome to come to dinner."

I didn't say anything. That Philon should hope for this was obvious enough, but it hadn't occurred to me, and now that it had been pointed out, I found myself annoyed. Theogenes was always admiring pretty girls, commenting on them, speculating about them. And Theophila flirted, modestly but persistently, with anyone. They both seemed suddenly smug, idiotic, unbearable.

Philon sighed again and began discussing my patient and the possibility of surgery, but I now found it hard to pay attention. When we had finished our lunch and walked back out of the park, I wondered whether there was in fact some substance to Philon's hope. It was hard to tell. But Theogenes had been coming more and more often, and paying more and more attention to Theophila when he did come. It was, I realized, very probable that he was at least considering marriage to her. That was good news for the family. Why should it annoy me?

Because, I admitted silently, Theogenes was an attractive young man and I liked him myself.

I bit my lip, staring at Philon's shoulders in front of me. Once admitted, it was absurd. I wasn't his sort of girl. I'd never be some "sweet little wife" waiting at home for anyone — and I was a better doctor than he was. Come to that, he wasn't the sort of man I'd be allowed to marry. I supposed his family's wealth was about equal to that of Thorion's friend Kyrillos, whom Maia had considered not good enough for me; but Theogenes' money came from a profession, not the land, and so was less respectable. And he was Jewish. I should put the stupid liking out of my head at once, and be pleased if Theophila had indeed captured his affection. Chariton the eunuch had no business liking charming young men, and Charis daughter of Theodoros had no business studying medicine. And I wanted to study medicine far more than I wanted Theogenes, or any other young man, for that matter.

But I was in a foul temper all the next day, and when Theogenes came to the house and spent half his time trying to make Theophila laugh, I had to complain of a headache and go upstairs to lie down. I lay flat on my stomach on the bedspread with the shutters closed and chewed on my fingernails, wretched. I had everything I wanted, I'd told Theogenes. But he had been right when he had said I hadn't thought much about it. I thought now. Love, the companionship of marriage, children — of course I wanted them. It would be inhuman not to want things so natural and good. And I did like Theogenes, his eyes and his smile and his quick hands. There was no way on earth that anything could come of the liking; no way that anything could come of any liking I felt, so long as I continued to study medicine.

I got up, went to my bookcase, and ran my hands over the backs of my medical texts. They were odd things to balance against a living, smiling young man and the possibility of home and children. I pulled out one of the volumes of Hippocrates and opened it at random. At first the lines of writing lay blurred before my eyes, but then they sharpened and became words, a case history. A man with a fever and abdominal pains; I read to the end of the account and saw that he had died. I put the book back and stood staring at it, resting my fingers on the yellow papyrus. The books did balance. I wanted the art of healing, wanted it more than anything else on earth. I would simply have to resign myself, and accept that I must remain a eunuch.

Winter came, my second winter in Alexandria. Theogenes continued to visit at least once a week and pay attention to Theophila, and Philon subtly encouraged him, but nothing was said about it. I tried hard to be pleased, and sometimes I succeeded. But I was not quite as happy as I had been.

That spring I had my nineteenth birthday. I spent the day attending a patient sick with typhoid. He was a wheelwright, married, with three young children; his wife went into a panic when she saw his fever rising that morning, and begged me to stay the day. I stayed, brought the fever down by means of sponge baths with vinegar, got the patient to rest with cinquefoil and opium, and saw that he managed to drink some broth and keep it down. When I left he was resting more peacefully than he had for some time, the fever seemed lower, and the pulse was certainly stronger and steadier than it had been for days. His wife caught my hand as I was leaving and clutched it tightly, tears in her eyes. "He will recover?" she asked me.

"I think so," I told her. "Let him sleep as long as he likes; if he's thirsty, give him some honeywater. He can have some barley broth in the morning if he likes, and I'll come visit then. If his condition changes during the night, call me."

She nodded. "I don't know what we'd do if he died," she confided.

"I think that, barring a relapse, he'll live," I said, after weighing her need for reassurance against the danger of creating false hopes. But privately I was sure he would live: he was strong, and the worst was over.

The woman's tears started, and she pressed my hand again. "Thank you! Oh, may God reward you!"

"Go and sleep while you can," I advised her, and set off home.

I arrived at Philon's to find the family at supper, and Theogenes with them. He was sitting next to Theophila, leaning toward her and smiling, while she smiled back with lowered eyes. Very well, I thought to myself, and I was glad.

"How's the patient?" Philon asked immediately.

"I think he'll live," I replied happily, and went upstairs to wash.

✠✠✠

One night that spring, when we had just returned from our rounds and the women were preparing the evening meal, there was a knock at the door. Harpokration went to open it. Philon sat down opposite me at the dinner table, listening. It had been a long day's work. I'd left him in the morning to attend another dissection at the Museum and joined him after lunch to find him frantically busy patching up burns and broken limbs from some fire, too busy to eat or think, and it had gone on like that all the afternoon. Philon was looking a bit gray, and knocks on the door at night usually meant somebody had suddenly fallen ill. "Would you trust me to take it?" I asked, as Harpokration let in whoever it was.

Philon grunted, smiled. "Trust you, yes, but let's see what it is first."

It was a woman with a childbed fever. The caller was her husband, a small, dark, hairy man in a tattered and filthy linen tunic and camel-hair cloak. He recited his story in a rapid singsong, shuffling his feet, nervously avoiding our eyes. He worked as a mule driver, he said. He was very poor, and he had to leave the city with a mule team the next day or they'd have no money for food; he had not been in the city long, and had no bread ticket for the public dole. His wife had given birth to their first child the previous week, and she had initially been fine but was now ill, very ill. He had given most of his savings to a priest, and the rest to a sorcerer, to cure her, but the cures hadn't worked. He and his wife had no family in the city. They were more or less Christians (that is, they were some kind of Gnostics), and what the man really wanted was for his wife to be admitted to the hospital. He was suspicious of Jewish doctors and had less faith in the Hippocratic tradition than in priestly prayers and magic spells, but he had heard that Philon helped the poor out of charity, and was trying his luck.

There are many varieties of childbirth complications, and it was impossible to tell which this was from the man's ramblings ("Very bad she is, burning" was all he said when we asked about her symptoms). Philon nodded, sighed, then smiled at me. "She'll need two opinions," he said. So Philon and I both went to see the woman; at least she was quite nearby, just across the Canopic Way near the shipyards.

We found the woman lying in a filthy bed in a tiny room on the top floor of a tenement. The room was hot, and must have been like an oven during the heat of the day: it was directly under the roof. Plaster was cracking from the walls; it covered the floor with a fine white dust, and dimmed the garish colors of the cheap terra-cotta statues of Christ and Wisdom that stood behind the lamp in one wall. The woman was holding the new baby when we entered. It was crying loudly, and its swaddling clothes were caked with excrement. The mother was rocking it and talking loudly and incoherently and singing bits of lullabies and Gnostic hymns, which mixed with her speeches to the empty air.

Philon picked up the baby and handed it to me; the woman screamed and tried to take it back. "Shhh," Philon said gently, taking her pulse. "We're just changing the swaddling clothes; you'll see . . . there." He handed her a cushion, and she fell back into the bed, cradling that. Philon went on with his examination while I saw to the baby. It was desperately hungry, but exhausted; it was crying because the filth had given it sores on its backside. I cleaned it up, anointed it with lanolin and cedar oil, and gave it to its father, telling him to rock it and let it suck on his finger. It soon went to sleep.

The woman was not so easily dealt with. She had a high fever and was delirious, with frequent attacks of shivering; she had been vomiting and passing small amounts of bloody urine; she complained of thirst. She was about seventeen. There was not much we could do, and we both judged it likely that she would die. But you never could tell; she was young and quite strong, and might survive if she had careful nursing and rest. The family had no clean linen, but we boiled some water and cleaned the woman up, and agreed with the man that we would try to get her into a hospital.

Philon set the man to find someone to care for the child. "You must have some neighbor who's nursing a child," he said. "Take the baby round to her and explain; she can hardly refuse to feed it until you get back to the city." The man muttered something, staring anxiously at his wife, and Philon said impatiently, "She has a better chance of recovery if she's allowed to rest! And she doesn't have any milk for the baby now; he'll die too if you can't find someone to feed him." The mule driver shuffled, nodded, and took the baby out. In Ephesus a child like that would probably have been exposed to die, but the Egyptians like children. Even as a stranger to the city, the man could probably find someone to nurse the baby for him.

Philon stayed to try a few drugs to lower the fever and make the woman more comfortable, and I set out for the hospital. I privately resolved to buy some bread and wine for Philon as well. It is hard to work properly on an empty stomach after a long day.

The street was narrow, dark, and empty when I hurried into it. The hospital we normally used was to the west, near the promontory of the Pharos, which divides the Great Harbor from the Eunostos. I paused before the door of the tenement, wondering whether to go up to the Canopic Way or to cut through the back streets down to the harbor. Then a sharp gust of wind carried the sound of something like a fight from the eastern end of the shipyards, near the citadel: indistinct chanting, shouts, the crash of something breaking. I wondered what it was about — religious differences or just a drunken brawl? Whatever it was, it settled the way I should go: back up to the Canopic Way. I was going to stay well clear of that.

I ran up the street, trying not to look over my shoulder; experience of the city had only increased my nervousness in the back streets, particularly at night. But the Canopic Way was safe; you might have your pocket picked there during the day, but you were unlikely to be assaulted, even at night — it was too public. I reached it with a sigh of relief, and slowed my pace to a brisk walk. A party of revelers stumbled along the other side of the street, looking for a brothel, but otherwise the road was strangely empty, occupied by only a few stray cats. The commotion must be keeping people home. I hurried up to Soma Square, then down the Soma Street to the harbor. There was more noise from the waterfront, but I saw no one, only the light of torches along the curve of water and lamplight in rooms above the black bulk of the citadel walls, deep gold against the haze-shrouded night sky.

The hospital was a large building of grayish brick with a tiled roof. It was built around an open square; it had a garden with a fountain in the middle, and three long corridors where the patients lay. On the fourth side of the square, the entranceway, was a large common room used by the attendants. It was a big, plain room with bare walls of whitewashed plaster; it opened onto the garden and was always unlocked. The monks ate and prayed and slept there, rolling their sleeping mats up against the walls during the day. When I arrived at the hospital it was brightly lit and packed with people: it seemed that all the attendants and their brothers were there. They were standing about in a circle, talking and praying excitedly in Coptic. No one had answered my knock, so I waited just inside the door, trying to catch someone's attention. Presently a monk whom I'd never seen before noticed me, stopped praying, and stared furiously, and the others stopped as well, looking alarmed.

"Who is that idolator?" asked the strange monk. He was wearing a rough woolen tunic, a long one that reached to his feet, and no cloak; he was barefoot, bearded, hairy, and very dirty.

"Sir," I said to him as politely as I could, "I am Chariton, an assistant to Philon the doctor; I have come about a patient. The brethren here know me."

"You are a eunuch," said the strange monk. He spoke in the nasal, singsong accent of the upper Nile. "The Arian heresy, which denies the Son of God, receives its support from eunuchs, who, since their bodies are fruitless and their souls barren of virtue, cannot abide to hear the word *son!* What do you want here among the virtuous, son of perdition?"

Oh Lord, I thought, has the archbishop died? "Sir," I said, remembering Philon's counsel of patience, "I am no Arian; I reverence the truth as you do. I am not a eunuch through any choice of my own. And I have come about a patient, a woman sick with a childbed fever. She has no family here, her husband must leave the city tomorrow to earn bread, and we wished to commend her to the care of your charity."

"He is no Arian," agreed one of the monks I knew, who called himself Mark, after the apostle. "He is the assistant to Philon the Jew, but a good Nicene Christian."

"A eunuch assisting a Jew?" roared the stranger. "A demon assisting a devil! What good can come out of a partnership like that? He has come to spy upon the faithful, and has lied to you to win your trust and betray you to the governor or the duke of Egypt!"

At this there was an uproar. The monks all jumped up and stood facing me, wild-eyed, and suddenly I saw that it was serious, not just talk. I became afraid. "Sir," I repeated, very slowly, trying to hold my hands still at my sides, "I have come about a patient. The brethren here know me. I have come often about patients. Never about anything else. You are mistaken, sir."

The glare faded from the eyes of a few of the monks. Mark nodded. "He's a good doctor," he told the stranger. "He and his master will treat the sick for nothing. We have no reason to believe he's our enemy."

"That is the subtlety of the devil!" said the stranger. "We have just heard that that false god, the emperor of the heretics, wishes to depose and exile our lord and father, Bishop Athanasios; we meet to pray and to decide what to do about it, and lo! A eunuch like a court eunuch comes in and stands listening to us, ready, no doubt, to go back and report all he has heard! He is a spy!"

I did not move; I knew that if I did at least some of the monks would set on me at once. They were frightened, I saw now, badly frightened. I wondered what they had been saying so excitedly in their native tongue — something to earn them the death penalty, perhaps. Was it true that the archbishop was to be exiled again? I remembered the fighting at the shipyards I had heard; presumably that was over the same rumor. But it could be no more than a rumor; there had been no proclamation; I would have heard it that morning at the Temple.

"I haven't heard anything," I said, "and I don't know anything about any exile. I doubt, friends, that it is true. I am not a spy. I don't even understand Coptic." I stopped, trying desperately to think of something else to say.

The strange monk spat and shouted, "Lies!"

"Don't believe me, then!" I snapped back, forgetting to be patient. "It's true, just the same. And I would have thought that these brethren here would know more about it than you do; you're a stranger here, aren't you?"

There was a rustling of feet about the room. The monks looked at each other, at the stranger, at me. Still no one moved to attack me. I doubted they would kill me even if they did. The discovery that I was really a woman, which they inevitably would make, would stop them short. The thought made me more confident. "Where did you hear about this exile?" I asked the stranger, pressing into the silence before he could denounce me again. "It hasn't been proclaimed in the city."

"They are moving troops down the Nile," the stranger told me, giving me a malevolent glare. "And the troops say that they are to keep order in the city, because rioting is expected. As you know, son of perdition. I have come down the Nile to warn the brethren of these things — you see, I am not afraid of you! I am Archaph, a servant of God and of the archbishop, and I will maintain my service to the death!"

"And these brethren here," I told him sharply, "are also in the service of God and the archbishop, and their service consists of looking after the sick, from which service, it seems to me, Archaph, you are distracting them with unconfirmed rumors about troop movements. My patient is really ill; she is very young, in pain, alone, with a new baby that no one is looking after — and what's happening to the rest of the sick here, while we stand about shouting? They could be dying, with no one left to attend them!"

At this Mark and some of the other monks looked worried. But Archaph said, "They will all die, if the heretics have their way. We will all be put in prison, persecuted for our service, and they will all be left to die. Do not listen to this creature, brothers, this spying half-man with his words set to create strife between us. Any patient of a

Jew and a eunuch must be a heretic. You should take no patients from such people; they will merely turn, like dogs, to tear the hands of those who healed them." He lifted his thin old arms toward Heaven, and I saw across his shoulders and upper arms the white scars of a whip, and noticed for the first time the calluses left by old shackles around his wrists. The other monks saw them too, gave a sort of growling sigh. "Remember how Gregorios beat us with thorns!" shouted Archaph. "Remember how Georgos racked and flogged the faithful! Remember the lists of the prefect Philagrios, which he compiled from the reports of his spies, and the torments he inflicted upon us when our lord Athanasios was exiled!"

The monks remembered and began to move toward me.

"I appeal to the archbishop!" I shouted, raising my voice to be heard over the clamor with which the attendants had greeted Archaph's words. It worked: at the mention of their precious Athanasios, they all fell silent. "If you really believe I am a spy," I went on, "you can tell His Holiness and have me sent out of the city. But in the meantime, will somebody please attend to the sick?"

For a moment there was silence. They all watched me, their eyes gleaming wildly in the lamplight. Then: "It is a good idea," declared Mark decisively. "Let us go to see our lord the archbishop. He will tell us what to do, whether this rumor is true or not. And we can ask him whether it is right to take patients from a eunuch and a Jew."

They all shouted and cheered, thronging around me suddenly as though I were a prisoner they had taken captive in some war and wished to lead in triumph to their leader. Some of them lit torches; Archaph and a few enthusiasts began to sing a psalm. So I was going to meet the archbishop. Well, he was at least a powerful man, and an experienced one. That ought to mean that he was less excitable than his followers. I thought it very likely that he'd acquit me at once and tell his followers to calm down. I just wished I could send a note to Philon and tell him what was happening. I was afraid he might try to come to the hospital himself if I didn't come back soon, and it would be worse for a Jew than for a eunuch. But there was no one to take any letter, so I contented myself with pointing out that someone should stay behind to look after the sick. A few of the monks agreed to do this, and the rest set off, jostling me into the middle, waving their torches and singing.

The episcopal palace was by the Eunostos Harbor on the west side of the city, near the Gate of the Moon. We marched along the waterfront, past the big church of Athanasios, across the ship canal, past the church of Theonas, and everywhere people ran out to join the monks. The rumor had spread throughout the city already, and the air was heavy with expectation of blood. Dock workers, shopkeepers, landless peasants who lived on odd jobs and the public dole all filed into line, waving clubs and knives, clapping their hands to the beat of the psalm, chanting and shouting. "O give thanks to the Lord, for he is good!" sang the monks, and the people shouted, "For his mercy endures forever!"

"It is better to trust in the Lord than to put confidence in man!"

"For his mercy endures forever!"

"It is better to trust in the Lord than to put confidence in princes!"

"For his mercy endures forever!"

"All nations compassed me about, but in the name of the Lord will I destroy them!"

"For his mercy endures forever, forever!"

"They compassed me about like bees; they are quenched as the fire of thorns: for in the name of the Lord will I destroy them! The Lord is my strength and song, and he is become my salvation!"

"For his mercy endures forever!"

We came to the episcopal palace at the head of a huge crowd, a mob that danced along the black edge of the harbor, its torches reflected in the eddies of the sea. At this, the far end of the harbor, there was a beach of stinking mud where the fishing boats were drawn up, bulked black against the dark sheen of the water. The palace was actually a far smaller house than my father's, with little to show whom it belonged to. I would have walked right past it, but the crowd knew who lived there; the people stopped short outside it, pouring over the low wall that divided the street from the sea, stamping their feet against the muddy beach, slapping the sides of the fishing boats, singing and chanting.

Some men in dark cloaks — monks or priests — came to the door and looked at us, then went back in. After a moment a small, dark old man came to the door and stood there, and the whole crowd shouted, "Athanasios! Athanasios! Athanasios!" I thought the ground would shake.

The archbishop raised his hands and the people were still. For a moment it was so silent that I could hear the crackling of the torches and the hush of the waves in the harbor behind us, the great sigh of the breath of this mob of people, the pounding of my own heart. I was closely pressed by the monks, and I felt dizzy; there was a smell of harbor sewage, unwashed bodies, and sweat.

"Beloved brothers," said the archbishop, "what is the meaning of this tumult?" There was another moment of silence, then many people began shouting at once. The archbishop raised his hand again and fixed his eyes on the monks from the hospital.

Archaph leaped forward; he prostrated himself to the archbishop. "Holy Father!" he exclaimed. "We have heard that the godless mean to take you from us, and we are afraid!"

Archbishop Athanasios sighed. "Do not be afraid," he said loudly and clearly; he had an extraordinarily powerful voice for such a small old body, and he did not mumble or hesitate over his words, the way many old people do; if you had closed your eyes, you would have thought it was a young man speaking. "I have heard this rumor too, but it is false. The duke of Egypt has brought his troops down to Alexandria for the Easter festival, for fear of tumults among the people, but there is no more to the matter than that. I have inquired of the duke and am content that nothing will happen, for the duke says that his troops will do nothing unless the people break into riot. Therefore, my brothers, I beg you to go home and to leave me to my evening's rest, for disturbances like this will do nothing but cause jubilation among the ungodly, who will accuse us of rioting."

The people all shouted loudly, "Athanasios! Lord of Egypt! Bounteous Nile!" They began to sing again, this time a psalm of victory. Someone restarted the clapping. Athanasios nodded to them, made the sign of the cross, and waved them off with a blessing. Most of the crowd began to disperse. My guard of monks milled about uncertainly, not sure whether to press the matter of taking patients from a Jew or not.

The archbishop decided them. "Is there anything more, my brothers?" he asked. "Archaph of the Thebaid! I did not know you were in Alexandria."

The monk looked very pleased to be recognized. "We caught this eunuch at the hospital," he told the bishop. "I think he is a spy. He wishes to slip his patients in among the faithful."

Athanasios looked at me, and I looked back. He was a small man, shorter than I was, and stooped slightly with age. He was very thin, had lost many of his teeth, and dressed very plainly in the gray robe of an ascetic. If it hadn't been for the crowd's reaction to him, I wouldn't have known who he was. He had a beard, white and thin, and white hair; but his eyes were perfectly clear. They were very large, dark eyes, like the eyes of some bird, but very expressive. One felt that they looked deep below the surface, gazing into the heart.

"You are a doctor?" asked Athanasios.

"A student, Your Holiness," I said. "I am the assistant of Philon the Jew. We have a patient, a Christian woman, whom we wished to have cared for in the hospital because she is poor and her husband has to leave the city to earn bread. I went to the hospital about her, but it seems to have been a bad time."

"What good can come of a Jew and a eunuch?" demanded Archaph vehemently. "They are spies, wishing to slip in more spies and heretics to watch us!"

"Is there anything for them to spy upon?" Athanasios asked him, smiling a little, then shrugged. "It is difficult to settle these matters on the doorstep. Come in — you, Archaph, and you, Mark . . . and you, eunuch. The rest of you go back to your work, and pray for peace. The city is troubled this spring, and we need the prayers of all godly men."

Reluctantly the other monks dispersed, and I went with Archaph and Mark into the episcopal palace.

Athanasios led us through an entrance hall and a small courtyard, and into a reception room. It was lit by several oil lamps. In one corner was a writing desk covered with books, in the other was a brazier. The room had a tessellated pavement floor, without mosaics, and was otherwise quite plain.

The archbishop sat down heavily at the desk, turning his chair about to face us; several deacons and another monk stood behind him. He gestured for us to make ourselves at home, but no one sat down; all stood, facing him. "Now," he said, "I pray you, brothers, explain yourselves. You object to taking patients from a Jewish doctor, and you think this eunuch is spying on you."

Archaph and Mark both began to speak at once, then stopped together. "I do not trust a eunuch who says he is a student of medicine," said Archaph. "They are a luxury-loving race, as you yourself have observed, Your Piety. And this one is foreign, but leagued with a Jew, though he claims to be a Christian. I have only just come to the city, I know no more than that. But Holy Father, you know how deeply we are hated, and how our enemies plot against us."

"God has protected us, and will protect us still," said Athanasios calmly. "I do not believe that the emperor will move against us now until I have died. But it is true that he has set men to watch those, like you, who support me. Mark, do you know this eunuch?"

Mark hesitated. "He is the assistant to one Philon, a Jewish doctor.

We have taken several patients on his recommendation during the past year; some have died, some lived. He and Philon are most assiduous in visiting them, though they expect no money for it. Indeed, if it were not that one was a Jew and the other a eunuch, I would have said that these doctors were both virtuous men."

"Do you have any reason to suspect that the patients have been spies?"

"The patients? No, indeed not, Your Holiness. They were ordinary people of Alexandria, poor people."

"Not Jews or eunuchs? Well, well. I see no harm in your taking patients from the Devil, if they are Christians and in need of charity. My brother Archaph is zealous and loyal, but truly, I think his zeal has overcome him a little here, eh? Eunuch — what's your name? Are you a Christian?"

"Yes, Your Holiness," I said, feeling greatly relieved. We now had it from the lips of the archbishop himself that the hospital was to take our patients. "I am Chariton, sir, of Ephesus, a Nicene Christian."

"Why then are you working with a Jew?" The bright bird-eyes fixed me again. "However virtuous your master is, it is surprising to find an Ephesian eunuch who is an educated gentleman studying medicine with an Alexandrian Jew. It is something that is bound to look suspicious to many who, like Archaph, have been given reason to suspect."

I smiled and shrugged, inwardly making a note of the old man's perceptiveness. I had said only a few words to him, and he already had me identified as a gentleman. That accent so carefully nurtured by Ischyras and Maia! "I applied to study with other doctors when I arrived in Alexandria, Your Holiness, but they did not wish to work with a eunuch. My master Philon is a very generous man, sir, a true Hippocratic, and I am well pleased with the instruction I receive from him."

"A true Hippocratic! And that matters more to you than whether he is a follower of Christ! I trust his instruction is limited to the medical domain and your Christian faith is secure."

I couldn't think of anything to say to that immediately, and Athanasios watched me with an expression of suppressed amusement. "Philon is a virtuous man," I said at last. "He would never impose his faith on anyone. And he keeps the oath of Hippocrates in every detail."

"I am glad to hear it," Athanasios said smoothly. "What, precisely, does he swear in that oath? Not to spy?"

" 'Whatever I may discover which I ought not reveal, I will keep secret.' I should think that that includes not spying."

"And his Christian patients trust him? You said that there was a patient you wished to have put in the hospital now, didn't you?"

"His Christian patients can trust him, Your Holiness. Yes, there is a woman with childbed fever and no one to look after her."

Athansios said nothing for a moment. He just stared at me, then suddenly frowned. Archaph noticed and stirred, giving me another look of suspicion and dislike, which the archbishop caught. "No," he told the monk, "you are quite wrong, brother: he is not our enemy. But God has revealed something to me. Young man, I must speak with you a moment privately. Mark, Archaph, I beg you to put aside fear and anger, and go and charitably look after this young man's patient. Pray for us, brothers, as we will for you." He gestured a blessing at them, and with a look of surprise toward him and a look of frank curiosity toward me, they left. Athanasios nodded to his other attendants. "Leave us alone for a while," he ordered them. "I must speak to this eunuch privately."

They withdrew, staring without surprise but with curiosity, as though divine revelations were nothing unusual but the nature of them a cause for profound speculation. I felt very uneasy. I did not like the archbishop's sharp eyes. What could God have revealed to him? I preferred to leave God out of it. Bishop Athanasios was quite powerful enough on his own.

"So," he said when the others had gone. "What is your real name, young woman?"

"What?" I asked him. "I don't understand."

He made an impatient gesture. "You understand perfectly. Chariton . . . Is it Charis, perhaps? Why are you dressed up like that, pretending to be a eunuch?"

I felt a bit weak at the knees, and my tongue felt dry. I once again could think of nothing to say. Deny it? Or admit it and beg him to tell no one?

"You need not be afraid," Athanasios told me. "I have a . . . Hippocratic oath of my own. Whatever I may discover which I ought not reveal, I will keep secret."

"Yes," I said, and swallowed. "Yes, it is Charis. How did you know?"

"God revealed it to me." He watched me carefully. "It was surprising to find a well-educated eunuch studying medicine with a Jewish doctor, but it is even more surprising to find a young noble-woman. Why?"

I swallowed again. Did God really reveal things to him, or was it just his keen and unprejudiced eyes? "I didn't want to get married, and I did want to study medicine."

I realized later that this was one of the best things I could have said. Bishop Athanasios was an ascetic. He considered marriage an inferior way of life; perfection was chastity and spiritual discipline. He had often supported Alexandrian women against their families, though this won him considerable enmity. But I didn't think of this when I spoke.

"Medicine," he said, with a peculiar little frown. "Well. Still, it may lead to higher things . . . Does anyone else know of it?"

"No one in Alexandria," I told him. "My brother helped me."

"Helped you to run off from your parents, but could not help you to a position with a prestigious doctor beforehand? I see. All suspicious circumstances are now explained. It is a pity that you are forced into such a masquerade. I have sometimes thought that the nuns should be permitted to study medicine — but there is no saying anything to the scholars of the Museum. Occasionally they acknowledge that a woman may study philosophy, but the sciences, never. Though I have known several nuns who would have made excellent doctors. And there was one . . . well. Are you really a Nicene Christian?"

"Your Holiness, I am ignorant of theology. I respect Your Holiness, and will believe as you do."

"You wouldn't say that if I were questioning you on some medical matter. You mean that you are not interested in theology, don't you? Well, perhaps you will come to it later. It is at the bottom of everything, what one believes about God. Study the art of healing, then, Charis of Ephesus. I thank you for being honest with me."

I stood there, blushing stupidly. A few minutes before I had felt like a student of the art of healing; now I felt like a silly little girl. "You won't tell anyone?" I asked clumsily.

He laughed. "Why should I? I cannot see that you are doing anything wrong. It is the vanity of the world and the ambition of men that forces girls to marry when they would rather not. And the art of healing is a noble one, which Our Lord Christ himself practiced, and there are too few doctors who take their oaths seriously these days. But I may ask you for help one day, Charis."

Our eyes met. His were steady, testing. No, it was nothing so crude as a threat of blackmail. But he knew he had power over me now, because he knew who I was when others didn't, so he knew that he could trust me. He had a hold on me.

I bowed very low. "If Your Holiness ever wants help from me, you know that I am your servant."

Athanasios laughed again. "Yes, I do know that, don't I? The blessing of God be on you, daughter." He made the sign of the cross, then added, "I will have one of my priests escort you back to the hospital. The city is still disturbed tonight, and even as a eunuch you would have trouble."

When I got back to the hospital I found that Philon was there making our patient comfortable. The monks, even Archaph, eyed me with considerable respect, as the subject of a divine revelation, and this respect seemed to be spilling over onto Philon as well. Philon looked very relieved to see me, but at first discussed nothing but the patient. He'd given her a small amount of hemlock to lower the fever, with gentian to dry up the flow of blood, and she was sleeping now; a wet nurse had been found for the baby, but Philon wanted the child brought back to the mother to nurse at least once a day, for fear that she would develop mastitis as well as childbed fever. All the monks were very cheerful and cooperative, and we were soon able to leave the hospital and start home.

"Thank Heaven you're safe," said Philon when we were alone on the road home. "There was shouting down at the dock, and that woman's husband came in saying that the archbishop was to be exiled again and the whole city was in an uproar. I sent him after you to keep you away from the hospital; I knew there'd be trouble with those monks. It was too late, though. They took you to see the archbishop himself?"

I nodded. "He told them that the rumor was false and that they ought to take our patients."

"Chariton, you're a wonder," Philon declared emphatically. "Anyone else would have got himself lynched . . . They told me that the archbishop wanted to speak with you privately."

I nodded. Philon looked at me for a minute, but I did not look back. "And what happened?" he asked at last.

"I think he would make a better emperor than Valens the Augustus," I said. "He wouldn't have people tortured. He wouldn't need to."

Philon stopped and caught my arm. "Chariton," he said, "he can't

. . . I know you've done nothing wrong, but I know there are some things you haven't told me about. It is obvious — a eunuch from a wealthy family doesn't suddenly arrive in a city like Alexandria penniless and without any study arranged, unless something's gone wrong. The archbishop can't use . . . whatever your reasons are, against you, can he?"

I was touched at his concern. "I don't think he will," I told Philon. "And anyway, I don't think he'll need to."

Philon looked at me searchingly. I smiled; he smiled back and dropped my arm. We went home.

"But what's the archbishop really like?" Theogenes asked me again. It was the evening after the Sabbath, and we were sitting in Kallias' tavern with a few other medical students. At first I hadn't said anything about my encounter with Athanasios, but Theogenes had heard the whole story at Philon's house the evening before, and people had been asking me about nothing else ever since.

"How should I know? I met him for ten minutes," I said irritably. "He struck me as very intelligent and very perceptive, but more than that I can't say."

"But how did he know this personal thing about you, when you won't even tell us what it was?" demanded Nikias.

"I don't know how he knew. Maybe God really did reveal it to him. Or maybe he just made a lucky guess."

"They say he's a sorcerer," Nikias said uneasily. Though as a pagan he tended to scoff at divine revelations to Christians, he believed in anybody's magic as strongly as he did in all the miraculous cures attributed to Asklepios.

"I don't believe it," I said firmly. "Accusations of sorcery are common as dirt, but about the only group of Egyptians I've never found actually practicing it are clergymen."

"But Athanasios can foresee the future," Nikias said earnestly. "Once he was going down the Soma Street in his litter when he passed the turning to the Temple. A crow had landed on the votive column there, and a crowd of people were discussing what it meant. Athanasios had his litter stopped and told them that the crow was saying '*cras*,' which means something in Latin . . ."

"It means 'tomorrow,' " I supplied. "But show me a crow that doesn't say something similar!"

"But *this* crow was sitting on the votive column of Serapis! And Athanasios declared that it meant that on the next day the procession in honor of that god would be canceled. And that's exactly what happened. The next day the prefect published an edict outlawing pagan processions."

I thought of the look of amusement in Athanasios' eyes, and I laughed. "I think he was probably making a joke," I told Nikias. "He must have heard about the procession being canceled from someone in the prefect's office." My wine cup was empty, so I refilled it from the mixing bowl that stood on the table before us.

"You always think you know more about it than anyone else," Nikias said angrily.

"Oh, for Heaven's sake! There's a perfectly obvious natural explanation for your little story, and you have to bring in sorcery and omens and whatnot. I think Athanasios was making fun of people like you. From what I did see of him, that would be completely in character."

"You're so prejudiced against miracles that you won't acknowledge one even when it happens to you!" Nikias returned. "Every time I tell you some wonderful cure worked by the great god Asklepios, you say either that it didn't happen or that it had a natural cause, and now —"

"And I still say that!" I replied heatedly. "Hippocrates says that diseases have natural causes, and that nothing happens without a natural cause. And your great god Asklepios was just a man; Homer doesn't talk about him as though he were a god, and he ought to know. Asklepios was no more a god than . . . than Hadrian's boyfriend Antinoos, who got deified by decree of the Roman Senate!"

Nikias flushed and started to get up; Theogenes caught his arm. "Calm down," he said. "Chariton's just shaken by what happened. You pay for the wine, Chariton: you know it's against the rules to discuss religion."

I went red in my turn, and tipped some coins out onto the table. "I'm sorry," I told Nikias. "I was entirely to blame for saying that. You worship your idea of divinity, and I'll worship mine." Nikias nodded rather stiffly. I got up. "I've got to get home; I have some drugs to prepare," I told the others, and started out. Theogenes jumped up as well.

"I'm supposed to reread Hippocrates' text on fractures," he announced. "Adamantios says that I set bones as though I were grafting fig trees, and wants me to go back to basics. Come on, Chariton, I'll go with you as far as the Broucheion quarter."

It was dark outside the tavern, the only light coming from the windows of the houses about us and the quarter moon in the hazy sky. We paused, letting our eyes adjust after the lamplight. "You've been very bad-tempered lately," Theogenes told me. "It's not like you to get into religious arguments. Though Nikias deserves it."

I shrugged. My friends' curiosity about me made me feel extremely uneasy. Picking quarrels with them seemed the easiest way out, but now I was ashamed of myself. And Theophila had asked me to sound Theogenes out about his intentions, a mission that made me uncomfortable and unhappy. "I was to blame," I repeated. "I said I was sorry." I started down the road, picking my way through the piles of dung and the rubbish tipped into the street. Theogenes hurried after me, stepped in a dung heap, and swore softly. I stopped while he wiped his sandal off on the stones.

"The archbishop guessed something that worried you, didn't he?" Theogenes asked. "Are you really a slave? Is that what he found out?"

"No! I am freeborn and was raised as a free person. Just let it alone, will you?"

"Sorry." Theogenes started walking again. "I just meant to say that I didn't care if it was true, you're still a better doctor than I or the others in there ever will be."

"Oh my friend!" I exclaimed, ashamed again. "You shouldn't say things like that when I've behaved badly. But thank you for the kindness."

We walked on in silence for a minute, then I said, "Theophila was talking about you this afternoon."

I sensed rather than saw the smile. "What did she say?" Theogenes asked eagerly.

I watched the dark ground before my feet. Theophila had been unhappy about her request as well, fidgeting, clasping her hands together, and finally speaking with an earnest uncertainty quite different from her usual cheerful enthusiasm. "She said she wished she knew whether or not you were serious. She said she thought she was falling in love, really in love, with you, and she was frightened."

"Oh," said Theogenes in a different voice. There was another minute of silence, and then he said, "Dear little Theophila! I shouldn't visit so often."

"Then you're not serious?" I said, caught between surprise and anger. "She ought to be told."

Theogenes kicked at a heap of donkey dung. "Of course I'm serious! The person I need to convince is my father. I wrote him last autumn, when I first began to get serious. You see, Chariton, he wanted me to marry some girl in Antioch; I think he'd even approached her father about it. I wrote him about Theophila, and told him all about Philon's learning and saintliness, and informed him that there wouldn't be any dowry to speak of but that the girl was as sweet as any girl alive, and devout, and a doctor's daughter, who knew what to expect from her husband, and I was in love with her. And I've been waiting for a reply ever since. I suppose it's been delayed because of the winter; I swear I've been meeting every ship that comes from Antioch, trying to see if anyone's got a letter for me. If my father's absolutely opposed to the match, I can't go ahead with it: I've got to obey him, haven't I? It's in the Law. But I think — I hope — he'll give his consent. I'm just waiting for that before I talk to Philon."

"Oh," I said in turn. We reached the Canopic Way. We were near the end of the Tetrapylon, and it was early enough that the shops were still open: the street glowed with lights and people. "Can I tell Philon that you're waiting for your father's consent?" I asked Theogenes after a moment. "They're beginning to wonder, you see. He wouldn't officially have to know, but it would make everyone feel better. And if your father doesn't give his consent, they'll understand that you haven't just been playing with them."

"Oh Lord! Yes, by all means tell Philon. And Theophila. But I hope my father will agree. It's good spring weather; I should get a letter soon."

We parted near the church of Alexander — parted warmly. I walked the rest of the way back thinking of Theogenes and Theophila. I no longer felt resentful of or angry with them. They were really in love now, and all I could do was hope that their love would find a happy end.

Theogenes received the letter from his father in May; he showed it to me. It was cautious, disapproving of the match, but concluded, "If you feel you must marry this girl, then you must. Let me know, and

I will write to her father on your behalf. But I hope that you have considered your standing and your dignity, and have already put her from your thoughts."

Theogenes was rapturous. He pulled me out of a lecture in the morning to tell me, and appeared at Philon's for supper, carrying a present of an amber necklace for Theophila. He beamingly asked to speak to Philon, and they went upstairs to the master bedroom for a few minutes and then came down smiling. Philon called all the house into the main room, then took Theophila and put her hand in Theogenes'. "My dearest," he told her, "Theogenes has asked my permission to marry you, and I have given my consent to the match."

Theophila went crimson. She looked at Philon with radiant eyes, then looked up Theogenes, aflame with happiness. He beamed again, and kissed her.

Of course it took some time to arrange the details of the betrothal. Theogenes wrote to his father, and his father wrote back, to him and to Philon, and Philon had a contract drawn up, and Deborah (overjoyed to see her daughter so well established) busied herself weaving and sewing the trousseau. But eventually a date was set: the new moon before the fast of Esther, a lucky time — early spring. "A long time to wait," said Theogenes with a groan. "But at least I know I have something to wait for." And he set himself again to the study of the art of healing. "After all," he told me, "I'll soon have a wife to support!"

✠✠✠

There was still no rioting that spring, not even at Easter, when the duke of Egypt went to the cathedral and left half his troops standing outside it to keep order. I went to that service; I had started going to the cathedral when I could, to hear what Athanasios had to say. For the first time I understood why the monks were so frightened. Those troops were drawn up, armed and armored, to punish the congregation if there was any trouble. People had been killed by them in riots before. There had been long episodes of violence several times since Athansios had taken the episcopal throne. Athanasios had certainly been a firebrand as a young man, but he was far from that now, and still the authorities clearly saw him as an enemy. He preached about peace that Easter, urging it on the congregation so passionately and eloquently that they came out of the cathedral almost ready to embrace the waiting soldiers, who didn't know what to make of it. He preached about peace quite a lot, but also about struggle, about the need for courage and resolution; it was quite plain that he too expected trouble.

I also bought the archbishop's theological work, *On the Incarnation*, and read that when I wasn't busy. I was busy most of the time, so I read it slowly. "Life is short and the art long" — I suppose that this aphorism of Hippocrates' really refers to the length of time it can take for a remedy to have any effect, but it seemed to me to apply very well to the amount of time it takes to learn anything. A doctor must know the symptoms of all the different diseases, and when to apply the remedies; he must know something about the different airs and waters which can carry diseases, and how best to guard the public health; he must know anatomy and surgery; he must be able to recognize the different medicinal herbs and prepare simples from them and calculate the correct dose. The more I learned, the more ignorant I seemed to myself. And then I realized that the most learned doctors are ignorant, and disagree among themselves not only over theories but over things that should be easily decided, like the function of the liver or the uses of bloodletting or black hellebore. And so often all art is useless, and the doctor might just as well tip his books and drugs in the sewer, for all the good they do.

"Can't we do anything?" I asked Philon one night in August, coming home after a patient died. "We're scarcely better than those quacks who try to cure with charms and incantations!"

"Well, we at least try to do no harm where we can do no good," Philon said. "And we try to follow and support nature. And sometimes we have cures. But it is true, it is hard to say when a patient has survived because of us and when he might have survived anyway. More die without a doctor than with one, though, and that's not true of charms and incantations."

I tried to smile, but I felt very low. The patient had been a young woman with an enteritic fever and an infection in the bladder. She had been about my age and apparently strong, dearly loved by her husband and her family, with a new little baby crying for her; and still she had suffered and died. "We know nothing," I said bitterly.

"No," said Philon. "We know a little. There is a great difference between knowing nothing and knowing a little. When you know a little, you do not guess blindly and invoke magical powers. We are still in the hands of God, but we have some knowledge of our limits."

"Tonight I feel that my limits should be the walls of my own house. What's the use of studying the art, if you can't help anyone for all your study?"

"We can help. We just can't promise a cure." Philon sighed and changed the subject. "When are you going to take your examination, Chariton? Or don't you mean to?"

That jerked me out of my depression. "What do you mean? I've only just started studying the art."

"It's been what, nearly two and a half years now since you joined me? That's true, it's not long. But you've gone at it like a starving peasant at a banquet, and you've a good memory. You'd pass your examination tomorrow. Don't look so alarmed: they don't ask you to *cure* anyone. You simply face a panel who ask you questions about the medical writers and about different treatments and diseases. You now know everything that everyone can agree upon, and they can't examine you on controversial theories or on experience. They can't teach you much more, up at the Temple. You're already notorious for picking holes in other people's theories, and the other day Adamantios told me that if you go on, they'll all conclude that nobody knows anything, which is a fine waste of scholarship. Though he'd like you to stay in Alexandria: he says you're stimulating company."

I laughed. When an Alexandrian says someone is "stimulating company," it means he argues with him all the time.

Philon smiled, understanding my amusement, but went on seriously. "You shouldn't go on paying them fees — or, come to that, paying me fees, either." We walked a few more paces, then he added softly, "Though I should be very sorry to lose you."

"I'd feel lost without you," I told him. "I don't have any experience. I would be afraid to do anything if I couldn't confer with you about it. I might kill someone."

Philon laughed. "That's not true. You've already treated people on your own. And any doctor might kill someone by getting a dose wrong. Although . . ." He stopped again, then stood still in the middle of the street, looking at me and pulling on his lip. Then he shrugged. "Well, I will put it to you: feel free to turn me down. In fact, perhaps you should turn me down. You're very gifted, and probably have a brilliant career before you, and I don't want to hold you back. But if you'd like to stay with me, for a few more years anyway, as a partner, I would be very pleased."

"Ai!" I exclaimed, like a washerwoman who's been pinched. I felt embarrassed, overwhelmed by Philon's offer. "You shouldn't say such things," I said at last. "You are an experienced and expert doctor, one of the best in Alexandria, and I am an ignorant student who has never been totally honest with you. I have no intention of taking the examination until I know a bit more about medicine."

"I don't want to disappoint you," Philon said, smiling, "but there isn't much more that anyone but experience can teach you." He started walking again. "Think about my offer."

We arrived back at the house to find Deborah and the slaves in a state of great agitation. Theophila was peering from the top of the stairs, and a stranger was sitting at the table, tapping it impatiently with his fingers; the gesture at once drew attention to his official-looking signet rings. He appeared to be a few years younger than Philon, and was clean-shaven and dark-haired. He was well dressed in a yellow tunic and fine orange cloak. He leaped up when we came in. "Chariton of Ephesus?" he demanded, staring at me. He had an educated Alexandrian voice, an accent carefully modulated but with the underlying singsong rhythm of Egypt.

"Yes," I replied, undoubtedly sounding nervous; I could think of no reason for this sudden descent by an official, unless Festinus had discovered something. "What is it?"

"I am Theophilos, a deacon of the church of the Alexandrians. Our father the most pious Athanasios wishes to see you at once," said the stranger. "Please come with me. And hurry."

"Why does the archbishop want him?" Philon demanded, looking anxious and angry. "What claim does the archbishop have on him? He's been hard at work all day, he's —"

The other hit the table. "Stop talking! His Holiness is ill; we want any doctor that he's willing to see, and he's willing to see this eunuch and no other. Now come. As for you, Jew, this news is not to be spread about the city. We don't want trouble, and there'll be blood-shed if it gets out."

Everyone gaped, and I clutched my medical bag. Theophilos gestured impatiently for me to follow him, and plunged out the door. I looked back at Philon and his family standing there in the dining room with their jaws hanging, then waved to them and went after him. Oh Divine Lord, I thought, running down the street, do I start my career as the doctor that killed the archbishop of Alexandria?

Athanasios had pneumonia. He'd had it for several days by the time I was called, but had suppressed the news for fear of causing a riot. By the time I reached him he was very weak, still lucid but with a glazed, exhausted look, the nose sharp, the eyes and temples sunken, the skin very dry — all bad signs. But he smiled when he saw me. His lungs were quite congested, and he had to struggle to breathe at all; he couldn't speak.

He was lying in a great canopied bed in a large, formally impersonal bedroom, his limp, shrunken body looking like a doll accidentally abandoned among the finery. He was surrounded by a huge throng of people — monks, priests, deacons, a couple of nuns, all the slaves in the episcopal palace, one or two bishops from elsewhere in Egypt. Some of them were sitting in one corner of the bedroom, praying and lamenting; the others were hanging over the archbishop and arguing about what to do to help him, when they weren't pressing him to arrange various church affairs. I turned most of them out of the room on the spot. Then I had the rest close the windows and fetch some braziers and water to fill the room with steam. I got a few cupping glasses and applied them to Athanasios' chest to loosen the phlegm, and I gave him oxymel and some horehound and iris root, which is good for the lungs. He began coughing and brought up a lot of watery phlegm, and then he was sick and brought up some of the oxymel and a little green bile, and then he coughed some more. His fever rose and his pulse became erratic, but it seemed to me that he was breathing more easily, so I persisted with the steam but ceased the cupping. The attendants wanted me to bleed him or give him purgatives, but it is not good to bleed old or exhausted people. Bleeding is good for those of middle age, particularly if they have a choleric disposition, and leeches on the temples will cure a headache, but otherwise I think bleeding is done mainly to impress upon lay people that the doctor is active. And purgatives won't help a man to breathe.

After much coughing Athanasios fell asleep, exhausted. His extremities stayed warm: a good sign. He was a strong man, but he was in very bad condition: old, and emaciated from years of asceticism. As soon as the attendants saw that he was asleep, they became terrified that he would die without naming his successor. The ones I'd thrown out came back in, and wanted to wake him up and have him name one on the spot. But I told them that I thought he would recover if they would only leave him alone, and I threw them out again. This time I turned everybody out, so that no one could be offended, and then I settled down to watch the sick man.

As soon as I was alone with my patient, my hands started shaking and I had to sit down and struggle for control of myself. It had been easy to seem confident when I was actually doing things. A doctor gets used to pretending more than he feels; he has to, to keep his patients happy. And you always feel at least something of what you act. But now, on my own, I was terrified. I was not yet twenty, not qualified, and here I was responsible for the treatment of the most powerful man in the city, only because he knew my secret and so felt that he could trust me. What if he dies? I asked myself, and clasped my hands together to keep them still.

Well, I thought, people do die. "Man born of woman is of few days, and full of trouble; he blossoms like a flower and is cut down. His days are determined, and the number of his months are with God," as Timon said. But the pneumonia isn't as bad as Timon's was, I thought, and there's no pleurisy. He has a chance. He's my patient now, anyway, and I must simply do my best for him, as I would for anyone else. Even the monks can hardly punish me for that.

I got up and checked the boiling water on the braziers.

He slept most of the night, soundly and without too much tossing about. His breath bubbled horribly at first, then steadied some. Then he woke up, whispering something about thirst; his fever had risen sharply. I gave him some honeywater with a small quantity of hemlock in it — a very small quantity, because I didn't want to suppress the cough which was clearing his lungs. He responded to this very well: the fever went down, and his pulse steadied. He still coughed occasionally, but these were good productive coughs. He fell asleep again, propped up on several pillows, and he was wheezing now more than bubbling. Was the crisis past? Too soon to tell. But there was nothing more I could do just then. I pulled a couch over so that I would hear at once if his breathing changed, and went to sleep on it.

I woke up about the middle of the morning and found Athanasios watching me. The light came in crisscross through the shutters of the room, and the braziers had gone out.

I sat up; my arm was asleep where I'd pillowed my head on it, and my tongue felt too big for my mouth. "Your Holiness," I said, "how do you feel now?"

He started to answer, then coughed. I stood up and supported his shoulders, then wiped his face and leaned him back on the pillows. He looked exhausted, but not as pinched and dried out as he had. The fever was gone.

"Don't try to talk," I told him. "Just nod. Would you like something to eat? Some barley broth?"

He nodded, so I went to the door and unbarred it. All the attendants seemed to be sitting outside in the corridor, even the other bishops. "He is much better," I told them. "Can someone fetch some barley broth?"

Various of the monks began to sing a psalm of praise; some more practical souls ran off to fetch the barley broth. The priests and deacons made a concerted effort to come in, but I wouldn't let them. "His condition is still delicate," I told them firmly. "I cannot have him excited, or the fever may come back. You can see him after lunch."

The barley broth arrived and was passed among the crowd like a holy relic. I took it and went back into the room, barring the door again. Athanasios was still watching me, with his old expression of suppressed amusement. "So," he whispered, "we see that women make excellent doctors."

I laughed and sat down on my couch. "Don't exert yourself talking," I told him. "Just rest. Here, I'll feed you this."

"Like a nurse feeding a child," he whispered, and coughed. I wiped his face off and pushed him back into the pillows, then spoonfed him the barley broth. His temperature stayed down, and his breath remained wheezing, not bubbling. I gave him a bit more horehound and iris root, then fetched him a bedpan. I checked the urine: fairly clear, with a sediment. Another good sign.

"Your followers want to see you after lunch," I told him. "But don't try to talk to them. Just wave or something, so that they can see you're not going to die. It is very important that you rest until you have recovered your strength."

He nodded. "I won't die this time," he whispered. "Read something to me. The Scriptures. The Gospel of Matthew."

I thought this would probably do a good job of keeping him quiet, so I found a book of the Gospels — there were several volumes of Scriptures in the bookcase by the wall — and began reading. While I was reading the fourth chapter, about the temptation in the wilderness, Athanasios sat up, listening intently, though surely he knew the whole book by heart:

"Again, the devil took him up to a very high mountain, and showed him all the kingdoms of the world, and the glory of them, and said to him, All these will I give you, if you will fall down and worship me. Then Jesus said to him, Depart, Satan, for it is written, You will worship the Lord your God, and him only will you serve."

The archbishop raised his hand for me to stop. I looked up, and saw him smiling a peculiar twisted smile. "The last temptation," he whispered. "All the others were easy." He coughed.

"You shouldn't speak, Your Holiness."

"Let me talk, girl. It will make me feel better. My followers are all sitting outside waiting for me to name my successor, aren't they?"

I admitted that they were.

"Yes, they are afraid," he said thoughtfully. "Even if I live this time, they want it settled. But it's hard to condemn a friend to exile and possible death."

I looked back down at the book. "And that will happen to anyone you name?"

"I know it will. Even if the rest of the world became Nicene. The emperor wishes to break the power of the church of Egypt. All I can do is to try to soften the blow." He coughed again, then lay back on the bed, his fierce dark eyes fixed on the ceiling. "It's safe while I'm alive," he said after a minute. "I'm too old for Valens to exile me again, and he hasn't forgotten what happened the last time. But, oh Holy Christ, it will start up again when I'm dead. The rioting, the exiles, the people thrown into prison. The torturing. It's gone on for years and years. Yes, and my own people are guilty too." He smiled his twisted smile. "Some of us, anyway. Passionate, turbulent, arrogant, violent Egyptians. But we always suffer more than we inflict." He lay still for a moment, his thin old fingers plucking at the sheets. "I will have to name two successors," he said after a moment. "One to be exiled, and one to take things in hand here in Alexandria. To contain the damage, and try to calm the people. I will have to arrange things with the prefect's office beforehand. But so much depends on the prefect, and they change all the time . . . What's the situation in Persia?"

"In Persia, Your Holiness!" I stared at him. He stared back, smiling. I shrugged and humored him. "The Great King has laid claim to Armenia again, and they say there's to be another war."

Athanasios sighed. "They've been saying that for years. I think they'll talk some more before doing any fighting. What about the Danube frontier?"

I was mystified by this interest in foreign wars. "All is peaceful in the East, Your Holiness. I've heard that there's a war in Africa, though."

"The troubles of Valentinian Augustus are no help. The western emperor doesn't meddle much in church affairs — indeed, my successor will probably have to go to the West to be safe. But if there were a war here in the East, perhaps Valens would leave us alone. Well, we can expect no help from the barbarians; I will have to strengthen the church to endure the worst. Charis daughter of Theodoros, I didn't mean to have you called."

"Did God reveal to you what my father's name is?" I asked him sarcastically, closing the book.

He jerked his head back, still smiling. "I worked it out. It is a pity, though. I hope I can still trust you."

"You can trust me. And you still know who I am: you have a hold on me."

"I fear that I do not. If I should reveal to the world that you are not a eunuch, I would have to reveal that I have just spent the night alone with a young woman, which would be even more damaging to me than it would be to you."

"But you were gravely ill with pneumonia, and you're old!"

He laughed, then coughed hard. "If I'm hypocritical enough to pretend to be an ascetic for seventy years, I'm hypocritical enough to pretend to have pneumonia. I've been accused of rape before, and tried for it. Rape, murder, sedition, sacrilege, and sorcery. Don't worry, I was acquitted. And the charges weren't true, except about the sedition."

"I'm not likely to accuse you of rape," I told him. "And I consider myself bound by the oath of Hippocrates. 'Whenever I enter a house, I will go to help the sick, never with the intention of doing harm.' If you don't think you can trust me, why did you send for me?"

"I didn't. Some of my attendants wanted to send for a doctor, and I couldn't think of anyone, not that I could trust. Then Theophilos remembered that I had talked with you. He asked if I could trust you, and I agreed that I could, so he ran off and fetched you. But here I am alive, so I suppose it was for the best. May I have a drink of water?"

"Plain water's not good in acute illnesses," I told him, and gave him a drink of honeywater. I checked his pulse: still perfectly steady, but his temperature seemed to me to be rising again. "You must stop exciting yourself. You'll have a relapse."

He jerked his head back again. "I'll name Petros to be my official successor," he said after a moment. "Another Archbishop Peter of Alexandria. The last one was martyred. That was in the great persecution. I can remember him: I heard him preaching when I was a boy. He never sat on the episcopal throne of St. Mark, but always on the footstool in front of it. I meant to do the same thing when I was consecrated, but the people cheered and it went out of my head. Do you know what it's like when they acclaim you? It intoxicates the will." He looked at me, the eyes no longer just bright but feverish.

"Please don't talk," I told him.

"Let me talk to someone. I have to give someone the throne of St. Mark, and that is even more uncomfortable than the imperial purple these days. And it's dangerous."

"You just said that you would give it to Peter."

"He's almost as old as I am. He's a brave man, an experienced man, but I will have to find someone else as well. Only it is hard. I must choose someone who is competent, who can manage the business of the church, who will judge fairly in the courts, who can hold his own against the authorities. But I cannot choose someone who is ambitious. 'The kingdoms of the world and all their glory' — a man who wants *that* can easily lead the church astray. It is difficult, when you are fighting against emperors and governors, to remember that your kingdom is not of this world." He looked up at the ceiling, closed his eyes for a moment, then opened them again. He seemed to be looking through the ceiling into some other place, somewhere where it was dark and very silent. "I should never have become archbishop," he whispered, quite clearly. "I wanted power too much. Well, it is in the hands of God." He began to sit up again.

"Lie still!" I ordered him. "I don't want to give you drugs, but I will if I have to!"

He smiled, but lay still. "I am not delirious, doctor. Only a sick old man prattling on." He stretched out a thin, blue-veined hand for the water, so I held it to his lips, then wiped his face for him.

"I know you are the governor of a great church, and a powerful man," I said, more gently. "But it would be better if you waited before trying to arrange any ecclesiastical affairs. Just wave at them this afternoon; leave the succession until tomorrow."

"I can never leave anything till tomorrow," he told me. "By tomorrow all the city will know that I am ill, and there will be trouble unless someone acts to see that there isn't. Go and fetch in Peter and Theophilos. I want to pray with them."

I tried to argue him out of this, but he was quite firm, and eventually I had to fetch them. Peter was another gray-robed old ascetic, but Theophilos was the younger man who had fetched me. When I went out of the room to call them, I found Peter sitting on the floor by the door reading the Scriptures, and Theophilos sitting in the next room on a chair, having a low-voiced discussion with some other deacons about what to say to the people. He looked surprised and alarmed when I said that the archbishop wanted to see him. When I had let them both into Athanasios' room, I warned them severely that they must not excite His Holiness, or I wouldn't answer for the consequences. Athanasios laughed at this, had another coughing fit, then sent me out of the room.

He prayed with them privately for what seemed a long time. I sat down in the corridor outside, with the others; they asked me how long I thought the archbishop would live. "Years, if he's sensible and rests himself," I told them sharply. "Otherwise, not long."

They again began variously praying for his health and debating in whispers what they should do when he died and the imperial troops arrived. I felt very tired, and sat with my head on my knees, trying to calculate doses of hemlock and foxglove.

After an hour or so, Peter and Theophilos came back to the door and called in the whole throng. Everyone filed into the room; it filled up so that it was difficult to breathe, and people were still waiting in the corridor outside. Athanasios was sitting up in bed, looking feverish but calm. He blessed them all. "Beloved brethren," he said in the clear, strong voice I had heard calming the crowd before (I don't know how he managed it, with the infection in his lungs). "Do not be troubled. God has delivered me from 'the pestilence that walks in darkness' as from 'the destruction that wastes at the noonday.' And I trust the Divine Power will protect us all. But I am tired, and need rest to recover. Therefore, I appoint Peter and Theophilos to care for you and bear my responsibilities while I am recovering." He would have gone on, but his lungs didn't permit it: he had another coughing fit. At this there was considerable commotion — praying and psalm singing and urgent questions from the deacons — but this time Peter and Theophilos moved to manage it, and helped me get the crowd out of the room. After this the archbishop consented to rest.

✠✠✠

I stayed at the episcopal palace for a week, feeling lost the whole time, what with the mobs standing outside the door singing, and the church officials consulting me as to what to tell His Holiness about the state of the city, and the imperial officials drawing me aside and offering me bribes for information about what the church officials had said. I got used to going to the door of the house and making announcements to all and sundry about the state of His Holiness' health, and I learned a few tricks for diverting the officials, but I felt out of my depth. Athanasios was a difficult patient, too, always trying to do too much and losing his temper when his body failed him. Moreover, I had very little privacy — the palace was apparently crowded at the best of times, and no one had a room to himself. I stayed beside my patient, but there was nowhere I could wash. I was worried that my period would start. There was no trouble concealing this inconvenience at Philon's house; for a doctor to have a couple of blood-stained towels soaking in a corner raised no comment there. But I'd refused to bleed Athanasios, and anything I did do raised endless worried discussion, so I could never have hidden it.

But the archbishop was a strong man, and determined to hold on to life a bit longer — at least until he had put the affairs of the church in order. He did recover steadily, and after a week even I felt that there was no danger of a relapse. I recommended to him that he leave the city for a few weeks, though, and stay in the countryside where he would be allowed more rest. He sighed and jerked back his head: no.

"I would like to go to Nitria," he admitted to me. "I would like to die there, in a monastery. It is so still in the desert; the only thing that moves is the light. You can think there, and pray. Here in the city they are always talking, plotting and counterplotting. But I must see how Theophilos manages."

"He's very competent," I told him. Theophilos was indeed more competent than old Peter, who couldn't keep more than one idea in his head at a time.

"Oh, I know he's competent," Athanasios said sadly. "What I need to know is how ambitious he is."

So the archbishop stayed in the city, and I went back to Philon's house. I continued to go to the palace every day to check on my illustrious patient, but I hoped that things could now get back to normal. But of course everything was changed. I was, incredibly, the doctor that had *cured* the archbishop of Alexandria, and I was fashionable. Even before I left the palace I was being called in to other cases, to sick monks and nuns, priests and deacons, and a few important lay people. As soon as the archbishop was back on his feet I was besieged with new patients, all of them Christian and some of them very distinguished. My fellow students asked so many questions that

I stopped going to the tavern to avoid having to answer them. I stopped going to lectures too. I was too busy for them.

"You had better take that examination," Philon told me one night when I returned after midnight, my head buzzing with ecclesiastical intrigues and anxieties. "The doctors at the Temple are very annoyed about you. They think that you're slighting them, not taking the examination so that you don't have to acknowledge that they taught you. I had Adamantios himself going on at me today when I went to the library to check a prescription. He thinks you must have become some kind of religious fanatic."

"Oh, by Artemis the Great!" I said. Philon gave me a strange look and laughed. It was a very stupid oath for a Christian physician, but a very common one in Ephesus. "Won't this just blow over?" I asked him pleadingly. "I'm not *old* enough for this; I don't know what I'm doing."

"You'll do your patients as much good as any other doctor in the city," he told me. "And it won't blow over."

He had met me in the front room when I came in. The rest of the household was asleep. It was a hot autumn night; the street stank of the harbor. Only one oil lamp was lit, the one that hung over Philon's writing desk at the corner. I sat down at the dining table and stared at the worn wood. When I had come to Alexandria I had never really thought of having a medical *career*. Of course, I had meant to go back to Ephesus one day. It had been enough just to study the art, and to practice it. But Philon was right: this wouldn't blow over. I was, if still unofficially, the private physician of the most powerful man in the city. I still did not know what I thought of Athanasios. I admired him, certainly, and I was beginning to feel a kind of exasperated affection for such an unruly patient. But on the whole I wished that he had not discovered me, and that Theophilos had not remembered it. I liked working with Philon, living in his house; I liked his generosity with his patients. And I liked many of the patients as well; the Jews of Alexandria were kinder and less excitable than their Egyptian neighbors. I found them easier to get on with than Athanasios' monks.

But I was being swept inexorably away from Philon's practice and pulled after the archbishop. I did not like the look of where I was being dragged. I supposed, thinking it over, that I was as good as or better than many of the doctors at the Temple — Philon was a good teacher. But I still felt ignorant and helpless, and when I thought about the church it was worse. Athanasios had been challenging emperors all his life, and the present uneasy peace in the city would last no longer than his life did. I was afraid.

Afraid of discovery too, I admitted to myself. If there had been a scandal when I ran away from Ephesus, there'd be more of a scandal if I was found out now. And if I became well known, someone might say to Ischyras, "Your young cousin has done very well at Alexandria," and he'd say, "What cousin?" and they'd say, "Why, the eunuch Chariton" — and then somebody was bound to put two and two together.

On the other hand, I had no intention of going back to Ephesus. And it was plainly impossible to just slip along as Philon's assistant any longer. I'd had to go to Athanasios, and I couldn't refuse the new patients. A career of my own it would have to be.

"Very well," I said heavily. "I'll take the examination."

It was not much of an ordeal, actually. I bought myself a new cloak and tunic for the occasion; the old ones that Thorion had bought secondhand in the marketplace at Ephesus were now very stained and shabby. Theophila presented me with a woven edge for the cloak; it had a pattern of birds and trees in red and green, and when it was sewn on and I'd had a haircut, I was agreed to look a perfect gentleman.

The whole family came up to the Temple to watch the examination, which was held in one of the annexes. It was one of the larger annexes, because there were quite a lot of observers: most of my fellow students, and many former patients as well. Philon's Jewish patients and the party of monks and churchmen eyed each other with mutual suspicion. There was a panel of six judges from the Museum — four physicians, two other scholars — sitting at a table in the middle of the room in their good cloaks, with official expressions on. But I could see the glint of pleasure under the official severity, and felt less nervous. Most of the judges were very pleased with the occasion. They did not like doctors from other systems of training to win important patients, and to have me standing there respectfully in my new cloak, preparing to answer their questions, vindicated the Museum. Athanasios' doctor was no Egyptian ascetic, no pious monk from the desert, but a Hippocratic trained at the Temple. The new philosophy still had to yield some areas to the old sciences.

I took my place, standing opposite the panel, and after the usual shufflings and rustlings from the audience and coughings and rappings from the judges, the examination began.

As Philon had promised, the questions were phrased so that everyone could agree with the answers, which meant they were easy and uncontroversial, drawn from the standard medical writers and the herbals. Describe the structure of the heart; how would you treat a dislocation of the shoulder; how do you prepare melanthion and what are its uses? Only one of the examiners even wanted trouble. He was one of the scholars on the panel, a philosopher, an astrologer, and an enthusiastic pagan, and he was determined to show that Christian physicans were inferior to the old pagan variety. His turn to question me came at last, and he gave me a malicious smile and asked, "What effect do the stars have on health?"

My mind went blank for a moment; I noticed Adamantios scowling. "Hippocrates notes that the solstices, the rising of Sirius, Arcturus, and the Pleiades, are critical times for health," I said at last. "But apart from that, there is no further agreement among medical authorities on which stars are helpful and which not."

"Just what Hippocrates would have said!" shouted one of my fellow students, and the rest of them all burst out laughing. Adamantios smiled. The philosopher, not seeing the joke, scowled and began to cite Aratus and other astrological writers; Adamantios stopped him. "These aren't *medical* writers, most perfect Theon. Their authority on medical questions must be considered unreliable, and you cannot expect the most esteemed Chariton to have read them!"

Theon stopped, though with the smug look of one who has made his point. "My young daughter, though a female, is as well read in these matters as she is in Plotinus," he announced. "I don't see why we shouldn't expect as much of this most *Christian* physician."

"Excellent sir," I said, "I applaud your daughter's learning, and wish her success in her philosophy, but I doubt that she's read Krateuas, so I don't see why I should have read Aratus and Plotinus."

At this some of the other Hippocratics applauded. Adamantios smiled again, then coughed and exchanged glances with his fellows on the panel. They nodded, and I was pronounced accomplished in all medical matters, a doctor of the medical faculty of the Museum of Alexandria. Then, because I'd offered in advance, I was invited to swear the oath of Hippocrates. Not every doctor wants to swear it; the provisions are very strict. But I had admired it for years, and would have kept its provisions even if I didn't have a room full of witnesses to hold me to it. Theon sneered at me for swearing in the name of "the most sacred and glorious Trinity" instead of by Apollo and Asklepios, but it was the same oath. For seven centuries doctors had sworn it. Now I too promised to respect my master in the art as my own father; to help the sick and harm no one; to give no drugs to cause death or abortion; to be chaste and religious in my life and practice; never to cut to make a man a eunuch (my audience whispered when I swore that); not to abuse my position in a house for sexual advantage (more whispers); to keep secret whatever I learned that ought not be divulged. "If therefore I keep this oath and do not violate it, may I prosper in my life and in my profession," I finished. "If I transgress and perjure myself, may my fate be otherwise."

Adamantios rose, came round the table, and shook my hand. "I am sure that you will prosper," he told me, smiling, then went and chatted to Philon. It was over. The other judges all came up and congratulated me, as pleased as if they had never sent me off when I first arrived. My fellow students came after them, shaking my hand, slapping me on the back, congratulating me, and offering to buy me drinks. I offered them drinks in turn, and so we all went noisily down the hill to the tavern, where I spent a considerable sum on wine. When the party began to get rowdy, I slipped out with Theogenes, and we went home to Philon and his family; I didn't like rowdy parties. "There's truth in wine," the saying goes, and the truth was something I wanted to prevent people from discovering. Deborah and the slaves had prepared a private dinner party to celebrate, and I enjoyed this much more than I would have enjoyed getting drunk and being thrown into the Temple fountain, which was the more usual way of celebrating the end of studenthood.

"What will you do now, Chariton?" Theophila asked me shyly, when the private dinner party was nearing its quiet finish. Her cheeks were pink with the wine: she'd had much more than she was used to. So had I, though I'd tried to be moderate. Philon's dining room seemed to me to be glowing of its own accord, bright with lamplight and the happiness I had felt in it.

I looked at Philon. He looked back at me. Oh God, I thought, if only he were my own father and not just my master in the art. I wished I could be open with him, tell him the truth, and then ask him if he still wanted me for his partner.

But he wouldn't have let his own daughter study medicine. It was true that Theophila was not really interested in the art. But even when she did ask some medical question, Philon always turned it gently away. The art, he said, was not an interesting topic for pretty girls.

"I don't know," I said. "It looks as though my practice will be largely among Christians. All your paying patients are Jewish. They're both likely to suspect me if I try to straddle the gap."

Philon sighed, then nodded. "They suspect you already. You don't need to apologize, Chariton. I know you will have to set up on your own."

"It's not what I wanted," I told him. "I was happy where I was."

"Don't be so gloomy! I hope we will still see much of each other." He lifted his wine cup. "To your success and long life!"

The others raised their cups as well, wishing me success.

A week after taking the examination I moved into a house in the Rhakotis quarter. The deacon Theophilos arranged this; he was pleased that I'd be closer to the archbishop, where I could be reached quickly if he fell ill again. "And it is better that you live with Christians than with Jews," he told me. "I'm not saying anything against your master, but it is improper for His Holiness' physician to be fetched from a Jew's house." To say nothing of how Philon's Jewish patients were worried by all the monks parading in and out.

I told Theophilos that I'd prefer just a room at present, so that I wouldn't have the worries of a householder; I said I couldn't afford any slaves just yet, and wanted to live simply. He found a house belonging to a wealthy Alexandrian nun, and she let me have a room in it for nothing, surprised that I wanted no more than one room. My room was once again at the top of the house; the lower floors were taken by some other nuns. My landlady worried slightly about letting me the room; she wasn't sure that the other nuns would like having a man in the house, even a eunuch, who couldn't endanger their reputations. But the nuns agreed that the archbishop's personal physician was an acceptable housemate, and were content to take on the chores of cleaning my things, fetching water, and cooking, for a small fee — though they lived very simply, having only one meal a day, usually of bread and vegetables, without meat or wine. I bought quite a lot of meals in the marketplace, had dinner at Philon's at least once a week, to discuss cases with him, and met Theogenes sometimes for lunch at the tavern.

But I liked the nuns more than I had expected to. There were three of them: Anastasia, Agatha, and Amundora. They were all of lower-class backgrounds (unlike the landlady, who had an ancestry to shame my father) and fanatically devout, but they all had a robust and surprisingly vulgar sense of humor, and they were not in the least retiring and ladylike. "Eh, Chariton!" Amundora told me when I gave her a prescription for her corns. "I thought a eunuch would be no good, and you've done more for me already than a week of monks' praying. It just goes to show: brains are better than balls, eh? Not that those monks have any of either, poor things." And she chortled, as she always did when she thought of a rude comment about the monks. She thought of plenty of these, perhaps because she did regard them as brothers — talkative and arrogant younger brothers, in need of someone to put them in their place. The nuns went about the city, attending to the poor; they wove clothes and sold them to support themselves, and they did work for the church. They were proudly independent, and resented the higher status of the monks. I had scarcely moved in when they were pointing out to me that they were just as capable of nursing as the monks at the hospital, and suggesting that I say as much to His Holiness.

"I'm sure it's true," Athanasios said when I told him. "But if I put both nuns and monks in the hospitals, the pagans will gossip. Perhaps I should found another hospital, and let the nuns run that one."

He still coughed occasionally, and tired more easily than he should, though it was now over a month since his illness. But he had never rested properly. He was now fully back in command of the church, hearing cases in the ecclesiastical courts, arranging church funds, appointing bishops and clergy, preaching and organizing, and writing long letters to bishops of the Nicene faction all over the whole of the East. (The imperial officials were very curious as to whom he wrote and what he said, and I was offered several bribes if I could discover this information. I told them he kept his correspondence private, and then tried very hard never to see any of it.) He worked furiously, getting up early in the morning and plunging into the church like a whirlwind. He also still practiced asceticism, eating as simply as my nuns and lying prostrate for hours on the church floor, praying. I did not like it at all, and told him as much. "You are going to make yourself ill again. If you must work like this, treat your poor body more kindly. Eat two or three meals a day, not just one, and take some wine. Water is bad for you."

He jerked his head back, though he smiled at me. "There is too much to do. I must make the church as strong as possible, so that it doesn't break when I am gone."

"I wasn't talking about the church work, I was talking about the asceticism."

"Chariton, my dear" — he had a secretary in the room, and so used my official name — "you are working too hard. A delicately reared young man like you, attending patients with diarrheas and enteritis, and most of those the common dregs of the populace who can't even pay you! Why don't you treat yourself more gently, like those excellent physicians up at the Temple: graciously visit one or two wealthy patients a day, read Oribasios, and admire the constellations?"

"What do you mean by all that?" I asked; I knew his biting sarcasm by this time.

"You're a doctor for love, not money or reputation. Well, I am an ascetic for love. The rest of what I do is for the church. But this I do for God, and for myself. If I am to die soon, let me seek God the more eagerly, even if it is bad for me. You're like a doctor coming to an athlete just before a great race and telling him to be careful not to strain himself by exercising too much. 'My soul thirsts for God, the living God.' Do you think I *want* to spend my time worrying about the Persians, and the duke of Egypt, and an argument between the monks of Nitria and the bishop of Karanis over where the monks are to sell mats? I do not take much time for prayer; don't bother me over what I do take."

"Why is it necessary to maltreat yourself to love God? You don't believe the flesh is evil. I read your book: you go on and on in it about how the material world is created by God and human bodies are hallowed by the incarnation. So why do you have to punish yourself this way?"

Athanasios sighed and looked around his room. Books and letters overflowed from the writing desk; the secretary waited with his tablets and stylus; a gold embroidered cloak, worn to preach a sermon, was tossed over the couch. "Our lives are so cluttered," he said, dismissing them with a wave of a hand, like a man wiping clear a tablet. "We need simplicity, stillness, but we invent unnecessary needs for trivial things, and they cluster about, distracting us from the Truth. The hermit Anthony once told me that a monk is like a fish: take him out of his element and he dies. Silence is his element. In silence you can trade this shoddy world for Heaven."

I did not understand it, but there was no mistaking the longing that came into his voice when he spoke of monasticism, so I had to let him be. Instead I asked Peter whether he couldn't divert more of the church business away from the archbishop.

"Do you think I'm not trying to do that?" he demanded. "But no one can tell Thanassi to do anything, particularly not if it's for his own good."

"Thanassi?" I said, amused. I hadn't heard this nickname before.

Peter grinned sheepishly. I was getting to know the old man better now, and I liked him: he was an earnest believer rather than an impassioned one, and he was thoroughly good-natured, eager to be of help to anyone. "We used to call him that when he was a deacon. No one could talk sense to him then, and no one can now. You know that I had to hit him over the head and drag him out of the church once, to get him away from the soldiers? There was Duke Syrianus and his men, marching right up to the altar to arrest him and beating everyone who got in their way, and there was Thanassi, standing on top of the episcopal throne and shouting that he wouldn't leave until everyone else had got out safely. I hit him with one of the altar candlesticks and we pulled him out the back door. When he came to, he thought God must have worked some miracle for him to escape, and we didn't disillusion him, since it convinced him that he shouldn't give himself up. You can't reason with him when he's like that. In fact, he listens to you more than he does to most people." He chuckled, then became very sober. "Will he recover if he doesn't rest?"

I shook my head. "No more than he's recovered already. The first disease he catches may kill him, in the state he's in now."

Peter bit his lip. "Well, Theophilos and I will do what we can. And we rely on you, doctor."

That was not reassuring. Still less comforting was the letter I got from Thorion about the archbishop. I had written to him about what had happened — some of it, anyway — and the letter he wrote back was the last one I received from him before the winter. "I read with astonishment your account of having cured Archbishop Athanasios of a pneumonia," Thorion wrote. "I found on inquiry that this same archbishop is profoundly hated at court: the praetorian prefect calls him a prating demagogue, and the master of the offices thinks he is depraved and dangerous. I hear that he was once charged with murder, rape, and sorcery, though Maia says that those charges weren't justified. However that is, it is quite certain that His Sacred Majesty plans to crush the Nicene party at Alexandria, and is only waiting for

Athanasios to die before he does so. He has chosen a successor for the archbishop already — one Lucius, a good Arian — and he has spies set throughout the city to report on what the archbishop is doing, for it is thought possible that Athanasios may attempt to raise Alexandria and Egypt in rebellion and cut off the grain shipments to Constantinople, which would certainly cause us no end of trouble. If I were you, Charition, I'd stay well clear of a troublemaker like that."

"Lucius?" Athanasios said when I told him what Thorion had written (I suppose I was a spy too, in my way). "Yes, I knew that they were thinking of sending him. A few bishops in Antioch consecrated him to the throne of St. Mark, from a safe distance, and when Valens first exiled me they tried to install him. But he had to be escorted out of the city under a guard; it's a wonder he didn't get himself lynched, coming in like that with only a few attendants. If he comes back, he'll be sure to surround himself with troops first."

"What will he do if he does come?" I asked unhappily.

Athanasios sighed, then shrugged wearily. "He's unlikely to be moderate, if that's what you want to know. He's a proud, hot-tempered man, and a passionate Arian; he won't trouble himself to conciliate anyone, and he'll be pleased to use force." He looked at me for a moment; his expression softened, the look of suppressed amusement came into his eyes, and he added, "But I don't think you need to worry about yourself. He won't bother to chase doctors when there are monks he can have flogged — unless you managed to attract the attention of his spies, of course."

I hadn't noticed the spies when I had first come to the episcopal palace, but after this conversation and Thorion's letter, I saw that they were everywhere. There were always a few odd clerics about, people from outside Egypt, some of them carrying letters from foreign bishops, some of them on less precise errands, and they asked lots of questions. There were the more obvious people from the office of the prefect, the governor Palladios. And then there were the agents. *Agentes in rebus*, "agents in things," is a wonderfully vague Latin title. They're couriers, carrying official messages and information from different parts of the empire to the courts of Their Sacred Majesties. But they, and particularly their inspectors, or *curiosi*, are also spies. They can be billeted in any rich man's house, and they report back on what they hear there, telling all the gossip and rumors to the master of the offices. One agent left the palace shortly after it became obvious that Athanasios was not going to die quite yet, and the next one showed up only six weeks later.

As I was finishing my check on the archbishop one morning in November, there came a knock on the door, and then, without waiting for a reply, a tall young man with a short military cloak and a swagger marched in, followed by an unhappy Theophilos. "Athanaricus of Sardica, *curiosus* of the *agentes in rebus*, to see Archbishop Athanasios," the stranger announced.

Athanasios regarded him with distaste, and gestured for me to hand him his cloak; he'd taken it off so that I could look at his chest. Athanaric — though it started like the archbishop's name, it wasn't Greek, or even Roman. It was pure Gothic. But the agents were in many ways more like the army than the civil service, and Goths are common in the army. This agent certainly looked like a Goth. He had light brown hair, which he wore fairly long; he had a short beard; he was carrying a sword on a harness by his side; and he was wearing trousers as well as his short military cloak. The trousers were dusty and the agent smelled of horses: he'd plainly just arrived in the city. He stood in the doorway with his thumb hitched through his sword belt, Theophilos peering in irritation over his shoulder.

"Greetings, most excellent Athanaricus," Athanasios said, standing up. The agent still towered over him. "May I perhaps see your license?"

Athanaric handed him a signet on a chain, and a signed letter. Athanasios examined the signet, read the letter, and handed both back. "The authorities require you to be billeted here?" he asked resignedly. "How long will it take you to . . . inspect the posts?" That, of course, was the official job of a *curiosus*.

"Oh, till spring I expect," the Goth said cheerfully. He had a peculiar accent, clipped and staccato, saying all the words separately instead of running them together the way Greeks do. "Maybe longer. One never knows." He looked at me and raised his eyebrows. "Your Holiness has his own eunuch chamberlains now?" I was used to looks like that, to the disgust with which an active man regards a eunuch, so I busied myself putting away my medical instruments.

"This is my doctor, Chariton of Ephesus. Theophilos, can Your Piety find a room for the most excellent courier?"

Athanaric gave a snort and went off with Theophilos. When I was leaving the palace next morning, though, he caught my arm in the courtyard and pulled me aside. "Chariton of Ephesus!" he said in an almost friendly fashion, keeping hold of my cloak. "How is His Holiness this morning?"

"Much as he's been the last month," I replied. "Could Your Excellency let me go? I have a patient to visit."

"What, others besides the archbishop! Do they pay you well?"

Here came the offer of a bribe. "Some," I told him. "Others don't pay at all. I have all the money I need."

"No one has that. Look, eunuch — Your Carefulness, then — the archbishop's health is a subject that provokes a great deal of interest, in Antioch and Constantinople as well as in Alexandria. And my masters would very much like to know what the Alexandrian church is doing about Bishop Athanasios' health. We'd be prepared to pay for the knowledge, of course. What would you say to a . . a consulting fee of ten *solidi* a go, eh? I'll bet that's more than the old Nicene pays you."

Of course it was. No one pays their doctors as well as they pay their spies. "I am sorry, Your Perfection," I said carefully. "I have sworn an oath, and cannot accept your generous offer."

"What oath?" he said, looking taken aback and suspicious.

"Hippocrates' oath. I am a Hippocratic, by training and inclination."

He laughed. "I thought you meant that the archbishop had sworn you to secrecy. All right, fifteen *solidi*. Is the oath less binding now?"

"The oath is not less binding under any circumstances," I told him. "You will excuse me. I have a patient, as I said."

"Don't look so bad-tempered!" he told me, but his face had grown a bit flushed. "You don't expect me to believe that a eunuch takes the Hippocratic oath seriously, do you? What do you spend your money on, to have enough of it, eh? Girls are of no use to you? What about wine, paintings, fine clothing?"

I thought it was particularly stupid to mention clothing, as I was dressed for work in my old blue tunic, which now looked almost disreputable. In fact money couldn't have tempted me at all, even if I hadn't felt bound to the archbishop; I was already earning considerably more than I was spending. All I wanted was knowledge of the art. "Books," I said. "But I have plenty of money for them."

"I'm sure you have plenty of money but could use some more. Twenty *solidi*. Very well, twenty-five. I warn you, I won't go any higher than that."

"My patient is expecting me," I said sharply. "Please let go of my cloak."

He let go. "What hold does the archbishop have on you?"

"He is my patient. Your Excellency, much health."

And I walked off, leaving him staring after me with a surprised expression.

"Some barbarian was asking about you at the Temple this morning," Theogenes said when we met at Kallias' tavern a few days later.

"A barbarian?" I asked, surprised and unhappy. "You mean that agent, Athanaric of Sardica?"

"That was the name." Theogenes filled our wine cups from the bowl on the table, swirled the wine in his. "He caused quite a stir, coming to the Temple in trousers and carrying a sword, flashing his license for the post. Everyone was wondering what you'd done."

"I turned down a bribe he offered me," I said bitterly. "What did he want to know?"

"Were you a good doctor, were you honest, were you interested in money. Yes, yes, and no were all the answers he got. Well, Nikias told him that you were a conceited ass and an enemy of the gods as well, but otherwise he agreed with everyone else. The agent said that a friend of his was thinking of offering you a job, but he didn't ask for any references, so nobody believed that. I thought that he was looking for something to blackmail you with. Don't worry, he won't have learned your deep dark secret reasons for leaving Ephesus, whatever they were. People can't tell what they don't know."

I sighed and rubbed my face. "Maybe I should just have accepted the bribe. He was so surprised to find a eunuch refusing money that he's suspicious. Only I couldn't give him any real information, and telling lies is too much work and makes trouble."

Theogenes laughed. "You've surprised a lot of people that way, haven't you? Look, don't worry! All he knows about you is that you're a good doctor and that you're not remotely interested in money." The serving girl brought us our lunch, a dish of broiled eels with beetroot. Theogenes dipped his bread into it and took a bite. "Now that he knows he can't bribe you, you don't need to have anything else to do with him."

However, I was waked up by a knock on the door one night not long afterward. I got out of bed. The brazier had gone out and the room was cold; I'd been wearing my tunic, without the corset, even while I slept. "Who is it?" I asked, shivering and looking for my sandals.

It was one of the slaves from the episcopal palace. Someone was ill; I must come at once. I told him to wait while I dressed, got on my corset, tunic, and cloak, picked up my medical bag, and went out.

It was a cold night; the street was full of a damp fog from the harbor. Off to the right the Pharos lighthouse cast its beams far out to sea, reflecting the light away from the city with its mirrors. It was past midnight, and there was no other light and no one else around. A rat screamed as one of the stray cats caught it in an alley. I stumbled in the darkness over some garbage that had been tipped into the way, and the palace slave remarked that it was a foul night. I thought suddenly of Ephesus, as I had not done for years. There I could have as much sleep as I wanted, with no work on cold nights or hot summer afternoons; there were gardens to sit in, comfort all around, cleanness, peace. I pictured myself in the small white room I'd shared with Maia, lying in bed after a bath (I hadn't had a proper bath since arriving in Alexandria), listening to my nurse sing and wondering what would happen when I married. Well, I told myself, you could go back, or go to Constantinople and join Thorion. Are you going?

Of course not. I set my shoulders, and we stumbled on to the episcopal palace.

Theophilos and Athanasios were both waiting for me in the entrance hall; they were squatting scribe-fashion on the ground and whispering intently. Theophilos kept shaking his head. I was pleased to see the archbishop: the slave hadn't said who was ill, and I'd been too groggy to ask him. "Chariton," said Athanasios when the slave opened the door for me, "is enteritis very common this time of year?"

"It's getting near the solstice," I told him, somewhat confused. "That's a bad time for health. And yes, I have seen quite a few cases recently. But it's better now than in the autumn."

"It wouldn't help if the whole city were dying of it," Theophilos said impatiently. "They'll still say that we poisoned him."

"Poisoned who?" I asked.

"That Goth," Theophilos replied contemptuously. "That Arian agent."

Athanasios shook his head reprovingly. "Do your best to cure him," he told me. "I don't want to give the prefect any excuse to bring a prosecution against us."

"I always do my best with a patient," I said. "Can Your Piety please go to bed? You shouldn't be up this late. You'll come down with whatever it is too, and you have less chance of surviving it than a strong young man does. I'll have you called if anything happens."

"Holy God, Holy Immortal One!" snapped Athanasios. "Doctors!

Once let them into your house and they think they own you! First let me know whether you think the man will live."

Athanaric had his own room at the palace, though it was small. We came in to find the agent lying curled up on his side, shivering. All strength and swagger were gone; he was exhausted, comatose. I'd disliked him, but it is painful to see a strong young person folded up by imminent death. The bed had been stripped, but the smell of vomit lingered in the air. Pulse weak and erratic; fever high. His eyes were half-closed, with the whites showing under the lid: a very bad sign. "Has he had diarrhea as well?" I asked the attendants, and was relieved when they said he had: eyes like that usually mean death, but diarrhea can do it too. I was astonished at the agent's condition; either he'd deteriorated with remarkable speed, or no one had thought to call me earlier. I examined the attendants about it. They said he'd felt sick that morning, had gone to bed but then commenced vomiting, and had kept it up until he collapsed into his present state. But he had not vomited or passed blood or pus, from what I could make out, and no particular part of his body seemed tenderer than any other, so I diagnosed an acute enteritic fever rather than an infection, and told the archbishop that I thought he had a good chance. At this Athanasios agreed to leave the sickroom and go to bed, and I told the attendants not to let him in again.

The agent needed very careful nursing. That first morning I half expected him to die during the day, for he could keep nothing down and was getting severely dehydrated. I tried suppositories, and kept the room cool. I repeatedly washed him off and gave him honeywater with aloe on a sponge, and I had the attendants burn some opium under his nose to ease the rigors by relieving the pain. But it was a delicate business. The combination of vomiting, diarrhea, and a high fever is a dangerous one, and it needs a very strong constitution to survive it. Fortunately, Athanaric was strong, and had been healthy and well fed, and he pulled through. I got some honeywater into him, and then a good dose of opium, and then more honeywater, and that evening he finally commenced sweating, which lowered the fever. After that I thought it would be simply a matter of making him eat sensibly and rest until he was better. But I stayed in the sickroom that night, just to be sure. He woke up in the middle of the night, muttering in Latin, the speech of his native Sardica. His fever was up again and he was delirious. When I tried to give him a dose of hemlock, he refused to take it and called me a poisoner — at least I think that was what he said. I had only a touch of Thorion's legal

Latin, and hadn't thought of it for years. I stammered out some of the words I did know, telling him that the drink was *medicina*. "Medicus sum," I told him, to which he replied, "Non medicus, mulier venafica!" "Medicus," I insisted, and eventually got it down him. The nausea seemed to be better, because he kept the drink down and eventually went back to sleep, still tossing and muttering. And the hemlock duly lowered the fever.

When he woke in the morning, he was lucid. One of the attendants shook me awake as soon as he noticed that the patient had woken, and I went over and checked his pulse. He stared up at me blankly. The morning sun made gold lights in his hair; his eyes were clear again, a vivid blue; and for the first time I noticed that he was very good-looking. "Chariton of Ephesus," he whispered at last. He looked disappointed.

"Your doctor," I told him. "How are you feeling?" The pulse was steady, and the fever was down to manageable levels.

He frowned. "I was poisoned."

"You had an acute case of enteritis," I corrected him. "Probably brought on by drinking water you weren't accustomed to. His Holiness directed me to do my best to cure you, and I have done so."

He kept frowning, glancing about uncertainly. "There was a woman here last night."

"*I* was here last night. You kept raving about some woman trying to poison you, while I was trying to give you a dose of hemlock."

"Isn't that a poison?"

"Of course. Most good drugs are. It all depends on the dose. Would you like something to eat?"

Barley broth, says Hippocrates, is by far the most suitable food for convalescents, and I saw to it that Athanaric ate barley broth for a week, gradually supplementing it with bread, then wine and the rest of a normal diet. But the agent recovered as quickly as he had succumbed to the illness, and wanted to be up and about. He got on with his job, too. Even before I would allow him up he was asking the attendants questions, and trying his luck with me again. "I hear that Archbishop Athanasios had some divine revelation about you," he told me when I made one of my visits to him. Well, he would have heard it; everyone in the household knew it, and reported it with pride. I was generally supposed to have been converted from an Arian to a Nicene during our conversation.

"His Holiness called it that," I answered. "Have you moved your bowels today?"

"Don't change the subject," Athanaric complained. "What did he discover?"

"Nothing that he could hurt me with," I said misleadingly. "Any more cramps, wind, nausea?"

He muttered something in Latin. "Are you really a passionate Nicene, then?" he demanded.

"How do you expect me to treat you if you won't answer my questions?" I asked him. "Are you really a passionate Arian?"

He shrugged. "To tell the truth, I'm not really bothered about theology. But I am loyal to Their Sacred Majesties. And it is dangerous to have this kind of instability in the richest diocese of the empire, with an old preaching demagogue putting his notions of divinity before the common good, putting Roman armies at risk from the Persians because he disagrees with the emperor about the relation of persons in the Trinity. You'd think he was an emperor himself, the way he acts! And he has no warrant for the power he has: the Sacred Offices certainly didn't give him the right to rule Egypt. You can't have two independent powers in the state; it endangers the public safety. Apart from fanaticism, I don't see why anyone supports him."

I said nothing and began packing away my medical instruments. I was, I decided, now a Nicene in my theology. I'd been sufficiently impressed by Athanasios' book to agree with him on that. But I certainly wasn't passionate on the subject. Still, I realized, I was not loyal to Their Sacred Majesties. I did not like to think of Roman soldiers at risk before the Persians, but this great tyranny that rules the world, the omnipotent imperial power, from which there is no appeal, which rules by force and inflicts its edicts on pain of torture and death — I had no love for it. I believed that the church ought to be allowed to determine its own destiny, choose its own theology, pick its own bishops, and not have them imposed by Constantinople. Apart from the church, there was no power in all the world that could oppose the emperors; apart from Athanasios, there was no man who had succeeded in struggling against them as an equal without claiming the purple for himself. Which was the fundamental reason why all the Egyptians, and not just the Christians, supported the archbishop. And it was why I would support him too.

But I could hardly say all that to Athanaric. "You should rest for a few more days," I told him. "And eat your barley broth. I'll see you tomorrow."

He swore again in Latin. "Of all the eunuchs in the world," he said as I left the room, "why does the only virtuous one have to serve the archbishop?"

"You haven't met all the eunuchs in the world," I replied, pausing and looking back. "How do you know the rest aren't virtuous too?"

✠✠✠✠

Two days after this I woke up feeling queasy and hot. It was a damp, chill day in late December, and usually I was cold in the mornings, but I found I had thrown off the blanket and lay there sweating.

I had patients to visit that day, five cases who had not yet reached a crisis and a dozen convalescents. But when I got up I found that my muscles ached and my stomach churned; plainly I was not up to a full day's work. Moreover, it would be extremely irresponsible for me to carry on with the visits and risk transmitting the fever to my patients; in their weakened state it could be fatal. I gave Agatha, one of the nuns, a couple of *drachmae* to run around to the patients and say that I was ill. I sent some recommendations for their treatment to each, and prepared some simples for them; I also gave them the names of some other doctors, in case they needed personal attention. Then I went back to bed. Amundora came up and offered me some fresh cumin bread and hot honeyed wine — both delicacies that she must have bought for me, as she never ate them herself. But I was feeling quite sick by then, and couldn't bear even the smell of them. I thanked her, but told her that all I needed was rest. She hovered uncertainly in the doorway. "Eh, you look ill!" she told me. "Well, I will be in the house all day; just shout if you need anything."

I told her I would. When she left the room, I vomited into the chamberpot.

I had never in my life been gravely ill. I'd had colds, of course, and a few tertian fevers, but nothing like this. I felt utterly wretched, and by the middle of the afternoon utterly exhausted as well. It was plainly the same fever as Athanaric's, though whether I had caught it from him or from some other patient it was impossible to say. I prepared myself a sponge with some opium and honeywater and sucked on that after vomiting, hoping to put myself to sleep and so calm the spasms, but it didn't seem to help much. I couldn't keep anything else down, though I tried hemlock for the fever, and nard and aloe for the nausea.

Amundora came in again in the middle of the afternoon and gave a wail of dismay. She took out the overflowing chamberpot and washed the floor, then wanted to wash me as well. "Just leave me alone," I told her. "I'll be all right. I know this fever: it comes on fiercely but it goes quickly."

She left me reluctantly, then came back with some more water. I asked her to dip the sponge in it and she did, then handed it to me, looking unhappy. Plain water's not good in acute illnesses, I thought instinctively. It ought to be honeywater at the least, or maybe a mixture of honeywater and brine. And the opium.

But it was too much effort to explain all this to Amundora. I took the sponge of plain water and put it in my dry mouth, shivering. The nun's face, dark and worried, seemed to float a long way off. I wished that Maia were there with me.

"You're too sick to treat yourself," said Amundora. "I will send out for another doctor."

"No!" I told her, rousing myself finally at this. "It's all right. No one else will do anything that I'm not doing now. All I need is to rest. Leave me alone!"

I put my head down on the pillow; I heard her footsteps go to the door, pause, then go on down the stairs. I started to cry, unable to help myself. It was very hot and dark here, and I wanted Maia. I was sick again, but didn't need the chamberpot: my stomach was clenched up and dry, full of nothing but wind and pain. The spasms went on for a long, long time.

It grew darker. Someone came in and shouted at me, shook me. Mumbling and sobbing, I told them to go away, but couldn't remember when they went.

The next thing I knew someone had lit an oil lamp and was standing looking at me. "Maia?" I asked. I tried to sit up, but the movement made me sick again. The visitor came over, put a hand to my forehead, and took my pulse. It was Philon.

"When did this start?" Philon asked, glancing over his shoulder.

"Just this morning," said Amundora. "I thought he looked very ill, but he wouldn't let me send for anyone. Then when I went up after evening prayers, he was in a stupor and didn't hear me, so I remembered that Your Beneficence was his master, and I ran straight over."

Philon was examining my eyes. "It's a very dangerous fever," he

150

said. "I've seen two or three cases of it this past month: they've all died. He should have let you send earlier: I'm glad you fetched me tonight. Come on, Chariton, you're awake now, anyway. Let's have a look at you."

"No," I said. "Go away. Leave me alone."

"Could you fetch a brazier?" Philon said to Amundora. "This room is very cold. And I need to boil some water."

"At once!" said Amundora, and bustled from the room. Philon turned back to me.

"Leave me alone!" I begged.

"Don't be ridiculous," said Philon. He started loosening my tunic, which stank enough to turn anyone's stomach. Then he stopped suddenly. "What's this?" he asked.

I began to cry. Philon stared at me; his face seemed to hang there for ages: the square beard and the familiar brown eyes, now wide with astonishment. The pupils seemed to flood with the darkness and the face to waver like a reflection in the water, trembling, fading out into the heat and the blackness, leaving me alone.

When I next woke the awful nausea was gone and I felt very thirsty. I tried to sit up, and someone put a supporting hand behind my head and held a cup to my lips. It was a mixture of honeywater and brine, scented with nard and with something bitter as well — hemlock, I thought. I drank some, then looked up to see who was giving it to me. Philon.

"Finish it," he ordered. I finished it, and he put the cup down. "How do you feel now?" he asked me.

"Much better," I said. My voice sounded foreign: a hollow whisper. I'd heard that tone from others, and noted the weakness of convalescence. It was strange to recognize it in myself. "Tired. You . . . did you —"

"Did I find out that you're a woman? I could hardly miss it, could I? I never felt such a fool in my life. My own assistant, who lived in my own house for more than two years, and I took his word for it that he was a eunuch when it should have been glaringly obvious that he was nothing of the sort. That *she* was nothing of the sort. Lie still! It's a cruel fever, that, and you need to get your strength back."

I lay still. "I'm sorry," I said, trying not to cry. "Have you . . . who have you told?"

He snorted and patted my arm, very gently. "No one. The nuns

151

in your house don't know, and I haven't so much as whispered about it to Deborah. I hold it under my oath. Is that what the archbishop discovered?"

I nodded.

"An old man, and a bishop, and he spotted it immediately! And I am a trained doctor and couldn't see it in two years!"

"I think anyone who did see it would see it immediately," I said; I'd thought about this. "Once you are used to one idea about what I am, it is that much harder to see me as something different."

Philon sighed. "I never felt such a fool in my life," he repeated. "I suppose that you're the daughter of Theodoros of Ephesus, then?"

"Yes."

"I thought that . . . well, never mind."

"I know what you thought. I overheard you one night, talking about it with Deborah. I'm sorry, Philon."

"Why did you do it?"

"I wanted to learn the art. I don't suppose I would have run away if it hadn't been for Father's wanting me to marry Festinus; but once I had fled, I had to come here. Can you understand that? I know it was indecent, and dishonest, but all my life I'd wanted to study here."

Philon gave an odd smile. "As a matter of fact, I can understand." He sighed, then took my pulse. "You'll recover," he told me. "This disease is a fierce one, but you should recover quickly."

"The patient I treated who had it recovered well," I said.

"Oh, so you've seen it too? As a matter of fact, you're the first one I've seen survive it. You must have managed your patient very well."

"He was a strong young man."

"And you're a strong young woman. I shall never get used to that. I never would have taken you on if I'd known. Don't excite yourself: I could no more advise you to turn your back on medicine now than I could turn my back on it myself. Do you know, I had to fight to study it too? My parents were very devout, and I was brought up to study the Torah. When I'd finished in Alexandria, they sent me to Tiberias to study at the patriarchal courts. I spent a year there, going through the laws of Moses, and then one morning I woke up and realized that I was twenty and I didn't care at all for the laws of Moses: I wanted to practice the art of healing. I was already married then, and we had the baby — and I hadn't read even a chapter of Hippocrates. But I ran away from Tiberias and came back to Alexandria. My father was furious. He refused to support me unless I went back to Tiberias. So I left home. My father-in-law wanted Deborah to divorce me and marry someone else, but she wanted to stay with me, bless her. There was a Jewish doctor at the Museum then, a man named Themistion. Adamantios was his pupil too. I went to him and begged him to teach me. He was reluctant — I knew nothing but the Torah, and he was like Adamantios, a well-educated man and a Platonist. He thought it would be better if I obeyed my father. In the end I offered to be his servant and undertake personal tasks for him if he would teach me, and he saw how desperate I was and agreed. I agreed to take you on because I could see the same passion in you. If I'd known you were a woman, I would have doubted that; I would have told you to go home to your family. But that would have been wrong, because we are alike. By the Holy Name, my girl, don't cry! Do you want some barley broth?"

As Philon had said, I recovered quickly. I was back on my feet, though still shakily, on the next day, but Philon advised me strictly not to strain myself, so I rested at home, reading Dioskourides' *On Medicines*. One of the archbishop's slaves came from the palace to ask how I was and returned reassured. (I gathered afterward that Athanasios had meant to come himself but had been talked out of it by Theophilos. "He said that you would be angry if I caught the illness myself," he told me later. "He said right," I replied. "I would have been angry and you would have been dead. You haven't looked after yourself properly, and something much gentler than that could be fatal to you." Athanasios chuckled.)

The next morning there was another knock on the door and in swaggered Athanaric. "Greetings, Your Grace," he said — a pun on my name that was rather better than he intended, since it's *charis*, not Chariton, that means "grace." "I thought I would look in and see how you were recovering from the little present I gave you. I'm sorry about that."

"I have other patients besides you," I said. "I might have picked this up anywhere. Would Your Excellency like to sit down? I'm sorry, I'm not really prepared for visitors."

"Don't trouble yourself," he said, sitting down at the writing desk. "Eternal God, you have a lot of books!"

I did by that time. Alexandria is a great city for books. Papyrus is cheap in Egypt, and scribes can make a fortune copying works and selling them by the library. My Hippocrates and Galen had been joined by Herophilos and Erasistratos, Dioskourides and Celsus, Krateuas and Nikandros and Oribasios — all the medical authorities. My bookcase was full, and my writing desk half submerged.

"I see that you did indeed give an accurate report of what you spend your money on," he continued. "Books. Certainly not clothes or lodgings or luxuries. Wouldn't it help, though, to have a bigger set of rooms, and a slave to keep them in order for you?"

I eyed him warily. Another attempt at bribery? "I don't like the bother of all that," I said. "This arrangement leaves me free to concentrate on the things that interest me."

"The detachment of the perfect philosopher. And who am I to question it? Tell me, Chariton, have you ever wondered about where your archbishop is leading you?"

Often, of course. But I didn't want to discuss it with Athanaric. "His Holiness Bishop Athanasios is my patient," I said. "It's my job to look after his health. What he does in his own profession is not my affair."

"Not when it could kill you? What he has done is to oppose the emperor. Oppose four emperors, one after another. His Sacred Majesty tolerates him now for the sake of peace in the city, but you must be able to foresee what will happen when he dies."

"Your Excellency, I would rather not talk about this."

"I think it would be better if you did. When Athanasios dies, there is going to be bloodshed. And being a doctor won't help you if you're involved; you could be arrested as easily as the craziest fanatic from the Nitrian desert."

I sighed. Not bribery. Threats. "I'm not going to shed any blood, except perhaps in surgery. Even the most fanatical Arian will hardly arrest me for simply treating my patients."

"What if your patients are fugitives and criminals? You would be better out of this altogether. Listen, I can give you a recommendation to the post of state physician in some other city. Our most pious Augustus, Lord Valentinian, has established a whole group of doctors in Rome, one for each quarter of the city. They treat the poor free of charge, and the state pays them a good salary. They'd be pleased to get you there, and you'd do very well. You could treat the rabble to your heart's content and expect a better reward than imprisonment. And if you don't like Rome, there are other cities. I would hate to see such a good doctor in trouble."

"Have you finished?"

He looked at me in irritation. "Very well, then, don't listen to sense!"

He *had* finished! I had expected a personal threat, something on the lines of "If you don't leave the city and abandon your patient, I will have to give your name to the authorities." But perhaps he meant me to assume that. "I thank Your Carefulness for the advice," I said. "At the moment I am happy to stay in the city with my friends. Don't let me keep Your Diligence; I'm sure you have a lot of work which requires your attention."

"Oh, damn your friends!" he exclaimed. "I was trying to help. Farewell, then, Chariton, and good luck!" And with that he went out, slamming the door. I sat in bed and wondered whether I should have paid more attention.

✠✠✠

I was still worrying the next week when I met Philon again. He had invited me to dinner, and we'd agreed to meet in Soma Square after the day's work, since most of my patients were in the west of the city and most of his in the east. I arrived in the square and found Philon sitting in the rubble of the old mausoleum, which was out of the wind. We started off at once down the Canopic Way. Some children were playing a game in the ruins of the old Museum; a goat, browsing among the stones, bleated as the woman who owned it came with her milking pail; a couple of whores smiled from the shadows by a wine shop; at the church of Alexander the lamps were being lit, saffron and silver in the dusk. Then came a shout and the sound of many feet tramping to a drum, and a troop of soldiers came marching up the street, their hobnailed boots ringing on the paving. Everyone else stepped aside and watched them: the children stopped playing; the woman sat holding her goat's head against her chest to keep it still; the lamplighters disappeared into the church; even the whores watched with set, unsmiling faces. The troops strode past, turned left, and marched off toward the citadel.

"How much trouble do you think there'll be?" I asked Philon when they were gone and we had started walking again. I didn't need to say more than that; he knew I meant "when Athanasios dies."

He sighed. "You know more about that than I do. You're in the middle of it. What do you think will happen?"

I said nothing for a minute. "The authorities will send in their own bishop, this fellow Lucius," I admitted at last, "and the church won't accept him. There will be a lot of rioting and arrests. I suppose

155

what I really meant was, is it possible to look after my patients and still stay clear of the trouble?"

"I don't know." Philon gave me a sympathetic look. "I suppose that depends more on the authorities than on your patients. I would have thought you'd be all right if you stay out of the actual rioting and are discreet about how you treat fugitives. What else were you thinking of doing?"

I told him about Athanaric's offer.

"State physician at Rome?" he asked. "That was generous of him. He must have been impressed with all he learned about you. Don't look so surprised — of course he questioned me. He wanted information from you, didn't he? He asked up at the Temple, and he asked me at home. I don't think he discovered anything. And I don't think he could guess . . . *that*, from what he did learn. So, are you thinking of accepting his offer?"

"No. I don't trust Athanaric. He can say what he likes here and to me: promises cost him nothing. But he wasn't actually promising a job, just a word of recommendation. And why should they listen to him in Rome? He's not Roman, or a doctor; his word won't mean a thing. They've probably hired all the people they need already. And I don't like the idea of deserting my patients just when they might need me most."

Philon pulled at his lip and nodded, giving the peculiar half-smile he used when I said something he understood from his own experience.

"No," I went on, "it was just . . . he made me nervous."

Philon smiled. "And who's to blame you? What would happen to you if . . . if the authorities found out?"

I shrugged. "I suppose they'd just send me home in disgrace. And once I got home, well . . ." I hesitated, glancing around at the few figures hurrying down the great street, and the shuttered houses. No one was nearby, but I continued only in a whisper. "I would sit there doing nothing for the rest of my life. I wouldn't have to worry about marriage. If anyone did marry me, it would be someone of lower rank who wants the money badly enough to put up with the disgrace. But even someone like that would demand respectable behavior from me. I would never be myself again."

We walked on in silence for a minute or so. Philon was frowning. "Well," he said at last, "I hope you can stay out of the trouble." We were nearing the street his house was on, and he paused on the corner, the frown fading. "Oh, I forgot to tell you. Theogenes is coming — yes, again! And my new assistant has arrived: you'll meet him at supper."

I'd heard of this proposed new assistant a couple of weeks before, and had tried to get used to the idea, though I couldn't help feeling jealous of him. I managed to smile. "Good. You need help, with all your patients. I never could understand why you didn't have an assistant before I came."

He chuckled. "Couldn't you? Let me explain. I don't earn much money. Most assistants find money useful. And even those who aren't worried about it like to be taught by somebody well known, and assume that anyone well known earns money, or at least has a few wealthy and distinguished patients."

"I know that," I said, smiling. "But you're as good a doctor as Adamantios — better. You could have lectured at the Temple too, and even picked up a few wealthy and distinguished patients."

He scratched his beard. "Perhaps that's true. But when I ran away from Tiberias, I made a bargain with God. You let me become a doctor, I told Him, and I will treat anyone in need, and not worry about whether or not they can pay me. I will use the art in Your service, not to gain a reputation or wealth for myself. So I never had time for the rich and important patients — and no one ever came posthaste to drag me across the city to treat one against my will, either. Still, perhaps I shall get my reputation at last." He gave me a grin. "The man who taught Chariton of Ephesus."

"Don't be absurd."

"I'm not! Why do you think Kritias has come to me instead of to Adamantios? He heard me mentioned as your teacher. And he's a hardworking, kind young man and should make a fine doctor, though he's not as clever as you. Poor lad, he's already tired of hearing about you. Come on, I'll introduce you!"

He pressed on up the street to his house, smiling again, and I trailed after him, wishing that I were worthy of such a master.

✠✠✠

Theogenes and Theophila were married just when the vines began to bud, while the winter-flowering hellebore in the Temple gardens was still heavy with fragrant white flowers. They were married at Theogenes' synagogue in the Broucheion quarter, a beautiful big building which had somehow survived the region's destruction; it was surrounded by a garden, colonnaded, and glowed inside with paintings and mosaics. Theogenes' brother had come by camel all the way from Antioch, and Philon's son, Alphaios, had arrived from Tiberias just two days before. I had been very eager to meet him, but in fact we didn't get on. He was a brilliant, passionate, narrow young man of about my age, and he cared about nothing but the Law. The first thing he did when we met was try to convert me. It was very embarrassing for everyone, and I found it thoughtless of him. If he'd succeeded, it would have caused considerable trouble for his family, since Athanasios' monks would not have approved of Jewish interference with their bishop's physician. But I suppose Alphaios thought that this was a small price to pay for the salvation of a soul from the Galilean heresy, as he called it. When he saw that I wouldn't be converted and couldn't argue the Law with him, he left me alone. But it was clear that he was suspicious of me. He'd heard of me from his father's letters, but that's different from knowing someone, and he (understandably) found it very strange that a foreigner, a Christian, a friend of the archbishop, and a eunuch was so deeply enmeshed in the affairs of his family. He didn't like Theogenes either: he thought him very worldly.

The wedding went very well. The couple stepped under the wedding canopy and exchanged vows, there were psalms and hymns of rejoicing, and finally we had a huge party in the garden. Luckily it was a clear, unseasonably warm day, a golden, perfect day, and it seemed that everyone on earth must be happy to see how happy Theogenes and Theophila were. There was eating and drinking and dancing. It began to grow dark, and torches were lit, fastened to poles, and burned brightly under the trees. Everyone gave presents to the bride and bridegroom, and then there was more eating and drinking and dancing.

I gave Theophila a piece of my mother's jewelry, a ring set with sapphires and amethyst. She gasped when she saw it, then held it up, turning it in the light so that the jewels burned. "Oh, Chariton!" she cried, looking at me. "It was your mother's, you shouldn't give it away!"

"Wear it," I told her. "It's better worn than sold. And I can have no one else to give it to."

Her eyes filled with tears. She slipped the ring onto her finger, then kissed me. Theogenes clasped my shoulder and pressed my hand. I nodded, mumbled something, and slipped out of the crowd. The synagogue was empty now, so I went and sat there. The lamps at the front, by the shrine of the Law, had been lit, but the rest of the building was in darkness, the painted walls full of vague shapes of animals and men. I sat down at the back and wept. I was no longer even half in love with Theogenes — but they were so *happy*. And I could never be happy like that. Never get married, be loved by some tall young man; never have children. Not if I wanted to practice the art. Not if I stayed myself. And if I stayed myself, I was simply my own grave, with no free outlet to the world until death came and claimed me.

I heard a cautious step entering the synagogue, and I hurriedly stopped sobbing. There was another step, and then a voice said, "Chariton?" softly. The voice was Philon's. I got up, wiping my face, and he hurried over.

"Sorry," I told him. "I know it's bad luck to run out on a wedding feast. But I couldn't help it."

He shook his head. "Everyone understood. That is, they can understand that a eunuch might feel unhappy at seeing so much gladness that he can never join."

I tried to laugh. "They understand rightly. I might just as well be a eunuch."

He sighed, peering through the darkness at my face. "I don't know what to say to that," he confessed at last. "I should say, 'Go back to your family, get married, it's natural and right and you obviously want it.' But I'm used to you as a eunuch. I can't imagine . . ." He stopped, then reached out and touched my cheek. "Poor Chariton," he said, feeling the tears.

I started crying again. I sat down. "I'll get over it," I said. "I won't go home. I can't imagine, either. Only just now I feel wretched."

"Perhaps one day you'll be able to tell everyone what you are," Philon said, squatting beside me. "You are very good. And if your reputation were really solidly established, it would survive a revelation like that. You could make your own rule, establish that women can study medicine."

"If that ever happens," I said, swallowing a sob, "it'll be when I'm old, too old to marry."

"You have friends," he told me. "And you could have students.

Students can become almost like your own children — as I have reason to know."

I flung my arms around him and wept onto his shoulder.

✠❖✠

Athanaric avoided me after the threats and the offer, though he remained at the palace, asking questions and occasionally going off to see the prefect or the duke of Egypt, presumably to compare notes. I did not have much time to worry about him. I was so busy with my patients that I began to wonder whether I should take an assistant at once. It seemed a very extraordinary thing for someone who had only arrived in the city three years before, who was under twenty and had only been practicing on her own for a few months, to take an assistant. But I was working so hard that I scarcely had time to sleep, and whenever a crisis came up, I badly wished I had someone else I could send to do the rounds, as Philon used to send me. But I didn't look for a job elsewhere. I was proud of my career. And Philon's suggestion had given me something else to hope for. One day, far away in the future, I might openly call myself Charis of Ephesus, a doctor of Alexandria, perhaps a teacher with a few student assistants, one or two of them women. It was something to think about, anyway.

Easter that year fell on the calends of April, or the fifth of the month of Pharmuthi, in the Egyptian reckoning — the Egyptians do everything differently from everyone else, and have a completely different calendar. The archbishop kept Lent very strictly, eating nothing but dry bread and drinking only water, and he traveled about the city and into the neighboring countryside, preaching and settling the affairs of the church. He was eager to set up reserves of money and places of concealment which might be useful to his supporters after his death. The Alexandrian church was very wealthy and owned a great deal of land in the area; Athanasios and Theophilos went through the accounts line by line, trying to attach the land and money to their own supporters so that any intruding bishop couldn't get his hands on it. Theophilos was good at things like that, but Athanasios was still worried about him. "He loves the church," he told me once. "But I don't know how much he loves God."

I was worried about Athanasios. He coughed more and more often, and occasionally became feverish; he was exhausted with fasting and hard work. But if I reproved him for it, he just smiled, no longer even bothering to argue.

On Easter Eve he and half the population of Alexandria kept vigil. They started the festival at the tiny shrine of Archbishop Peter the Martyr, which is near the sea, outside the city wall. There was a huge crowd, thousands of people, and I was in the middle of it with my housemates, the nuns. There was a great deal of singing as the evening fell; musicians played on the lyre, the flute, and the cymbals; some of the people danced. When it was dark, we saw the Pharos lit: first a little yellow glow as they struck the kindling, then a bright saffron flare, and then the great swath of light crawling over the dark sea, reaching further and further as the fire took hold. You could see the outline of the city itself, a web of little lights crisscrossed by the great avenues of the Canopic Way and the Soma Street; on the other side of the city was the Lochias promontory, the citadel of the government, its stone fortifications black against the sea. The musicians stopped playing, and everyone fell silent. You could hear the night sounds of the birds, and the hush of the sea. Then someone began to sing.

It was a hymn of rejoicing, praising the time when all light started, when the Lord led his people out of slavery into freedom, out of death into life, out of darkness into day. One voice began it — one of the deacons, I think — but it was soon taken up by the rest of the clergy, and then everyone was singing, the music rising in great waves through the darkenss. It swept me up with it, and I stood among the others with my mouth open, singing as well. Then, in the shadow in front of the shrine, someone lit the bonfire that had been readied, and suddenly I saw Athanasios standing in the firelight, his best gold cloak reflecting the glow around him. His white hair stood out around his face, and his eyes were staring into the light, wide and illimitably happy, focused on something beyond the fire. I knew then what I should have seen all along: he was eager to die. He had tried to stay alive as long as was absolutely necessary, out of love for his church, but he had long ago set his mind on death. He would not live for another Easter, and he wanted to celebrate this feast perfectly.

Athanasios lit a torch at the bonfire, and the people cheered, that deep, rhythmic Alexandrian applause that is unlike the acclaim of any other people. The clergy lit their torches, and the people poured forward with lamps and candles and anything else they could find to burn and give light. The musicians began to play again, and the procession moved off, twisting down the road into the city through the Gate of the Moon, like a sunrise in the west. By the time they reached the church, people were dancing again and giving the long whooping cheers they use at the racecourse. I did not sing now. I walked along in silence, wondering if the others would be so glad if they knew that within the year they'd have another archbishop, one installed by troops.

The service for Easter Eve is a very long one. First there were prayers and singing in the cathedral; then everyone who wanted to be baptized that year was brought into the baptistry and plunged into the water; then there was more singing and a procession back into the main church. The congregation settled itself to listen. Thousands of faces were packed into the great, barnlike cathedral; the light of a thousand lamps glittered off the stern mosaic saints along the wall; incense and the smell of the great hot crowd surrounded us. And Athanasios preached. It was a fierce, passionate, glad speech based on the text "death is swallowed up in victory." "This is the season of death," he told the people, "and it is the season of rejoicing. For where what is human comes to an end, what is divine does not. Thus when we are dead, our poor nature tired out, God himself raises us up, and what was born of earth he leads into Heaven. For God has restored to us in Christ the image of his own eternity. Death, beloved, has no power over us. The lord of this world has no power. Death is swallowed up! Consuming our mortality, he consumes himself, and only victory is left for us!"

"Athanasios!" roared the people; his name, of course, means "deathless." Athanasios sat on the episcopal throne carved with the lions of St. Mark, looking deathless indeed, his eyes sweeping the hall. He set down the Gospel he was holding and stood, stretching out his arms, and the crowd shouted his name again and again until his voice stilled them. I remembered what he had told me, that acclamation intoxicates the will. He looked intoxicated with the acclaim now, and he spoke for over an hour, the crowd cheering him at every pause. Then he celebrated the Eucharist, and there was more singing, and afterward eating and drinking and dancing in the street until day; and then he preached and celebrated the Eucharist again, and finally, in the clear spring morning, he dismissed the people with a blessing.

I did not go home. I went straight to the episcopal palace, and arrived, bumping into the slave who had been sent to fetch me, shortly after the archbishop. Athanasios had fainted on the way home from the church. When I went into his room I found him doubled up on the bed, coughing up blood.

I did everything I could: steam, cupping, warm compresses, and various drugs, even black hellebore, which I normally avoided. But the "deathless" Athanasios floated through my treatment with a smile, responding to none of it, his eyes still fixed on whatever it was that lay behind the fire. He was quite lucid, and insisted on interrupting the treatment to talk to all his clergy.

On the second day he sent me out of the room and had a long session with Peter and Theophilos. Peter came out weeping; Theophilos looked white and shaken, and went off somewhere private. I went back into the room and looked at the archbishop. For the first time since his collapse, I was the only one there. He hadn't allowed me to lock out the others. Since I had the opportunity, I bolted the door. There was not much hope that he'd recover, even if he was allowed to rest, but it was always possible.

He had been lying still, staring at the ceiling, but when he heard the bolt click he looked at me. "Charis," he said, and smiled.

I went over and sat down beside him.

"You are still angry?" he asked, smiling.

"You might have lived for years," I told him.

"If I had heeded my doctor," he finished. "Well, I have lived for years already. Longer than I could have expected. And as my master Anthony the Hermit said, exchanging this world for Heaven is like exchanging a copper *drachma* for a hundred *solidi*." He looked at me for a moment, the eyes, though sunken, as deep and penetrating as ever. "The faith still doesn't mean much to you, does it?" he asked. "Not compared to Hippocrates."

"Oh, Holy Christ!" I said. "You don't want to spend your last hours converting me." I tried to give him a drink of honeywater; he refused.

"I can think of worse ways to spend the time. But not everyone is called to asceticism and divine service. Your way is good, though not the most excellent one." He stared at me again, this time with regret. "You will marry."

"What? I have no intention of marrying. I am married to Hippocrates."

"You will get a husband though," he said slowly, "as well as your Hippocrates. You are too fond of people, Charition. Ai, I never meant to become archbishop. I meant to become a monk. But I was too fond of power and acclaim, and it trapped me. The world holds us by what we love. But all that is over now. No more battles now." He paused, then smiled, the expression of intoxicated happiness returning to his face.

I felt helpless, furious, profoundly grieved. "You should have lived!" I told him. "Think what will happen to us without you! Your death will extinguish all the light in Alexandria!"

He jerked his head back — no — very weakly. "Not all the light. One man doesn't matter that much. And no one can live forever, even with the best doctor." He smiled at me again. "You mustn't lock the door, my dear; the people want to see me. Tell the others to come in now."

He died after midnight on the second of May. He was lucid till the end, and happy, fiercely happy, watching for his death. Most of the city was watching too: mobs of people encircled the house, waiting for the news. I kept trying to cure him, even when it was clear that all I was needed for was to say that the breath was gone. When it was over, I knelt by the bed with the others and, like them, wept bitterly. He was a proud man; I could easily believe that he'd been high-handed and violent in his youth, but his mind had soared above his age like an eagle, and there was no one else like him. When we announced his death, it was as though the whole of Alexandria went into mourning. All the shops were closed, the churches shrouded in black; even the Pharos was hung with black streamers. A light had gone out, and the city waited for its invaders.

I cropped my hair in mourning and tried to buy a black cloak and tunic, but the merchants told me that there were none to be had. When I went to the palace in my old blue tunic (I had to give a dose of opium to Peter, who was quite sick with grief) Theophilos asked me why I wasn't in mourning, and when I explained he gave me an old cloak of his own. Only Athanaric seemed unmoved by it all. Before the archbishop's body was cold, he'd taken his license and some letters from the prefect, mounted a post horse, and set out for Antioch and the court.

✠✠✠

The Arian bishop, Lucius, arrived in the city in the middle of June, considerably sooner than expected. He had come at once from An-

164

tioch; he brought with him the imperial treasurer, Magnus, and some letters giving him the use of the city guard — and, as Athanasios had predicted, he made sure he had the troops before he actually ventured into the city. The duke of Egypt was already in Alexandria, with troops from most of the five provinces of Egypt. As soon as Lucius disembarked, the harbor was shut up, and every ship that left had to have a pass from the prefect. The gates were closed and guarded; the troops came down from the citadel and watched the lakeside. And then the Arians went through the city looking for Athanasians.

They got Archbishop Peter. Elected by the clergy and people of Alexandria, according to the canons of the church, he'd taken the episcopal throne of St. Mark two days after Athanasios' funeral, but he'd been ill frequently since then; it was the shock of grief and fear following the long fast and months of waiting that had made him ill, I judged, rather than some serious disease. At any rate, he reacted to the sudden descent of the Arians with confusion and uncertainty, and the soldiers caught him at the episcopal palace and carried him off to prison. Lucius took the throne of St. Mark, and scourged the church over which he presided.

There were riots, of course. All that time I had lived in Alexandria and never seen one; and now there were riots every day, breaking out in one part of the city after another, always bloodily quelled by the troops. It would be a still, hot noon, the streets empty and baking in the Egyptian sun, and then from somewhere far off would come the sound of shouting. The noise would grow into an indistinct yammering howl, an inhuman sound, rising and falling, coming closer or going further away. People would appear, running — toward the sound or away from it, but running frantically over the glaring stone of the pavements. I would stay inside, in my own room if I could, otherwise at some patient's. The troops would come marching past, armor chiming, shields on their arms, striking out at anyone they saw; the noise would turn to screams, break up, fade into the hot silence. Then I would go and treat the casualties. The worst was when the mob tried to get Peter away from the soldiers as he was being led off; the troops left a hundred and fifty-two bodies in the streets that time, and I don't know how many injured, though I treated quite a few of them. I forgot all about diseases and complex prescriptions; I spent my time splinting fractures, treating shock and contusions, stitching up sword and knife wounds. I ran out of opium, and couldn't buy any more: the marketplace was closed most of the time. I dosed with hellebore and borrowed drugs from Philon; his patients weren't involved much. Then the authorities began questioning the people they'd arrested. Some were executed, some just tortured and released. Muscles and tendons torn, bones dislocated by the rack, marks of the whip and the rod and the fork and the fire, teeth torn and eyes gouged out — I had to treat them all. The hospitals were closed, the monks all either arrested or fled. But eventually the markets opened again, and I could buy more opium.

They didn't get Theophilos. The deacon had disappeared quietly during the first round of arrests and installed himself in one of the prearranged hiding places. From there he busied himself with smuggling other leading Athanasians out of the city. He sent for me often, to treat patients. But his first concern was Archbishop Peter.

"If they kill him," he told me, "then we don't have a canonically consecrated archbishop any more than the Lucians do, and our case will be that much weaker when we ask for support in the West. And we're not likely to be allowed to assemble and choose someone, either. We've got to get him out."

But Peter was locked in the citadel, which was on the Lochias promontory and walled off from the rest of the city. No one had been allowed to visit him. We thought he was still alive: he was of fairly high rank, and could not be tortured or executed without trial. And there was nothing he could really be tried for, so he should be safe. But Theophilos was gloomy. "They murdered Bishop Paul of Constantinople," he said. "Locked him up in a dark cell for six days without food or drink; when they came in and found him still alive, they strangled him. But I don't think they'd need to strangle Peter. He wouldn't last six days. And if he dies, they can say that he was ill anyway, and pretend it wasn't their fault." Then he sat up and looked at me thoughtfully, with a faint light in his eyes. "They might let his doctor see him, though. Just to prove that it wasn't their fault."

"They'd search me," I told him.

"You wouldn't have to carry anything," Theophilos said, warming to the plan. "Not the first time, anyway. It would be useful to know exactly where they are keeping him."

I said nothing. Peter was my patient, and I felt responsible; I liked the old man, and it hurt me to think of him chained up in prison, and perhaps starved to death. But if I was searched, I'd be found out. It would be my ruin, and no use to the church, since I'd undoubtedly be packed straight off to Ephesus.

"What's the matter?" Theophilos asked impatiently. "Are you afraid?"

"Yes," I told him. "I don't like torture."

"We'd get you out of the city afterward," he said reassuringly. "We wouldn't let them catch you."

I still said nothing.

Theophilos hit his desk, eyes bright with anger. "Is this your loyalty to your church and your archbishop?" he demanded. "What does it matter if you have to flee the city? Archbishop Peter has every right to expect you to help him! He is your spiritual father, your friend who's given you hospitality I don't know how often, and your patient, which I thought counted for something with you. Do you value your career more than his life?"

I winced. I was very tired. It was late at night, and I'd been treating the injured all day. Two of my patients had died of blood poisoning that morning, and I thought another would go that night. I felt guilty and ashamed that amid so much suffering, I had been spared. I had not rioted, tried to free the archbishop, fought at all; I had shut myself into my room until it was safe to go out again. Theophilos' words hurt me.

"What do they do when they search you?" I asked.

When a noble prisoner is visited by his doctor, the doctor is hardly searched at all. I had envisaged being stripped, or at least having my clothes examined for messages or knives stitched into them, and I had surreptitiously constructed a phallus for myself, and wore it in the appropriate place to deceive any questioning hand. But in fact the jailers watch the prisoner the whole time and rely on this to catch anything the prisoner's friends might try to smuggle in to him.

I applied to the prefect for permission to attend on Peter, and was sent a letter authorizing a visit. The citadel was heavily guarded; when I presented myself at the gate, my letter was examined carefully before I was admitted. Then I had to wait in the guard room until an escort arrived. I had never been in the citadel before. Through the guard-room window I looked out at the wide streets, the marble and porphyry columns of the public buildings, and the date palms standing tall and green behind the walls of private gardens. It was much quieter than the city.

One of Peter's guards, a beefy soldier who wore a black cloak over his bronze and leather armor, eventually appeared, eyed me suspiciously, and examined my letter of authorization. Then he nodded and led me into the quiet street. It turned out that the archbishop was being held in one of the watchtowers that overlook the Great Harbor. My escort brought me there and handed me over to another guard, who examined my letter again. When the seal had been checked, he searched my medical bag, and then led me up to see Peter.

The archbishop was being kept in a fair-sized room. The window was barred, but it might otherwise have been any room in a private house, a neat white room with a red and white tiled floor, a bed, a bench, a chamberpot, and a writing desk devoid of any books or paper. Peter was lying on the bed when I came in, and two more guards were sitting on the bench playing dice. The archbishop's hands were chained together and the chain was fixed to a bracket in the wall, but it was quite a long chain, and a fine one, with loose shackles. I'd treated plenty of injuries caused by tight ones, and was glad.

"Chariton!" Peter exclaimed when I came in. He sat up, beaming at me. "Bless you, my dear brother! I was beginning to think myself quite forgotten!"

"Greetings, Your Holiness," I said, and kissed his hand. "No one has forgotten you. How are you?"

None too well. He had a slight fever and some dysentery, and he was very low in spirit. I checked him over and recommended barley broth for the dysentery. I could not say much with the guards listening, but I assured him that his friends held him in their thoughts and prayed for him.

"And I pray for them," he told me. "I've heard about what's been happening." He was silent for a moment, staring at his shackles, then looked up with tears in his eyes. "I wish Thanassi hadn't nominated me to the throne. I am not worthy of it. All those people suffering martyrdom on my behalf, and I've failed them already."

"You've been unwell," I told him. "It's too soon to talk about failing. And you know that Athanasios always said that *he* was unworthy and should never have taken the throne, so you're in good company regretting it."

He shook his head. "Thanassi was different. He was afraid of what power would do to him, and what he would do with it, but he always knew how to get it and use it. He tried to avoid the throne — he even had himself sent off to Constantinople when Archbishop Alexandros was dying — but no one ever doubted that he was destined for it. But me! I can't keep my own head straight, let alone direct anyone else in an emergency. The throne should have gone to Theophilos."

I saw that the guards took note of this, but I just smiled and said, "His Holiness nominated you, and you admit that he generally knew

168

what he was doing. Have courage! We'll do what we can to make you comfortable."

"Can you get me some copies of the Scriptures?" he asked. "I have nothing to read here, and it's hard to stay faithful when your mind is idle."

I promised to ask the authorities on his behalf, and was escorted out of the room.

Before I left the citadel I was taken to a small room at the prefect's residence and questioned for a long time by two officials, one of them a notary who made notes in shorthand of everything I said. They wanted to know about Theophilos and some of the other clergy. I pretended to believe that they had fled the city. They offered me a bribe, which I turned down with apologies, saying that I was only a physician and that no one had trusted me with any information. I told them all about Athanasios' illness and the state of Peter's dysentery, giving them a wealth of unwanted medical detail. Then I passed on Peter's request for books, deprecating it slightly and playing smug doctor to the best of my ability. They sent to ask the prefect about it, and he sent a note authorizing me to give Peter a set of Gospels. Eventually my questioners let me go. My escort showed me firmly back to the gates of the citadel; the heavy doors were opened, and I stepped back into the hot, noisy, free city. I gave a long sigh, and had to go sit down for a little while to calm myself. Only when the ordeal was safely over could I admit to myself how deeply it had frightened me.

When I was sure I wasn't being followed, I went to Theophilos and told him about the interview. He was very pleased. "A watchtower!" he said. "If we could get him out of that, it would be an easy matter to get him into a boat and away from the citadel. And if we could get some money to him somehow, and bribe the guards . . . yes, you've done very well, Chariton. Thank you."

"Do you want me to leave the city now?" I asked nervously.

"No, don't do that! They'll be watching you now. It will make them suspicious if you disappear. Just go about your normal duties; I'll get word to you if I think of some way to get the archbishop out."

"What about the books?"

"Oh! Yes, I'll have Peter's own set of Gospels sent to you, and you can drop them off tomorrow. Or perhaps . . . can I see your letter of authorization?"

I handed it to him and he read it, then folded it over and put it in his purse, smiling. "The letter just authorizes the bearer to deliver some Gospels to the house where Peter is being kept. I'll give it to one of the bishop's friends, and he can send someone to deliver the books this evening." He sat still a moment, staring at one of the signet rings on his hand; he twisted it back and forth, then looked up at me and smiled again, a peculiar smile. "How do I reach you quickly if I need to warn you?" he asked.

I told him that I would leave a list of my patients at my house, and he nodded and thanked me again as I left.

Two days later I returned to my house late in the evening and found no one there. The door was unlocked; I went in and called the nuns, but no one answered. I started up the stairs. As I was climbing the second flight, the door to my own room opened, and a soldier looked down at me. I stopped, and he ran down the stairs and grabbed my cloak. "Chariton of Ephesus?" he asked, pushing his face close to mine. The whites of his eyes were yellowed, and under the bronze guard of his helmet he had a broken nose.

"Yes," I said. "What is the matter?"

He snorted and dragged me up the stairs without answering. My room was brightly lit by both my own oil lamps and a burning torch. Two other soldiers were going through my things. The one who had hold of me shoved me through the door, then came in himself, closing the door behind him. "Here he is," he told his fellows. "Didn't run off after all."

"I've been attending my patients," I told them, trying to pull myself straight. "Who are you and what do you want? I've done nothing wrong." I tried to sound confident, but I was very frightened. I didn't think I could be punished simply for being a man's doctor, but Bishop Lucius might do anything.

"Peter of Alexandria," said the soldier who had grabbed me. "Where is he?"

I stared. Theophilos had said that he'd get me out of the city, that he wouldn't let them catch me. Surely he hadn't managed to get Peter out already? Surely he'd have told me first if he was going to do such a thing? "He's . . . he's in prison," I said. "In the citadel. I saw him there day before yesterday."

They sneered. "We know you did. You were the only one of his faction that did see him there. Where is he now?"

"I don't know what you're talking about."

One of the soldiers grabbed me and twisted my arms behind my back, and another one hit me across the face, twice. It stunned me, and I started to slump down, until the pain in my arms stopped that. "Holy Christ," I said.

"Stop praying," said the soldier, and hit me in the stomach. I doubled up; the other man let go of me and I fell onto the floor. The soldier kicked me twice, once in the ribs and once in the crotch; it would have been agonizing if I were really male, and it was still very painful. I cried out, and the one behind me grabbed me and pulled me up again, twisting my arms.

"I am a gentleman," I said when I could talk again. "You can't do this to me." I was shaking badly, and could feel something running over my chin; blood from a cut lip, I supposed.

"You? Eunuchs are slaves."

"I am freeborn and of good family!"

"You're a filthy ass-licking Athanasian slave!" said one of the soldiers. But they didn't hit me again. It's illegal to torture gentlemen, and a victim's "good family" could ruin a soldier.

"We'll check who he is when we get him to the prison," the chief soldier said to the others. "Tie him up."

They tied my hands behind me with a long leather thong, leaving an end loose to hold on to. Then they shoved me into the far corner, out of their way, and continued going through my things. "By Kybele!" one of the soldiers said. "What a lot of books!"

The chief soldier picked out Athanasios' treatise on the Incarnation and snorted; one of the others picked up the Galen. It fell open to an illustration of the heart and lungs, and he gaped. "Is it sorcery?" he asked his superior nervously.

"It's a medical text," I put in hurriedly. "On anatomy."

The soldier gave me a dark look, and held the book out toward the torch to see whether it would burn.

"No!" I shrieked. "Please don't! It's very valuable!"

At this they regarded it speculatively, with more respect. "Better take it as evidence," the chief commented. "And the letters."

So they packed all my books and the few letters on the desk into my clothes chest. They took my medical bag away and shoved that in on top. They looked for money, but there wasn't much in the room: I still kept all valuables at my bank. They took the loose change there was and pocketed it. Then, with two of them carrying the chest and cursing the weight of the books and the other holding the thong that tied my wrists, they took me down the stairs, through the empty house, and along the streets to the prison in the citadel.

An archbishop's doctor doesn't rate a private cell. I was put in the common prison, with about twenty others. My guards marched me in by torchlight, and stood for a moment looking for somewhere to tie me. The prison was dark, the walls of unfaced stone; the floor was covered with a little dirty straw full of fleas. Wild eyes stared up at the torches; a few filthy bodies picked themselves up off the floor and crouched warily, watching us, while others lay heaped in exhausted sleep. There was a clanking of chains, a little moaning. The whole place stank. There was only a ditch along the wall to serve for a latrine, and it was crawling with sleepy flies. It was too late for the jailers to forge chains for me. They found a free bracket set into the wall, kicked one of the sleepers away from it, dragged me over, and tied the lead thong to it. One of the guards kicked my leg so I fell into the straw. "You'll be questioned tomorrow," he told me. "And racked, if you're eligible for it. We can worry about the chains after that. Sleep well." And he and his fellows marched out with the torches, leaving the prison dark.

I had no time to lie there wondering what had happened. As soon as the guards had gone the other prisoners began asking questions: Who was I? Was I imprisoned for the faith as well? Was it true that Archbishop Peter had escaped? Then one of them began shouting in great excitement. I recognized her voice with a shock even through my numbed horror: the nun Amundora. "He has rescued our lord, Archbishop Peter!" she told the others.

She told them all about me: I was a foreign eunuch who'd been converted to the Nicene faith after a divine revelation to Archbishop Athanasios; I'd followed the path of true religion and asceticism, treating the poor for nothing and attending on the saints of the church; I'd visited Archbishop Peter and helped him escape. She had been arrested earlier in the day when the authorities had gone to look for me, and was sitting chained in a filthy dungeon because of me, ignorant of where her sisters were, but she thought nothing of this. She gabbled out a pious, passionate speech full of admiration for me. All the prisoners began to praise my resolution and encourage me and each other with the glory of martyrdom. I felt quite sick, from the beating and from fear. If Amundora's tale was believed by the authorities, I might be tortured even after they discovered that I was a woman.

I was worried about what would happen to my hands if I stayed in the leather bonds all night — I'd treated too many fingers gangrenous from tight shackles not to be aware of the danger. I asked my neighbor if he could help me loosen the rope. He was chained to the wall, but managed to catch the thong with his leg and twist it into my fingers so that I could work at the knot. I couldn't do much, but managed to loosen it a little, then pull and twist it outward with my wrists until the blood flowed stinging into my hands again.

Even when the other prisoners had settled and the room was still except for the occasional moan or clank of a chain, I sat in the dirty straw exhausted and wide awake. I thought about calling the guards and telling them that I was not Chariton, a doctor of the Nicene faction; I was Charis, daughter of Theodoros of Ephesus, whose father would reward them for sending her home.

But I was ashamed to run away, and it didn't even seem true. I was not that noble maiden. I never really had been. The thought of returning to my father's house was like the thought of being buried alive, or rather, of being smothered like a baby in pillows. Part of it — most of it — was the art. The more I studied it, the more I loved it; nothing could be more fascinating, or more moving, than the intricacies and mysteries of the body, nothing more wonderful than the realization that you had saved a life. And beyond that, I was so accustomed now to ruling myself and ordering my own affairs that to depend on a man to do all that would be like having my tongue cut out. No, I would keep up the pretense as long as I could, until they actually stripped me for the rack. And it might not come to that. Perhaps I could convince the authorities that I was as ignorant of Peter's disappearance as they were.

I wondered if Theophilos had tried to contact me to tell me to leave the city, and simply failed to find me in time — or if he hadn't even tried. Probably he had seen some good opportunity to rescue the archbishop and taken it, deciding to help me afterward if and when he could. Of course I wasn't important to Theophilos. Peter wasn't important either, as a person. We were just tools for the construction of the freedom of the church of Egypt. Athanasios had seen that: that had been why he distrusted the deacon. Athanasios had never seen people as tools. He was as fascinated by them as I was by the art of healing. And of course he had genuinely loved God more than he loved power.

At that thought I tried to pray. It was exactly what Amundora's fanatic might be expected to do, but it helped. I went to sleep.

I woke when the gray light of dawn crawled through the narrow slits in the opposite wall. My bruises ached miserably, I was desperately thirsty, and my new collection of flea bites itched. My hands, caught by the rope as I'd slumped in sleep, had gone numb again, and I crouched in the straw flexing my fingers until I felt some pain in them as well. The light showed me that several of my fellow prisoners had been questioned already, and were marked by the whip and twisted by the rack. They woke, noticed my stare, and told me proudly that the torturers had wanted to know the whereabouts of some of the leaders of the church, and had wanted them to confess to various crimes so they could be executed. None of them had cooperated. I could do nothing for them.

About an hour after dawn there was a clanking of metal, and then the guards came in. They set out a few cups of water for the prisoners, then picked out several for questioning, unfastened their chains from the wall, and pulled them out in stony silence. The other prisoners began to pray for the victims, and the guards cursed them, kicked one or two, and went out, bolting the door.

I couldn't even reach the water in the cup the guards set out near me. The rope was too short. I tried to think of some way to help the torture victims, and couldn't manage that either. It was no use advising the sufferers to keep the wounds clean and to rest: that was impossible in this damp and filthy prison. So I sat and waited for the guards to fetch me, imagining the treatments I would have prescribed if I had been at liberty and had my medical bag. I was afraid to think about my own position. Eventually, though, I ran out of treatments and had to face the issue. What should I say to the authorities?

I felt a wave of bitterness toward Theophilos, a sudden desire to make him regret that he'd betrayed me. But that would be a pointless piece of vindictiveness. And at once I realized that he must have meant to warn me; no one can be relied upon to stay silent under torture, and I knew too many of the secrets of the church. Now that I'd been arrested, Theophilos wouldn't be in his hiding place anyway — though others might be. My only course was to deny that I'd seen the deacon since he first disappeared, and to continue my role of competent but dull physician, obsessed with medical detail and not trusted by the church authorities with any other knowledge.

But would the prefect believe that? Believe it without having me tortured first? What had Athanaric told him about me?

I remembered all the victims of torture I had ever seen, and I felt so sick with fear that I forgot almost everything else. I tried to pray again, for strength, and couldn't. I mustn't panic, I thought, it's all over if I panic. Desperately I began running over the Aphorisms of

Hippocrates in my mind. They came back to me easily, despite everything. "Life is short and the art long"; I didn't panic.

About noon the jailers brought the prisoners back, dragging the ones who couldn't walk, and chained them up again. Then they looked around, found me, cut the rope loose from the wall, and dragged me out; my legs were asleep and I was staggering. The other prisoners began to pray loudly for me as we left, and the jailers shouted for them to stop it or they'd get no food that day. They didn't stop it. "Obstinate Egyptian pigs," said one of my guards, and kicked me in the leg to relieve his feelings.

I was led out of the prison and along the quiet streets of the citadel to the prefecture. It was a fine building, fronted with marble columns, domed, and surrounded by gardens. My guards took me through the tiled atrium with its mosaic of the seasons, through a courtyard full of peach trees, and into an office. It was a large room, the floor covered with a very fine mosaic of dolphins, the walls painted with city scenes and hung with draperies. It seemed like something in a dream to me, after the rioting and the soldiers and the prison. The prefect, Palladios, was reclining on a cedarwood couch, finishing a cup of wine; he was freshly bathed and wore a green cloak with a purple stripe. He was a middle-aged man, an Illyrian. I'd met him a few times at the episcopal palace, where he'd come to see first Athanasios and then Peter. On the couch next to him sat another man, a thin, nervous man with a goiter, curling brown hair, and large, restless hands; his cloak too had the purple border to it. He was wearing on his finger a gold signet ring carved with the lion of St. Mark the Apostle; Athanasios had worn it, and then Peter. So this was Lucius.

Behind these two, sitting at a writing desk, was the notary who'd taken down my words after I'd seen Peter. He had his tablets ready now and his stylus in hand; he looked up and nodded to the soldiers, and they saluted. "The eunuch Chariton of Ephesus," they announced, and everyone looked at me. I'm sure I looked criminal enough. I was wearing the old black cloak that had been Theophilos', on which several patients had bled or vomited, and my stained blue tunic, now filthy from the prison, and I was covered in dried blood and dirt. I knew that I stank; the prefect wrinkled his nose in distaste. I couldn't open one of my eyes properly; it had swollen from the blows the night before. I stood between my guards, my hands tied behind my back, and looked at the floor.

"Umm, yes," said the prefect. "Well then, eunuch, have you any notion of the whereabouts of the false bishop, Peter of Alexandria?"

"He was in prison here in the citadel," I said. "I saw him here three days ago. I was going to see him again later this week."

"Where were you going to see him?" put in Lucius angrily.

"In prison in the citadel," I returned evenly. "If he's not there now, I know nothing about it."

"Heretic and liar!" Lucius said, sitting up straight, a flush coming to his thin cheeks. "You arranged for him to receive some money in a book! You had the books sent to him, so that he could bribe his guards and escape!"

"What?" I asked, staring.

The notary coughed and looked at some notes. "The prisoner requested, on behalf of the false bishop, some Gospels; His Excellency Lord Palladios acceded to this pious request, and sent a letter authorizing the books to the prisoner."

"Yes, I did ask for some books for Archbishop Peter, but —"

"He confesses it!" Lucius said triumphantly.

"— but Peter asked me for them! I thought he just wanted something to read. I don't know anything about them. I didn't bring them to him, I just passed the request on to his friends!"

"Which friends?" asked the prefect patiently.

I hesitated, then named a couple of wealthy laymen who were supporters of the church but who had not been molested by the law.

The prefect shook his head. "Where is Theophilos the deacon?" he asked.

"I don't know. I thought he'd fled the city."

"Young man," said the prefect solemnly, setting down his wine cup, "this will get you nowhere. We understand that you are claiming immunity from torture on the grounds of noble birth, but the status of any eunuch is highly questionable. You must have been a slave at some time. I will have no hesitation in having you put to the rack if you refuse to cooperate with us and tell us all you know."

"I don't know anything," I said, feeling very cold. "I'm just a doctor."

"An Athanasian fanatic!" said Lucius hotly. "Have him flogged, and see if he won't talk then! It's no use trying to reason with these people!"

Suddenly the door of the room swung open and in walked the agent Athanaric, followed by a nervous scribe. "Your Excellency," he said, nodding to the prefect; "Your Holiness," to Lucius; and "Greetings, Chariton!" to me. We looked at each other for a moment, and then he turned back to the prefect. "Your Excellency, I hope you will forgive my intrusion, but I have an interest in this prisoner. May I sit in?"

The prefect nodded, and Athanaric sat down on the nearest couch, perching on the end of it to allow space for his sword.

"I didn't know you were in Alexandria," I said. I didn't mean it to sound like an accusation, but it did.

"Oh, I came with a message for His Excellency," said Athanaric easily. "Were you involved in this escape?"

"I was Archbishop Peter's doctor," I said, glad of the chance to state my position exactly. "I went to check on him when he was in prison. But I had nothing to do with smuggling him any money; all I did was recommend that he have some barley broth, and pass on a request for some Gospels."

"Well, there you are!" Athanaric said to the prefect. "Is there any evidence he produced these Gospels himself?"

The prefect frowned; the notary checked his notes. "The books were given to the guardsman by an unidentified citizen, together with His Excellency's letter of authorization. The magistrate Apollodoros, a friend of the false bishop, sent another set of Gospels to the prison after the escape, together with another letter of authorization, which on examination proved to be a forgery copied from the first. His slaves have denied, under torture, that they know anything about it."

Apollodoros had been one of the men I named. I wondered whether he had known about the plan and sent the second set of Gospels to protect himself — or whether Theophilos had deceived him too.

"So," said Athanaric, "Chariton told Apollodoros that Peter wanted some Gospels, and gave him the letter of authorization; Apollodoros arranged to have them sent; some friend of Apollodoros heard of it, stole the letter, and sent another set of Gospels with the money hidden in the binding. I don't see that Chariton can be held responsible for that."

Everyone looked at Athanaric in some bewilderment; I was more bewildered than any of them. I'd thought he'd come in to give evidence against me, to tell the prefect about how I'd refused his bribes. But instead he seemed determined to defend me — and he was doing quite a good job, too. The prefect Palladios looked a bit less sure of himself.

"He's one of those damned fanatics," Lucius objected. "He'd do anything to support their heretical faction."

Athanaric snorted. "He's a fanatic, all right. The True Word of

Health was revealed to the prophet Hippocrates, only begotten son of Divine Healing, whose word is law — except perhaps on the custom of dosing with hellebore, about which Chariton has a heresy of his own. Go on, you searched his room. Did you find Gospels, psalters, theological tracts?"

The notary checked a list. "Bishop Athanasios' treatise *On the Incarnation*; all the others . . ." His eyes ran down the paper. "All the others are medical texts. Sixty-two of them."

"Not even an epistle?" asked Athanaric.

The notary shook his head, smiling a dry little smile. "Your Excellency," he said to the prefect, "I am inclined to agree with the most esteemed agent's assessment of the prisoner. I was present at his interview following his meeting with the escaped prisoner, and all he talked about was the state of Bishop Peter's bowels. As regards personal correspondence, the prisoner's effects contained only this, which is far from incriminating."

The notary held up a sheet of papyrus. Athanaric took it from him. "What's this? A letter?" I saw that it was from Thorion, his most recent one: it had been written in response to mine about Athanasios' death, but before Lucius arrived in the city. " 'Theodoros son of Theodoros to Chariton of Ephesus,' " read Athanaric. " 'Very many greetings,' et cetera — here! 'I understand that Bishop Athanasios was your patient and you felt you couldn't turn your back on him, but, by Artemis the Great! he's dead, and you'd do well to get yourself some less controversial patients, or even none at all. Even if it doesn't pay as well. There's bound to be trouble in Alexandria now, Chariton, I don't want you caught in it. You know you couldn't care less about any damned theology, so why don't you drop the lot and come stay with me in Constantinople? Maia would be overjoyed to see you.' " Athanaric lowered the letter and looked at me assessingly. "Sensible man, your friend. Why didn't you listen to him?"

"Peter was my patient too," I said. "And lots of the others. And the hospitals were closed, and there was no one else to treat them."

Athanaric handed the letter back to the notary. "This man here," he said, indicating me, "is a very good doctor, and nothing more. When I offered him a bribe for information, back before Bishop Athanasios' death, he couldn't think of anything to spend it on. I checked on that; I couldn't find that he ever does anything but practice medicine, read about medicine, go to lectures about medicine, and talk about medicine with his old teacher, who's not even a Christian. For all I know he spends the rest of his time thinking about medicine and dreaming about medicine. He's not one of *your* fanatics, Your Holiness. If some of Archbishop Peter's friends used what he told them about the old man's request, it wasn't his fault and I don't think he knew anything about it."

"He was in the thick of that viper's nest of heresy," Lucius said obstinately. "He knew all the men we want. Even if he wasn't part of the plot to free the false bishop — and I still think he was! — he must know where Theophilos and those other serpents are hiding. I'd wager my life that he's treated half the fugitives from justice who leave this city, and I wouldn't be surprised if he's seen and treated that false bishop Peter since he escaped. Put him on the rack!"

Palladios hesitated, then reluctantly nodded agreement. He turned back to me. "Will you talk, eunuch, or do I have to do as the most pious archbishop suggests?"

Once again Athanaric interrupted. "Whatever he might know of any fugitives he would hold under the Hippocratic oath," he said. "For him, that's better than an imperial edict. I don't think he'd tell you a thing, unless you broke him utterly. And, most excellent and charitable Palladios, I beg you not to do that. As a favor to me."

"Why are you defending this . . . this gelded heretic?" Lucius demanded furiously.

"Because he saved my life," Athanaric returned flatly. "I would have died of a fever if it hadn't been for him. And where I come from, we think that creates a debt."

"Blood debt!" said Lucius, getting to his feet and sneering at Athanaric. "A pagan notion; a barbarian notion; a foolish and worthless Gothic sentiment!"

Athanaric flushed. "Perhaps. But I prefer it to your Roman savagery, most Christian archbishop." He turned back to the prefect. "Moreover, Your Excellency, this Chariton could be of great service to the state, if you let him live. If you kill him on the rack, he might give you a few worthless names of people who would be gone already by the time you went to seek them. But if he lives, he could be a means of strengthening the armies of Their Sacred Majesties, and also a means for you to do a favor to your colleagues in Thrace."

"Eh?" asked Palladios, almost visibly pricking his ears up. "What's that?"

"Send him to work in a military hospital," said Athanaric. "Have you been to the ones on the Danube frontier? There are also some in Your Excellency's home province of Noricum. The doctors in places like that are incompetent quacks. I didn't know how bad they were until I met a real Hippocratic like your prisoner here. They kill more men than they cure. But real Hippocratic doctors don't want to work in military hospitals at the ends of the earth; they'd rather spend their time soothing ladies' nerves or even treating the Alexandrian rabble, leaving our soldiers to butchers and witches. Well, I know the army duke who commands in Scythia; he'd be delighted to have a real Alexandrian physician, a graduate of the Museum, to run his hospital. If Your Grace would have a contract drawn up and Chariton would consent to sign it, you would have the pleasure of rendering Duke Sebastianus your debtor, serving the interests of the state, and ridding your city of an adherent of the Athanasian faction, all in one."

Palladios let out his breath in a little puffing sigh and looked at me speculatively.

"Why should you let him go?" demanded Lucius, seeing that he was losing and growing still more vehement. "He must know something about our enemies. Have him racked and see if he talks."

"Have him racked, have him flogged, have him killed!" Palladios snapped, turning on the archbishop. "That's all you ever say. I swear by all the gods, you bishops are more bloodthirsty than barbarian anthropophagi! What's the use of killing a doctor? The most noble Athanaric is right: the eunuch would be more use to everyone stitching up soldiers in Thrace. Well, Chariton of Ephesus." He turned back to me and left Lucius biting his nails with anger and glaring. "Would you consent to sign such a contract?"

I felt very weak at the knees and had to swallow several times before I could answer. I hadn't felt the depth of my fear until I began to believe I would escape. "Gladly," I said at last.

It was not entirely clear who should draw up a contract for me to become an army doctor. In the end the notary was sent to the office of the duke of Egypt, who would arrange things with the assessor. I was to wait until the contract arrived; Athanaric stayed with me, as though he didn't trust Lucius not to have me racked in the interval.

The waiting room was a little box in the back of the prefecture. It had a bench down each side and a window overlooking the prefectural gardens. The guards escorted me there, this time without roughness, but Athanaric dismissed them when we arrived. Astonishingly, they didn't question his right to do this; they just went. I sat down hard, shaking a bit. I had to lean forward because my hands were still tied. Athanaric noticed and grinned; he took out his knife and sawed through the leather.

"Thank you," I said, and examined my wrists, which were rubbed raw. My hands were trembling. "Thank you very much."

He shrugged; I just caught the gesture as I looked up again. "The debt's canceled now?" he asked.

"There wasn't any debt," I told him. "A doctor doesn't refuse to treat a sick man. And you might have recovered from that fever without me."

"Might I? Shall I go back and tell them that?" He laughed at my alarm. "There was a debt. Besides, I like people who refuse bribes. It's unprofessional, seeing how much I depend on their acceptance, but I can't help it. And I don't like to see honest men tortured for keeping faith with their friends, particularly not by bloodthirsty bishops. You thought I'd come to help them, didn't you?"

"I knew you'd helped them in the past."

"My job is to take information to the court and edicts out of it. I don't make policy, and I don't lie to His Illustriousness the master of the offices of His Sacred Majesty. I don't have to like every act every servant of His Sacred Majesty may take it into his head to commit."

I thought of him riding off with the news of Athanasios' death. If he hadn't ridden so fast, Lucius might not have been here yet, and Peter would never have been captured. But still I could believe that he disliked cruelty. And he had saved my life, or at least my life as a doctor. That counted for something. "What are military hospitals like?" I asked. "Do I have to sign on for twenty years?"

"Oh no!" he said, answering the second question first. "Doctors aren't enlisted, or commissioned either; the contracts of employment vary. We'll probably sign you on for ten years or so, to keep you out of Lucius' way. The hospitals are fairly standard things of their kind, a bit more regulated than your ecclesiastical hospitals here. I imagine you'll be sent to Noviodunum. It's a big fortress on the Danube, and the hospital there is particularly bad. The troops always say that it's better to cut your throat and have done with it than go to Noviodunum. It'll keep you busy." He paused, then added, "I'll probably see you there from time to time. My appointment here is finished, and I have a lot of contacts in Thrace; some family too. I'm usually posted there. So you see, I'm interested in improving the health care of the region."

I smiled at that. "I'll improve it if I can."

We sat in silence for a minute, and then Athanaric asked, "Since you've finished here, and I have too, perhaps you could tell me: What was that divine revelation that Archbishop Athanasios had about you?"

"Something personal," I said.

"Which you don't mean to tell me. Very well, I'll just have to suspect the worst. Your conscience was burdened with some appalling crime and the archbishop made you treat monks as a penance. All I have to do now is to imagine the crime. Did you attribute a work of Herophilos to Hippocrates?"

He looked so cheerful at this prospect that despite everything I had to smile. "Imagine away," I told him. "Thank you again."

✠✠✠

I left Alexandria a week later, sailing on an army supply ship from the Great Harbor. I had not seen Theophilos, nor any other of the church leaders. I did manage to get my three nuns out of prison, but I didn't stay in their house. Philon had heard of my arrest. When I had signed the contract and was allowed to walk out of the prefecture, I found him waiting in the atrium: he had been applying, unsuccessfully, for permission to see me. When I appeared, still stinking and filthy from the prison, he came running over and caught my shoulders. "I thank God!" he exclaimed, and hugged me.

He took me straight back to his house, and we arrived to find Theogenes and Theophila both over from their home in the Broucheion, waiting anxiously for news of me. Everyone was so glad to see me free and untortured that I had great difficulty in getting enough time to bathe.

I spent my last week in the city at Philon's house. It was perhaps a mistake, as it made me wish that I didn't have to go. Everything I loved in Alexandria was there: Philon and his family; medicine and books; freedom. Alexandria's freedom is like Christ's peace: "not as the world's." Alexandria's freedom is a liberty to search for truth and to define your own law. The city has a hundred different laws, all in conflict, trying to impose on each other, violent and alive. In that last week in Philon's house, I knew that if I stayed in Alexandria I would one day be able to fulfill my dream, to say plainly, "I am a woman, but I will still practice medicine," and have it accepted, a law of my own, not really any stranger than the Torah or the hierarchies of Plotinus. But I could never survive under Lucius. And Alexandria had become a sad place for me. Too many people were dead or imprisoned. Too much had died with Athanasios.

I was not terribly frightened of going to work in a hospital in Thrace. As Philon had said, my greatest teacher now would be experience anyway. And the great Dioskourides had been an army doctor. I didn't mind the idea of the work. I knew that I would miss the stimulation of lectures at the Temple, and the many bookshops around its annexes; I would miss consulting with Philon, and the "stimulating company" of the other doctors from the Museum. I gathered I might have difficulty in finding various common drugs up on the frontier. I could certainly expect the army doctors and most of the men to despise me, at least at first, as an effeminate Asian eunuch. But all this was considerably better than the rack — or, for that matter, being sent back to Ephesus and forced to behave as a disgraced gentlewoman. I would be paid, once in rations and again in the value of those rations in money, and I would be free to take private patients on the side. I'd see something of the world, particularly if I managed to attach myself to a mobile unit during a campaign.

I'd arrived in Alexandria almost penniless, with a chest containing my jewels, three books, two spare tunics, and a pair of boots. I left in somewhat better state, with most of the jewels, sixty-three books, three tunics, two spare cloaks, a complete set of medical supplies, and nearly fifty *solidi*. I also had a medical qualification from the Museum, and the dubious distinction of having been private physician to the archbishop. All in all, I had not done badly. And, I told myself, a few years' experience on the Danube frontier wouldn't hurt me. From what Athanaric had said, good doctors were in short supply up there: I might make a career for myself yet. I managed to put a brave face on it when I said farewell to Philon and his family.

But when the ship glided past the Pharos and lifted its sails to the land breeze, I looked back at the city, shining around its harbor, and I wept. Alexandria, the most turbulent city in the empire, dirty, dangerous, violent — I wept at parting from it as I had not wept when I left my own home. It is not confined by the limits of its nation or its people. Like the Pharos, it rises from stubborn rock and casts its light a long way through the wastes of darkness.

III

THRACE

The Provinces of the
IMPERIAL DIOCESE
OF THRACE
in the Fourth Century

Novidunum

Histria

Tomis

SCYTHIA

RIVER DANUBE

DIOCESE
OF
DACIA

MOESIA

DIOCESE OF THRACE

Odessus

Marcianopolis

HAEMIMONTUS

EUXINE
SEA

THRACE

RIVER HEBRUS

Philippopolis

Hadrianopolis

RHODOPE

EUROPA   Constantinople

DIOCESE OF
MACEDONIA

Thessa-
lonica

MIDDLE SEA

HELLESPONTUS

BITHYNIA

I ARRIVED IN THRACE in early October of the year that Athanasios died. We had a smooth journey from Alexandria. Because it was unseasonably fair weather, and because it was late in the season, the shipmaster did not sail up the Syrian coast but took his vessel directly across the deep sea to Crete. There we took on fresh water, and then, hurrying to catch the last of the good weather, proceeded through the islands and up into the Bosphorus. We arrived in Constantinople early on the twenty-fifth of September. The harbor shimmered in the soft morning, and the city seemed to rise out of the water like a vision of the Heavenly Jerusalem, its domes and palaces turned to gold by the early light. By the docks vendors were crying their wares: fresh figs, new melon, hot sesame cakes! Seagulls flapped white wings over the bright water, scavenging amid the rubbish tipped into the harbor.

The ship was due to unload part of its cargo of grain into a smaller vessel, which would take it, and me, on up into the Euxine Sea; the cargo would be unloaded at Histria and from there shipped up the river. This smaller ship was already waiting in the dock when the Alexandrian one put in, and immediately its master came on board. "I want to leave tomorrow!" he announced to the entire crew. "Who knows how long this wind will hold? I want to get the voyage done before the winter. You don't make any money sitting in Constantinople docks!"

So the hatches were opened, and the dock workers began dragging the bales of grain up, loading them onto handcarts, and wheeling them over to the other ship. When I managed to catch the master in a free moment, I asked him whether I had time to go into the city to see someone.

"You're going to Scythia?" he asked, looking at me dubiously. The master obviously thought Scythia an unlikely destination for an Asian eunuch.

I explained who I was, and he looked still more dubious. "I have a friend in the city," I said. "Do I have time to see him?"

"If you're back on the ship before dawn tomorrow," he answered. "That's when I'm leaving. The wind won't wait and neither will I."

I agreed to this, and set off.

Constantinople is a new city. Very little is left of the old town of Byzantium which the Most Glorious Emperor remade into his capital and named after himself. But some of the shine had come off his work in the fifty years since it had been built. Many of the buildings had been put up hastily and carelessly and were now coming down again; I found that the carpenters and plasterers of the city were well employed, and the streets were littered with chunks of plaster and broken roof tiles. But the city was still beautiful, with wide streets, and full of public gardens. In one square I found a statue of the great Alexander, taken from his mausoleum in Alexandria and now standing among the plane trees of Constantine's city. A public fountain flowed from the pedestal beneath his feet, and his glass eyes, under the hair of gilded marble, seemed to stare sadly at the world he had conquered and lost. Constantinople is full of art treasures pillaged from all the greatest cities of the empire. The Most Pious Emperor had wanted the city that bore his name to be of unrivaled magnificence.

I made my way to the city prefecture, then stopped. It was nearly noon, and I had to be back on the ship that night. Was it worthwhile, troubling Thorion for that short a time?

I went back to the public square of Alexander and sat down on a wall. I wanted to see Thorion. It had been three years and more, and I missed him. And I wanted to see Maia too. I ached with wanting to see them. But I was afraid. I knew that Thorion wanted me to give up my pretense. He now had a job as an assessor, legal adviser to the provincial governor. He had a good salary and earned as much again in bribes and perquisites, and he was no longer dependent on our father and no longer so worried about Festinus. So much he had told me in his letters. He hadn't trusted more than that to paper, but I could guess the rest of his plans. He meant to bring me — his sister, whom he had "rescued" from Festinus and "concealed" for three years — back into respectable society, and he meant me to marry one of his friends and lead a normal life. And I didn't know how to begin to tell him that I would do no such thing. The gap between us had grown too wide — and Thorion was scarcely even aware yet that it existed. I would cause my family nothing but misery if I appeared in Constantinople now. And there wasn't any time to talk to them properly, not with the ship leaving next day before dawn.

I sighed. Some women from the quarter were drawing water from the fountain, and they stared at me suspiciously. I smiled at them in apology, got off the wall, and walked back to the docks. The shipmaster gave me a strange look, but no one asked any questions.

From Constantinople we sailed northwest along the Euxine coast. The weather held, and the Euxine produced none of its treacherous storms; the master began to relax, and put in at several small ports along the way to take on water and fresh fruit. At one of these, Odessus, we learned that Sebastianus, who was duke of the Thracian province of Scythia, was consulting with the count of Thrace in Marcianopolis. Since I would be under Sebastianus' command, it made no sense to go on to his headquarters in Tomis and wait there for him, so I disembarked at Odessus and set off for Marcianopolis, which is twenty miles upriver from the seaport.

There were plenty of boats going up the river from Odessus to Marcianopolis, carrying fish and imported goods from the port as well as passengers, and I paid a few coppers to install myself and my traveling chest on one of these. Two other passengers climbed in, a woman with a package of imported woolen cloth and a man with some fish and two large amphorae of wine. They both looked at me sidelong, but said nothing. The boatmen cast off from the quayside, raised the sail, and sat to their oars; I sat on my chest in the stern and watched the countryside go past. I hadn't had much chance to see it from the ship — just beaches and rocky shores backed by mountains; many forests of dark pine and oak; a few towns huddling at the mouths of muddy rivers, surrounded by open fields; one or two cities. Going up the river, I found Thrace even wilder and more desolate than I thought it would be. Odessus was a very much smaller city than the ones I was used to, and Marcianopolis, when we reached it, was not much bigger. Between the two the river wound through a narrow strip of cultivated land toward the Haemus mountains. Cows grazed in the rich pastureland; a few peasants were taking in the last of the harvest, stooping and rhythmically slashing the rich gold of the grain. For the first mile or so the landscape looked indefinably strange to me, and then I realized what was missing: olive trees. They won't grow in Thrace; it's too cold for them. The inhabitants follow the barbarian Gothic custom and make a paste from milk, which they call butter, and this they use in cooking and on bread in place of olive oil. The vine too has difficulty growing in Thrace, and the local wine is thin and sour.

I gave an uncomfortable shiver and looked up, away from the cultivated lands. Beyond it were the dark, shadowy shapes of the mountains and miles of empty plain and forest, alien and savage. There was a lot of land lying waste. Thrace is a sparsely populated region. It was so even in ancient times, except around the coast, and it suffered greatly in the wars before the accession of the most illustrious emperor Diocletian. It is quite a large diocese, too, comprised of six provinces. It is bounded on the south by the Aegean, on the east by the Euxine, and on the north by the river called Hister or Danube, beyond which are the tribes of the barbarian Goths. On the west it borders the imperial diocese of Dacia, which is Latin-speaking and under the control of the western emperor. The southern four provinces of Thrace speak a kind of Greek, but the two northern ones, Moesia and Scythia, are bilingual, Greek and Latin — that's not counting the Gothic spoken by many of the soldiers and the Thracian of the peasants.

We arrived in Marcianopolis in the evening. Though not much more than a town by Asian standards, it was strongly fortified. The stone walls towered black against the sunset as our little boat approached them, with the Haemus mountains looming behind them and shutting out the light. Even the river passage was fortified with gates, though these were standing open when we entered the city. We landed at a stone quay in the dusk, and the passengers climbed out, stiff from sitting in the cramped boat. Neither of them had spoken to me during the journey, though both had done some more staring, and they had whispered to each other. I could scarcely understand what they said even when they spoke in a normal tone, their Greek was so peculiar and the accent so unfamiliar. I felt tired and downhearted. I hired a porter for my chest and found a room at the nearest tavern.

The next morning I went to present myself to Duke Sebastianus. I felt nervous of the meeting, so I dressed carefully, putting on my newest tunic and my best cloak, the one I'd bought for my medical examination in Alexandria. I didn't have a mirror, but there was a black earthenware bowl of water in the room, and I looked at myself in that. It had been some time since I looked in a mirror. It was a thinner face now than I remembered, and older. The detached, assessing look had deepened, become one of wariness, even of suspicion. I smiled at it, mentally prescribing rest and regular meals, and the face smiled back, becoming professional and assured: the face of a doctor trained in Alexandria. I'd do. Feeling more confident, I set out to see Duke Sebastianus.

I knew he would be staying with the count, the military commander of the whole of Thrace, who had his headquarters in Marcianopolis. I had no trouble finding the building: it was the largest one in the city. It stood fronting the marketplace, dwarfing the governor's residence and the cathedral church next to it. Two gilded standards stood crossed over the doors: a dragon and the labarum of Christ. A troop of guards stood beside them. They were in full uniform, helmeted and booted, carrying shields over their backs and spears in their hands. They wore trousers under their tunics, and carried long swords slung from belts across their shoulders. Many of them were fair-haired and bearded, and besides their regulation Roman uniforms they wore a variety of jewelry. One man had a wolfskin fastened over his helmet, the teeth hanging savagely above his eyes, the paws tied under his chin; another had a necklace of boar's teeth; yet another wore a bearskin for a cloak, tossed casually back from his shoulders. They looked like Gothic barbarians, not Roman troops at all. Then I realized that all the men in the marketplace wore trousers too, and I noticed that many of the women were wearing stockings under their sandals. Presumably the dress made sense; it must be cold in the winter. But the scene was barbaric, for all the Corinthian colonnades of the public buildings. I stood in the marketplace for a moment, staring at it and feeling horribly out of place. I didn't feel well dressed and confident anymore: I felt foreign. Chariton the eunuch with his Alexandrian education was totally alien to this frontier world of camps and barbarians, and as for Charis, the mind could not conceive a less "proper" place for a young lady. I even wondered for an instant whether I should have jumped ship in Constantinople, gone to Thorion, and given up my masquerade.

But of course I could never give up medicine. Well, I reasoned with myself, you stood out in Alexandria as well, as a eunuch and a foreigner. It was hard there at first; it all looked foreign to you when you arrived. Pull yourself together and go see Duke Sebastianus.

I went over to the guardsmen and explained who I was, and they let me into the headquarters and told me to wait.

There was no one else in the waiting room, but I sat there for more than an hour before one of the palace scribes came and called me. "His Prudence the Duke is with Count Lupicinus," the scribe explained as he showed me the way. "They were arranging troop movements, but they've finished now. They'll both see you." He knocked on a door, then opened it. "Chariton of Ephesus, a physician," he announced.

There were two men in the room, sitting at a table littered with papers. Light from a window high in the wall poured onto the middle of the papers, making the rest of the room dim. The legionary emblems were carved into the wall and gilded; a bearskin rug snarled by a couch in a corner. One of the men was young, golden-haired, and absurdly handsome. He wore a gilded breastplate and a red cloak; a red-crested gold helmet rested in the middle of the patch of sunlight, shining. The other was of late middle age, stocky and dark-going-gray, with heavy jowls. He too wore a red cloak, but his armor was plain leather and iron. The older man was leaning back in his chair and scowling; the younger was sorting the papers. But when I was announced he put them down, jumped up, and came over to me.

"Greetings," he said, and shook hands, smiling to display a set of even white teeth. "I'm Sebastianus, duke of Scythia; I had a letter about you from my old friend Athanaric only two days ago. You've traveled swiftly!" His Greek had the same clipped, staccato accent as Athanaric's. I'd taken the accent to be Gothic, but I learned that it was simply Illyrian.

"Who's that?" asked the older man — Lupicinus, he must be, the supreme commander of the troops in Thrace. He had a low, growling voice, and an accent I found disturbingly familiar. I couldn't place it for a moment, and then I remembered: Festinus. Was Lupicinus a Gaul as well, then?

"A doctor from Alexandria," Sebastianus told him, going back to the table and shuffling the papers together. "Palladios, the prefect of Egypt Augustamnica, and Athanaric the agent have arranged for him to come work in the hospitals here. I need someone skilled to set Novidunum in order."

Lupicinus looked at me suspiciously. "Some Ephesian eunuch," he concluded. "If he's any good as a doctor, what's he doing here? Well, eunuch?"

"I was private physician to His Holiness, Bishop Athanasios," I said. Athanasios was famous, or rather notorious. It took a moment, but both men understood; from the expression on Sebastianus' face, I judged that Athanaric's letter hadn't mentioned this detail. I wondered what it had said.

Lupicinus laughed. "So you shoved enemas into that old rabble-rouser! You some damned Nicene fanatic?"

"No, Your Excellency," I said, glad of Philon's training in patience. "I am a Christian and a Nicene, but not passionately so."

Lupicinus grunted. "Good. I've seen enough of theological disagreements. The state post is always cluttered up with bishops rushing about to their synods and shouting at each other. And that Athanasios was the worst of the lot, tickling the ears of the Alexandrian mob with his seditious preaching. Though I hear that now he's dead, the Alexandrians are indulging their taste for riot. They ought to be whipped."

"Many of them are being whipped now," I said — quietly, since I didn't want to offend a man who could command me.

"I fear you'll find work in a military hospital a considerable demotion after service with a great bishop," Sebastianus put in, hastily trying to preserve the decencies of conversation.

I smiled to show that I appreciated his courtesy. "It's a case of 'I save myself. What care I for the shield?' " I told him.

Lupicinus looked completely blank. Sebastianus smiled, but suppressed his smile hurriedly. "What shield?" asked Lupicinus irritably.

"He was quoting poetry," said Sebastianus. "Archilochos' poem on having thrown his shield away."

Lupicinus gave me a look of profound contempt. "Damned over-educated Greeks," he said, to no one in particular. "I don't see that there's any need to go bringing in some lisping Asian eunuch to treat the men, some girl-faced gelding with lily-white hands and a white liver too. What do you mean to do, eh, Chariton of Ephesus?" He imitated an Asian accent with the too-heavy lisp of a clown in the mimes. "Treat them with hot baths and perfumes? The old way of medicine is good enough for me. Here, if a man doesn't get better, he dies, and you're well rid of the burden of him."

"Most excellent Lupicinus," I said, keeping my voice level, "it's true anywhere that if a man doesn't get better, he dies. The thing is to make him get better. I don't know what the old way of medicine is. Quite possibly it's as good as anything I've learned in Alexandria. But I understood that doctors were required on the frontier, and I am content to serve as one."

"I am delighted to have a skilled physician for my hospital at Novidunum," Sebastianus put in quickly. "Most of the men who go there at present seem to die, and the rest are crippled; I hope you can improve on that. If you'll come with me, I'll give you letters to the tribune of the camp, and licenses to use the state post to get there." He picked up his papers and his helmet from the table, and bowed to Lupicinus. "Most excellent count, much health!" he said, and hurried me from the room.

When we'd walked down the corridor a little way he suddenly stopped and laughed. "Oh Holy Christ!" he said. " 'The old way of medicine is good enough for me.' You'd never catch Lupicinus using an army hospital!"

"Did I offend him?" I asked, nervously aware of the man's power.

"Him? It's hard not to offend him. He's dirt-ignorant. He didn't like your quoting poetry; he thinks Archilochos is a kind of fish."

"I thought everyone knew that one," I said.

"Anyone with an ordinarily decent education. Any gentleman. But he's not only ignorant of Greek letters, he scarcely knows the Latin ones. Money, that's what he likes — though he's an experienced commander, I'll give him that. Don't worry, he's forgotten all about you now — he'll only remember if he himself falls ill, in which case he'll have me send you from the hospital to look after him. He calls me an overdressed lover of luxury and puts on airs of antique Roman virtue, but he cooks the account books for all that, and his house is like a Sybarite's mansion. 'The old way of medicine' — hot baths and perfumes are what he'd like himself, don't worry about that!"

"I don't use them," I said. "Unless he meant steam baths and drugs like myrrh. It's drugs and anatomy that I learned at Alexandria."

He gave me a quick assessing look. "Athanaric says you cured him of a deadly fever, and that you're the only honest eunuch in the world. I don't see Athanaric going in for perfumes, I must admit. Well, I hope you can do something at Novidunum. I'll give you authority to rearrange the hospital as much as you need to. There's plague among the troops stationed on the Danube further west, and I don't need it here. The barbarians are warring among themselves, and it makes them restless. If our forces were weakened, they might try to cross the river."

I murmured something about doing my best, and Sebastianus smiled. "Perhaps you'll have dinner with me this evening?" he asked. "I don't meet educated men often here in Thrace, and I like to have their company when I do."

I ate dinner with Sebastianus that evening. He had a set of rooms in the presidium, and had brought some of his slaves with him from his headquarters in Tomis; I found myself treated to the most civilized meal I'd eaten since I left Ephesus. We reclined on our couches, drinking our wine (Chian, in fact — my father's favorite) and eating our way slowly through the three courses, eggs to apples. I dredged up my training in the classics and capped the duke's frequent quotes of poetry, so that he continued to think me cultured. The only difference from one of my father's dinner parties was the singing girl who played the lyre while we ate; the sort of party I went to in Ephesus never had any entertainments but poetry recitals. She was an exceptionally pretty girl, as golden as Sebastianus, and she was wearing the thinnest of silk tunics, showing off a sight Sebastianus evidently enjoyed.

Sebastianus was very pleasant company, talkative and amusing. I soon found out why he felt so free to abuse his superior: his father was the commander of the Illyrian and Italian legions and one of the foremost generals in the West. "Though I'm not the only one on the frontier with a father to live up to," he told me. "There's my friend Theodosius, in the Dacian Moesia — his father's the count, the one who just defeated the rebel Firmus in Africa, the one who restored Britain after Lupicinus made a mess of it. He's worthy of his father, too; he makes no end of trouble for the Sarmatians. Daphne, my dear" — to the lyre player — "play another song! That one's as tedious as Lupicinus' accounting!" Daphne giggled and played another song. "But most of the dukes here are dirt-ignorant," Sebastianus continued sadly. "Goths, mostly; a few Pannonians and Illyrians — professional soldiers, worthy men, but dull. Initially I had hopes that our friend Athanaric would be posted here, but his father wanted him to go into the civil service instead; he wants him to end up a consul at Rome. A pity, because he's good company — and of course the Goths will do anything he says."

"Is he very well educated, then?" I asked. "I never talked to him in Alexandria, except about his health, or mine."

Sebastianus shrugged. "Tolerably well educated. Not excessively, I suppose. But of course he's of very good family. And he's never dull."

"He's noble? I thought his name was Gothic."

"Of course it is. He's the nephew of the king of the Theruingi, didn't you know that?"

"The who?" I asked stupidly.

Sebastianus laughed. "There we are. I get caught up in this region, I forget that most of the world has never heard of King Athanaric of the Theruingi. Some call them the Visigoths. They're the Gothic tribe that live across the river from us, a very powerful tribe — though not as powerful as they used to be. They caused trouble a number of years back, supporting the pretender Procopius. His Sacred Majesty invaded their kingdom to teach them a lesson. He burned some towns and some fields and chased King Athanaric and his people up into the mountains. But he couldn't catch the king, and the campaign was expensive, so after a while our most illustrious lord decided to offer Athanaric another treaty of peace. But Athanaric refused to come to Scythia to sign the treaty; he said he had scruples about treading on Roman soil. The most illustrious Lord Valens, master of the world, had to conclude the treaty on a boat in the middle of the Danube, to satisfy the scruples of a barbarian king; they say he still resents it. Well, the reason King Athanaric had scruples was that his brother, our friend Athanaric's father, crossed the river with a troop of federates years ago, fought in the Roman army for years, married a Roman girl, and settled in Sardica to bring up his son to the civil service and, he hopes, to marry an heiress with a good Roman fortune. King Athanaric doesn't approve."

"It must be very strange, to be a Gothic commander fighting against Goths," I said thoughtfully.

"They don't seem to mind it," Sebastianus said cheerfully. "They fight against each other all the time, with or without Roman assistance. The Theruingi are preparing for some war now, with the Halani to the northeast. And the Greuthungi to the east of us are at war too. And they say that the Quadi to the west of them are invading Pannonia, and our Lord Valentinian, Augustus of the West, is having to campaign against the Alamanni in Gaul. There's trouble all along the frontier." His cheerfulness faded and he sat silent for a moment, looking grim. Daphne still sang in the background, a witty little song about a shepherdess; but Sebastianus suddenly reminded me of the Alexandrians, waiting for their archbishop to die and the troops to come.

After a moment he shook himself. "Still, barbarians are barbarians and Romans are Romans, and the latter always win wars against the former. Though it's good to be prepared. I hope you can do something with that hospital at Novidunum."

"I'm no Asklepios," I said, "but I'll try."

Novidunum is one of the larger fortresses on the lower Danube. It's at the head of the Danube delta, about fifty miles from Histria and sixty from Tomis, on the Euxine. The camp is set on a bluff, overlooking the flat countryside for miles around. The walls of the fort frown down on the brown flood of the river, forbidding the barbarians entry to Roman lands, but in fact Novidunum is as much a trading post as it is a fortress. Its main business is collecting duties on trade. Plenty of boats cross the river, taking gold, spices, silk, and crafted work into Gothic Dacia and taking slaves and a few trinkets out. It also has a hospital, which is supposed to care for all the troops in Scythia.

I arrived in Novidunum in a two-wheeled cart with a mixed load of papers and wine sent from Marcianopolis. It was my first experience of the imperial posts, and it was an unimpressive one, jolting along, sitting on top of my traveling case. The cart got fresh horses every twelve miles, but the passenger had no chance to get down, stretch her legs, and find something to eat. I arrived at the fortress very tired and hungry. I climbed down from my trunk and stood on the blessedly firm earth, one hand on my case. I looked around. If Marcianopolis had been barbaric, Novidunum was the end of the earth. Within the stone walls of the fortress was a Gothic town: thatched houses of stone, stucco, and timber; cows staring from sheds beside them. Even the barracks looked un-Roman, despite their neat, legionary squares. They were thatched rather than tiled, and their doors were decorated with the ever-present legionary emblems but were draped as well with arms captured from the Goths and with the skins and heads of wild animals. In the center of the camp was a taller building, entirely of stone, with a tiled roof. I supposed that that was the camp headquarters, the presidium. Where was the hospital?

"Novidunum," said the cart driver, in case I hadn't noticed. "Beyond here there's nothing but barbarians."

"I ought to see the tribune of the camp," I said, thinking aloud. "Where can I leave my trunk?"

The driver spat. He had a low opinion of foreign eunuchs cluttering up the post, and had not said much during the journey. "Where are you staying?"

"The hospital."

"I'll drop it there for you. Don't worry, nobody's likely to steal anything from *there*. No one goes there unless they have to."

With that he shook the reins and drove off, leaving me staggering.

A few off-duty troops had come to the posting station to see the cart arrive: they stared curiously. I gave a feeble smile and said that I must see the tribune of the camp, and they stared harder. One of them offered to show me to the presidium.

The camp tribune was called Valerius; he was an older man, an Illyrian from a family of professional soldiers. His scribe showed me in to him as soon as I appeared, and when I said who I was, he stared. "I'd been told we'd have a new chief physician, a very learned Alexandrian," he said. "But I thought you would be older and, umm, that is . . ."

"You weren't expecting a eunuch," I said. "Well, it's not what I'd have chosen myself, if I'd been consulted."

He didn't laugh, only looked surprised. "Yes, well, the present chief physician — that is, the former chief — must be twice your age. It's, umm, awkward. He isn't happy. But I suppose the most distinguished Sebastianus knows what he's doing. When is His Honor coming back north, did he say?"

I handed him some letters from Sebastianus. He glanced through them, then looked uncertainly back at me. "And you really are in charge of the hospital, then? His Excellency says that . . . well, you really are in charge. I, umm, suppose you'll want a house."

"I don't need a whole house. I can manage with a room, provided it's private — or I could stay at the hospital."

"I should think you'll want a house," Valerius repeated, but he shrugged. "Well, leave it for now. I had better show you to the hospital."

The hospital was in the town, outside the main body of the camp. It was an attractive building, an open square of stone and stucco, thatched, with a covered colonnade along the inside. The hollow of the square was filled by a garden of medicinal plants. When Valerius and I arrived we found three men standing in this garden examining my trunk, which had been deposited in lonely splendor beside the well. They all looked up and stared hard as we approached. Two of the men were of middle age, and might have been brothers: they were both dark and grizzled, thin and wiry, with heavy brows and bad teeth. The third was younger, a couple of years older than myself, with light brown hair and a beard; he smiled as I approached. The other two scowled.

"My dear Xanthos," said Valerius nervously to one of the dark men; "esteemed Diokles," to the other; "Arbetio," to the last. "This is, umm, your new colleague, Chariton of Alexandria."

"Of Ephesus, actually," I said, and smiled at all three. "But I trained in Alexandria. I am delighted to make your acquaintance."

There was a moment of icy silence. The two older men were now frankly glaring. Valerius coughed, said that he had to examine Sebastianus' letters, and retreated to the presidium.

"Well," I said, "could I perhaps see the hospital?"

The senior doctor, Xanthos, grunted. The younger man, Arbetio, smiled nervously. "What about this, Your Wisdom?" he asked, indicating the trunk.

"Is there some room I could have here, at least for the time being?"

"Oh, yes, there's lots of space. I'll take it — by Teutones, it's heavy!"

"It has all my books in it. If it's safe here, you could have a couple of slaves move it later."

"Arbetio's a slave," said Xanthos. He had a rough voice, deeper than one would expect from such a thin man. "He can take it."

"He'll need some help. I have a lot of books." I took one end of the case, since the other two men were now glaring with disdain. Arbetio took the other end, and we carried it into the hospital.

The hospital had a long ward room down the back part of the square, the east side, with beds for forty patients. There were another ten beds on the north side, and a kitchen; the south had some operating rooms, storerooms, and the like. But there were only six patients in the ward. Two were recovering from amputations; one had a stab wound in the shoulder, which was infected; one was a case of smallpox, off by himself at one end; the other two had fevers. But they were all in a bad way. The fever cases in particular were extremely pale and lethargic, and when I examined them, I saw why. They had been bled white.

I had never truly appreciated the wisdom of Hippocrates until I saw the way medicine was practiced at Novidunum. Hippocrates says that doctors must work with nature to effect a cure, only assisting the body in its own efforts to heal itself, never trying extreme and violent remedies unless everything else has failed. Xanthos and Diokles were ignorant, brutal, and incompetent butchers, and the suffering they inflicted on their patients was enough to turn my stomach. They had not the least idea of hygiene. The water for cleaning in the hospital came from a stone trough set against the side of the building to catch the rain. It was green with slime, and the camp horses drank from it. Xanthos and Diokles would use this water to wash the patients' infected wounds, and the wounds would fill with worms. "But rainwater is pure!" Xanthos told me when I objected to this. "It's pure when it falls, but it becomes rotten very quickly on standing!" I told him. "You should use boiled water and a cleansing solution with vinegar on wounds, and pure well water or spring water even for cleaning the rooms!" "We've been using that water since the hospital was built," sneered Xanthos. "But of course Your Wisdom knows better than army doctors of years' seniority." "It's not just my idea; Hippocrates recommends it!" I said. "Book-learning!" said Xanthos with deep contempt.

Besides knowing nothing of hygiene, Xanthos and Diokles were very free with their knives, and bled patients who were ill with anything from mild enteritis to lockjaw, bled them repeatedly until they were quite white, bled them to death. And they also liked dosing with hellebore after the bleeding — a course of treatment calculated to kill anyone, since the hellebore purges whatever the bleeding misses, and leaves the patient a dried-up husk. When I told them how dangerous this course of treatment seemed to me, they just sneered at my book-learning again. They had both learned the art of healing from Xanthos' father, who had been the previous chief physician of the camp. They did things the way they had always done them, and that was the right way to do them, and if the patient died, well, it just went to show that he was feeble and would have died soon anyway. On my first day I gave up trying to conciliate either of them. They despised me because I was foreign, a eunuch, young, and overeducated; I despised them because of their travesty of the art of healing. Xanthos in particular was difficult: brutal and superstitious, and always in the way. Diokles did not in fact spend much time at Novidunum; he had private patients in Histria, and only spent the odd week back at the camp.

Arbetio was another matter. He was a very clever surgeon. The other two had bought him to help them out after seeing him practice dentistry with his previous master, a peddler. They worked him very hard, giving him all the messy jobs, so that he ate, slept, and lived at the hospital and had almost no time for himself. He was not their personal slave; he'd been paid for out of camp funds. That didn't stop them from sending him out on personal errands, though, and generally treating him as though he were one of the camp servants, born to chop wood and cook. This was doubly deplorable because he was a better doctor than either of them and genuinely loved the art. He was literate and intelligent; he had clever hands and a fine instinct for correct treatment that not even Xanthos and Diokles had been able to debase, and, unlike the other two, he was eager to learn. As soon as he was certain that I genuinely did know more than Xanthos and Diokles, he was my firm friend and ally. The fact that I treated him with more respect had very little to do with it. I was glad of his support. I needed an ally, even a junior and servile one. I made a lot of changes at that hospital.

I realized within a week that my plan of staying at the hospital was impossible. I had no privacy there. There was nowhere that I could wash without being watched, and people kept coming into my room, wanting things, even when I was asleep. So I handed Valerius another piece of my mother's jewelry (a pearl necklace that fetched sixty-five *solidi*), and I bought a house. Valerius owned it, and he let me have it cheap. It was a pleasant house, fairly standard for the camp, which meant it was a mixture of Roman and barbarian that would have been gaped at anywhere else. It had a large kitchen in the center, with a loft over it where the slaves slept, and two other rooms, one on either side of the main one. The kitchen had an oven, which provided heat during the winter. The house was near the hospital, and had a cowshed and garden. (I added a bathhouse after the first winter, so that I could wash in comfort rather than shiver over a basin in my room.)

Then I had to buy two slaves to keep the house for me. Slaves are cheap on the frontier. I paid twelve *solidi* for Sueridus, who was a man about my own age, a Theruingian Goth by birth, good with horses, fair at gardening, strong enough to do all heavy work; for Raedagunda, a housekeeper and a good cook who was fifteen when I bought her, I paid ten *solidi* — less than what I later paid for my horse. In Ephesus or Alexandria I would have paid three times as much. But most slaves in the great cities are born slaves, and very few are ever sold. It's different on the frontier. Sueridus had been captured when he was twelve in Valens' campaign against the Theruingi. Raedagunda had been sold to a trader by her parents when she was seven, because they needed a new plow ox and some money to restore what the campaign had destroyed. There are thousands of Gothic slaves with similar histories. I suppose my Maia's father had once been like Sueridus — he'd come from Scythia too.

I got on quite well with my slaves, except that they thought that I was a sorcerer. They thought this first because I was a eunuch, and they accounted such sexual mutilation a very powerful charm. Second, I brewed drugs in the kitchen, planted herbs in the garden, and did the occasional dissection in the cowshed: all clearly sorcerous practices. They also thought that I had some distinctive sorcerous marking, perhaps a tail, which I did not want them to see — this because I insisted on bathing and dressing myself behind locked doors. They never, so far as I knew, tried to observe this supposed tail. Perhaps they were afraid I would curse them. However, Goths do not despise sorcerers the way Romans do, so my household remained friendly toward me, and even, I discovered, boasted of my magical powers in the marketplace. Which was just as well, because I had quite enough trouble at the hospital without having to worry about things at home.

The hospital had problems other than the incompetence of its doctors. Perhaps because of its systems of treatment, it was much dreaded by the troops. If a man up the river fell ill, he and his friends kept it secret as long as they could. So a man would come down with a fever, and instead of receiving treatment, he kept on at his work as long as he could stand; when he couldn't stand and was found in bed burning and vomiting, he was packed into a little supply boat with a load of chickens or wheat, without receiving any sort of nursing, and sent downriver, sometimes for a two- or three-day journey; and if he was somehow still alive when he arrived at Novidunum, Xanthos and Diokles would kill him. The soldiers also tried to treat for themselves any wounds they received in fighting with the barbarians (or among themselves), and this was even worse than their "treatment" of fevers. They would tie tourniquets very tightly around the affected part to stop the bleeding, and pack the injuries with moss and spiderwebs and magic charms composed of bits of animals, and the inevitable result was that the wounds became gangrenous. When the patients arrived in Novidunum, if they were lucky they had to have an arm or leg amputated, and if they were unlucky they died, usually of injuries from which they could have recovered easily if they had received proper treatment.

The third class of problems had to do with money. The regional troops are not funded, paid, or privileged as well as the field armies, and there was a shortage of funds for anything other than pay, and that of course included the hospital. There were no regular attendants when I arrived; instead, the troops stationed at the fort worked at the hospital on a rota. The hospital duties were hated by all of them, since they found the work slavish and were afraid of catching something, so it was felt to be fair to have all of the men taking their turn. I can think of no better way to insure that if there is some serious disease about, everyone in the whole Scythian army is exposed to it. It also meant that the standard of nursing was very low, since no one bothered to learn any standard procedures for a one-week tour of duty. Moreover, there was no money for drugs. Xanthos and Diokles grew a few of the commonest medicinal herbs in the hospital garden — hellebore, of course, and wormwood, and hemlock and foxglove and the like — but apart from that, there was nothing. They had never heard of opium, let alone some of the more exotic Indian herbs I'd been accustomed to use in Alexandria. Arbetio had to perform his amputations on conscious patients, as his learned chiefs didn't even know the use of mandragora as a general anesthetic. I went through my copy of Dioskourides and worked out a number of substitutes for the herbs I was accustomed to — ivy juice instead of cedar oil as an antiseptic; nightshade instead of melilot for earache — but I couldn't find any substitute for opium except hellebore. Now hellebore is all very well; it is a powerful narcotic, and does dull pain. But it is also a powerful purgative, and to give it to the old, the young, or those weakened with disease can be fatal. But giving a patient nothing for his pain can be fatal too, since the pain exhausts him and makes him sick. Opium, a narcotic that is not a purgative, is the perfect solution, and in Egypt it's cheap and so common that some of the peasants eat it for pleasure, as we drink wine. But there was no authority that could order opium in quantity from Egypt and pay for the shipping of it.

After I'd been at Novidunum for a couple of weeks, I sat down at the kitchen table in my new house one evening and thought about what I should do. I'd had a couple of futile shouting matches with Xanthos that day, and one with Diokles; I'd seen another man die who should have lived, and I was angry. Sebastianus had put me in charge of the hospital, trusting in Athanaric's recommendation and in my Alexandrian qualifications. But Valerius refused to support me in any of my proposed changes. I would tell Xanthos not to bleed a patient; he would sneer, then bleed the man behind my back. If I complained, Valerius hummed and fidgeted and concluded that Xanthos and I had different methods. "You have one way of treating patients; the most respected Xanthos has another. We here can, umm, judge of the values of both." If I recommended a new rule, Valerius said that he would think about it. He was suspicious of change, and Xanthos was an old friend of his. If I was do to any good at all, I had to put Sebastianus' support to the test, and get a clear declaration that I was in charge and could reorganize things as I liked. That would certainly cause a lot of resentment, but the present system was impossible. It was killing and maiming the troops it was meant to help.

And it couldn't be reformed gently from within; there was too much wrong. I would write to Sebastianus with a list of concrete recommendations and a plea for help in implementing them. If he helped, good; if not — well, then I would have to see. I could always go to Constantinople.

The first thing to do must be to establish a good system of hygiene. Well water for washing floors and linen, cleansing solutions and boiled water for injuries, and the place cleaned at least once a day. To do this without Xanthos' cooperation would mean changing the system used for hospital attendants, which I wanted to do anyway. I determined that the best system of recruitment would be to take on men who were former patients — the cripples and amputees. These men had an insecure and unhappy position in the army. The tribunes of some forts thought it most important to keep up the front-line strength, and they dropped cripples from the rolls, turning them out to beg. At other forts they were kept on at half-pay, doing menial tasks while their officers kept the other half of their pay in return for this favor. To use them in the hospitals wouldn't cost the state a copper *drachma*, and would give me a group of attendants that I could train into what I wanted.

The second thing was to curb Xanthos' and Diokles' blood lust. I would prefer to get rid of them both, especially Xanthos, but that was beyond my authority. It would have to suffice to get a declaration from Sebastianus, and from Valerius the tribune, that they were not to bleed or dose patients without my consent. That would be humiliating for them, but it couldn't be helped. If they wouldn't agree to that, perhaps Sebastianus could transfer them somewhere else; I wouldn't have them butchering men before my eyes. Come to that, I ought to establish a rule that Arbetio should perform only medical duties. It shouldn't be too hard: it was what he'd been bought for.

The third thing would probably have to wait until the end of the winter. I would have to go and talk to the troops upriver. I had to convince them of the dangers of tourniquets, give them instructions for treating the milder fevers on the spot, and tell them when to send someone to Novidunum. If, as Sebastianus had said, there was plague further to the west, it would also be a good idea to set up some mechanisms for isolating plague cases and purifying the camps.

I would have to find someone to get me opium and a few other drugs, too — Thorion could probably buy them for me in the capital, if he was willing. But I could afford to leave that for the moment.

So I went to my room at the back of the house (I'd been sitting in the kitchen, as it was early November and the rest of the house was already cold) and fetched some papyrus and a pen. "Chariton of Ephesus to the Most Excellent Duke Sebastianus," I wrote. "Esteemed Lord, very many greetings." Then I stared at the papyrus, wondering how I could best convince the duke to do what I wanted. I thought of him reclining on his couch in Marcianopolis, enjoying his concubine and his Chian wine. But that was an inaccurate picture: at Novidunum, Sebastianus was greatly admired for his energy and efficiency in his command. I would do better to be energetic, efficient, and straightforward myself.

I wrote him a very long letter, sealed it, and sent it off with the first courier. A week later Sebastianus himself appeared at the fort. I was in the hospital, cauterizing a wound, when he arrived. It was the second time I'd had to do this to the same patient. The injury, on the man's shoulder, had been gangrenous when I had arrived. I'd dosed the patient with mandragora (I had a good supply of this drug, and could obtain more, as I'd found it growing wild not far from the fort) and cauterized the rot, then cleaned and bandaged the wound. It had stayed clean for a few days, then suddenly taken the rot again. I was surprised, and asked the patient about it; he told me that Xanthos had cleaned it for him once when I was busy. Cleaned it with that damned rot-water. I told him that if Xanthos tried to do that again, he should scream for help, and failing that, kill the man the way he'd kill a deadly snake. I dosed the poor man again and heated the irons, hoping that I could stop the infection; if it went any deeper it would certainly kill him, and as it was he'd lose much of the strength of the arm. I'd had to use the mandragora very lightly, too, because of the patient's weakened state, and he began to wake up in the middle of the operation, giving the most heart-rending whimpers of pain. I had to stop and have him held down. I hate cauterizing: using red-hot iron on a patient makes me feel like a torturer.

I was just in the middle of this task when one of the staff messengers came in and said, "His Excellency Duke Sebastianus wishes to speak with all the doctors."

I sent Arbetio, who was helping me, up to headquarters at once, and finished the job. I didn't know where Xanthos was; Diokles was down in Histria lining his pockets.

When I had the patient settled again, I took off the butcher's apron I wore for these jobs and went straight up to the presidium. I knew the way to Valerius' office by heart now; I'd been there often enough, complaining. The dusty little antechamber, the legionary emblems on the door, the office itself with its desk of pine, its bearskin rug, and its red-covered couch with the dragon-claw feet . . . Sebastianus was sitting not on the couch but at the tribune's desk, tapping his fingers with impatience. Xanthos was standing nearby, looking smug because I'd kept the duke waiting; Arbetio and the tribune Valerius just looked uncomfortable. I was angry enough not to care. Anger like this, steady, burning anger that churns unceasingly in the stomach, was something I was not very familiar with. I wanted very much to get rid of it.

"Your Excellency," I said, "I am sorry to have kept you waiting. I had a patient."

"So I've been told," said Sebastianus. He glanced round at the others.

"Yes, and the operation should have been unnecessary," I went on, not giving the duke a chance to open the meeting peacefully. "The wound was reinfected by cleansing procedures I expressly forbade. I told the poor patient that if anyone tries to clean his injury like that again, he ought to kill them as he would a snake."

Xanthos gave a jump. "You worthless gelding! You and your book-learning! Do you think —"

"Silence!" snapped Sebastianus, and Xanthos fell silent, glaring. Sebastianus sighed and looked at me. "Well," he said. "You have stirred up a hornet's nest, haven't you?"

I bowed slightly. "Your Excellency wanted me to reorganize the hospital."

At this Sebastianus laughed. "Oh Immortal God! So I did. And I meant you to do so. But I thought you'd be able to do it without jumping at your colleagues' throats. And I don't see why you needed to write me such a passionate letter about it. I thought I'd given you the authority already."

"At the moment, Your Prudence, my authority doesn't stretch very far. I can't even recommend one method of treatment and have it stick."

Xanthos looked outraged. "Your Excellency!" he protested. "I have been practicing medicine all my life! I don't see why this . . . this creature should be allowed to overturn all the traditions and procedures that we have always used, all on account of what he's read in some book!"

Valerius was nodding. "Indeed, I think Your Excellency is being too hasty. Let Chariton treat his patients his way, and let Xanthos continue to treat his patients in the old way. That way we can see the advantages of both methods."

"There are no advantages to Xanthos' methods," I said hotly. "If I had half a *solidus* for every patient he and his father must have killed, I could buy all of Novidunum! And he uses his butcher's methods on my patients behind my back. I won't have it; it's a disgrace to the Hippocratic tradition!"

Sebastianus looked at me and laughed. "Behold the ruling passion!" he said. "Very well, you shall have what you want. I'm sorry, Valerius, but I gave Chariton responsibility for the hospital, and he's to keep it. What's the use of importing learned men if you don't listen to their advice? And the Hippocratic school in Alexandria is the best in the world, and carries more weight than the old ways they use here. I like these ideas, Chariton." He picked my letter up from the desk and waved it at us. "Particularly the arrangement for the attendants. I don't want any more men exposed to plagues than I can help. And going upriver and talking to the troops is another excellent plan; I'll see that you get a horse so you can start this winter."

Tenella kallinike! Victory! I could hardly stop myself from shouting, and I smiled at Sebastianus so that I thought my face would crack. "Thank you, Your Excellency. I had one other request as well."

Sebastianus sighed, then eyed Valerius and Xanthos thoughtfully. "If you must. Though that sort of thing causes as many problems as it solves."

"I cannot have my patients interfered with."

Sebastianus nodded resignedly. "Very well. Xanthos, you and your colleagues are to obey the most esteemed Chariton and to follow his instructions on all matters of bloodletting and dosing with strong drugs."

Xanthos went red, then white. "I won't," he said flatly.

"Then I relieve you of your post," said Sebastianus evenly.

Xanthos gasped, tried ineffectively to say something.

"You can think again, if you like. I give you till tomorrow morning to make up your mind," offered Sebastianus. "But you must either follow Chariton's advice or leave the army: I give you no other choice. What about you, fellow — what's your name?"

"Arbetio, Your Prudence," Arbetio said eagerly. "A slave of the legion. I'll be very happy to follow Chariton's advice. I value it highly."

"Good. You're the slave, then, that Chariton wants to confine to medical duties? Another good idea: we have plenty of less valuable slaves for domestic chores. In future, if anyone tells you to do something outside your duties, I order you to disobey him." Arbetio swallowed, stared, and bowed. Sebastianus smiled. "Wasn't there another one?"

"He's in Histria, Excellency," said Valerius.

"In Histria? What's he doing there?"

There was an awkward pause. I said nothing. "Seeing his private patients," Valerius admitted reluctantly.

"Private patients in Histria! That's a long way to go to see them! Tell him from me that any private patients he takes are to be not more than half a day's journey from Novidunum. We don't pay his salary for him to spend all his time down in Histria. Well, I think that's settled, then. Valerius, Chariton, perhaps you would join me for lunch? Though I would appreciate it, Chariton, if you'd go and wash first."

I looked down and saw that my hands were still covered with my patient's blood. "Of course, Duke Sebastianus," I said, still smiling. "Thank you."

Things went smoothly after that. Xanthos swallowed his pride and stayed on, and though it was plain he hated me, I had no more trouble with him about patients. Diokles was equally angry when he got back from Histria, but he didn't cause any trouble for me, only vowed to return to his private patients whenever he wanted, and damn the duke. Arbetio was quite touchingly grateful.

I collected my band of attendants and trained them in cleaning procedures and basic nursing, and had the immense pleasure of seeing the changes pay off at once and dramatically in our patients' rate of recovery. I also sent a letter to Thorion. I sent it by state courier — as an army doctor writing to an imperial official I was able to do this. I'd written him just before I left Alexandria, telling him something of what had happened, and now I told him about the fort and begged him to buy some opium for me and send it by the state post, which he should be entitled to do.

In the middle of December, when there were only a few patients to worry about, I went to the camp stables to choose a horse for my first trip up the river. When I turned up, the grooms regarded me contemptuously. The troops disliked me because I was a eunuch and a civilian from a notoriously soft province, and the changes I had made in the hospital had not yet been impressed on them. However, the head of the stables was polite, and showed me the spare horses. He recommended one to me, a sleek little mare. I had a look at her.

"It won't do," I told the stablemaster. "She's broken-winded."

There was a moment's silence, then, "So she is," said the man. "Perhaps you'd care for this one instead?" indicating a bay gelding. I pointed out that it had split a hoof fairly recently, and wouldn't do for a long ride. He recommended another horse, healthy but far too old, judging by its teeth; then another one that was afflicted with the spavins. I turned both down, and suggested a remedy for the spavins. Somebody laughed.

"Do *you* know something about *horses?*" the stablemaster asked incredulously.

"I grew up in the house of a rich man who was crazy about chariot racing," I replied. "Most of my first patients were horses."

My status rose dramatically. The grooms began a discussion of worms, hoof galls, and colic; the stablemaster gave me a decent mount; the veterinary appeared out of nowhere and began talking about spavins and the rampass; and finally we all went off to the camp tavern and discussed equine disorders and chariot racing. The troops in Novidunum were inclined to the belief that no one who could treat horses could be all bad.

Riding, though, was another matter. I had never sat on a horse in my life. I couldn't control it. When I started out upriver for the next fort with a party of soldiers and some supplies, the soldiers had to keep rescuing me from snowdrifts when my mount tried to go back to its nice warm stall. Even when they put me on a lead rein, like a child, I had difficulty. Riding uses muscles I didn't know existed, pounds them the way a cook pounds meat. And it was bitterly cold — I hadn't dreamed it could be so cold. The Danube delta was beginning to freeze, and chunks of ice floated on the dark river, turning slowly. The sky was white, and the earth was white with snow; the clumps of woodland were heaped with the stuff. The local people stayed sensibly by their warm fires; wolves came sniffing up to the very doors at night, leaving their footprints icy on the snow. It had snowed sometimes in Ephesus, but such snows always melted quickly, gone within a day or two. In Scythia the snows piled up, one on top of another, till the whole world seemed to be made of nothing else. I'd swallowed my civilized prejudices and bought two pairs of trousers from a fort trader, together with some stockings and the loose boots they wear on the frontier, and then I had had to go back and buy a fur cloak, since my old ones, though fine for Egypt, were woefully thin for a Scythian winter. Even so I shivered when I started off up the river, and felt chilled through before we'd ridden a mile. I arrived in the next camp feeling exhausted, cold, contemptible, and very sore.

But contemptible or not, I went on with my lecture to the troops, showing them a couple of their cripples and explaining the evils of tourniquets. I set up a system for treating the milder fevers on the spot. I checked the arrangements for sanitation — perfectly adequate; the army always does that well — and for drinking water, and gave the local tribune instructions on what to do about contagious diseases. I felt very pleased with myself when I went on to the next fort.

I didn't manage to visit all the camps that winter. It took me until the end of the next year to do that. But even by the spring the troops had heard of me and would listen to me. I might as well have been talking to the wind for all the notice they took of me at first, but my changes at the hospital produced spectacular results. Xanthos predicted that patient after patient would die from my methods, and patient after patient recovered. Not all of them, of course — disease is a far more deadly enemy than the barbarians, and the best doctor can't cure lockjaw or blood poisoning. But the troops were in fact an ideal group of patients: young to middle-aged, well-fed, active men, inherently better able to recover from an illness than the miscellaneous assortment of elderly and impoverished Alexandrians I'd treated before. More of them recovered than died, for the first time in the history of that sorry hospital. Xanthos began to mutter darkly about sorcery. Sebastianus was delighted.

Thorion was not. That first January, when I returned from my trip up the river, I discovered that he had sent me a letter by the imperial courier. It was waiting for me on my writing desk at home. It was closed with several seals, and I could only hope that they were as unbroken as they appeared to be, because, though on the outside it was addressed to "Chariton the Doctor, Novidunum," on the inside it began, "Theodoros to his sister Charis, many greetings."

"Have you gone out of your mind?" Thorion asked.

I'm sorry I ever agreed to your schemes. Going to Alexandria and studying medicine for a few years was bad enough, but it did keep you out of

Festinus' way, and I knew you'd enjoy it. But you said you'd come back! Charition, it's been almost four years; I have my own household now, and I can introduce you among civilized people without being ashamed of what I did. I'm strong enough now that Festinus can't touch us. My friend Kyrillos is here at Constantinople, he's an assessor and looks set to do well. He'd marry you quite happily; he asks about you sometimes, and I give him ambiguous answers about how I have news that you're well. But, by Artemis the Great! nobody on earth would marry you if they knew you'd been an army doctor. The longer this goes on, the harder it will be to explain where you've been all this while. And soon you'll be past marriageable age. Come to Constantinople at once. I can't believe you're doing this. I've never heard of a woman acting so shamelessly. Do you mean to stay a eunuch all your life? No children, no man? That's only half a life. It's unnatural.

The letter hurt. I didn't know how to answer it. I burned it and scattered the ashes, afraid that someone would read it, but the words stayed in my memory and stung. Now at last Thorion knew what had happened and saw the gap between what I had been and what I was, and so between him and me — a gap now as wide as the Danube. But he still thought I could recross it and go back. How could I? I'd been private physician to two archbishops of Alexandria, I was chief doctor of the fortress of Novidunum, I'd fought for my practice and won. Oh, to be sure, married women have more freedom than young girls, but still a noblewoman is bound by an iron propriety to do no serious business in the world.

A week after receiving this letter, I dreamed that I was in Ephesus. I was dressed in my Thracian doctor's clothes, trousers and all, but I was standing outside the front of my father's house. I had a patient to see there, I sensed. I went in, walking through the First Court and then the Charioteer Room. No one was about, but I heard wailing. I went into my father's bedroom, and there he lay, pale, drawn, and still. I touched his forehead, and it was cold. A bad sign, I thought, and looked in my bag for some opium. "I don't want it," Father said. "I don't want to live. I will trade this world for Heaven. My son hates me and my daughter is gone." "I'm not gone," I said. "Here I am; I can cure you." At this the color came back into his face. He smiled radiantly, sitting up; he embraced me. For a moment I felt deliriously happy; like Asklepios, I could call back the dead. Then his arms tightened around me. I couldn't breathe. I began to struggle; when I pulled my head back I looked at his face, and it wasn't Father anymore, it was Festinus, baring his teeth in a smile. I tried to cry out, and he put his mouth over mine; I was suffocating, helpless. He pulled my short tunic off my shoulders and pushed me down on the bed; he pulled a pillow over my face to choke me; somewhere I heard people singing a marriage hymn. I woke up screaming.

Someone banged at my door. "Who is it?" I asked, sitting up in bed and shivering, not knowing where I was. It was bitterly cold; the windowsill was white with ice, and the moonlight crept through the shutters.

"It's me, master." The voice was my slave's, Raedagunda's. "Are you all right?"

"Oh. Yes. Just a nightmare."

I heard Raedagunda's footsteps going back to the loft where she slept. I was still shaking. Sleep was impossible, so I got up and dressed, putting on my fur cloak against the cold. I sat down at my writing desk and answered Thorion's letter.

"To my dear brother Theodoros, many greetings," I wrote.

Yes, I do mean to stay a eunuch doctor all my life. Thorion, dearest, try to understand. I love the art more than anything on earth. And I'm good at it. It would kill me to be confined to people's idea of what's proper, or I'd kill myself. I couldn't bear it, I'd suffocate. Perhaps this is only half a life, but it's the half I prefer. Don't expose me. You know that if you do, you'll have me on your hands for the rest of my life. You said yourself no one would marry me if they knew, and what would be the point of my sitting in your house, disgraced, unmarried, and without my career? If you can't forgive me, tell people I'm dead, and forget me as if it were true.

I sealed it very carefully, terrified that someone would read it, then went back to bed. Before I went to sleep I realized I'd have to find some other way to get the opium.

In the end I wrote to Athanaric about the drugs. He had seemed interested in the well-being of the troops on the frontier, and I thought he quite liked me, so he might be willing to arrange to have the drugs sent from Alexandria. He could certainly license Philon to send them in the state post. I wrote him a very respectful letter, begging him to arrange for Philon to buy me the opium and a few other simples, and I enclosed a sardonyx ring to pay for them; I also enclosed a letter to Philon explaining the situation. I sent this letter and the letter to Thorion by imperial courier to Constantinople. Then I threw myself into my work and tried not to worry about it.

The first long winter passed, and the earth renewed itself with flowers. The whole delta seemed to be a mass of purple, white, and gold; violets flowered by every stone, the bushes were white with hawthorn, and every stretch of open land shone with buttercups. I had never seen so many birds: ducks and herons, hoopoes, swallows, cuckoos, swans, crows, and hundreds of others whose names I didn't know. Storks nested on the roof of the presidium. More temperate lands have a temperate spring, but the Thracian season was a bacchanalian revel. It was impossible not to be happy. And on one radiant morning in late May, Athanaric walked into the main ward of the hospital while I was doing my rounds.

He swaggered in, carrying a heavy pair of saddlebags slung over one shoulder. "Chariton of Ephesus!" he shouted down the building; and when I turned from examining my patient, he swung the saddlebags round in the air and tossed them to me. "There're the drugs Your Grace requested."

I caught them and staggered. I looked at the bags, then looked at Athanaric, who stood with his thumb hitched through his sword belt, grinning. "Bless you!" I said fervently, and began undoing the straps. There indeed they were: everything I'd asked for, and even some opium-poppy seeds, all ready to be planted; a thick letter from Philon too. I could have kissed Athanaric. I stood there and gloated.

"Your friend Philon packed them up for you," said Athanaric. "He says there's some change left from the sale of that ring. I told him to keep it, and gave him a license to use the post to send more."

"Bless you," I said again, and beamed at Athanaric. He looked very well. The trousers no longer seemed so barbaric now that I was wearing some myself, and his face was bright from the wind and with his smile. "What are you doing here?" I asked him. "— Your Excellency," I added hurriedly: the last thing I wanted was to offend him, after the favor he had just done me. "Do you have time to stay for dinner with me?"

He grinned again. "No time for dinner, no. I'm taking a message from the court to Sirmium; I just came through Novidunum to deliver those. Some other time, perhaps? I should be in Thrace for a while now; I've been sent to rearrange the posts along the frontier."

"You'll let me buy you a drink, at least?"

"There's a thought." He glanced round the hospital. "You don't seem very busy." Most of the beds were empty.

"It's the weather," I told him. "Anyone who's going to die does so in the winter, and I can't say I blame them. It would be too painful to leave the world when it looks like this."

We went to the camp's tavern, and I bought a flask of the finest wine they had, a rather sticky, strong red brought up the coast from the province of Europa. It was the middle of the morning, and quite a few of the men who were off duty were sitting about having something to drink; there was nowhere for us to sit. Athanaric whistled, and everyone looked at him. "I am Athanaric, the son of Ermaneric of Sardica," he announced. "I need somewhere to sit with my friend."

Immediately all the Goths in the tavern scrambled to their feet, grunting and bowing. Athanaric took a seat at the best table, and I put the flask of wine down, then started to fetch the water. But I didn't need to. The tavern-keeper rushed over with a flask of fresh water and his finest mixing bowl; he rushed off and came back with a pair of his own Egyptian glass drinking cups. He bowed to Athanaric and said something in Gothic; Athanaric responded in the same language and dismissed him with a wave of the hand. He looked at me and laughed. "Barbarian royalty," he stated.

"I heard about your uncle," I said. In fact, since coming to Novidunum I'd heard quite a bit about him; many of the soldiers were Theruingian Goths, and all the rest had fought against King Athanaric's people.

"Everybody's heard of him in this part of the world." Athanaric poured the wine and some of the water into the mixing bowl, and I tipped the mixture into his cup. "That's one of the reasons I enjoy visiting the region. What does Your Grace think of Thrace?"

"I like it," I said, finding to my surprise that this was true. Partly it was just that the countryside was so beautiful just now, in the spring. But I liked the open space around me, after the dirt and crowding of Alexandria; I liked the responsibility of the hospital, felt pleasure and pride whenever I thought about what I was doing with it. I liked being master of my own house and respected in the fort. I was even starting to like riding, now that my muscles were getting used to it and it wasn't so cold. "In many ways I like it as much as Alexandria."

"Do you indeed!" said Athanaric. "Well, you seem to have fitted yourself in, all right. The grooms at the posting station told me that you were the cleverest doctor in Thrace, and could cure colic and the mange. I wouldn't have thought it of such a perfect Alexandrian. And you are certainly doing your job. Sebastianus thinks you must be a lineal descendant of Asklepios. He says you cure the sick like a miracle worker."

"That's not true," I told him. "We can't cure everyone, and the cures we do have are the result of Hippocratic medicine, not miracles."

He grinned. "Of course. How could I ignore the immortal Hippocrates?" He raised his cup. "I'm pleased it's all worked out so well. My friend Sebastianus is happy, the troops are well looked after, and even you are not displeased. Much health!"

"Much health!" I returned. "But I will need a steady supply of the opium. The seeds may not grow here, and even if they do, it will take time to establish a supply from them."

"Send money to your friend, and I'll see that the posts take it."

"Next time you're in Novidunum, you'll have to come to dinner," I told him happily.

"So you can be sure that, as your guest-friend, I've got to help you? Very well. But I'd do it anyway, you know: I want the men to be treated well."

"You can give me the news, too," I told him, smiling.

He gave me a bit of it before leaving. It seemed that Archbishop Peter was safely at Rome, enjoying the hospitality of the Roman archbishop, Damasus. The western church was inclined to the Nicene theology, and the western emperor disinclined to interfere with it: Peter was safe as he would not have been anywhere in the East. His Arian rival, Lucius, had tired of persecuting Alexandrian Nicenes and gone off to the Nitrian desert to flog monks. Philon and his family were well; yes, Athanaric had seen them himself; he had brought them my letter in person after delivering some messages to the prefect. Theogenes had taken his examination and gone back to Antioch with Theophila, but Philon had another student. "I like your Philon," Athanaric declared, finishing the wine. "He's a brilliant doctor, I suppose?"

"The best in Alexandria," I said warmly.

"Well, he would be, wouldn't he? To teach you." Athanaric put down his cup and rose. "I'm off to Sirmium, then! *Ave atque vale*, as they say. I'll see you next time I pass through Novidunum."

He went out of the tavern directly to the posting station and jumped on a horse. It was standing ready saddled for him, with another set of saddlebags over its shoulders. He turned it, waved, and rode off splendidly, dashing through the fort at full gallop, sending the pigeons and chickens flying in a scatter of wings. Down the hill, out the gate, and onto the road. Only couriers ride like that: gallop, gallop, gallop, twelve miles in an hour or less to the next posting station; off one horse and onto the next, and gallop, gallop, gallop again. It must be four hundred miles from Novidunum to Sirmium in the West, and Athanaric would do it in a few days.

I sighed, watching him leave, then went back to my work. I could find it in my heart to wish him back in Novidunum soon.

I got another two letters from Thorion in the next week. The first had been written some time before but sent by ship and delayed during bad weather. It was indiscreet, but did not have the open confession in its address that had been so frightening in the last one. "What do you mean, telling me to say you're dead?" he asked. "I wish you would come away from that godforsaken spot on the edge of the world, but I can't do anything about it if you won't, and I'm not going to turn my back on you. But do come to your senses, Charition, please! You can't go on as you are now. Someone's bound to find out. What's wrong with a normal life, what do you mean, 'suffocate'? I don't understand you. My house is yours when you change your mind."

The other letter had been written in April, and was far less cheerful. "I've just heard that Father's dead," Thorion wrote in it. "He died of a pleurisy during the winter; I've only just heard. Johannes is managing the estates now, till I can come live on them. But I can't go home yet, and there's no point. I feel wretched; I should have gone home before. He was very unhappy these last years, with you gone and me in Constantinople and half his horses sold. I should kill that Festinus, it's all his fault. Father was a good man; he couldn't help being a coward. I wish you could be with me, Charition."

I remembered my dream. But that seemed to cheat grief, to picture my father dead. I tried for another memory, and saw him scrabbling at the floor, pleading his innocence of treason to Festinus. But as Thorion had said, Father couldn't help being a coward: it was unfair to remember him like that. We had never been close, but he had been kind and affectionate. At last I thought of him coming home after presiding over some public festival, taking off his gilded laurel wreath and throwing it into the air, whooping with pleasure because his chariot had won the race, hugging me and Thorion and Maia and giving presents to everyone in the house. Then I did cry a little. I cut my hair and put on my black Egyptian cloak in mourning. When people asked me what it was for, I told them an old friend and patron had died. But I didn't mention my father's name. It had been necessary in Alexandria to have a story to explain myself, but it was not necessary now, and it was better to bury the past. I had abandoned my father — but if I had not run away, I still wouldn't have been with him in his illness. I would have been with Festinus, suffering God knows what while he governed some distant province. Despite what Sebastianus thought, I was no Asklepios. Even in my dream I had been unable to heal the dead.

It was only a month or so later that I saw Athanaric again. I was at a camp two days' ride up the river, doing my lecture on tourniquets. This camp was quite small: a watchtower with a half-dozen men to guard it. The men sat at the foot of the tower in the open air and gaped at me while I talked to them. It was still early in the morning, but already the sun was hot; the shade of the woods was full of mosquitoes, and no one was paying much attention. Then suddenly one of the soldiers gave a yell, and Athanaric rode up at a gallop, his cloak tossed over his shoulder and the sun glittering on the hilt of his sword. He pulled the horse to a stop almost on top of us and leaped down. "There you are!" he told me. "Are these all patients, or can you leave them?"

"What is your name?" demanded the decurion of the watchtower officiously, ashamed at having been caught out in his lack of vigilance.

"Athanaric son of Ermaneric of Sardica, *curiosus* of the *agentes in rebus*."

This produced the usual effect; the men all stood up and grunted respectfully. "Do you have a patient for me?" I asked.

He grinned. "Yes. A private patient, if you like. The wife of a rich and powerful man, who'll pay you well if you cure her."

"I'm not supposed to take private patients more than half a day's ride from Novidunum," I said doubtfully. And why was Athanaric riding posthaste to fetch me to somebody's wife? Whose wife? A governor's?

"Sebastianus won't mind this one," he stated, waving aside my objection. "And she's less than a full day's journey from Novidunum."

Not a governor's wife. The governor of Scythia was based at Tomis, twenty miles down the coast from Histria. That was more than a day's journey, unless you used the imperial posts.

"Where?" I asked bluntly, unable to work it out.

"Across the river." Athanaric waved his hand at the brown flood of the Danube and the forests the other side of it. I gaped, and he went on. "It's probably quickest to cross at Novidunum. But we must hurry. Take your own horse from here, but leave it at the next posting station; I want to be there by tomorrow evening. The woman's been ill for a week already, by my reckoning. You have your medical things? Good, let's go."

The next thing I knew I was in the saddle and galloping after Athanaric. I didn't bounce about quite as much as I used to, but I was no courier, and was too hard pressed with keeping up to have time to think about much else.

Gallop, gallop, gallop; change horses; gallop, gallop, gallop. And so to Novidunum by late afternoon, though it was two days away for me at a normal pace on the one horse. I felt jolted to bits. But Athanaric didn't give me time for rest; he dragged me straight down to the river and into a boat, shouting at the boatmen in Gothic to make them hurry. I sat in the back of the boat in a stupor for the first part of the crossing. Then I shook myself and asked, "Whose wife?"

Athanaric gave a jump, as though he'd been thinking of something else. "Lord Fritigern's," he said. "Her name's Amalberga. They say she gave birth to a son just over a week ago, after a difficult labor, and has been ill since — unless she's dead already. If she's not dead and if you can cure her, Fritigern will be very grateful."

"Is he a cousin of yours?"

He glanced at me and smiled. "More or less. It's his wife who's my cousin. She's a remarkable woman; I hope you can help her. But he's one of the chief men among the Theruingi, second only to the king. He's inclined to be friendly to Rome — he's a Christian, and admires Roman law. I'd like to keep him friendly. And I want some information from him."

"So you're now 'inspecting the posts' in Gothic Dacia," I said sourly. "Are there any?"

He laughed. "None. I am moved by pure family feeling to try to help my noble kinsman in his need. But it won't hurt him to talk to me — in fact, I heard that he was asking to talk to me. People are swarming like ants who've had their nest flooded, all up and down the Danube. They say a new race of men has sprung up out of the earth and is sweeping like a blizzard from the high mountains, killing all before it. The king has been fortifying the passes through the mountains to the northeast. His Illustriousness the master of the offices of His Sacred Majesty wants to know what's going on. So I arrive at Fritigern's with a skilled Greek doctor to treat his wife, and hope that Fritigern will be pleased and informative. Does that satisfy Your Grace's scruples?"

"Not really. I don't like being made part of a spying mission. But I will treat the patient, if no one objects to me."

"Why should they object?"

"I'm a foreigner and a eunuch, I've come to spy on them, and I don't even speak their language."

"You speak some Latin, don't you?"

"A little." I'd had to brush up on it since arriving in Scythia; some of the troops spoke nothing else.

"Well, everyone who's anyone among the Goths speaks Latin, and Fritigern and Amalberga speak Greek as well. And you're a mighty sorcerer, whose fame has reached them already. They'll be delighted."

"Oh, by Artemis the Great!"

Athanaric stopped smiling and looked at me rather grimly. "Half Novidunum believes you're a sorcerer. More than half. Some of them are pleased about it, others are afraid. I'd be careful if I were you, Chariton. Sorcery is a dangerous thing to be charged with. There was a man put to death at Carnuntum only last month for cutting up a donkey; he said it was just to stop his hair from falling out, but no one believed him. And he was the nephew of the praetorian prefect, too. And it's rumored that you cut up a man."

I bit my lip. "Who told you that?"

"One of your colleagues at the hospital. An older man, dark, with half an ear missing. I went to Novidunum first, looking for you, and he was very eager to tell me all about your sorcerous practices."

"That's Xanthos," I said, relieved. "He hates me because I supplanted him. Everyone knows that; they won't take him seriously."

"Chariton, your own servants think you're a sorcerer! I don't know whether it's true that you cut up a dead man or not. I know that they do dissections in Alexandria. But you're not in Alexandria now, and people on the frontier don't understand these things."

I said nothing. I had in fact done a dissection on a patient who died of lockjaw. The disease is fairly common on the frontier, and I thought I might understand it better if I knew how it affected the body. I'd done it in a spare room at night and stitched the body up again afterward, then dressed him and had him buried; I'd thought nobody knew. Xanthos must have been spying on me. Athanaric was probably right: it was better to leave such researches to the scholars at the Temple. My dissection had not brought me much knowledge anyway.

Athanaric continued to watch me carefully. "It would be a great pity if I got you away from the rack in Egypt," he said, "only to have you die on it in Thrace."

I sighed and nodded. The boat bumped against the opposite shore and we climbed out. I almost tripped; my legs were still unsteady from the riding. Athanaric, of course, ran up the bank, shouting for horses. I clutched my medical bag and looked around, realizing with a shudder that I was outside the Roman Empire.

It didn't look very different from Novidunum — the same kind of stone and wooden houses, similar Gothic men standing about in trousers. Only there were fewer walls in this trading post, because it was only a trading post and not a fort. The barbarians built no walls against the Romans. I'd never reflected on this before, and it seemed odd: they certainly had reason to fear the Romans. But then, the Romans would only invade to punish them. They didn't want the barbarian lands, and the barbarians did want the Roman ones.

Athanaric came back with two horses, extorted from some Gothic trader or perhaps from a nobleman. We were up and riding into the lands of the Theruingi before I had any more time to think. It was just starting to get dark.

We did rest that night, though I had feared we wouldn't. Athanaric stopped at some little town about an hour after sunset (gallop, gallop, gallop) and went up to the biggest house. We were shown in by the slaves, there was considerable discussion in Gothic, and then we were hospitably treated by the nobleman of the house, who seemed acquainted with Athanaric. The bed was full of bugs, but I was too tired to care.

We proceeded at a more moderate pace the next day, because we had to keep the same horses. Even so, we arrived at Fritigern's settlement well before the evening. It was a town about the size of Novidunum, set in the midst of a broad patch of farmland. In the middle of the town, which was the usual rough thatched stone-and-timber affair, stood a large Roman villa with a tiled roof and Corinthian columns. It looked quite old; the roof of one of the wings had fallen in and been replaced with thatch. Gothic Dacia had been a Roman province once, in the long-ago days of the Good Emperors. Perhaps this villa was a relic of that short occupation.

We were surrounded by a crowd of people from the moment we entered the town, but Athanaric paid no attention to them. He rode straight up to the villa, drew rein, and made a little speech in Gothic; I caught his name and my own, but little more. Some people came out of the villa, then went back in again. Athanaric sat on his horse and waited.

"One thing I didn't tell you," he said suddenly, turning round in the saddle. "The lady Amalberga will have some attendants who'll have been treating her, some women. Don't be too dismissive with them. They don't have doctors here, and all the nursing work is done by women, midwives and wisewomen. Some of the wisewomen are quite well born, and are respected. Don't just assume that they're slaves."

I was astonished. Before I could think of anything to say, the doors of the villa opened again and a man came out, followed by a crowd of armed attendants. He was tall and thin, very fair, with a beard that was almost white; his strong nose was sunburned and his eyes a very pale blue, glasslike. He was dressed in a rich cloak with an imported purple edging, and he wore a gold chain around his neck. The cost of the jewels on his sword hilt could support a family for life.

Athanaric jumped off his horse. "Most excellent Fritigern!" he exclaimed; he went over to the other and they embraced.

Fritigern was pleased to see us. When I was introduced he shook hands with me, and thanked me for coming in faultless Greek. His dear wife, he said, was indeed ill; her attendants had thought at first she might recover, but now they weren't so sure. He could not but be overjoyed to have a Roman doctor for her. My fame had reached across the river, and he had thought of sending for me himself but had been uncertain of how this would be regarded by the Roman authorities. He was most grateful (turning back to Athanaric), most grateful that his noble cousin had seen fit to bring me. Did I need some refreshment before visiting the patient, or would I see her right away? The eyes rested on me for a moment, with an indecipherable expression.

"I would prefer to see the lady immediately," I said, reckoning that I could always eat after starting the treatment.

Fritigern's eyes darkened slightly and he smiled. Apparently I'd said the right thing. He gestured to two of his attendants and barked a command in Gothic, and they escorted me off. As I left, Athanaric was taking Fritigern's arm and starting to ask questions.

Lady Amalberga was in one of the larger rooms at the back of the villa. My escort stood outside the door and knocked; from beyond it came the sound of women arguing shrilly in Gothic. The escort knocked again; one of the women shouted something, then continued arguing. We went in.

The room was magnificent, but dirty. There were rushes across the mosaic of the floor, the brocade coverlet of the bed was stained with blood, and a bowl of vomit stood in the corner beside a full chamberpot, both swarming with flies. A baby was in a cot in the other corner, sleeping. The two women who were arguing stood in the middle of the room. They were both of middle age. One was small and dark, and wore a plain gray woolen gown; the other was tall and fair, in a fine blue cloak and much jewelry. Amalberga lay motionless on the great bed, awake but exhausted. She was a beautiful woman, very blonde, with a gentle face; she was a year or two younger than I. She was extremely pale; her eyes were bright with fever. Her white arms were covered with blood-swollen leeches.

The small dark woman screeched at my escort, and they shouted back, waving at me. I bowed vaguely toward the lady. "I am Chariton of Ephesus," I said slowly in Latin, "a doctor from the camp of Novidunum. The most excellent Athanaric brought me to treat the lady Amalberga."

There was considerable commotion. The small dark woman shouted at the men, and they gobbled in their barbarian tongue. The fair woman in the jewelry stared, then flushed red, then asked in Latin if I would excuse her, but was it true that I was a eunuch? (The Goths have no eunuchs among them.) When I replied that it was, she said that it was most improper for a man to touch the lady Amalberga. The small dark woman gave another screech and started laughing. I found out afterward that she found the whole idea of eunuchs ridiculous, and was convinced from the first that I was a woman.

Suddenly Amalberga herself intervened. "If you can help me," she said in a firm clear voice and good Greek, "I will be grateful."

"I will do my best," I said, and went to examine her. The small woman moved to stop me, but Amalberga prevented her with two sharp words, and she contented herself with hustling the escort out of the room. I went on with the examination.

The lady was not gravely ill, to my relief — if she had been I could have done very little about it. She was feverish and in some pain, but it was nothing from which she couldn't have recovered. But she had lost quite a lot of blood, and the wisewoman, the one in the jewelry, had insisted on "imitating the Romans" and bleeding her, weakening her further. The dark woman, who was a midwife, had the sense to dislike this procedure, and it was this that had caused their argument.

I took all the leeches off, telling the wisewoman as I did so that the Romans who employed frequent bleedings were ignorant quacks — though I tried to be tactful, and praised her own moderation in using leeches rather than the knife. The body has its own wisdom, I said, and when the patient is already losing blood, the doctor must never force out any more. The wisewoman listened carefully, ashamed rather than angry; I found out afterward that like many well-born Goths, she deeply admired all things Roman. She probably wouldn't have tried the bleedings to reduce fever if she hadn't thought it the Roman thing to do. But she gave my words an exaggerated respect, because I was a Roman doctor and, what was more, an imported one from the other end of the empire. The midwife spoke no tongue but Gothic, but was pleased to see the leeches go.

I then gave the lady some honeywater and opium — a small quantity on a sponge, since she'd been vomiting. Then I had the other two move her and clean her up with boiled water and a cleansing solution. (They refused to let me do this myself; no man, not even a eunuch, could touch Lord Fritigern's wife about the private parts!) I gave her some warm compresses to ease the pain and asked the slaves to clean the room. By this time the opium was having some effect, so I gave Amalberga the rest of the dose in some oxymel. With the earlier dose and the compresses and the clean sheets to soothe her, she managed to keep it down, and in a few minutes she went to sleep. She had been very tired, but, kept awake by the pain, she hadn't been able to rest properly since giving birth a week before.

The other women were delighted to see her resting so peacefully, and they praised me to Heaven. They found I'd had nothing to eat, so asked the slaves to bring me something, and then the wisewoman asked me about the opium and the rest of my medical gear. We were unpacking it all and discussing herbs when Fritigern and Athanaric knocked at the door. I'd been sitting there with a piece of bread in one hand and a box of dried bryony in the other, but I put them down and jumped up. The women did too. They opened the door, talking in an excited undertone in Gothic and making hushing noises.

Fritigern came in silently and stood staring at his wife, who lay there peacefully asleep, her blonde hair spread over the pillow. He walked up to the bed, took one of her hands and kissed it, stroked her hair. Then he went over and looked at the baby, who was just waking up and grunting into the mattress. Then he looked at me. Without a word, he took the gold chain from around his neck and put in into my hands. He stared at his wife for another moment, then left in silence.

"He loves the lady Amalberga very dearly," Athanaric told me when we were riding home three days later. "As far as he's concerned, you've earned not just that gold trinket, but his friendship for life. She will continue her recovery, I hope?"

"No fear about that," I said. All Amalberga had really needed was a good rest and a sensible diet with plenty of fluids. I hadn't said as much to Fritigern, but the real cause of her illness had been her attendants. When I took my leave she was already sitting up and wanting to nurse her baby. She too had asked whether it was true that I was a eunuch. When I said yes, she'd told me that the midwife thought I was really a woman. "No," I said, "among the Romans, women don't study medicine." She frowned at this, looking at me with some surprise; then she smiled. "So there is one way in which our customs are superior to yours." I laughed, and said that many would think so. "Well, then, Chariton," she said, "I thank you for your attendance on a foreigner like myself. Please take this as a token of my gratitude." She offered me a ring set with pearls. I told her that her husband had already been most generous. "Then let me be generous as well," she said, smiling. "I don't wish to be outdone by him!" I told her that I was amply rewarded by her recovery, but I took the ring.

"You don't need to worry about her," I told Athanaric now. "And that wisewoman, Areagni, has tolerably good sense when she isn't trying to imitate Xanthos. I don't think she'll go in for bloodletting again. It's a pity she can't read; I'd like to lend her my Hippocrates."

Athanaric chuckled. "I thought you'd be offended at the very idea of women practicing medicine."

"Why should you think that?" I asked, before reflecting that this was dangerous territory for me. "There are plenty of midwives in Roman lands, and many of them are sensible and competent women," I added hastily. "On the whole they do less harm than quacks like Xanthos. With a proper Hippocratic training they could be as skilled as any other practitioner."

"In other words, Hippocrates is so powerful he could even make a doctor out of a woman?"

"If you like," I said, "yes."

"Idolator," Athanaric said pleasantly. "Well, it's good you got on with the wisewoman; they're more likely to call you again if Areagni likes you too."

"Do you need to do more spying, then?"

Athanaric ran a hand through his hair. "I wasn't spying. I was consulting with the most noble Fritigern. I won't need an excuse when I come to do it again." He dropped his hand and looked at me keenly for a moment, smiling. "If I tell you what we consulted on, will you hold it under your oath?"

"Of course," I said, surprised that he would tell me at all.

"There is a new race of men who have come from the northeast, from beyond the lands of the Halani. They do not build houses, nor do they ever set their hands on a plow, but, like the Halani, they live in wagons and spend most of their lives upon the backs of their horses. They are without law or religion, inconstant to their allies, but they burn with a desire for gold and for the goods of their neighbors, and they are most savage fighters. They are called the Huns, and there are many thousands upon thousands of them. They have already defeated the Greuthungian Goths, and King Athanaric has led the Theruingi against them — and lost. They have been devastating the northern part of Gothic Dacia, and many people have been ruined by them. They say that it is useless to oppose them, and the only course left is to flee. The question is, where should the people go? They are penned in between the river and the Huns, with the Sarmatians to their west and the Euxine to the east. King Athanaric has fortified his borders, but even he openly talks of invading Sarmatia and taking the land, if the defenses fail. But Fritigern has another idea." Athanaric smiled, his hands tightening on the reins until his horse curvetted nervously. Plainly the idea excited him. "Fritigern wants to take the Theruingi into Thrace."

I caught my breath. "Invade? And he told you that?"

Athanaric shook his head, then tossed it back, laughing. "Fritigern fight Rome? He adores Rome! You must have seen that. No, he wishes to beg His Sacred Majesty to receive the Theruingi as a federate state within the empire and grant them some of the Thracian lands that are now deserted. The emperor would then be able to tax the lands, and would have a source of Gothic recruits for his armies." Athanaric grinned at me. "Fritigern asked me whether I thought the emperor would like this plan. I didn't tell him plainly that I knew the emperor would jump at it; I just said that I'd report it to the master of the offices, and bring him the answer when I could. But the emperor will jump at it, all the same."

"What about King Athanaric?" I asked. "Would he agree to become a client of Rome?"

"Never in a thousand years." Athanaric laughed, dismissing his uncle with a wave of the hand. "This is Fritigern's idea. And Fritigern is quite keen to keep it secret. He wants to lead the greater part of the people across the Danube, and be king of the client state. You wouldn't have thought he was that powerful, would you, from looking at his house? He looks no more than an ordinary country gentleman. Well, he can summon up a thousand swordsmen within a few days. He'll probably be crossing the river by this time next year."

We were both silent for a time. Athanaric rode with a smile on his face, his eyes bright. I thought of the Goths crossing the river, settling on the wastelands of Thrace, paying taxes to the emperors, and the thought somehow made me uneasy. There could not be two powers in the state; and if the emperor was one, where did that leave a Gothic king?

"Will they want to live as Romans?" I asked Athanaric. "I know they admire Rome, but it's easier to admire it from a distance than when you're sitting under the eagles."

"Of course they want to live as Romans!" Athanaric exclaimed in real annoyance. I realized only then that the prospect of the Goths coming into Thrace delighted him. Of course; it was what his father had done, and what he had been brought up to. Perhaps he felt that when others came, he himself would have a home.

"You look at them from the other side of the Danube and think 'noble barbarians,' don't you? There's nothing noble about the way they live. They are almost always at war — the nobles among themselves, the Theruingi with the Greuthungi, the Goths with the Sarmatians, and all of them with us. They live by the sword, and they're ruled by whoever is strongest. Sebastianus calls Lupicinus ignorant because he's never read Homer; Fritigern can't read at all, not even his own name. Where would your Hippocrates be without books, eh? Lost in oblivion, and you'd be practicing like Xanthos, out of what you learned from your father. You look at Rome and you see a force that killed your friends in Alexandria; they look at Rome and see a power that rules the world through law, peace, and learning. From Armenia to Britain, from Africa to the Rhine, one government, two common languages, and a thousand years of civilization. Here we are, a Greek eunuch from Amida and Ephesus, and the son of a Gothic prince and an Illyrian lady, differing in our native languages, our customs, our faiths — and we are both Romans. That is stronger than any of the divisions between us; that keeps the peace. Why shouldn't the Theruingi love Rome and live happily under Roman rule?"

I couldn't answer. I was watching his face and listening to his voice, and the words suddenly didn't seem to matter much. He had a wonderful light in his eyes, and he spoke rapidly in that quick staccato Greek, driving his words with the dashing splendor with which he rode his horses. My throat felt tight.

"What's the matter?" Athanaric asked, breaking from his enthusiasm into a surprised concern.

"Nothing," I said. "I hope you are right. When do we reach the Danube? I'm not a Hun; I'm not used to living on horseback."

He laughed, and I concentrated on my riding. It was not true, of course, that there was nothing wrong. I could have checked my symptoms off one by one, but from an authority other than Hippocrates.

> But my words are broken on my tongue
> Over my skin light fires run
> I see nothing, and my ears hum.
>
> Violently a cold sweat shakes me
> Paler than grass the fever makes me
> Near to death your presence takes me.

Oh Holy Christ, I thought, why should this happen to me now? Why should it happen to me at all? I mustn't let it happen. Nothing can come of it, and I don't even trust Athanaric. Not really. And I wouldn't give up medicine for him, even if he'd have me, and he wouldn't have me, not having known me as Chariton all this time. Oh Christ, when did this start to happen? For I knew it must have been creeping up on me for some time, and it was only when my whole body felt the force of it that I admitted to myself, in an instant, that I was in love.

I had innocently believed that I'd been in love with Theogenes; that the mixture of affection and regret I'd felt for him had been the worst I had to fear from "Desire, tyrant of gods and men." I learned my mistake. I hadn't dreamed of him, and waked, sweating, to lie half the night burning and biting my nails, or gone hot at the sound of his footsteps. Of course, I should have avoided Athanaric as I would a poisonous snake. Nothing could come of the passion but exposure and disgrace. Marriage was out of the question — his father meant him to marry an heiress, and no one would marry an army doctor. I felt quite dizzy with longing, and even dreamed of going to him secretly and saying, "I am not really a eunuch; my name is Charis, not Chariton; I'm still young and I used to be thought rather pretty. Sleep with me and keep it secret, please!" But what would that lead to? Athanaric was particularly unlikely to keep it secret. He'd ask questions and more questions, find everything out, and more than likely send me back to Thorion. And even if he didn't, would the passion extinguish itself on fulfillment, or would it just grow, binding me to Athanaric with invisible chains? Or, worse, with visible ones. I supposed that I could get pregnant as easily as the next woman; indeed, Hippocrates says that women who are healthy and accustomed to hard work conceive more easily than delicate gentlewomen. I knew a few drugs that were supposed to impede conception, but I doubted that they'd work for long; like aphrodisiacs, such things tend to be unreliable. That would leave me in a fix: disgrace myself before all the world by bearing the child, or mix myself some purgative to get rid of it, breaking my oath and risking my life. No, it was impossible. I should simply avoid the man and do everything I could to put him out of my head.

But I hadn't the strength. I wanted to see him. I tried to talk myself out of the passion. Why, after all, should I love Athanaric? True, he was well born and intelligent and looked splendid on horseback, but was that really so very unusual? Sebastianus was better-looking and more cultured, but though I did find him attractive, I certainly didn't lose sleep over him. Why should I over Athanaric?

It didn't work; I only discovered more reasons why I did love Athanaric — the way he made me laugh, the way he swaggered more when he knew he was disliked, the way he stood with a thumb through his sword belt and the sun in his hair, grinning. And beyond that, something deeper; I suppose a passion as fierce as mine had to have deep roots. Birth and training, rank and responsibilities did not make him, as they make most of us. I felt that he had chosen the rules he lived by, and chosen well: that he was free, that the world could fall to pieces around him and he would gallop off through the chaos, still distinctly and indefinably himself. And I cursed myself for my reasoning, and stopped it. But I couldn't bring myself to avoid him.

Indeed, I pressed him to be my guest whenever he was in the fort, saying, as Sebastianus had done, that I missed the company of educated men and that I was eager for news. And he usually accepted my invitations. Since he was in the region most of the time now, I saw quite a lot of him. I knew that he quite liked me — he respected my skill, for all his jokes about it, and he respected what he called my honesty. He seemed to enjoy my company. Of course I had to be extremely careful to show nothing of what I felt. If he suspected anything of that, I knew I'd never see him again. He was not the sort to like boys or eunuchs; I wouldn't have fallen in love with him if he had been. So I would say, "Come to dinner if you've time, next time you cross the river!" and he would come, and find me still at the hospital, pretending to have forgotten the invitation. Then I would apologize, and wash myself up and take him back to my house for a dinner during which he would tell me the news of the empire and I would deliver at least one Hippocratic lecture; and then he would go off, either across the river or up to the presidium, and I would go have a cold bath and chew on my fingers, nearly crying with frustration. My only consolation — and it was a cold one! — was that such a strong passion must fade with time, ebbing, so I hoped, into an ordinary friendship.

One thing that made it easier was that there was a lot of news that year, so we had a lot to talk about. The western emperor, the Augustus Lord Valentinian, died late in the autumn at Brigetio in the diocese of Illyricum, where he'd been preparing a campaign against the barbarian Quadi. He had ruled the world for nearly twelve years, and he was senior to his brother, whom he had appointed. The news struck the troops like an earthquake. (It would appear that he had died of apoplexy, outraged at the insolence of some envoys from the Quadi, and that he had had no doctor on hand to treat him at once; I had to discuss apoplexy with everyone in Novidunum.) He had long before appointed his son Gratianus as co-Augustus with him, but this young man was only eighteen and was far away in Gaul at the time of his father's death. It was feared that one of the Illyrian generals might try to claim the purple on the spot. The one under particular suspicion happened to be Sebastianus' father, the count of Illyricum, who was very popular with his troops. The commander of the household troops, Merobaudes, kept the news of the emperor's death secret as long as he could, and sent the elder Sebastianus off on a fool's errand to Mursa, hundreds of miles away. Then he had the emperor's other son fetched and proclaimed Augustus on the spot, to insure the succession of the house of Valentinian. This little boy was only four years old, and had been living in the region with his mother. Sebastianus was greatly annoyed.

"My father is a loyal and honest man, and Merobaudes might just as well have accused him of treason!" he told Athanaric and me one evening. He and Athanaric were both visiting Novidunum, Athanaric on his way across the river and Sebastianus during an inspection of the troops. Sebastianus had invited us to dinner. He habitually invited me when he was in the camp, and invited Athanaric whenever they met: he enjoyed company.

"People have been made emperor against their will," Athanaric said soothingly. "The troops like to have an emperor present, everyone knows that, and if they had acclaimed your father, what could he have done? He wouldn't have been able to convince Gratianus Augustus that he didn't plan it. He would have been forced to keep the title just to hold on to his life — and more than likely he would have lost his life anyway, after a costly war."

Sebastianus grunted. "Merobaudes could have told him that he was worried about something like that. Father would have taken his own steps to prevent it, gone off on his own somewhere. Then he wouldn't have this stain on his reputation. And making that child an Augustus! Valentinian the Second! What will he do, declare war on the Alamanni unless they hand over all their toys? 'That's His Sacred Majesty's rocking horse!' "

Athanaric sighed. "He is Augustus now, and we should keep our mouths shut. No good ever comes of making fun of an emperor. My friend, no one's accused your most esteemed father of anything; he still has his command, the trust of the new emperor, and the respect of his troops."

"And so he should!" said Sebastianus, but he was mollified.

That spring there was another upheaval along the frontier to outrage Sebastianus. The father of his friend Theodosius was suddenly relieved of his command in Africa — where he had bloodily distinguished himself — and summarily executed at Carthage. No one knew why. No charge of treason was officially brought, and the younger Theodosius was allowed to keep the family estates, though he too was relieved of his command. The men said that the count had been executed for sorcery, but Sebastianus rejected this idea. "Oh, it's true the count was bloodthirsty," he told me when he was next at Novidunum. "But he was honest; you wouldn't find him consulting oracles."

At the mention of oracles I felt a peculiarly cold sensation at the back of my neck. "Maybe it was because of his name," I said.

"His name?" asked Sebastianus irritably. "What do you mean?"

"There was an oracle received by a conspiracy a few years back, predicting who would succeed the present Augustus."

"It said that a Theodoros would succeed. Everyone heard that."

I shook my head. "The conspirators asked it who would succeed Valens, and it spelled out THEOD. Then they said 'Theodoros' and didn't ask it any more. It could be interpreted to mean Theodoros or Theodotos or Theodoulos — or Theodosius. Perhaps Valens didn't like to see someone with a name like that in such an eminent position, and sent a message to Gratianus about him."

Sebastianus looked uneasy, but he shook his head. "I can't believe that a man like Count Theodosius would be put to death on the strength of that alone. Though that damned oracle has killed a lot of men. They say that our lord the Augustus Valens takes it very seriously. It predicted ruin for him as well."

"What?" I hadn't heard this part of the oracle, and stared in surprise.

" 'Tisiphone's deep wrath arms evil doom, when Ares rages upon Mimas' plain.' That's what it's supposed to have said, anyway. They say that His Sacred Majesty is afraid to visit anywhere in Asia — I believe there's a mountain called Mimas there."

"Yes, near Erythrae. But I wouldn't trust an oracle. Even if there's any truth in it, it's sure to be couched deceptively. Like the man who was told he would die in Alexandria and spent all his life avoiding the great city, only to die in a posting station at a tiny village of the same name."

"Oracles are deceptive, that's certainly true. Immortal God, I wish that one had never been delivered! I'd hoped it was forgotten already."

That spring I also had some news from Thorion. He sent me a jubilant letter from his latest position as assessor with the court in Antioch. He had hopes for another promotion, this time to a governorship. "The prefect Modestus hates me," he wrote, "but the master of the offices is my friend. I've had two terms as an assessor now, and I met His Illustriousness at the hippodrome last week. I never thought

Father's chariots would be good for anything, but I got into conversation with Eutherios, and I discovered that he's keen on racing. So, not to let the opportunity slip, I gave him Father's prize blacks. He was delighted and invited me to dinner. While I was there he asked me very kindly about my prospects, and then said that I seemed an able young man and was wasting my time in assessorships and ought to have a province. I said I felt able to run one, provided it wasn't too large, and he laughed and said he'd see what he could do. I named one province in particular, but I won't tell you which, in case I don't get it. I hope I do get it, though. You can make some money in assessorships, but to repair the damage to our estates I need a governorship. Speaking of damage, have you heard that that brute Festinus is going to get a province in Thrace? Moesia, I think it is. I hope he dies there."

I shoved the letter to the back of my writing desk; I had no time to answer it just then. I was working very hard: the plague to the west was threatening to spread to our troops, and I was always being called up the river — or across it. Fritigern had taken to sending one of his attendants for me whenever a member of his household or one of his friends fell gravely ill. I was generally able to go; I now had several assistants on whom I could more or less rely, so I could be confident that my patients in the hospital would be well looked after in my absence. I'd let Arbetio copy all my books, and, as he was naturally gifted, he had absorbed them all and could run the hospital just as well as I could. I had also acquired a student, a Goth by the name of Edico. He was the nephew of the wisewoman Areagni, and he had come across the river especially to learn the art of healing from me. He was a tall, fair young man, extremely bright and capable but, unfortunately, illiterate, so it was no use telling him to go look anything up in Dioskourides; I had to explain it all myself. I arranged for him to be taught letters by one of the attendants, but he found it slow work, though he was quick enough to pick up how to mix a drug or set an arm.

Besides these two colleagues, several of the attendants were by now able to administer a few of the basic remedies as well. Xanthos was still about, but he had little to do except glare; Diokles, despite Sebastianus' prohibitions, was down in Histria more and more often. Nonetheless, I was not altogether happy about spending much time among the Goths. I had come to Thrace to treat Romans, and I had always disapproved of Diokles' having so many private patients. I worried that people would think I was acting from greed — the Gothic nobles were very generous, because they consider it a sign of high rank to give many gifts, and I was earning from them several times what I was paid as a salary. The money was quite welcome — it isn't easy to support two slaves, a cow, some chickens, and a horse on an army doctor's pay — but it was much more than I needed, and I didn't want to set a bad example for my colleagues. I began to refuse to go if the Gothic patient was further away than a half-day's journey, unless it was a really exceptional case and Athanaric intervened.

Even so, as the spring wore on I seemed to be crossing the river at least once a fortnight, and usually once a week. By this time many Goths from the northern part of their country had moved south, down to the river, and were preparing eagerly to cross into Thrace as soon as the Romans would allow them. They were fleeing from the Huns. Many arrived penniless, all their possessions lost to the invaders; some were injured or had old, infected wounds. They camped near the river, fishing, picking berries, and begging for food. Fritigern tried to distribute supplies to them from the southerners who had not been affected by the invasions, but there was barely enough to go round. Disease was rife among these northerners, weakened as they were by traveling and hunger. Fritigern wanted my advice on how to control the spread of plagues, and Sebastianus was eager for me to help: he didn't want the diseases spreading across the river. So I went over and back frequently, and I tried to get my slaves to teach me some Gothic.

Late in May, when Diokles was returning from Histria up the delta, his boat struck a submerged log and broke up in the river. The passengers were rescued by another vessel, which happened to be passing, but Diokles came back wheezing and shivering to Novidunum. He went to bed and never got up again: either the soaking or something he'd picked up in Histria had settled on his lungs. I was across the river seeing to the treatment of plague cases when this happened; I came back to find Diokles being treated at home by Xanthos. I'd never liked him, but I went to see how he was and offered to help with the treatment. They both glared at me like basilisks; Xanthos told me to get out. I got out, after pleading with him to go easy on the bleeding and the hellebore. I felt, perhaps wrongly, that I could do nothing more than plead in this case: I couldn't impose on a fellow doctor a method of treatment he detested, or take a patient out of the hands of his friend and put him into those of his enemy.

Xanthos ignored my advice, of course. When Diokles died a week later, he'd been bled white. Xanthos was at least consistent: he used the same abominable methods on his friends as he did on strangers.

I suppose a few patients must have survived them and he was convinced that they could cure. But Diokles' death he blamed on me.

I had scarcely heard that Diokles was dead when Valerius had me summoned to the presidium. He still didn't like me, but he was deeply impressed by all I had done with the hospital, and treated me with great respect. "Umm, yes, most esteemed Chariton," he said, sitting at his desk and fidgeting with a paper. "I'm very sorry, but, umm, your colleague, the most respected . . . that is, your colleague Xanthos has accused you of sorcery."

I stared. The dissection, I thought. but why has he waited so long? "What does he say I've done?" I asked cautiously.

Valerius pursed his lips in distaste and picked up the paper he'd been fidgeting with. "He says here that you came once to visit the most unfortunate Diokles, and that Diokles took a turn for the worse immediately after the visit. He says that after Diokles' death, a search of the room revealed a rabbit's foot wrapped in a sheet of lead under the clothes chest. He says that you have sorcerously mutilated the bodies of several animals, and even that of a man, and that it is common knowledge that you are a sorcerer and effect your cures by magic. He says that he is taking the case to the provincial courts in Tomis, and he wants me to put you under arrest and search your house for evidence of sorcerous practices. I hope you won't mind if I do have your house searched? I am sure, most excellent Chariton, that it is all nonsense, but I would not wish to be found remiss in my duty before the governor."

One look at Valerius' nervous face showed that he was not at all sure that it was nonsense, and that he expected me to refuse to have my house searched, at least until I had had time to remove any evidence of sorcery. I said nothing for a moment, trying to clear my head of shock and think. "Can Xanthos charge me before the governor?" I asked at last. "I would have thought we should use a military court."

"Oh! He's not commissioned, and neither are you; he *could* use a military court, but he's not *obliged* to."

Sebastianus would have been judge in a military court, so it was plain that Xanthos would avoid it if he possibly could. "You are welcome to search my house," I said; I'm sure I sounded as angry as I felt, because Valerius winced. "Just let me oversee the search, to make sure you don't damage anything. But first let me talk to Xanthos."

Xanthos was at his house. When I knocked at the door his slave opened it, saw who it was, gave a shriek, and closed it again. I knocked again, and after a minute it opened, and there was Xanthos. He made the sign against the evil eye and stood there staring with hatred around the edge of the door.

"Don't be ridiculous; you must open that and talk to me," I said. "I hear that you're accusing me of sorcery. You don't have a case. I know you hate me, but I'm not guilty, and you can't prove that I am. Why don't you spare both of us the expense and trouble of the provincial court?"

Xanthos spat. "Do you think you can fool me? I know you murdered Diokles with your spells; I want you dead before you kill me too. And all Novidunum knows that you're a sorcerer: I'll have no trouble proving it."

"You're the one who murdered Diokles, with your bleeding and your hellebore!" I said, losing my temper. "Taking me to court will prove nothing but your own incompetence!"

Xanthos grinned unpleasantly and shook his head. "I don't think so. I'll see you on the rack yet, Chariton! Now get away from my house." He closed the door. I beat on it again, but no one answered.

When I got home some of the soldiers and Valerius' scribe were waiting to search my house, and Sueridus and Raedagunda were standing in the door looking nervous. Raedagunda was now pregnant: she and Sueridus had taken it for granted that since they were living in the same house under the same master, they would sleep together. Their whispers and giggles after dark had often annoyed me, particularly when I felt lovesick myself, but when I saw them standing huddled together in the doorway I felt cut to the heart. If any credence was given to Xanthos' case, they would both be tortured.

The troops went through my things very respectfully, and the scribe made a list of everything they found. My spare corset caused a moment's puzzlement: "What's this?" asked the soldier who found it. "Bandage for cracked ribs," I said unblinkingly, and the scribe wrote "1 lge bandage" down on his tablets, as he'd already listed several smaller ones.

Of course there was nothing directly incriminating. I'd been slightly worried that perhaps Xanthos had slipped some foreign object in, but it would have been very difficult for him to do so, as one or the other of my slaves was usually about. However, as the search went on I became uncomfortably aware of just how many poisonous drugs I kept about the house. Poisoning is the natural companion of sorcery. And it was true that all my books were medical texts, but I remembered how the soldier in Alexandria had reacted to the illustration in my Galen. A governor or his assessor examining that scribe's list would probably feel that there was something there to require further investigation, particularly if Xanthos recited many of his sorcery stories and called in witnesses to show how widely they were believed. It was in fact very likely that my slaves would be tortured. It was even likely that I would be, after their evidence. Holy Christ, I thought, not again.

But Thrace wasn't the same as Alexandria. I had powerful friends here; Sebastianus could probably fix things with the governor, and Athanaric should have some pull as well. The thing to do would be to have the case thrown out at the preliminary hearing, before the judicial investigation swung into action and tried to wring confessions out of everyone. Sebastianus was presently up the river; Athanaric should soon be coming back across it. I would speak to them both and enlist their help.

The men left, apologizing for their invasion. Sueridus and Raedagunda looked at me wretchedly. They'd been told the purpose of the search, and had by now worked out what it could mean for them. I smiled. "Don't worry," I told them. "I'm not guilty, and the governor will find it so at the first hearing. The duke and Lord Athanaric will protect us."

They both looked relieved. The duke was the ultimate authority in Scythia, as far as they were concerned, and Athanaric was a person of unparalleled distinction, both as a Goth and as a Roman. With their protection, we had to be safe. They went confidently back to their work. I went to my room, wishing I could be as certain as they were.

Immediately after Diokles' funeral Xanthos went down to Tomis to present his accusation to the provincial courts. He must have spent fairly heavily in bribes, because the preliminary hearing was set for the end of June, only two months away. By rights I should have been arrested and imprisoned until then, as murder by sorcery is a serious criminal charge; but the civil courts have no ability to enforce a warrant in an army camp. A couple of officials came up from Tomis and talked to Valerius and then to me. I promised to attend the hearing and they went away again, relieved that they had as much cooperation as this.

Sebastianus was furious when I told him what had happened. The first thing he did was summon Xanthos and threaten him with immediate sacking unless he dropped the charge. But this Xanthos refused to do. I had murdered Diokles, he said, and I would murder him unless he had me killed first.

"Damn him!" Sebastianus said to me afterward. "I should have sacked him when you first came here."

He had asked me to dinner at the presidium to discuss the case, but he was too angry to eat. He stood scowling out the window for a moment, then finished his cup of neat wine and glared at its empty bottom. "I never thought that malice and jealousy would take him this far; I thought he'd be alive to self-interest."

"He really believes what he's saying," I said wearily. "Perhaps he is even genuinely afraid for his life. He hates me enough to believe anything. I've handled him very badly."

Sebastianus grunted. "He's a damned incompetent butcher. If he costs me your services I shall flog him myself. To lose the best doctor on the frontier because of the ravings of some deluded quack!"

"You haven't lost me," I said, feeling more frightened with every word he said. "Not yet, anyway. Can't you do something to protect me?"

Sebastianus shrugged. "You will have to go to Tomis. I would like to tell you to ignore the charge, but I can't. Sorcery is a very dangerous accusation; if you're not cleared of it publicly, it could hurt you in the future — and hurt me too, if I protected you. It would be different if you'd just cut Diokles' throat: I could tell the governor to take his warrant and sink it in the Euxine, I'm not having one of my men tried by some ignorant civilian. No, you'll have to go to Tomis." He came back to the table and poured himself some more wine, then looked up and noticed how distressed I was. "Oh, I think you'll still get off!" he told me. "I'll write the governor's office tonight, saying that the charge is frivolous, malicious, and unsubstantiated. And I'll come to Tomis with you. That should be enough to convince the governor not to find you guilty. If it were up to the present governor, I could promise you a full acquittal at the first hearing — but his successor is due to arrive about the time set for the trial, and I don't know who it will be. Even so, you should get off: governors don't like offending a military duke, particularly one with a powerful father. The only danger is that the new governor will be some ambitious climber, out to make a name for himself by scourging the emperor's enemies. Men like that love sorcery cases. Do you know anything about the magic charm Xanthos says he found in Diokles' room?"

I shook my head. "I don't even know whether it's really supposed to put a curse on someone or it's a good-luck charm; I don't know whether it was Diokles' own or someone else put it there, or Xanthos made it up to support his case. You won't find any works on magic charms in the Hippocratic writings."

"So we can't prove anything. Well, we will simply have to overawe the governor with the majesty of Scythian arms."

In the end both Sebastianus and Athanaric accompanied me to Tomis. By this time Athanaric's prediction had come true: the Goths were starting to cross the river into Thrace. But they weren't coming into Scythia; the imperial authorities had decided to bring them across further up the river, into the neighboring province of Moesia. The crowded camps on the other side of the river from Novidunum were gone now, their inhabitants off for their crossing into Moesia. From there they would be directed into the wastelands in the heart of the diocese. The emperor and his court were enthusiastic about the idea of a Gothic state in Thrace. The thought of the Goths paying taxes on land previously waste and providing recruits for the imperial armies was irresistible to the treasury and the army alike. Athanaric had played a delicate part in the negotiations between the emperor and the Theruingi, but now things were out of his hands, and he had plenty of time to assist a friend at his trial. He did point out that he had warned me, but he was eager to help.

And it looked increasingly as though I'd need the help: the new governor sounded the wrong sort for me altogether. "A young man, that's all I've heard," Athanaric said. "Got the governorship at the last minute by outmaneuvering another man; eager to make a name for himself, it seems."

"He should also be eager to avoid offending anyone," said Sebastianus, but he was almost as unhappy about it as I was.

I was so used to life on horseback by this time that I didn't even think of taking a boat down to Tomis. We rode to the provincial capital, and Sebastianus, as always, rode at the head of a troop of cavalry. It is hard to feel helpless and terrified when you're riding at the head of a troop of cavalry, and I was glad of this. We planned to arrive a few days before the hearing, to allow time for Sebastianus to work on the governor. It took us two full days to get there. Athanaric left us on the second day and galloped ahead via the posting system, to tell Sebastianus' people in Tomis to get his residence ready. That was his excuse, anyway; I think he had simply forgotten how to ride at a trot.

Tomis, the provincial capital, is a large city, by Thracian standards — a mere town, by Asian or Egyptian ones. It has a pleasant situation on the Euxine, facing eastward to the dawn, with a wide sandy beach and a good harbor. Like all Thracian cities it's strongly fortified, its walls built of the light-colored local stone. It looked bright and spacious when we approached it that evening. The marketplace was impressive enough, surrounded by the governor's residence, Sebastianus' headquarters, a pagan temple, and a fine portico of shops. There wasn't much else in the town, though, except the church.

Athanaric was already at the headquarters; he'd arrived there around noon. The staff had everything ready for us, and we were able to get off our horses and go straight in to dinner. Though based in Tomis, Sebastianus did not actually spend much of his time there. He was a very active commander, and preferred to supervise his troops in the field, settling their problems on the spot. But he kept his personal slaves, and his lyre-playing mistress, at his headquarters, so he was able to make us comfortable. The three of us reclined to an excellent meal, though I was too nervous to have much appetite. I kept remembering the prison in Alexandria. The lyre player came in, but Sebastianus sent her out again. "No time for pleasure tonight, my sweet!" he told her. "Not until later, anyway."

"It's good that we came when we did," Athanaric said during the first course. "The governor has arrived, and he's brought the case forward by three days — the hearing's now scheduled for tomorrow."

"*Sacra Maiestas!*" exclaimed Sebastianus. "Why has he done that? We haven't even engaged a barrister yet! Who is he, anyway?"

"I don't know why he's done it," Athanaric said. "I complained. He's a countryman of yours, though, Chariton, a fellow Ephesian. His name's Theodoros."

I had been sipping my wine, and at this it went down the wrong way; I had a coughing fit and nearly spilled the rest of the cup over myself.

"Do you know him?" asked Sebastianus in surprise.

"What's his full name?" I asked Athanaric. "Did you meet him?"

"Theodoros son of Theodoros. Yes, he received me at the prefecture. He's a young man, dark, wide across the shoulders, crooked teeth. He said he was sorry I was annoyed about the change in date, but he didn't think it mattered."

I started laughing; it was a while before I could stop, and the other two watched me suspiciously. "He was right," I said at last. "You needn't have bothered to come to Tomis, either of you. I could walk into that court tomorrow wearing a cloak embroidered with magic symbols and chanting a hymn to Hermes Trismegistus, and the governor would acquit me. Holy Immortal One! Thorion, governor of Scythia! Oh Lord God!"

Athanaric's look of puzzlement cleared. "There was a letter from a Theodoros among your things in Alexandria."

"It's the same Theodoros."

Athanaric smiled, and explained to Sebastianus. " 'Dear Charition, stop treating that dangerous archbishop and come stay with me in Constantinople; Maia would love to see you.' Where does Your Grace know *him* from, then?" He snapped his fingers and answered his own question. "Now I remember, I did hear that you were the client of a Theodoros of Ephesus. But he wrote as though you were a member of his household."

"I was — sort of. I was a dependent of his tutor. We grew up together, studied Homer together. He made me learn some Latin so I could help him with the plural of *magister militum*. He wrote to me that he expected to get a governorship soon, but he didn't say where; he was afraid it might fall through. And I suppose he meant to surprise me."

"He's done that, then," said Sebastianus, now smiling as well. "Are you sure he'll acquit you?"

"I feel sorry for Xanthos," I said.

"Well. Do you suppose it would bring bad luck if I called Daphne back in and we had a party before the event?"

He called Daphne back in and called for another jug of wine, and we had a party. It was a fairly decorous sort of party, actually, with only the four of us, but we drank too much. Daphne sang some extremely funny and vulgar songs, and Sebastianus eventually stumbled off to bed with her, leaving Athanaric and me to finish the wine. "Lucky devil," said Athanaric, staring morosely after Sebastianus.

I said nothing. My first elation had worn off, and I was beginning to worry about meeting Thorion again. Scythia must have been the province he named to the master of the offices. It was not really surprising that he'd got it, either, as it's not one of the provinces everyone wants — not wealthy like the Asian or Egyptian ones, or prestigious like Syria or Bithynia. Thorion had wanted it for my sake, to have a chance of arguing with me, of persuading me to go home. What would he think when he saw me?

"I wish I had a girl like that," Athanaric said, still gazing after Daphne. "But I suppose I couldn't keep her. I travel about too much. The hardships of an agent's life! I suppose you didn't notice her."

"I thought she sang well," I said feebly. Thorion fell out of my thoughts like a stone falling through seawater, sunk without trace. My mind was like a mirror, reflecting nothing but Athanaric. "And she's pretty."

"She's certainly that," Athanaric returned. He stopped looking at the door and stared at me for a moment, his eyes vividly blue in the lamplight. "There's something I've often wondered, Chariton. Do eunuchs ever — that is, have you ever wanted a woman?"

"No," I said. I was a bit breathless; my ears hummed. "Others may, sometimes. I don't know."

"You're probably better off without it." Athanaric sat up and stretched, ready to go off to bed. "Desire's a torment."

"Yes," I said fervently, before I could think.

Athanaric looked at me again, surprised. "You think that? Chariton the doctor, the perfect philosopher, practitioner of Stoic detachment? And you just said . . ." He stopped, suddenly suspicious. "Not women? Men?"

"One man," I said, and bit my lip.

"I suppose a eunuch can't help it," he said, but with an expression of distaste. "And you must have been a beautiful boy."

"It wasn't like that. Nothing at all happened."

At this the look of distaste and suspicion changed to one of amusement mixed with sympathy. "He didn't like boys? What did you do?"

"Nothing," I said. "I never said anything, and neither did he. One gets over these things, eventually. That is the whole of my experience of desire. It doesn't add up to much, does it?"

He laughed. "Poor Chariton!"

I shook my head. "There's always Hippocrates."

We went to the court early next morning. I put on my best cloak, the one with the red and green border. Sebastianus called in "the majesty of Scythian arms" and came to the court magnificent in his gilded armor and short crimson cloak, followed by a guard of a dozen men. Athanaric joined in the spirit of things and put on a clean cloak — a good one with a patterned border — and hung the signet that was his license to use the posts on a gold chain around his neck, and swaggered along with his thumb through his sword belt. Even if the governor had been unfavorably inclined, I thought, this show would have swayed him.

The courtroom was on the ground floor of the prefecture, squarely fronting the first of its courtyards. It was embellished with statues of

Justice; an altar to this goddess had been torn out of one wall, condemned as excessively pagan, leaving peeling chunks of plaster behind it. The ushers admitted me, Sebastianus, and Athanaric, but stopped all but two of Sebastianus' attendants, apologizing for a lack of space. The building was already crowded with citizens of Tomis. A sorcery trial always provokes considerable interest, and the people also wanted to have a look at their new governor.

Xanthos was already there, in his best clothing, and with him were a number of others from Novidunum, all presumably ready to testify that I was a sorcerer. The ushers showed me to a place to the left of the dais, behind a railing; my friends sat down in the front of the court. There was no space on the benches, but the court ushers brought chairs for them and fussed about finding cushions.

Thorion came in promptly on the hour, as measured by the water clock. He had scarcely changed at all. He was a bit heavier, his face slightly fuller, and he was dressed with more care — he never used to keep the purple stripes on his cloak straight, but now you might have measured them with a plumb line. Even before he sat down his eyes were sweeping eagerly about the court. He looked at me and away twice. He sat down and looked again, and I smiled. He stared, and I saw his lips move as he swore under his breath.

The proceedings were opened. Xanthos had engaged a barrister, a rotund old rhetorician who stood up and made a long speech about the merits of his client and about my wickedness, depravity, impiety, hypocrisy, and cunning. Thorion kept looking at me and shaking his head in astonishment. The watching citizens whispered to each other and stared at me, first just curiously, then, as the barrister warmed up, with fascinated revulsion. The old barrister stated the precise charges, and produced the incriminating rabbit's foot with a flourish. Whispers and horrified gasps. Xanthos smiled. Sebastianus looked uneasy. The barrister concluded, bowed to the judge, and sat down.

"Right," said Thorion decisively. "What does the accused have to say to all that? Do you have a patron here, Chariton of Ephesus?" He pronounced my assumed name with a certain degree of dislike and with an air of lofty disdain, as though he'd never met me.

"I will speak for myself, Your Honor," I said, and I got up and proceeded to do so. I described Diokles' accident and the treatment Xanthos had given him, and protested my total ignorance of magical arts. "I trained in Alexandria, and I am a Hippocratic, both by training and by inclination," I concluded. "We believe that diseases have natural causes and natural cures, and we are too busy studying these to pay much attention to magic. Besides that, we swear to use our knowledge to heal, never to harm. I am entirely innocent of this charge." I sat down again. The people of Tomis whispered to each other, unconvinced, giving me sideways looks of horror and suspicion.

Thorion nodded and leaned forward. "As I understand it, the accuser used to be chief physician at the fort of Novidunum, until the arrival of the accused. Can anyone tell me what sort of job he did?"

"My client has practiced the Apollonian art all his life!" said the barrister in measured tones. "As his father before him, he fearlessly treated the sick, alleviating their pains, soothing —"

"Yes, yes, but what sort of job did he do?" asked Thorion. "Any witnesses?"

Sebastianus rose gracefully to his feet.

"His Excellency the most noble Sebastianus, duke of Scythia!" announced the usher.

"Your Excellency," said Thorion, giving the old crooked-tooth smile, "I am delighted to make the acquaintance of so eminent a gentleman. I am honored that you have seen fit to attend our court."

Sebastianus made a disclaiming gesture. "May I witness on behalf of the accused?"

"A gentleman of your quality could witness on behalf of the Devil."

Sebastianus proceeded to revile Xanthos forcefully as incompetent and bungling, and to praise me. "The year before the most esteemed Chariton arrived," he stated, "the hospital at Novidunum treated eighty-three patients, of whom seventy-two died. Last year it treated a hundred and forty-eight, of whom a hundred and two recovered. Moreover, the number of men sick throughout my troops has dropped dramatically. I value Chariton's services very highly. He is an exceptionally skilled and dedicated physician, and this talk of sorcery is nonsense." He sat down.

Thorion nodded at intervals throughout the speech. "Your Excellency was good enough to say as much before, in a letter Your Diligence wrote to my predecessor," he said when Sebastianus had finished. "So. Xanthos was chief doctor and did a bad job; Chariton arrives, supplants him, and does a good one. This fellow Diokles falls into the Danube, gets pneumonia, is treated by Xanthos, and promptly dies. Xanthos blames his enemy, who supplanted him."

"Your Eminence!" cried the barrister. Xanthos sat up straight with his mouth open, gasping.

"Oh, be quiet!" said Thorion impatiently. "You can't hide the fact

243

that your client has a grudge against the accused. Do you have any evidence to link Chariton to the death?"

"He's a sorcerer!" said Xanthos, jumping up before his barrister could get a word in. He gripped the court rails as though they were some kind of weapon he meant to hurl at me, and spat his words out, glaring around as though challenging the court to call him a liar. "Everyone in the fortress knows it. His own slaves boast about it. He gets his cures by magic. He mutilates the bodies of animals, yes, and of men too!" An excited rustle ran about the benches. "I have witnesses here who can attest to that!" Xanthos' voice was rising with excitement, though his barrister was trying to get him to slow down, to produce this evidence for maximum effect. "Alaric and Ursacius here examined the body of a man, a Roman soldier, cut up by this gelded magician for some necromantic purpose! I myself saw him doing it, and they can swear to what he did!"

Horrified exclamations. I hadn't realized that Xanthos had got himself some witnesses to the effects of my dissection: I'd thought it would just be his word against mine. The evidence was damaging.

But Thorion waved it aside. "They can swear, perhaps, that a dead body showed signs of having been cut. You'll swear, so you say, that you witnessed your colleague cutting the body. Was it the body of the deceased, Diokles? No? Well, how do you know the cutting wasn't done as part of some standard surgical procedure? The accused is a surgeon, I presume? Well, there you are! Will your witnesses swear that the signs of cutting they saw were necromantic, and not administered before death in some attempt to save the patient's life?" The witnesses looked nervous and unsure of themselves; they shook their heads.

"I saw him cutting the body after death!" Xanthos exclaimed. "He did it in a back room of the hospital at Novidunum, at night when he thought no one was watching, but I looked through the keyhole and saw him at it!"

More rustling about the benches. Thorion raised his hand for silence. "Even if I accepted your evidence that the cutting took place after death — and given your evident hatred of the accused, I don't know why I should — can you give me any evidence that it was part of a necromantic procedure and not a standard medical dissection? Of course there are such dissections! Any educated man knows that learned doctors sometimes perform such operations, to gain knowledge about how to treat similar disorders in future. Have you read Galen, or Herophilos? What? And you a doctor, too! It is plain to me that you're as incompetent as the most respected duke says. Do you have any other evidence?"

"Everyone knows he's a sorcerer. I can call witnesses —"

"What everyone says isn't evidence. Do you have any witnesses that he made a magical charm for anyone, or cursed someone to cause sickness, or practiced astrology? No? Any other evidence, then? No? Right, case dismissed."

Uproar in the court. Thorion raised his voice and went on. "And I assess damages against Xanthos the son of Polykles, for bringing a malicious and frivolous charge against the most excellent Chariton. Assessor, do we have anything else for this morning? Right, the court rises until this afternoon."

Xanthos and his barrister began to protest. Xanthos wept, beating his hands against the railings. The fine for bringing a frivolous charge is a large one, and he had obviously already spent heavily on bribes and barristers: the loss would ruin him. And he'd lost his job too, and would be unlikely to get another after this branding as an incompetent. He rushed up toward the dais, ready to beg Thorion for mercy; Thorion gave a sign to the ushers, and they pulled him out, still weeping. The barrister followed him, glancing over his shoulder at Thorion. The public got up, arguing loudly among themselves. Thorion sat back in his chair, thumbs through his belt, whistling soundlessly. He caught my eye and grinned.

When the public had left, Sebastianus and Athanaric rose and went over to Thorion; I got up as well. "Esteemed Theodoros," said Sebastianus, offering Thorion his hand, "you don't waste your time."

Thorion shook the hand, grinning. "I heard enough windy speeches while I was an assessor; I don't see why I should listen to more of them now I'm a governor. And I think I would have spotted that fellow as a liar and a cheat even if I hadn't known about this case beforehand. But I suppose Charition has told you he's an old friend of mine. Excuse me a moment, Excellencies." He hurried over to me, stood staring for a moment, then shook his head in wonder. "By Artemis the Great! Lord God, Charition, I really didn't recognize you. It *is* you, isn't it?"

"Of course it is," I said, and embraced him. He gave me a bear hug in return, then let go and stepped back, staring again.

"Trousers, too!" he exclaimed. "Eternal God, you look like a barbarian!"

"It's cold here in the winter."

"It'll be pretty damn cold before I wear gear like that! Excuse me,

245

Your Eminences." He grinned at Sebastianus and Athanaric, who were both trousered. "It takes a bit of getting used to. I thought the trial went well, though I say so myself. I didn't want to make it too obvious that I knew Chariton. God, everyone will think I'm marvelously learned now! It was Herophilos and Galen who did dissections, wasn't it, Chariton? Did you do one, or did that fellow just make it up? It was a stupid thing to do, if it's true. I was never so surprised in my life as when I found you were supposed to be coming here for a sorcery trial; I was just sending a letter to you, inviting you to come visit, when the assessor says, 'But sir, this Chariton is to be here next week!' Anyhow, we've got that mess out of the way now; you'll have to come to lunch with me, so we can talk — if Their Excellencies will excuse us." He turned back to Athanaric and Sebastianus, still grinning. "I haven't seen my friend for years; we grew up together."

"So he informed us," said Sebastianus. He looked somewhat taken aback, as well he might.

"Then you will excuse us. Though I'm delighted to make Your Honor's acquaintance — and yours, most noble Athanaric. You'll have to forgive me: I didn't recognize your name last night; I remembered it after you'd gone. The most illustrious Eutherios mentioned you to me, saying I could rely on your assistance if I had any trouble with the Goths. I gather some big transportation of them across the river is going on, though not in this province. I would be delighted if Your Excellencies would honor me with your most esteemed company at dinner. I have much to learn if I'm to do a good job here."

Sebastianus and Athanaric bowed and murmured that they'd be delighted to attend His Excellency at dinner; Thorion bowed back and thanked them, then towed me off rapidly into the rear of the prefecture, where he had his residence. One of the court scribes followed, but as soon as we'd crossed to the house Thorion turned on him. "What are you doing here?" he demanded. The scribe gaped and offered him some papers; Thorion snatched them. "Why are you showing me these?" he said, glancing through them. "I'll look at them later." He shoved them back. "I want to talk to my friend and I don't want to be disturbed," he announced loudly, glaring from the scribe to two or three of the prefectural slaves who'd come up. They bowed and retreated hastily. "But I've invited their eminences Duke Sebastianus and the agent Athanaric to dinner: see to it!" he shouted after the slaves, and they bowed again.

Thorion took my arm. "Never get any privacy here," he told me,

pulling me into the building. "By the holy apostles, Charition, I
didn't know you had such powerful friends! You should have seen
the letter that Sebastianus wrote — and the one from the agent
Athanaric! You're a reincarnation of Hippocrates, according to them.
I didn't know what to think!" We went upstairs: up one flight with a
carved stair rail and plaster walls painted with seascapes; up another,
steeper flight with plain walls and a plain railing, into the servants'
quarters. "We'll have lunch with Maia. She's expecting us," Thorion
explained as he reached the top and stopped, panting a little from the
climb. "It's no use trying to be private downstairs; people are always
coming in. Could His Excellency sign this, would His Excellency
look at that. His Excellency will see no one till this afternoon!" This
last was directed at one of the slaves, a girl who had come out of her
room to see who was talking; she gave a gulp, bowed, and went back
in. Thorion strode down the corridor, stopped so suddenly that I
bumped into him, and rapped on a door. It opened instantly.

Thorion had not changed at all; my Maia had changed a great
deal. The hair that I remembered as red was gray now, and she seemed
smaller, dried like leather. Her eyes slid eagerly past Thorion to meet
mine directly; they widened. She stood back from the open door and
let us past, then closed it, bolted it. "Oh, my dear!" she said breathlessly, staring at me.

"I didn't recognize her," remarked Thorion.

"Oh, my poor darling!" said Maia, and embraced me, standing on
tiptoe to do so. Had I grown that much? Or had she shrunk?

"The trial went beautifully," Thorion told Maia, going on into the
room without waiting for her to let go of me. The room was a fair-
sized one, with orange-painted panels, and a bed, a couch, and a
stool drawn up around a small table set with delicacies. Thorion sat
down on one end of the couch and picked a bunch of grapes off the
table. "The man bringing the accusation was a piece of spite and
jealousy; anybody could see how he hated Charition. And His Honor
the duke was there in person, and this Athanaric man, and the duke
made a speech about how wonderful Charition is and how she's cured
all these people and is the cleverest doctor this side of Alexandria. I'll
say one thing for you, Charition, you've made a great job of this
doctoring. I didn't know what to think!"

Maia was still holding me; she put her hand against my cheek,
looking into my face. Then she shook her head. "My poor dear!" she
said again. "And you were such a lovely girl!"

"Leave her alone for now!" Thorion told her. "Let her find her feet. Come and sit down. Immortal God, stuffed dormice! You really have made an occasion of this, haven't you?"

"It's for the reunion," said Maia briskly, letting go of me. "And I don't have much to spend my money on, do I? You don't like me giving it all to the church."

"You do what you like with it, that's all I keep telling you," said Thorion through a mouthful of grapes. "It's just a shame to see money I give you as a salary going into church coffers, that's all. It's much better spent on stuffed dormice."

I sat down on the other end of the couch; Maia took the stool. "What's this about money?" I asked.

"Maia's salary," explained Thorion. "As housekeeper."

I looked from one to the other. "You didn't tell me you freed her!"

"Didn't I? Well, I did. I inherited her after Father died, and had the papers drawn up at once. Not that it makes any difference. I freed Philoxenos too, and made him farm manager. You remember Philoxenos?"

"Of course. Maia, how wonderful! I never drank to your freedom; let me do that now."

Maia smiled rather wanly and poured some wine into my cup; it was standing in a jug, already mixed. "Though as his excellency Lord Theodoros says, it doesn't make much difference," she told me.

I laughed; I'd forgotten how fond she was of titles. "To my Maia," I said, lifting my cup, "Elpis of Ephesus, a free woman!"

Maia smiled again, then poured some wine for herself and Thorion and joined the toast.

Thorion talked while we ate the stuffed dormice, telling me about the estates in Ephesus and all the slaves and dependents of the house, and about his friends, and about Constantinople. I was quite happy to sit and listen, asking the odd question. I knew that sooner or later the talk would settle on Me, and that would be difficult.

Maia watched me silently, not eating much. Her eyes were red-rimmed, one more so than the other. It seemed a bit rheumy as well, and she rubbed it occasionally as though it itched. There was a pause in Thorion's account while he downed another dormouse, and Maia noticed me looking at her eye. She smiled. "Will you give me a prescription for it?" she asked.

"I was just thinking of one," I said truthfully.

"I'm sure it will be a good one," she said evenly. "I think you must be a very good doctor. Are you happy, my dear?"

"Yes."

She gave a long sigh, staring at me wistfully. "I wanted you to come home. I wanted to see you married."

"I know you did. I wish . . . I wish I could, and still practice the art. But I can't; I had to choose one or the other."

She nodded slowly. "I never thought you would come back. When you left Ephesus, I told Thorion that it was forever. He told me not to be silly."

"And I think you're both being silly now," said Thorion. "I don't see what's so wonderful about this art, though I suppose I am pleased you've done so well at it, Charition. But you've learned it, and you've practiced it, and you've been away for more than five years, and I don't see why you can't come back and get married now. And don't look so mulish. You've spoiled your looks a bit, but nothing that a few months and a bit of make-up won't cure: you're pretty enough, and still not too old. And I'll see that you get half the estate as a dowry. You can marry whomever you like, and set whatever conditions you want. You can even play doctor to your own household. I know you used to plan to do that. Well, what's wrong with that? It's no good living without a family, pretending to everybody that you're something you're not. Do your own slaves know? No, I thought not. It's no good. And you keep getting into trouble, first that damned heretic archbishop in Egypt and now this!"

"He wasn't a heretic," I said sharply.

"He was a damned rabble-rouser, then, and in trouble with the authorities! You should have let him alone. And doing dissections? That was asking for trouble. You may be clever, but you never had any sense. I thought about having you arrested properly on this charge and smuggling you out of the prison; I thought that then you'd have to see reason. But I didn't want to have your slaves tortured; I don't like it. Not since Festinus did it to Maia."

"It would kill me to go back to being a lady," I said. "I won't do it. Let it alone, Thorion, please. I don't want to argue."

"I just don't understand!"

"How would you feel if someone told you it was improper to hold a governorship, or an assessorship, or any office; that you couldn't appear as a witness on your own behalf in court, and your consent wasn't required for your own marriage — which somebody else would arrange for you? Wouldn't you do everything you could to avoid an enslavement like that?"

"Yes, but I'm a man!"

"Well, in the eyes of the world, so am I. Now. You're used to the freedom, and so am I. And I do love the art, probably more than you love your governorship."

"I told Your Excellency it would be no good," said Maia.

Thorion sighed, frowning at me. "I'm sure no one else in the world has a sister like you. Very well, leave it for now. Maybe you'll fall in love one day and change your mind. Love's a very devil for changing minds. I only hope it isn't too late by then."

Maia smiled into her cup. "Charis, my dear," she said, "have something more to eat. You haven't been eating properly."

"You're thin as a fencepost," Thorion agreed sourly. "Flat and bony. What do you do at that hospital?"

I felt a wave of relief. I'd got off quite lightly. And I'd never expected Maia's tacit support; she'd always disapproved of my doctoring in Ephesus. I told them a bit about the hospital.

"One thing I want to know," Thorion said, interrupting my description of the problems with drugs. "Can you tell what sex a baby's going to be before it's born?"

I was taken aback, and blinked for a moment. Maia was smiling again. "Hippocrates says you can tell something from the way it leans in the womb. But they mostly move around a lot, so it's not very reliable." Maia was still smiling, and I looked at Thorion suspiciously. "Whose baby is this?"

"Mine," he said proudly. "I'm hoping it's a boy. A girl might take after you, and cause no end of trouble."

I stared at him for a moment, wondering if he'd forgotten to tell me that he had married. But no, I would have been aware of that. This must be some mistress or concubine.

"Congratulations!" I told him. "Is the mother slave or free?"

"Oh, free," he said happily. "She's a baker's daughter from Nicomedia; I met her at the law court there. I've given her a good settlement of property, so if I ever do get married, she'll be all right. But I don't intend to get married for a long time; it would be hard to part with Melissa." He stopped, looking wonderfully contented at the thought of his concubine, forgetting for the moment about the improper behavior of his sister. "We think that the baby's due in September," he confided, grinning at the thought of it.

"Melissa's a sweet girl," put in Maia. Maia was, if anything, more excited than Thorion himself at the prospect of this child. She had always been eager to have children of mine to play grandmother to, but a child of Thorion's, even an illegitimate one, was entirely acceptable.

Inwardly I blessed the unknown Melissa. I would have had a much harder time of it with my family if it hadn't been for her. "Well," I said, smiling, "I hope for your sake it is a boy. If you'll introduce me to Melissa, I'll have a look and see if I can predict the baby's sex, but none of the methods is really reliable. But I can probably recommend a few things to make her more comfortable, if she needs them. If you like, I'll try to come from Novidunum and deliver the baby for you."

Thorion grinned and nodded. "I told Melissa I'd get her either the best midwife or the best doctor in the province. It seems you're the best doctor. And I was already thinking of calling the baby Chariton."

I returned to Novidunum a week later. I felt utterly exhausted. Thorion and Maia on their own had been fine, after the first lecture; Thorion seemed genuinely impressed by my skill at medicine, and by my powerful connections. ("His Illustriousness the Master of the Offices thinks the world of this fellow Athanaric," he told me. "He said his advice was as good as an edict when it came to Gothic affairs. I'm glad to make a friend of him.") But Thorion with anyone else had me continually cringing with anxiety. He never let my proper name slip — he'd always called me Charition anyway — but he occasionally referred to me as "she." Of course, some people do this in reference to eunuchs, but only to be rude. It wasn't quite frequent enough that people were sure of what they heard, but it was enough to make me very nervous. Athanaric noticed the slip, and asked me privately if Thorion was "the man you mentioned." I couldn't think what he meant for a moment, and then I remembered my confession of the torments of desire. "Heavenly God, no," I declared. "He's just a very old friend."

Athanaric looked at me thoughtfully, and I tried to look unconcerned. But I knew that he was trained to notice such things, and I wondered if now he would guess the truth. I wondered how I would feel if he did discover my secret. But he said nothing more about it. And in fact he galloped off on an "inspection of the posts" two days after the trial. Sebastianus remained in Tomis: he would stay for a month or so, sorting out supplies for his men. I was obliged to return to the hospital as soon as possible, since midsummer is a bad period for contagious diseases. But I talked with Sebastianus before I left, about Xanthos.

"Now that he's lost his case," I said, "you don't need to sack him. I don't mind him working under me, provided he doesn't interfere with my patients."

Sebastianus stared at me, then gave a wry smile. "Why the Christian forbearance? The man is your enemy. He wanted to have you tortured and killed. And I've already sacked him."

I shrugged. I kept remembering Xanthos being pulled weeping out of the courtroom. I wondered if he even had enough money to pay his fines. "It was partly my fault," I told Sebastianus. "I handled him badly. I supplanted him, and then I behaved arrogantly, humiliating him and abusing his methods. It's not his fault he's such a bad doctor; he's not responsible for his own training. And he really did believe that I was a sorcerer and killed his friend. I don't want him tortured because he can't pay."

Sebastianus laughed. " 'O integer vitae scelerisque pure!' Well, if you ask it, you may have him back. I'll send him a letter to that effect. He's back in Novidunum now, collecting his things. But I'll tell him that it was you who interceded for him, and he may not want to come back. I've seen hatred like that before. It's a deadly poison, and if it can't kill its object, it kills its owner. But you wouldn't know about that, would you?" He gave me a look of real affection and wrote out the letter. I took it, mounted my horse, and rode home.

I didn't gallop all the way — the horse wouldn't have stood it — but I did press harder than I had on the way to Tomis, riding with Sebastianus, and I arrived at the fort around noon on the second day after leaving Tomis. As I rode through the camp, various of the soldiers cheered and waved, pleased to have me back, pleased that I'd escaped. I might be a sorcerer, but they'd rather have me for a doctor than Xanthos. I waved back, but I didn't stop until I reached the hospital. Arbetio and Edico both came running out, grinning and shouting congratulations. I felt that I was home.

The hospital was quiet: no plague cases — at least, not yet. I looked at a couple of cases who had arrived in my absence and checked on some of those who had been ill when I left. Only one had died. Arbetio and Edico had done a faultless job, as usual, and I complimented them on it. They complimented me on my teaching, and then Edico produced a flask of Chian wine. "I bought it to celebrate your acquittal," he told me, grinning.

We took it out into the hospital garden and sat beside the well to drink it. The sun was warm; cinquefoil, gentian, and my opium poppies were flowering in the garden, and the mosquitoes weren't too bad. I told the others something of the trial, and they laughed. "Xanthos got back three days ago," Arbetio told me. "He was saying that you'd cast a spell on the governor. And he came round here and tried to steal half our drugs. I told him to go away or I'd report him to Valerius. He cursed horribly."

"He was fined for bringing a frivolous charge," I told my colleagues. "He probably needs the money. I asked Sebastianus to give him his job back."

"What?" asked Edico, staring at me.

I explained.

Arbetio and Edico looked unhappy. "He is a dangerous man, Your Grace," said Edico. "I would prefer it if he were far away. He is your enemy."

"I don't like having enemies," I said. "I'm willing to forget the charge if he is — and surely he'll be willing to, if he gets his job back?"

They still looked unhappy about it, but said nothing. I finished my wine, then got up, saying that I must take my horse home and have it stabled.

At home, Sueridus and Raedagunda were as pleased to see me as Arbetio and Edico had been. Someone had told them that I was back, and they were both waiting for me in the doorway. Sueridus took the horse into the cowshed and began to rub it down.

"I put some water on to heat if you want to bathe, Master," Raedagunda said, smiling a bit shyly. "And I made some sweet wine cakes and bought some Chian wine for you, because we had escaped the courts."

"Bless you," I told her. I hadn't been aware that so many people had been studying my tastes, to buy Chian wine and get baths ready for me. I hadn't had a proper bath the whole time I was in Tomis — I hadn't had the privacy. And I felt very grubby from the riding. I felt grateful, at ease, myself again. In Tomis I had been walking a tightrope between Charis and Chariton; now I was on solid ground again. I smiled at Raedagunda and went into the house.

Raedagunda followed me, her smile waning. "That wicked Xanthos came here this morning," she told me.

"What did he want?"

"He wanted to know when you were coming back."

Perhaps he was going to beg me to intercede for him with Sebastianus. He'd swallowed his pride before. If so, I could simply hand him the letter and make peace. I liked the picture, and smiled.

"Well, tell me if he comes again. I'm willing to talk to him." I put the letter down on the kitchen table and went into the bathhouse. It was only one room, and a small one, but it was private. Raedagunda put the water for the bath in a sink behind the oven, where it grew warm. The sink was set against the wall of the bath itself, on the other side of the kitchen wall, and you could let the hot water run in from inside the bathhouse. Raedagunda always filled an amphora with cold water from the well and left it beside the bath, so that I could mix the water for myself in privacy. The room had two doors: the entrance from the kitchen, and a back door, which Raedagunda used to empty the dirty water into the garden; I locked both. There was also a stool, a shelf for the oil and strigil, and a couple of empty amphorae standing in the corner. My towel hung over these today, and I was a bit surprised: Raedagunda usually left it against the opposite wall, where it would grow warm. But it was a hot day. I ran some hot water into the bath; I heard Raedagunda on the other side of the wall, leaving the kitchen to fetch some more water from the well. I untied my riding boots, kicked them off, threw my cloak over the spare amphorae, undid my belt, took off the horse-scented trousers, and then reached under the tunic to unfasten the corset. I checked the water and added some cold to it. Then I took off the tunic.

I was just stepping into the bath when I heard a noise behind me, a gasp of astonishment. I spun around and saw Xanthos standing behind the amphorae. He had the towel which had concealed him in one hand. In the other he held a long knife.

Oh God, I thought. For a moment I was actually unable to move, paralyzed with the shock. Then I stepped back against the rim of the bath and grabbed my tunic, held it protectively in front of me. I felt quite sick.

"It's too late for that," whispered Xanthos. He grinned, a very slow unpleasant grin. "I already got an eyeful. I never yet heard of a eunuch where they not only cut everything off, but left a hole. You're a lot more interesting to look at than I thought you'd be — *Chariton.*"

"How did you get in?" I whispered. I had to whisper; I was afraid of alerting my slaves.

"Through the back door. Your slave left it open while she prepared the bath. I was going to wait until you were in the water, and then kill you. I don't think I will now. It would be a waste."

"Get out," I said, a bit more loudly. Sueridus was in the cowshed, Raedagunda had gone to the well: they would only hear a shout. "I already asked Sebastianus to reinstate you here, and he's agreed. I'll pay you what you like to keep this secret. You know I get money from the Goths. You can have all of it, if you'll keep this quiet."

"Oh, you'll pay," said Xanthos, still grinning. "Who are you really? One of the duke's mistresses?"

"No. He doesn't know. Nobody knows this. Nobody must know."

"It would be the end of your career as fort doctor, wouldn't it? You'd be sent back to your family in disgrace — or to your master. Are you somebody's slave? I suppose it doesn't matter. Put that tunic down. I want to look at you." He pushed one of the amphorae aside with his knee and came out from behind them, then stood in front of me, staring. I stood there clutching the tunic to my breast, unable to move. He pushed the tunic aside with the point of the knife and looked at my groin, then lifted the knife slowly, collecting the folds of cloth up until the point rested at the base of my throat. I started shaking. I could feel the blood mounting to my face. "You're even beautiful," he said. "Thin, but the right shape. I should have realized that you were too pretty to be a eunuch. Beautiful big eyes." He sneered. "You will pay me everything you earn from the Goths." His voice went hard on the terms. "You will get me my job back. And you will sleep with me."

"No."

"Yes. What would you do if I took you right here and now? Scream? Then they'll all know, even if I don't kill you: they find you like this and the whole camp will know you're a woman. That will be the end of you, won't it?" He laughed. "By all the gods, I never dreamed this. The perfect way to put you in your place!" He pushed his hand between my thighs.

I might have reasoned with him. I might have said that I was a noblewoman, and that he would suffer horribly if the rape were discovered; after all, an executioner who had led a noblewoman convicted of adultery naked to her death was burned alive for his insolence. I might have told him that the governor was my brother, and that he could guess what would happen to a man who raped the governor's sister. But I wasn't sure by then whether I wanted to reason with him or whether I just wanted him dead, and I couldn't bear for him to touch me. When Xanthos moved, so did I. I threw my tunic over his head, catching the knife in its folds, and I hooked my foot around his ankle and shoved him in the face. I was strong with desperation, and he was off guard with gloating and lust: he fell over backward, crashing to the floor with a grunt. I kicked him in the groin, then pulled the tunic off him. The knife was imbedded in its folds. I pulled it out. He rolled over onto his knees, groaning with pain — though my wild barefoot kick couldn't have really hurt him. He looked up at me with the old basilisk stare of hatred and began to climb to his feet. I jumped onto him, knocking him down again. I put the knife into his side just under the armpit, caught the big artery that runs to the arm, twisted slightly, and took the knife out. Xanthos screamed, and his blood splashed out over me; I jumped back. He collapsed onto his face. The blood jetted out, again and again. Then it slowed. I stood there naked, trembling, the knife in my hands.

Someone was beating on the door. "Master!" came Raedagunda's voice, then Sueridus', shouting, "Master!"

"Yes," I said vaguely. They stopped beating on the door and shouted questions — what had happened, was I hurt? I had to get dressed. I picked up my tunic, but it was soaked with blood. There was blood everywhere; I was covered with it. I stepped into the bath and splashed some of it off myself, then pulled my cloak on. Holding it closed in front of me, I opened the door. Sueridus and Raedagunda tumbled in; they looked at the body, and Raedagunda screamed.

"He was hiding in here," I said. "He tried to kill me. He was hiding behind the amphorae."

In the eyes of the camp, I was a hero. I had been acquitted on the charge of sorcerous murder, and had magnanimously interceded for my accuser. Xanthos had hated me; Xanthos had come back threatening vengeance; Xanthos, worst of all, had not attacked me openly but prepared an ambush in a cowardly fashion. I had bravely wrestled the knife away from him and killed him. Even Valerius was impressed. Sebastianus, when he heard the news, wrote a congratulatory letter and made jokes about my superiority to the hero Agamemnon, who hadn't managed to escape his final, fatal bath. Xanthos, everyone agreed, had got what he deserved.

Perhaps he had. But I knew that I was guilty too. I was not sure whether I had killed him to defend myself or to preserve my secret. If I had indeed been a eunuch, Xanthos would certainly have succeeded in killing me. It would have been a simple matter to wait until I was busy washing my hair or whatever, then jump out, stab me quickly, unbolt the back door, and slip out of the camp. Vengeance and escape. Because I was a woman, he had changed his plans. Vengeance and blackmail. Rape is a good substitute for murder, less permanent but more humiliating to the victim, and he was not immune to greed. But I might have been able to talk him out of the rape. And if I had refused to be blackmailed, if I had screamed for help, it wouldn't have ended in blood.

The whole incident was hateful to me. I never used that bathroom again, and I burned the blood-soaked tunic. Valerius had Xanthos' body burned and the ashes thrown into the Danube, to wash his ghost far away — but I thought that it would always haunt me.

About a month after killing Xanthos, I decided to buy a new slave.

By this time my workload had eased somewhat. The Goths were long gone up the river for their crossing into Moesia, and there was still no plague among our own troops; I had little to do, and time to think about my own house. Raedagunda was now heavily pregnant, with the baby due in a couple of months, and she was unable to do a lot of the fetching of water and washing of clothes that she normally did, though she'd had very little trouble with sickness, thank God. I decided to buy a girl to help her — one about twelve years old, perhaps, who would run errands and help with the baby after it was born. I would need a larger house when the child was more than a few months old, of course, but I would be glad to get rid of the present one. I couldn't bring myself to enter the bathhouse, and kept it locked up like a tomb.

There were plenty of traders coming down the river with cargoes of slaves; I gathered that the Goths in Moesia were selling off some of their children so as to have money to settle with. It always seems to me tragic for a parent to sell a child, but it's something that happens, and something that always has happened, like war and disease, so I wasn't unduly worried about it. One bright morning in early August I went down from the fort to the trading station at the docks and had a look around. There was a fair-sized slave boat there, standing moored against the bank. It was roofed over with thatch and watched by a few guards; the trader himself was inside the station, buying food for his merchandise. I told one of the guards what I wanted, and he ran off to fetch his master. In a moment the slaver, a large blond man with a red face, came out, smiling in what was meant to be an ingratiating fashion. But his eyes kept flicking over me in a quick assessing fashion, calculating how much I was worth. Eunuchs are very valuable slaves. Still, I was plainly an army official, and this slaver was hardly going to kidnap me from the Novidunum docks. "Your Prudence wishes to buy a slave?'" he asked.

I nodded. "A girl, about twelve years old, by preference. Biddable and good with children."

"Of course, of course! I have plenty like that, though I was, umm, planning to take them down to Histria. One earns more that way; you'll have to take that into account, eh? Would Your Discernment care to step on board?"

I stepped on board, and the slaver showed me under the thatched canopy. The boat was packed with children, far too many for the size of the craft. They ranged in age from about four to fifteen. They were sitting cramped in the bottom of the boat, the older ones shackled together in groups of three, the little ones loose. There was a terrible smell. They didn't have a cloak among them, and many of the boys were without tunics either, wearing only their tattered Gothic trousers: you could count the ribs in their thin chests. They looked in ill health, as though they had been worn out by hunger and rough living over a long time. I remembered the camps on the other side of the river. But the children there had looked healthier than these, surely? And these children came from Moesia, where conditions should be better. When the slaver came in with me, they stared up at us hopefully; one or two smiled nervously. It was very hot under the canopy. Flies buzzed, the boat rocked slightly on the river, but the children were eerily silent. One little girl was playing with a straw doll and an older child was rocking a four-year-old boy on her lap, but the rest sat still, waiting, hoping perhaps for the nightmare to end and their parents to take them home.

"Here's one that might please you," said the slaver, indicating the girl with the four-year-old. She was a thin, pale waif with dirty white-blonde hair and staring eyes. "Loves children, as you can see, very helpful and obedient. She's thirteen; cost you six *solidi*." He added to the girl, in Gothic, "Here, baggage, sit up! The gentleman wants to buy you!" I'd learned enough of the tongue by then to understand quite a lot, though I spoke it very badly. The girl sat up and stared at me in horror. The little boy looked at her and started to cry.

"Is that your brother?" I asked her. She stared at me blankly, and I repeated my question in Gothic. Her eyes widened; she shook her head. But she clutched the boy tightly, and he clung to her, sobbing pitifully.

"He's just taken a fancy to her," said the slaver. "Your Kindness need not worry about breaking up a family."

"I'll give you five *solidi* for both of them," I said. I had not the least need of a four-year-old boy, and I didn't have the space for one, but I decided all at once that I would buy the two. They had lost their families and clung together in their enslavement, and I didn't want them separated.

"Eight," returned the slaver. "He's a healthy child, a pretty one too — look at those blond curls! He'll grow into a fine strong man; you can train him to whatever you like." He grabbed the child and held him up so that I could see how healthy he was; the boy screamed in terror and kicked sticklike legs wildly in the air. The slaver handed him back to the girl, where he clung like a limpet.

"I already have a manslave," I said, determined not to pay this carrion crow a copper *drachma* more than I needed to. "I'm buying him out of charity. Neither of them speaks a word of Greek, and I think they both have worms. Five."

We bargained for a bit, and then the slaver let me have both the girl and the boy for five *solidi*, which I had not expected: his prices had been very low to start with. I had expected to pay more than that for one slave. But he had a bigger cargo than his boat could carry, and was probably worried about making the others sick.

We shook hands on the bargain, and then the slaver had the girl's shackles struck off, and his guards pulled them out of the boat and stood them up on the dock. I paid out the money, five small gold coins stamped with the face of His Sacred Majesty, Lord Valens the Augustus. The girl stood there looking at me, still clutching the little boy in her arms, the eyes of both wide with fear and confusion. The slaver asked me if I needed help to get them home, and I said that I thought I could manage on my own.

"I have bought you from that man," I told my new slaves in my clumsy Gothic. "I have a woman slave, she have baby soon, she need — needs — help. You come home with me."

"You've bought Alaric too?" asked the girl uncertainly.

"Yes. If you like, he is your brother. Now come." I pointed up the hill. The girl stared at it unhappily, stared back at the slave boat, then started up. After the first few steps she set the boy down. He took her hand and walked beside her.

When we reached the house, we found Sueridus and Raedagunda in the kitchen; I heard them giggling together before I opened the door. When I came in, I found Raedagunda sitting at the kitchen table kneading dough for bread, while Sueridus was making a model cradle from the extra. They stopped giggling and sat very straight when I showed my purchases in. I'd told them I meant to buy some-one else, but they stared at the little boy with astonishment.

"This is my house," I told the girl in my bad Gothic. "This is Sueridus, that is Raedagunda. You are —?"

"Gudrun." She looked around the kitchen, then looked at Raedagunda, then looked at me. "Please, are you a man or a woman?"

Sueridus laughed.

"She is a woman dressed up as a man," said the little boy, Alaric, confidently — the first words I heard him say.

Sueridus and Raedagunda both laughed at the child's simplicity. Raedagunda jumped up and came over to the little boy; she knelt in front of him. "He is not a woman, he is a very wise and powerful wizard! You are very lucky he bought you. Would you like a sesame cake?"

The child's mouth went perfectly round. He stared hard at me, then looked at Gudrun. "I would like a sesame cake," he told her, rather than Raedagunda. But Raedagunda laughed and fetched two cakes, one for Alaric and one for Gudrun. The little boy bit into his hungrily, but the girl stood holding hers, still watching me doubt-fully. Not surprising, since she'd discovered that her new master was a powerful wizard.

"I am a eunuch," I told her. I had to use the Greek word; there isn't a Gothic one. "Do you know what that is?" She shook her head. Sueridus explained to her; she looked horrified.

"You won't do that to Alaric!" she declared. It sounded like an order.

"I don't do that," I said, wishing I spoke the language better. "I have an oath. I am a healer." Then I gave up on the Gothic and continued in Greek. "Raedagunda, tell her that this is her home and that I won't hurt her or her brother; give them some food. Sueridus, get some clean clothes for them — here's five *solidi* for it; if there's any change, buy some bedding for them. Buy them some boots, too." They were both barefoot.

"You don't want to buy boots," said Sueridus while Raedagunda conveyed my instructions. "I'll buy the leather and make the boots myself."

"Very well, but go." He went. Raedagunda gave the children milk and some bread and cheese, which they ate as though they'd been starved a long time. Then I helped her to wash them. The Goths don't bathe often, and they were both terrified of the warm water, but submitted; I was so busy that I didn't even think twice about entering the bathhouse. They had lice, which I treated with a rinse of ivy and vinegar; the bath got rid of the fleas. They did both have worms, for which I recommended eating large quantities of garlic and applying an ointment of gentian. Gudrun had sores from her shackles, and had been beaten. I treated these injuries while Raedagunda assured the two that I was the cleverest healer in Thrace. Sueridus returned with the clothing, and soon the children were sitting at the table, looking presentable, clean, and comfortable, and eating garlic.

"There was a healer in the camp of Lord Fritigern," Gudrun volunteered. "He too said that eating garlic cured worms."

"Perhaps that was me," I said to Gudrun. Then: "Why did your parents sell you?" I was very anxious to hear her story. It is true that traders have always sold Gothic slaves. But a boat like that, crowded to the gunwales with children who are sold very cheap, for as much as it costs to clothe them — that's unusual. And it wasn't the only boat on the river. I thought I'd seen more than usual, heading down to Histria and the Euxine ports, but I hadn't thought much about it until now.

"We needed food, sir," the girl answered, putting her garlic down. "We had none. My mother said at least the Romans would not let me starve. The Romans gave them a dog in exchange for me, so Mother could eat the dog."

"Merciful Christ," I said, and I stared at the girl to see if she was joking. Exchange a human being for a dog?

Raedagunda stared too. "My parents sold me for a young plow ox and a gold *tremissis*," she said.

"That was before the people went across the river," Gudrun said confidently.

"Begin again," I told her. "You are from the north? You fled the Huns?"

She nodded. "The Huns came, and they burned our house," she said in a flat voice, then looked at me curiously. After a moment she went on. "They killed my father. My mother took me and my little brother out before the Huns came, and we hid in the forest. The Huns looked for us for a little while, but then they rode off again.

We walked south. We had heard that Lord Fritigern had agreed with the king of the Romans that we could cross the river and find lands there, where there are no Huns. We walked south a long way. Mother sold her bracelets and bought food, and I picked berries. Then we reached the river, and things were better. Mother found another father for us — his wife had been taken away by the Huns. Lord Fritigern gave us some wheat to make bread. I picked acorns and reeds and meadowsweet, and I tried to catch fish; my brother and I caught lots of frogs — we had plenty to eat. Then Lord Fritigern had it proclaimed that we could cross the river, and brought wagons to move the little children and the sick and all our possessions. We walked along the bank for many days, together with many other people, until we reached the place where the boats were. But we were very happy when we reached it. We got into a little boat and it took us across the river into the Roman lands. But when we got there, there was no food. My new father wanted to go look for some food, but the Romans wouldn't let him. They had very many soldiers there, and wouldn't let anyone go forward; they said that we must wait for lands to be allotted to us. We waited, but we had nothing to eat. I couldn't even find any frogs or berries; the people who had crossed before us had eaten them all. The Romans had lots of food, but they wanted money for it, lots of money. Mother sold her cloak and her earrings. My new father had a mail coat that he sold — the Romans had taken his sword away when he crossed. After a while I wanted to go back across the river. But the Romans wouldn't let us do that either. Mother sold my necklace and my cloak, and all our shoes. Then she said that we would all starve unless she sold us to Romans who would give us food. So she sold me first, but all they gave her was a dog, and when she protested they laughed at her. They gave me to the man you bought me from, sir, and he put chains on me and put me in the boat. I told him he didn't need the chains, but he put them on anyway. I tried to get away, and he beat me. Alaric was in the boat already when I came there, lying on the floor and crying. I'd seen him before in the camp, so I tried to comfort him. He's just like my little brother used to be. Thank you for buying both of us."

I said nothing. My five *solidi* suddenly felt like blood money, linking me in guilt to the people who had offered dogs in exchange for human beings. People in dire need have always sold their children, but the need is not usually created by unscrupulous men simply to acquire slaves. Those lands should have been allotted before the Goths ever crossed the Danube; I was sure Athanaric had mentioned certain parts of Thrace as already designated for settlement by the Theruingi. I tried to picture the camps beside the river in Moesia: worse than the ones I had seen in the spring. Cramped masses of people living in a few wagons and some makeshift shelters of bushes and leaves, with a few hides stretched out as roofs; people feeding on grubs and acorns and whatever they could afford to buy at extortionate rates from the well-supplied Roman force beyond them. People dying of disease, freely, inevitably — dysentery, typhoid, dropsy. People with no good drinking water, no privacy; children crying with hunger, the dead buried among the living or else thrown into the river. And the Romans taking jewelry, mail coats, clothing — and people.

"Who were the Romans who did this?" I asked at last. "Did you hear their names?"

Gudrun nodded, staring at me wide-eyed. "The commanders of the soldiers were called Lupicinus and Maximus. And there was a leader called Festinus, too, who had no soldiers but who should have sent food — that's what my new father said."

Festinus. Yes, Thorion had said that he was now governor of Moesia. He'd be capable of a thing like this. And I remembered what Sebastianus had said of his commanding officer's greed. Maximus was the duke of Moesia, and I knew nothing about him, but he must have been of a similar stamp or Lupicinus would not have been able to inflict such suffering.

I was utterly appalled by what the girl had told me. Moreover, it frightened me. I did not think Fritigern would endure too much more of this treatment; I suspected that already he was plotting some way to rally his people. They had had to surrender their arms when they crossed the river, but probably they had not all done so; they would be weaker than the opposing force of Romans, but still armed and dangerous. Or would they even be weaker? How many of them had crossed? I knew from Athanaric that there were thousands of the Theruingi.

Someone had to stop this. The authorities in Moesia were plainly in collusion, but Sebastianus and Thorion might be able to do something. And Athanaric? I couldn't believe for a moment that he was a part of this corrupt scheme, or that he wasn't aware of it already. I hadn't seen him since the trial. Presumably he had discovered how the Roman commanders were handling the Goths and had ridden posthaste to the court at Antioch to report them. Perhaps orders were already flying from the court to put an end to the disgraceful practices of Festinus and Lupicinus.

But corruption is a part of the way the empire is governed, and it can be difficult to get anyone at court to take notice of it. And I knew that Festinus at least had powerful friends. It would be difficult to stop this business. In fact, I was in as good a position to move people as anyone. I was a friend of the duke and a sister of the governor of Scythia. I would have to talk to both of them.

"Gudrun," I said, then stopped, baffled by my ignorance of her language. "You stay here now," I said. "I give you to your parents later, when — Raedagunda, tell her that I will not profit from this trading of people for dogs, and that I will return her and Alaric to their parents as soon as the Theruingi are settled on their own lands. And tell her that not all Romans are like Lupicinus and Festinus, and that I am going to tell her story to the duke and the governor and ask them to send food to her people."

Raedagunda stared for a moment, then gave me a radiant smile and translated. Gudrun stared too, and then her whole face lit with hope. She fell onto her knees and kissed my hands. "You will send me home?" she asked. "You will send food up the river?" Alaric stared at her, then ran over and hugged my knees in imitation.

"I will do everything I can," I promised them, in the language that they didn't understand, then: "All I can do, I will do," in Gothic. I only hoped that what I could do amounted to anything at all.

Sebastianus was still in Tomis, arranging supplies for the winter, and of course Thorion had never left it, so I determined to go to the city and speak to both of them personally. I told Valerius I was taking leave indefinitely but that I hoped to be back within a week. Then I arranged the hospital's affairs and left Arbetio and Edico in charge. They were delighted when I told them where I was going. Edico had heard from his family something of what was happening in Moesia, and from the looks that passed between them I gathered he'd expressed himself fiercely on the subject to Arbetio. At first I couldn't understand why they hadn't said anything to me. Then I realized that they believed that the cruel exploitation of the Theruingi was what the Romans had always intended, and that my friends Sebastianus and Thorion were party to it. They hadn't trusted me. Indeed, they plainly still suspected Sebastianus and Thorion, and were unsure of how much success I would have, but they wished me luck. I asked Arbetio to check on my new slaves occasionally while I was gone, and to check Raedagunda as well, and then I got onto my horse and set off. I had a spare tunic and my medical bag, and I took twenty *solidi* and some Gothic jewelry in case I needed to bribe someone. I left Raedagunda with a good supply of copper money for the shopping. In an emergency, she could buy what she needed on credit.

I reached Tomis in the middle of the afternoon on the second day after leaving Novidunum, and went straight to the prefecture. The prefectural slaves told me that the governor was seeing no one. I offered them a bribe, and they looked unhappy and said that it was really true: the governor had given orders that he would see no one. I said that he would see me. They whispered among themselves, then one of them went off to see if this was true, while I was left standing in the public waiting room, my horse tied up outside in the street. There was one other person waiting there, an old man with a petition, and he stared at me uneasily, recognizing me, no doubt, as the sorcerer whom Thorion had acquitted.

After a few minutes the door was flung open, and Thorion crashed into the room, his cloak with its purple stripe all askew and his hair sticking out like a twig broom. "Charition!" he shouted, and embraced me. "Thank God you've come; how did you manage it so soon? I only sent for you this morning!"

I gaped stupidly, and he laughed and began to pull me from the room. The gentleman tried to present him with the petition, but Thorion waved him angrily aside. "My concubine's in childbirth, this is a doctor for her, you want me to look at some bit of paper? Get out of my way!"

"Oh," I said weakly, and followed Thorion. The plight of the Goths would clearly have to wait.

He had not really needed to send for me at all, and if I'd come in response to his message, I wouldn't have arrived in time, even if I had used the imperial post — which I would have, as Thorion had sent a courier with a license to fetch me. Melissa (who was, as Maia had said, a sweet girl, though a bit dull) produced a healthy son about two hours after I arrived. She had a perfectly competent midwife with her already, and the birth was absolutely straightforward. I had nothing to do but mix up some cleansing solutions and hand her soothing draughts afterward. Still, I was very pleased to have assisted at my nephew's birth. He was a fine baby, with dark hair curling over his scalp, and he yelled with outrage as soon as he emerged into the world, and suckled lustily about an hour later. He was plainly not premature, as I had feared; Thorion and Melissa had simply judged the dates wrong. I sometimes think that the ten months Hippocrates allots for gestation is a mistake anyway: it often seems less than that.

Maia had been helping the midwife, fetching water and so on, and when Melissa was settled and comfortable after the birth, she ran to fetch Thorion. He was waiting in his room, and came running. When he saw Melissa cradling the baby he beamed; he was almost shaking with pleasure when he stroked his son's head. He kissed Melissa, kissed Maia, kissed the midwife, kissed me, kissed Melissa again. He kissed the baby. You would think that no one had ever had a son before. When the midwife finally persuaded him to leave the room and let his concubine get some rest, he took Maia and me with him, to hear again our opinion of the health, strength, and evident intelligence of his son.

"But how did you manage to get here so soon?" he demanded once more, after we had said most of what he wanted to hear. "I only sent for you this morning!"

"Actually," I told him, "I came to talk to you about another matter. But leave it till tomorrow; let's have only good things spoken on your son's birthday!"

Thorion beamed again. "Let's drink to his health!"

Thorion drank heavily to his son's health, and had to stay late in bed next morning, moaning about his head and his stomach. I gave him some hot, weak, honeyed wine with green cardamom, checked on Melissa and the baby (both doing well), and went to see Sebastianus.

The duke was busy with some traders when I arrived, but he had me admitted at once to his office. He smiled and waved me to a seat while he settled with them. He wanted so many tons of grain to go to Novidunum, so many to Salices; so much of wine and so much of lentils, to be delivered before the beginning of October. The traders shook their heads and said that there was trouble in Egypt — the Alexandrians were rioting again over some bishop, the port was closed half the time, the grain shipments were irregular — and they couldn't promise that the grain would get to Thrace by the proposed date.

"Your friend Athanasios is still causing trouble, even after his death," said Sebastianus after he had threatened the traders with penalties if they failed to deliver on time, and sent them out.

"The blame belongs to my enemy Lucius," I responded. "There

wasn't any trouble when Athanasios was alive. And there wouldn't be any trouble now if the Alexandrians had the archbishop they chose."

"Alexandrians are always rioting over something," Sebastianus said sourly. "But what brings you here? Or has your friend's mistress borne her infant hero yet?"

"Oh, you've heard about that?"

"I had dinner with the most excellent Theodoros last week. He spoke of little else. He almost made me wish Daphne were pregnant, he was so pleased with the idea of being a father. Do I gather I should send him a christening present?"

"It would be appreciated. The child is a boy; he was born last night, and his father thinks that Achilles was less bold and Adonis less beautiful. But in fact I came here to discuss another matter with Your Honor."

Sebastianus gave a snort of laughter. "Discuss away."

I told him Gudrun's story, and the smile faded from his face. When I finished he sat silent for a minute, turning a stylus in his hands. "And what do you think I should do about it?" he asked at last.

"Stop it."

"Stop Lupicinus? My commanding officer? I have no authority in Moesia."

"Report him to the master of arms, then. Or to your own father: he'd have influence with anyone."

Sebastianus put the stylus down and stood abruptly. "I'd heard something of this," he said. He went to his window and looked out into the courtyard. "Athanaric came through almost a month ago and shouted at me about it for an hour. I wrote to Lupicinus and to my father. I sent the letter west by a fast courier, and Athanaric galloped off to Antioch to report the affair to the master of the offices. Perhaps he's convinced someone to stop it by now." Sebastianus did not sound very confident that this was the case.

"Can't Your Excellency do anything more?" I asked.

"No." Sebastianus turned from the window. "My father has written back. He doesn't want to interfere with Lupicinus in his command, and he doesn't think I should either. He says it's not a military matter, but the concern of the governor."

"Isn't it a military matter? Do you think Fritigern will endure this treatment quietly?"

Sebastianus winced. "My father says that if the Goths do make trouble, we can always defeat them. The Romans have never been beaten by barbarians."

"So the Theruingi are to be crushed by Roman arms, and thousands of them and hundreds of our people no doubt killed in the process, all to satisfy the greed of a few corrupt men? Do you think it's right that they force people to trade their children for dogs?"

"Of course I don't!" Sebastianus snapped. "But it's out of my hands. Why don't you go tell your friend Theodoros to do something?"

"I came to Tomis to do just that. But can't you do something too? Report Lupicinus to the emperor?"

Sebastianus gave a deep sigh. "Chariton, I respect you more than I respect most, I'm sure you're motivated by the most perfect Hippocratic philanthropy, but I can't go interfering in a brother officer's command. And I can't go reporting my commanding officer to the emperor. It's against the honor of Roman arms."

"Oh, damn the honor of Roman arms! Can't you at least talk to Lupicinus yourself? Point out to him that if Fritigern and his people do rebel and have to be slaughtered, the emperor will be displeased? The settlement of the Goths in Thrace was something that delighted the officials at court. They won't be happy if it goes wrong."

"Lupicinus is making enough on this trade to buy half of Italy. Do you think he'd listen to me?" But Sebastianus frowned as he said this, as though he weren't sure whether Lupicinus would listen or not.

"He respects you, doesn't he?" I asked, pressing my point. "Wouldn't he listen if you told him he must guard his own back?"

"He might." Sebastianus sighed again, and looked at me speculatively. "He might. Very well, I will go see him in Marcianopolis. I don't want trouble with the Goths on this side of the river. And you can come too."

"Me?"

"The duke of Moesia wants to meet you. Or rather, he wants his doctors to meet you. Maximus may be greedy and unscrupulous, but he is worried about those damned Goths catching the plague and spreading it to his troops. He noticed that we've had no trouble here, thanks to your systems, and he wants you to tell his doctors how you've done it. There: you can come and argue with him yourself. Let's see . . . we can get away day after tomorrow." Sebastianus pounced back on the papers on his desk, shuffling through provisioning orders, orders for horses, a license for the post.

"I told Valerius I'd be away for about a week," I said, thinking of all my work back in Novidunum, of Raedagunda's baby, of Melissa.

"Well, you can write to him and tell him otherwise." He looked up from the papers and grinned. "You started this, not me. Why don't you go see your friend Theodoros and get to work on him as well?"

"At this rate I'll find myself headed for Antioch," I said, wishing I'd brought another tunic and another cloak. "But I will. And thank you."

Sebastianus laughed. "Thank you. I'm just as glad to do something about this. Athanaric left in a rage because I wouldn't do more. I have to do something to appease him."

I went back to the prefecture. Thorion was up, and was sitting in his office doing business. A horde of local decurions and magistrates were waiting to see him with petitions (and bribes) to be excused from some of their responsibilities. But the scribes recognized me this time, and sent me straight in. Thorion beamed as soon as he saw me.

"Did you see Melissa?" he asked at once. "How is she? I saw her when I first got up; I thought she looked perfect. That was a damned good hangover remedy you gave me, too."

I said that I too thought Melissa looked very well, but that she must rest, keep very clean, and drink plenty of fluids — well-watered wine, and perhaps some milk. The first week or two after childbirth is a dangerous time. Thorion nodded and looked knowing.

"Maia's helping with the baby, so Melissa doesn't have to get up," he told me. "But I'm glad you're here as well. How long can you stay?"

"I'm leaving for Marcianopolis day after tomorrow."

"What? But you just said that the next week or two would be dangerous . . ."

"You've got a perfectly competent midwife here in Tomis, there's no reason to suspect any danger for Melissa, and I'll leave a few preparations for some of the commoner problems. I have to go, Thorion. Duke Sebastianus wants me to talk to some of the doctors in Moesia about methods of preventing the spread of plagues."

"Oh, damn Duke Sebastianus! He seems to think he owns you!"

"Well, he is my commanding officer. I've just come from seeing him. He sends his congratulations on the birth of your son."

Thorion looked disgruntled and disgusted. "A woman has no business having a commanding officer. What were you seeing him about? Plagues?"

"No. Goths."

"Has that fellow Athanaric been at you too? He came round here a month ago, wanting me to send half the grain supplies in Tomis and Histria up the river to the barbarians in Moesia. I said it was the responsibility of the governor of Moesia to supply them and I'd hang myself before helping Festinus, and he swore at me."

I was beginning to feel quite proud of Athanaric. "You should send the grain," I said, and I told him Gudrun's story. He looked disgusted, but shrugged.

"I heard something of this," he admitted. "In fact, I've been collecting stories like that, and sending them back to the court. Maybe somebody there will listen. Or maybe not. Everybody knows I hate Festinus, and so they discount everything I say about him. I told Athanaric that when he came through."

"Couldn't you send some food, though, as well? Those people are starving."

"Lord God Eternal! How can I? We've scarcely got enough in the public granaries to last the winter, and Sebastianus will take some of that if he doesn't get his shipments from Alexandria for the troops. And why should I bail out Festinus? Let him get into trouble. The more trouble he gets in, the better, that's what I say."

"Thorion," I said urgently, "these people who are starving aren't Romans. Romans understand about official corruption, they accept it, they work at bribing other officials and pulling strings to get what they want. Goths don't know any of that. They used to think that the empire was perfect and that imperial officials were just and wise. They won't think that anymore, and they won't try to bribe somebody to report Festinus to the emperor. They'll fight. People will be killed. Sebastianus thinks that if it comes to fighting, that will be the end of the Theruingi and the whole affair, but . . . but there are a lot of Goths. And if there's a disturbance near the river, we may get more of the Gothic tribes crossing over, the ones who weren't invited. And behind them are the Halani and the Huns. Oh, I know that the empire always wins in the end, but 'the end' could be a long way off. If there's real trouble because of this, it won't be limited to Moesia: you'll be looking at a Gothic army outside the walls of Tomis."

Thorion stared at me, looking very uneasy.

"And think what would happen if you prevented that!" I went on. "I know you want to make a good job of this governorship. Prevent a war and you can go to the court covered in glory and walk into any office you like!"

"Yes, but that sort of glory costs," said Thorion unhappily. "If I let a lot of people off paying their taxes, I not only earn money in bribes from them, but they all praise me to the emperor as well, saying how just and moderate I am. But to get enough grain to have a surplus to send up the river, I'd have to exact the last scruple of an ounce due out of the locals, and they wouldn't like it. It's much more likely that instead of being covered in glory, I'd be covered with complaints. Then when my term of office is over here, I'd have to hang about the court taking lawsuits and kicking my heels in the chamberlains' waiting rooms. And I wouldn't be able to earn a copper *drachma* here, either. By Artemis the Great! Don't look so disapproving. You know why I want the money: Festinus cost us dear. Father had to sell off one of the farms with all its stock and twenty slaves in the last year of his life. I was hoping to buy them back with the proceeds of this governorship."

"Thorion, how much do the estates bring in every year?"

"Last year it was produce to the value of three hundred fourteen pounds in gold," Thorion replied promptly. "Twenty-two thousand, six hundred *solidi*. That's down by forty pounds in gold from what it was five years ago. What am I supposed to do if I want a consulship in Constantinople? The games cost more than that, even out of season."

"Do we spend twenty-two thousand, six hundred *solidi* in a year?"

Thorion looked embarrassed. "Well . . . no. But I have to keep up my position here, and the house in Constantinople as well as our house in Ephesus and all the estates. And that damned harbor in Ephesus always needs dredging, and people are always wanting me to contribute to it; they've even written to me here about it. And Johannes the steward says that . . . Oh, damn you, Charition! Very well, I'll send some grain to your damned Goths! Just watch, though, if Festinus doesn't manage to get the credit for it!"

I kissed Thorion. "You're a credit to your governorship, and a worthy father for your son."

"Yes, well. I wish that damned Sebastianus weren't dragging you off to Marcianopolis. What's the use of having a sister who's a doctor if she goes off just when you need her? Oh very well, I'll write up the orders, and you can take them to Marcianopolis with you. But you'll have to convince somebody there to accept the grain shipments. Lord, I suppose I'll have to write to that brute Festinus about it. I only hope you're right, that I do get some credit for this. It's hard to be virtuous and punished for it."

It's nearly a hundred miles from Tomis to Marcianopolis; we rode there in five days. Sebastianus said that he sometimes did it in three, but there was no particular need to hurry, as we were taking the coast road and the accommodation along the way wasn't bad. He was also taking Daphne and some of his household slaves. "She likes a change of scenery," he explained. "And there's no saying how long this will take; I might as well be comfortable while I'm in Marcianopolis." So Daphne rode in a covered carriage in the middle of the troops, Sebastianus' chattels bounced about on mules, and we traveled slowly along the coast in the bright summer sun. It was hot weather: when the road ran next to the sea, the men would all drop their arms and dash into the waves, splashing the cold water over each other and laughing. Once Daphne's carriage driver ran after them, and the lyre player jumped out into the salt water. Sebastianus rode his horse into the sea after her, fell off it chasing her, then caught her and put her back, dripping and laughing, into the inlaid interior. She had the curtains of her carriage pulled back nearly all the time, and she joked with the men and sang marching songs. She teased me because I didn't go into the water, and I responded that sea-born Aphrodite, goddess of love, was notably hostile to eunuchs. It was a wonderfully happy journey. I don't think there was a single member of the party who was pleased to see Marcianopolis looming black against the mountains the evening we arrived.

It was strange to remember how barbarous the city had first appeared to me. It looked such an ordinary place now. Sebastianus dismissed his troops to their barracks and invited me to stay with his household in a wing of the headquarters; he had sent a courier ahead to announce his arrival, and his usual rooms were prepared for him. Sebastianus also offered me one of his slaves to attend me while I was there, but I declined the offer, with thanks. So I had some privacy. I washed, changed into my un-horse-scented tunic, and resolved to buy another pair of trousers. Sebastianus' slave knocked on the door and conveyed an invitation to dinner from his master. I thanked him and went down to the dining room in which I had first had dinner with the duke; the first person I saw when I entered it was Athanaric.

I hadn't expected to see him, and was caught off guard. I stopped short in the doorway, my heart leaping; I could feel my face going hot. Fortunately, there were no lamps by the door, so no one noticed the blush. But as soon as he saw me Athanaric gave a smile of delighted welcome, hurried over, and took my hand. "Welcome, Chariton!" he said. "I gather that it's to you I owe Sebastianus' presence here. Well done!"

I said nothing; I was trying to control myself. Athanaric's greeting made me quite dizzy, as though I were swinging out over some great void.

"He got Theodoros to agree to send grain, as well," Sebastianus informed his friend.

"Immortal God!" Athanaric said. "How did you manage that? I tried arguing with him, but got nowhere: he said he couldn't get the grain."

I managed to sneeze, to excuse my silence. "Any governor can get more grain if he wants to squeeze the landowners," I said. "It was just a matter of convincing Thorion that it was necessary. He's a kind man, he doesn't like suffering. And I'd just helped deliver his first-born son."

"The advantages of the Hippocratic method!" said Athanaric, grinning. "Well, I am pleased to have such a powerful ally."

"I thought you were in Antioch."

"I've just arrived from there." The grin was gone, and I saw that he looked tired and careworn. "Allies there are less capable. The most illustrious Eutherios will listen to me, but Festinus, the governor here, is a friend of the praetorian prefect. Eutherios may say one thing to His Sacred Majesty, but Modestus just dismisses it all, and the emperor listens to Modestus. And everyone is preoccupied with Persia. No one wants to know what's happening here; no one will do anything. It will go on until the Theruingi revolt. Unless you can convince Lupicinus to stop it," to Sebastianus.

"I will try. But can we forget the Theruingi for tonight? I'll have to do quite enough talking about their problems tomorrow."

We reclined at table, Daphne and Sebastianus on one couch, Athanaric and I separate on two others. Daphne was yawning, tired from the journey and her swim. She rested her blonde head on Sebastianus' arm; they made a very pretty picture. Athanaric looked at them sourly, and started on the problems of the Theruingi again before the first course was finished.

"Will Theodoros really send the grain?" he asked me. "He and Festinus are notorious for the way they detest each other; neither will do anything that might benefit the other. And it is Festinus' responsibility to provide supplies for Fritigern's people."

"I have letters from Theodoros, asking Festinus to arrange distribution of the grain when it arrives for Scythia," I said simply.

Athanaric gave a whistle of admiration and shook his head.

"Why are they enemies?" asked Sebastianus, sipping his wine and looking affectionately at Athanaric over Daphne's head.

"It's a personal grudge," said Athanaric. "Theodoros' sister was supposed to marry Festinus. She disappeared a month before the wedding, leaving the bridegroom looking foolish — there was a scandal about it in Asia a few years back. Theodoros is supposed to have arranged the disappearance so that he wouldn't have to call an auctioneer's son 'brother.' Festinus was furious, and used all his influence to make things difficult for Theodoros and his family."

"What happened to the sister?" asked Daphne.

Athanaric shrugged. "No one knows. Something must have, or she'd have turned up again by now. She pined to death, her delicate nature crushed by the scandal and the concealment. Or she ran off with a charioteer. Those are two of the rumors: take your pick."

"Oh, I'll pick the charioteer!" said Daphne with a laugh. "I like races."

Sebastianus laughed and kissed her. "I'll bear that in mind," he said. "No charioteers will be invited to this house. Slaves! More wine. And Athanaric, no more talk about the Goths!"

The following day Sebastianus went to see Lupicinus, and I gave Athanaric Thorion's letters about the shipment of grain to take to the governor's office. Athanaric was surprised that I wouldn't take the letters myself. I said that I thought a *curiosus* of the *agentes in rebus* would receive more attention more quickly than an army doctor.

"You don't have any conciliatory messages from Theodoros to Festinus, then?" he asked, looking worried. "There's a danger that Festinus will refuse to receive the grain, particularly if it's Theodoros who sends it. The two hate each other very dearly. And Festinus may want to continue his trade at present, and may not be eager to receive supplies for the Goths, even at someone else's expense."

"Even if Theodoros would agree to send a conciliatory message," I replied, "I'm not the person to carry it. I'd rather not meet the governor."

Athanaric stood watching me carefully. "He knows you?"

I shrugged. I'd thought this over carefully, and decided that it was highly unlikely that Festinus would recognize me. He'd only actually seen me a few times, years before, and my own brother had failed to recognize in me the curled and perfumed young lady of his memories. Nonetheless, I was not keen to speak to the governor. "He probably doesn't remember me," I told Athanaric. "We have met, but there's no reason that he should notice me. Only I remember him. Most Ephesians do. Or perhaps you never heard how he acted when he governed us?"

"I heard. Well, well. You got into trouble not only in Egypt and Thrace but in Asia as well. You seem almost as good at finding trouble as you are at medicine. What was it that time? Did you help Theodoros to arrange his sister's disappearance?"

I laughed, and handed Athanaric Thorion's letters. " 'Sufficient unto the day the evil thereof,' " I told him. "Let old grudges sleep. Good luck with Festinus."

Sebastianus had notified Duke Maximus of Moesia that we were coming, and I accordingly presented myself as the learned doctor he had asked for. The duke was a tall, bronzed man with the looks, manners, and morals of a bandit. He had summoned two of his doctors to Marcianopolis as soon as he heard I was coming; he took me down to the barracks, introduced me to his men, and left us to discuss plagues. The doctors were marginally better than Xanthos and Diokles, but only marginally. I asked about supplies of water in the camps by the river; they said the people had the river. I asked about sanitation; they said the Romans had the usual arrangements, but the barbarians wandered up and down the banks looking for food and fouling everything. I asked about provisions for the sick; they said that the troops cared for their own on the spot and sent severe cases to the hospital. No provisions of any sort had been made for the barbarians. The doctors were highly resentful of the Theruingi, who were lashed by various illnesses which they passed on to the Roman troops; the doctors seemed to think they did it deliberately.

I gave a long lecture about how contagions affect the air and water, about the importance of insuring supplies of clean water for everyone, about quarantine and the use of sulfur to purify the air. I ended by stressing the urgent need to settle the Goths in their own land. When I left, the doctors were dissatisfied with me because I'd offered no magical cure for plague, and dissatisfied with their commander for keeping the plaguey Theruingi so near their own troops. I was dissatisfied too. If the doctors followed my instructions carefully, they might manage to control the spread of disease among the Roman troops. But I had done nothing for the Goths. I walked back to the center of Marcianopolis in a temper, cursing Roman greed.

When I reached the headquarters building, I found Sebastianus and Athanaric in an equally bad temper. "That Festinus is a fat red bloodsucking leech," Athanaric declared in a low voice. "I gave him Theodoros' letters and invented a few compliments, but he wouldn't say what he'd do about them, or if he'd do anything at all. He invited me to some banquet tonight. He's done the prefectural palace up like a Sybarite's mansion and stuffed it with Theruingian slaves to attend on him. He's in the thick of this business."

"Lupicinus credits him with considerable ingenuity," Sebastianus said with distaste. "When I brought the matter up, he tried to lay all the blame on the governor. Though it's plain the basic idea was his. Well, they've had a good few months of profiteering now: Lupicinus may agree to end the business. He's heard some rumors that the Goths may revolt, and he's beginning to worry. Festinus has invited him to dinner tonight too, as well as the three of us, and Lupicinus promised me he'd say something about the Goths there."

"Not me too?" I asked.

"He's invited all the army commanders and their staffs, and your name was specifically included. It's hardly surprising: you're a learned man, and could hardly be left out. Why, what's the matter?"

"He got into trouble in Ephesus when Festinus was governor," said Athanaric, grinning. "He won't say why."

"Serious trouble?" asked Sebastianus sharply, looking exasperated.

"I was never accused of anything," I said, now annoyed with Athanaric's easy deduction and concerned to prevent him from guessing anything else. "I doubt very much that Festinus will even remember me. I might as well go; I imagine I'll be seated at one of the bottom couches anyway." I went up to my room to wash, then sat on the bed in my good cloak and worried.

I needn't have. The banquet was a very large affair. Sebastianus took one of his staff officers as well as me, and on arriving in the banquet room we discovered that the duke of Moesia had a party of seven (and he hadn't included his doctors) and Lupicinus was there with a group of ten. Festinus greeted the arrivals at the banquet hall door. He was stouter than I remembered him, and more of the veins in his face had burst, leaving it blotched with red, but the glassy blue eyes were the same. He smiled as he shook Sebastianus' hand: the baring of teeth I remembered, like an animal's snarl. Sebastianus introduced me — "Chariton of Ephesus, my chief physician" — and the eyes skimmed my face, a fat damp hand rested in mine for a moment, and then he was baring his teeth at Athanaric, and one of the slaves was showing me to my place for the dinner, on the bottom couch with one of the junior staff officers. I sat down, feeling a bit limp. One of the prefectural slaves gave me a cup of honeyed white wine.

The banquet room was large and magnificent, recently replastered, repainted with hunting scenes, and hung with new brocade curtains. It was lit by three racks of oil lamps which burned a sweet oil scented with frankincense and cast a brilliant light over the whole room. The table was of citron wood and maple, highly polished, and it glittered with a dinner service of silver and Corinthian ware. At one side of the room sat three fair-haired girls playing flutes and lyres; the lyre player was rather clumsy, and looked nervous. Other slaves, girls and boys, hurried about filling the guests' cups and handing out rolls of white bread. They were all young, attractive, and quite clearly Gothic.

The guests were seated, and the banquet began. Lupicinus shared the host's couch, but Athanaric and Sebastianus were given the place of honor to Festinus' right. The slaves brought in a plate of oysters; three slim girls in thin red tunics served the upper part of the table, and some other children handed out food at my end. The staff officers around me began discussing campaigns, and I could hear nothing that anyone at the other end of the table might be saying.

The oysters were followed by stuffed dormice and grilled mullet with leeks; then chicken in white sauce, wild boar with honey and asafetida, and a peacock, roasted and carried in covered with its own splendid plumage. Lupicinus was given the privilege of ordering the wine, and he called for it strong and early; it was an unfamiliar red wine, old, highly fragrant, the sweetness balanced with the vinegar of age. I later learned that it was an Italian vintage called Falernian, which westerners esteem very highly and which is priced accordingly. We didn't get too much of it down at the bottom couch, but the slaves seemed to be constantly filling the cups at the top, and before long the guests at that end were all flushed and loud with it.

The staff officers went on about sieges and fortifications for most of the second course, pausing only to pinch the serving girls. But toward the end of the second course there was a lull in the conversation, and then Festinus said, loudly and clearly, "That damned insolent Theodoros wants to send grain supplies to the Goths." He looked at Athanaric as he spoke.

Lupicinus sneered; some of his staff officers jeered.

"The most careful Theodoros heard that Your Honor was unable to supply the Theruingi with the necessities of life," Athanaric returned evenly, "and he has most generously agreed to send some grain from the surplus of the province he governs, to assist Your Beneficence in your task of providing for them. He explains this in the letters I gave Your Prudence this morning."

"What I do in my province is no business of Theodoros'!" Festinus said contemptuously. "I've thought about his offer, and the more I think, the more insolent it seems. The fellow has done it simply to insult me! It's just a way of saying he thinks I'm incompetent. I've been governing provinces since he was a gaping adolescent; I saw him in his father's house in Ephesus, sulking over his schoolwork. He can sink his grain in the Danube before I'll take it."

"Nonetheless," said Athanaric, still in a level voice but now with an edge to it, "it is unquestionable that the Goths have suffered greatly from hunger since their crossing into Roman lands. And it is possible that the barbarians, being too ignorant to understand the most excellent reasons Your Prudence and the most esteemed Lupicinus have for keeping them beside the river with nothing to eat, may try to find some food by force of arms — unless something is provided for them."

Festinus gave a snort of contempt. Lupicinus glared at Athanaric. "We have commanded the barbarians to leave the river and to come see us here in Marcianopolis," he growled.

Athanaric stared at him for a moment, leaning forward on his couch, his face flushed. "To receive their lands?" he asked.

"To receive the lands His Sacred Majesty allotted them," agreed Lupicinus.

"I thank God." Athanaric sank back onto the couch as though overcome by the weight of relief and exhaustion. He looked at Sebastianus, who raised his eyebrows and shrugged.

"I've had reports that there are more Goths in Thrace than there ought to be," Lupicinus said, to no one in particular. "The Greuthungi were petitioning to be allowed to cross as well, and I think some of them may have slipped over with the help of that fox Fritigern. I want to bring the brute here and get him to explain."

The staff officers all began talking, like a pack of hounds catching a scent, protesting that they would soon put an end to the unauthorized intrusion of the Greuthungi. Athanaric began to look worried again. The Theruingi were a great tribe, even defeated and divided as they were; the Greuthungi were also powerful. If they had joined forces and if they were both across the river, they were an enemy to be feared.

"So Theodoros can keep his grain," Festinus added when the hounds had finished baying. It was plainly true that he hated Thorion even

278

more than Thorion hated him, and he was not letting slip a chance to abuse his enemy. "God rot him and it! He's an arrogant and bigoted lout, and has no business interfering in my province."

"Especially not after interfering in your wedding," said Lupicinus, grinning maliciously.

Festinus swore. He had had too much to drink already. "Everyone tells that story to disgrace me," he said savagely. "It's Theodoros that it ought to disgrace. I was thinking of settling in Ephesus, I'd acquired some land there, I looked around for a wife. The elder Theodoros practically throws his daughter at me — a frigid little virgin of fifteen, all big eyes and a touch-me-not air. I agree to take the girl, and her father is delighted. Next thing I know, she vanishes. Her father is distraught. Theodoros the younger as good as admits that he hid her somewhere, all out of arrogance and vanity, thinking himself above an alliance with my house, just because his grandfather scrambled to power and saved him the bother of doing it himself. Is that the way a gentleman behaves? But in fact he did me a favor. I was well out of the match: I heard that the girl ran off with a gladiator."

"With a gladiator?" asked Sebastianus, smiling. "How unusual. I wasn't aware that they had gladiators in Asia. I thought that was a western taste."

Festinus gave him a venomous look. "I meant a charioteer."

Lupicinus sniggered and called for more wine. Some fresh Gothic girls came out, in even finer and shorter tunics, and began to dance. The staff officers applauded.

I had disliked the banquet before it started, and by now was very eager to go. It didn't matter that I was supposed to have run off with a charioteer, but to have Festinus talking about me made me very uneasy. And the sight of the commanders feasting themselves and getting drunk on the profits they'd made from people like Gudrun, preparing to bed down with girls who'd been sold to ward off starvation, made me sick with anger. Fortunately, Sebastianus left early, pleading fatigue from his journey, and that meant his party could leave with him. We walked back to the headquarters in silence. The staff officer went off to bed, but Sebastianus invited Athanaric and me to join him in a drink. "Not Falernian," he stated.

"Did you convince Lupicinus to summon the Goths here?" Athanaric asked when the wine — Chian, mixed with warm water and fairly weak — was produced.

"I talked to him about the dangers of a revolt," said Sebastianus, swirling the wine about in his cup. "I hadn't heard that the Greuthungi wanted to cross as well, though. I expected it was that which decided him. Well, I hope it's over now."

"I hope it is," said Athanaric heavily.

"But you fear that Fritigern may have already set some kind of revolt in motion."

Athanaric waved the point aside. "If Fritigern's got an alliance with the Greuthungi . . . well, even so, it probably won't come to war. If Lupicinus handles him right, it may pass off without any trouble at all." But he was still frowning.

"There are always the legions," said Sebastianus.

"You trust too much in Roman superiority at arms," Athanaric said sharply. "My father commanded a federate troop armed and trained exactly like Fritigern's men, and they weren't noticeably worse than the regulars when it came to the battle cry."

"The Theruingi will be worse now, though, won't they?" Sebastianus said. "Defeated by the Huns and starved all these months, and most of them disarmed at the crossing. But I hope it doesn't come to that. It needn't."

"It needn't," agreed Athanaric.

"Where are your father's old troops now?" Sebastianus asked in a casual tone.

"Here in Thrace, at Hadrianopolis," Athanaric returned evenly. "Under the command of my cousins Bessas and Colias."

"You might recommend to someone that they be moved somewhere else. No, I'm not questioning their loyalty. But they are Theruingian Goths, and they are still federates, not regular army. I wouldn't like to lead them against their own people."

"They wouldn't follow you, not in a cause like this," Athanaric said, still in the even tone. "I will recommend in my report to His Illustriousness that they be moved to another diocese. I wish Festinus had been willing to accept that grain, though. The Theruingi can hardly be expected to march to Marcianopolis with empty stomachs."

Sebastianus laughed harshly. "There you see the result of spurned desire!"

"Of fallen pride, rather. Chariton, what's the truth of that story about the marriage that wasn't?"

I looked down at my hands, glad that Festinus' slaves had been niggardly with the wine to the lower couches: I needed my head clear. "Shortly after arriving in Ephesus as governor, Festinus accused the elder Theodoros of treason — on the strength of his name.

It was just after that conspiracy with the oracle, and he made a great show of zeal to impress His Sacred Majesty. There was no evidence to connect Theodoros with anything of the sort, but Festinus had some of the slaves tortured and the house searched, and he made the master of the house grovel to him and beg for mercy. When the elder Theodoros did agree to marry his daughter to the governor, it was because he was afraid of him. My friend, the younger Theodoros, was furious about it. I think anyone would have been, under the circumstances. He tried to talk his father out of arranging the match, but he was a dependent at the time, and could do nothing legally. Well, the girl disappeared. I couldn't tell you more about it than that."

"I can't really blame Theodoros," Sebastianus said thoughtfully. "Though it's a disgrace to a gentleman, being left with his marriage garlands and no bride. Still, I don't imagine the girl was keen to marry him, even if there was no charioteer waiting in the background. Though it's hard to tell what a noble maiden is thinking. I never can. Except they never seem keen to marry anyone."

Athanaric smiled. "Has your father introduced you to some prospects, then?"

"One or two. I never see more of them than the tops of their heads; they're always staring at the floor. Mindful of my responsibility to marry and breed Romans, I try talking to the young lady in question. Does she like literature? If Greek, she allows that Homer was a great poet; if Latin, she admires Vergil. Pressed hard, she may quote a few lines. Does she have any hobbies, perhaps like, well, gardening? She agrees that gardens are nice. Isn't it nice weather for the time of year? I ask, growing desperate. Yes, she says, and stares at the floor. When I get home I discover that I am supposed to be madly in love with her. Fortunately, the financial arrangements have always fallen through, and Father has yet to cobble up a match to his satisfaction. I don't know what I'd do if I had to get some young gentlewoman into bed."

Athanaric laughed. "I've always thought I'll have to spend my wedding night reading Vergil to her; it seems to be the only acceptable topic of conversation. Bless their finances, though; Father can find few girls whose dowries he thoroughly approves of. What will you do with Daphne when your father does arrange a match for you?"

"Don't get any hopes up: I'm not giving her to you, that's certain. I'll set her free, buy her a house, and give her a decent portion to live on. If she chooses to marry someone, that's her business, but otherwise I may need to go back to her, and I don't want anybody else meddling with her. She's a great girl."

"She is that," said Athanaric. He leaned back on the couch, considering her excellence, the Theruingi at last forgotten. "And she has a wonderful sense of humor."

"And she can sing, don't forget that," put in Sebastianus. "Oh, she's not my ideal woman — I'm not any Chaireas or Charikles, swearing love until death — but she's pretty and she's fun and I can talk to her. That seems to be about as much as you can expect from any woman, and it's a lot more than what you see in one suitable for marriage."

"All too true." Athanaric sighed. "What's your idea of an ideal woman, then?"

"Ah!" Sebastianus sat up and put his wine cup down. "Now, I've thought about this, and I decided that I'd take one like Catullus' Lesbia any day. 'Nimis elegante lingua,' 'dulce ridentem.' I wouldn't mind if she fitted the rest of the description as well — tall and slim, with a trim ankle and dark eyes — but for me, it's more important that she knows how to talk and how to laugh. I'd like to marry an intelligent woman of my own class, who knows her value, whom I can talk to. Catullus was lucky. If she did betray him later, I'm sure it was his fault for writing such damned slobbering poetry about her. 'Lingua sed torpet, tenuis sub artus flamma damanat —' "

"But that's Sappho!" I exclaimed.

"Catullus adapted it," returned Sebastianus. "You Greeks never read anything that's not in your own language."

"Why should we bother, if all the Latins do is 'adapt' Greek poems?"

Athanaric laughed. "Have you ever heard any Latin poetry, besides what Sebastianus is always quoting?"

"I heard Festinus quote some once in Ephesus," I said rashly. "It went 'Vitas inuleo me similis, Charis,' and I didn't think much of it."

"Chloe, it should be," Sebastianus corrected at once. "But I agree, it is one of Horace's weaker poems. And I don't suppose you see the point of love poetry anyway. I'll let you off reading Catullus. But what about you, Athanaric? What's your ideal woman?"

"Unlike you, I've never thought about it," he said. "I suppose . . . well, an honorable woman. Honest."

"Impossible!" Sebastianus exclaimed, and laughed.

"I don't mean one that tells the truth!" Athanaric said, laughing as well now. "What would be the use of that? But one that knows her own value, to use your phrase. Not corrupt, not cowardly. Noble and generous, a woman who can run a house and hold her own against the world."

"A Gothic princess," Sebastianus said, smiling. "That's the sort of woman you're describing."

Athanaric looked embarrassed. I thought of his cousin Amalberga. "Like Fritigern's wife," I put in, trying not to sound bitter. It was foolish and useless, but I couldn't help wishing that Athanaric had been the one to express a taste for intelligent, tall, slim women with dark eyes.

"What's she like?" Sebastianus asked with some interest.

"Brave," I said. "And she keeps her head. I attended her for a childbed complication; she was in some pain, but still able to give orders to her attendants and overrule their objections to me. I suppose she's beautiful as well — very fair and delicate."

"She is," Athanaric said. "Yes, I suppose I was thinking of someone like her."

"What does your father think of that?" Sebastianus asked. "When last I saw him, he was pretty damned keen for you to marry some Roman heiress."

"That fell through," Athanaric returned automatically. "But no, my father wants me to marry a Roman. Still, there must be Roman girls who don't spend their time staring at the floor."

Sebastianus shook his head dubiously. "I think they're brought up to it. Haven't you ever noticed nursemaids shouting at girl children: behave yourself, keep your tunic clean, don't talk to that strange man? By the time they're grown they can't do anything else. Sometimes by the time they're middle-aged they get over it; you meet a few intelligent older women. But never a marriage prospect like a Lesbia or a Theruingian queen. No, you and I are doomed to marry silly tongue-tied virgins with fat dowries, and settle into a matrimonial state of stupefying dullness. If we're very lucky, after ten or fifteen years the girls may turn into quite interesting women. But we can't tell beforehand whether they will or not, we'll just have to wait and see." He glanced at each of us, then gave me a look of chagrin. "I'm sorry," he said. "I have been tactless, discussing marriage in front of a eunuch."

"I don't mind," I replied. "You don't make it sound an attractive prospect." I got up and stretched; it was late and I was tired. "I'll quote you some love poetry. 'The moon has gone down, and the

Pleiades have set; Midnight is past, and soon comes dawn.' "

Sebastianus laughed. "And you're off to bed alone!"

"Well, with Your Excellency's permission, I'd like to start back to Novidunum tomorrow. I've talked to Duke Maximus' doctors, and there's no reason for me to stay here longer. And to tell the truth, apart from the present company I find this city disagreeable."

"So do I," said Athanaric. "I was planning to take Lupicinus' orders to Fritigern. We can take the same road out of town."

"Very well," said Sebastianus. "But you're not to go dragging him off to treat Goths."

Athanaric gave him a look of irritation. "Why not?"

"Because if Fritigern is planning a revolt, I don't want him to kidnap my chief physician. If there's a war, I want Chariton to spend his time treating Romans, not Goths."

"There probably won't be any war," Athanaric protested. "And the Theruingi need doctors."

"Then Lupicinus ought to provide them. I don't see why he doesn't; it's in his interest to keep the Goths healthy. I'll mention it to him tomorrow. I'm not leaving; since I'm in Marcianopolis, I might as well discuss some more business with the count. And I have Daphne here to keep me company."

"Don't be insufferable," snapped Athanaric. "Goodnight."

Athanaric rode with me as far as the first posting station beyond Marcianopolis. He was still annoyed with Sebastianus over the prohibition on taking me to treat the Goths. "You would have come, wouldn't you?" he asked me.

I agreed that I would have. There was not much work waiting for me in Scythia, and I was certain that the Theruingi in Moesia did need medical help. The idea of Fritigern having me kidnaped seemed flatly ridiculous, and I said so.

"Exactly," Athanaric said. "I don't think there will be a war now, unless Lupicinus commits some atrocity, and at any rate you're Fritigern's guest-friend, and immune from violence. The Goths take hospitality much more seriously than the Romans do. But Sebastianus judges everyone by what a Roman commander might do in his place."

"I thought you admired Roman commanders."

"Oh, there's more to Rome than the Lupicini of the empire. More to Rome than there ever will be to any Gothic kingdom. But it's true that the Goths are less corrupt." He rode in silence for a few minutes, frowning, then asked suddenly, "What's the truth of that story about Theodoros' sister?"

"Why do you need to know?" I asked.

"Just curious. There's something wrong there, somewhere; I have a feeling about it. I've missed something I should have noticed, something obvious. You won't help?"

"To tell the truth, I don't see that it is any affair of yours. There's no suspicion of treason involved, nothing that would concern the state."

"I didn't say there was. My reason for wanting to know what really happened is personal. I like to know the truth about things. I like to understand what's happening around me."

"Oh by Artemis the Great! Understanding is all very well, but you're talking about rooting out somebody else's secrets. It might hurt people to be exposed, haven't you thought of that? Curiosity in a case like this is indecent."

"I wasn't going to expose anyone; I just want to know the whole story. If you were involved in the girl's disappearance, you needn't fear that I'll make some statement about it to Festinus. It's just that . . . it's like an itch in my ear, feeling that I've missed something and not knowing what: I keep trying to scratch, and can't get at the place where it itches. Perhaps it isn't a decent sort of curiosity, but I can't help it. And you in particular ought to understand and be more sympathetic. You've gone poking about in people's bodies after their death, a thing that wouldn't have been approved of by them and that is dangerous to you as well. That's an indecent curiosity, isn't it?"

"If I do a dissection, it's so that I can understand how better to heal the sick," I said virtuously, though uneasily aware that there was a strong element of "indecent curiosity" in my motives as well. But it was true that my curiosity hurt no one whereas Athanaric's could ruin me. "Leave the matter, please," I begged him.

He looked at me, surprised but still obstinately curious. "You're afraid it could hurt *you*, aren't you? What if I promise to keep quiet about it? No? Well, maybe Theodoros will tell me more about it himself. I'll ask him the next time I'm in Tomis." He sighed, and added, "Which won't be for a long while."

I hoped it would be a sufficiently long while that he'd forget all about it. But I said nothing.

At the first posting station Athanaric changed horses and set out directly north at a gallop. I watched him ride off, the summer dust streaming from the hooves of his horse, his short cloak flying over one shoulder, strong hands on the reins, eyes narrowed on the road, hair pulled back by the wind. I thought of some more love poetry: "Not knowing it, you drive my soul." But he was dangerous to me; it was wrong to want him to discover my secret. Wrong to want him at all. I had to stop at Tomis before going back to Novidunum, to tell Thorion about the failure of my mission and to check on Melissa and my nephew. I would also use the visit to warn Thorion to be very careful what he said to Athanaric.

It was late in September before I finally got back to Novidunum. Thorion and Maia had wanted me to stay a long time at Tomis, and I agreed to remain until it was quite clear that Melissa and the baby were out of danger. Not that they were ever in it. Melissa was a strong young woman, and the baby took after his father and had a constitution of iron.

Thorion had already acquired a surplus of grain, though I'd been gone little more than a week. He had hit on the plan of allowing some of the landowners in the south of the province who had previously paid taxes in specie to pay in kind. This had allowed them to get rid of surplus grain and save money, and had been a popular move. Thorion had even managed to get some of them to bribe him to allow it. Of course, it is too expensive to move grain in inland regions, which is why the landowners had paid in specie to begin with, and why the army brought in some of its supplies from as far away as Egypt — it's cheaper to send grain by sea from Egypt to Tomis and up the Danube than to cart it a hundred miles overland. But Thorion worked hard at finding new routes to ship by canal and river and bought some boats at imperial expense (more discounting on taxes), and was busily piling up grain, gold, and good will. Only the imperial treasury was likely to be annoyed, and Thorion was ready for it with arguments about the present difficulties in getting shipments from Alexandria and the need to insure a supply for the army. He was disgusted to hear that Festinus wouldn't make the arrangements to receive the grain after all. But by this time he was enthusiastic about his new tax structure and kept on with it, storing the surplus grain in the public granaries and looking around for some good use for it.

And it turned out to be very lucky, for him and for Scythia, that he had done this, because that winter the world fell apart.

I had no suspicion of that when I rode back into the fortress, though. It was a bright, warm autumn day, and I was once again glad to be home. Everyone was very pleased to see me — Arbetio and Edico, the attendants and patients at the hospital, the troops, my own household. Gudrun and Alaric had settled happily into the house, and greeted me as though I were a minor god. I told them that I would return them to their families as soon as their families had homes for them to go to, and they knelt and kissed my hands. Raedagunda had managed not to have her baby yet; it arrived two days after I did. It was a girl, and healthy. Gudrun adored it. Alaric loathed it. Sueridus and Raedagunda asked my permission to name it Charitona. I told them that I could not countenance a barbarous name like that, but they could call it Charis if they wanted. And I looked around for a larger house.

Then, at the very end of October, my Gothic assistant at the hospital, Edico, disappeared. He'd had a visitor the night before, another Goth whom the guards at the fort gate had recognized as his cousin, and in the morning he and the visitor were both gone. I was surprised and perplexed. He'd finally learned how to read, and had been learning very quickly; he had a real gift for the art, and I was sorry, as well as hurt, to lose him. He'd taken half my supply of opium with him, and some hemp and mandragora, and my copy of Dioskourides' *On Medicines*, which I'd loaned him not long before. I felt as though he'd lowered himself to the level of a common thief, and was ashamed for him. I supposed that some members of his family must have fallen ill, but I didn't see why he couldn't have told me as much; I would have given him as much time off as he wanted.

Then, two days later, at the beginning of November, we had the bad news from Moesia that Edico must have already received. The Theruingi were in open revolt.

They had gone to Marcianopolis, but had taken a long time to get there. First they had insisted on building some wagons to carry their children and what goods they had left, and then they had marched very slowly to the city, pausing to beg, borrow, and steal food along the way. When they finally did reach the capital, Lupicinus invited the Gothic leaders to a banquet. Fritigern and a noble called Alavivus went, and their usual guard of armed attendants went with them and waited outside the headquarters while the chieftains feasted. The rest of the Theruingi were left outside the city walls. They were still hungry, and a large group of them went up to the city, wanting to trade for some food. The soldiers on guard laughed at them and tried to send them off; the Goths grew angry and hurled insults. Then the townspeople joined in and threw stones. The Goths began to throw stones back, and some threw spears — whatever they could find. The guards ran to tell Lupicinus that there was fighting at the gate. Lupicinus' first fear was for his own safety and the security of the city. He looked outside his own doors and saw Fritigern's companions sitting there waiting for their leader. He had them all killed and the chieftains seized.

The news of this reached the Goths outside the walls very quickly, and the rest of the Theruingi came swarming up to besiege the city. Though weakened by disease and hunger, they were very numerous, and many had kept their weapons when they had crossed. They beat their swords on their shields and demanded that the Romans release their king, as they called Fritigern. Fritigern at once spoke to Lupicinus, saying that all this was a misunderstanding, and that bloodshed would be avoided if he and his companion, Alavivus, were allowed to go and calm their people. Lupicinus sent them out past the bodies of their slaughtered companions, and of course as soon as they were out of the city they were off and away. They began to devastate the country regions around Marcianopolis, seizing food, horses, cattle, and whatever else they could get their hands on.

The next news was worse, and arrived a few days later. Lupicinus and Duke Maximus had managed to gather their troops and had led them against the Goths — and been routed. Most of the legions were simply wiped out, as were nearly all the staff officers who had talked so tediously of fortifications at Festinus' banquet. The standards of Roman legions were in barbarian hands. Moreover, the Goths had armed themselves with the dead Romans' weapons and were stronger than ever, and it now seemed certain that the Greuthungi had crossed the Danube as well, and that Fritigern had already formed an alliance with them. (Lupicinus was still alive: he'd fled his army when he saw it was going to lose, and had barricaded himself in Marcianopolis and sent for help.) The Goths were now free of all the restraints that fear of the Romans had imposed on them. They were desperate and, once they had tasted blood, hungry for revenge. They attacked towns and country houses throughout the southern provinces of Thrace, burning, looting, and raping. They killed all the men old enough to bear arms, and drove the women and older children off as slaves; babies and toddlers too young to walk far they snatched from their mothers and slaughtered. Officials, even innocent town magistrates, they killed by torture. One of Lupicinus' staff officers was caught: they flogged, burned, and blinded him, and ended by tearing him to pieces.

But Roman arrogance, the cause of the war, still hadn't finished making trouble for the Roman state. A letter from the emperor himself was sent to Hadrianopolis, commanding the Gothic troops there to leave Thrace and go at once into Hellespontus, in Asia. These troops were Athanaric's father's men, and they were in their winter quarters. They'd already put aside their weapons for the winter, and the town council had had these locked up when the trouble started. The Gothic commanders were not eager to involve themselves in a war, and simply asked for two days to prepare for the journey, for supplies of food, and for journey money. The chief magistrate of the city didn't have journey money, and the emperor hadn't sent any. The magistrate's country villa had been sacked by Fritigern's people, and he was furious with the Goths. He armed the citizens, and told the Goths that if they didn't leave immediately, he would have them all killed. The commanders tried to reason with him. The populace shouted and threw things. At last the Goths broke into open rebellion, killed great numbers of the citizens, seized arms — there's a munitions factory in Hadrianopolis — and left the city. They joined up with Fritigern's forces, and now Hadrianopolis was under siege by a vast and well-armed Gothic army.

Sebastianus had returned to Scythia before the rebellion started. The troops were put on alert, preparations were made to join up with other imperial forces — and then nothing happened. Sebastianus did not have enough men to face this huge Gothic army on his own. He sent letters to the emperor, sending them by sea so that they'd be safe, asking what he should do.

Thorion sent letters too, some to the emperor and some to me. "Come back to Tomis at once," he wrote. "I'm sending you and Melissa and the baby back to Constantinople. A province at war is no place for women."

"There are plenty of women in every province in every war," I wrote back. "And I am responsible for this hospital: I can't just abandon my patients. Don't worry. I'm as safe here in Novidunum as you are in Tomis."

I sent the letter with the official courier. I climbed the walls of the fortress and watched the man ride off across the flat fields, white now with the first snow. The sky over the delta was gray and swollen; only on the horizon did it brighten, with the peculiar lightness that the air has over the sea. The courier moved across the white snow under the heavy clouds, a small black ant crawling along a stretch of dust. Nothing else stirred. I looked down the delta, then walked slowly along the circuit of the walls. Smoke from a few houses eastward; cows in a field; a woman gathering wood. Then the vast brown tide of the river, dark and steaming in the cold air, running into the brightness of the distant, invisible sea. Beyond it the walls of the abandoned Gothic settlement on the other side were just visible, and more fields and trees: no motion, no life. There were no Goths there. But there might soon be other barbarians — Halani, Huns. I closed my eyes and thought of the empire, a ring of cities around the Middle Sea, spreading up the Euxine, up the Nile, up into the inland wildernesses, from remote Britain to the Persian frontier, from the Rhine and the Danube as far south as the deserts of Africa and the lands of the Ethiopians. Alexandria with its beacon tower, Caesarea, Tyre, imperial Antioch, Rhodes, Ephesus, my home, with its splendid temple to the goddess Artemis. Radiant Constantinople. Athens, mother of us all and still a city of learning, even in its long decline. And the cities of the West, which I knew only by report: Rome, Carthage, Massilia, and remote inland capitals like Treviri and Mediolanum. People of Britain, Gaul, Africa, Egypt, Syria, Asia: a babble of different languages, different histories, religions, races. One empire, two common tongues, and nearly a thousand years of civilization. For the first time in my life, standing there on the walls of Novidunum, I tried to imagine life without the Roman Empire, and for the first time I understood why Athanaric loved it.

I climbed down from the walls and went to my work at the hospital. I should have realized before that I was entirely a creature of the empire, formed by it through my education, fed by its learning, nourished by its peace. But Ephesus is an old city, and one takes things for granted, assuming that something is a natural state when really it is a hard-won privilege. It had never seemed odd to me that only soldiers bore weapons, that the laws were the same everywhere, that people could live by their professions, independently of any local lord, that one could buy goods from places thousands of miles away. But all of that was dependent on the empire, which supports the structure of the world as Atlas is said to support the sky. All of it was alien to the Goths. I had hated the imperial authorities at times, for their corruption, their brutality, their greedy claim on all power in the world. But now that there was a challenge to the imperial government of Thrace, I found myself completely a Roman. What I could do to serve the state now, I would. Others might abandon their posts; I was resolved that I wouldn't abandon mine.

Sebastianus came through Novidunum in the next week, checking on the troops on his way upriver. I gave him my report on the state of the legions' health (it was fairly good) and reported Edico's defection. Since this left me shorthanded, I asked Sebastianus to do two things: first, to promote the cleverest of the hospital attendants to the rank of doctor, and second, to legally manumit Arbetio and give him a salaried position. I'd asked this last several times before, but on this occasion I stressed the demand. I didn't want my other assistant disappearing as well, and I was fairly certain that Edico had promised him his freedom if he joined the Goths. Sebastianus saw my point, and didn't put the matter off as he'd done before; he had his scribe draw up the documents at once, called Arbetio in, and told him he was a free man. Arbetio gaped at him, and Sebastianus handed him the contract of an army doctor for him to sign. Arbetio looked at it, stunned. He signed it, his hand trembling. Sebastianus took the hand and shook it. Arbetio stared at the contract, his eyes very wide. I went over and offered him my hand as well; he took it, then looked at my face and embraced me. "Thank you," he said.

Sebastianus laughed. "You're right to thank the author rather than the executor of your freedom."

"I thank Your Generosity as well," Arbetio said, turning to him in embarrassment.

Sebastianus waved the thanks aside. "I should have done it the first time Chariton asked me — only we've been short of money. It's pleasant to see somebody happy these days. Will you perhaps join me for dinner this evening? You too, of course, Chariton."

"I didn't know you'd been asking him for my freedom," Arbetio told me as we left the presidium.

"I didn't want to raise false hopes," I returned. "I'm glad you've got it; it's long overdue. Congratulations."

Arbetio stopped and caught my hand again. "You are like a god to me," he said, his voice shaking. "You have transformed everything. First you taught me the art, and now you've given me my freedom.

I have no words for it. I would be willing to die, to thank you properly." He was crushing my hand, and starting to weep. "I could kill myself for happiness! Freedom!"

I felt ashamed. I had done nothing unusual; he had no cause for this passion of gratitude. And I hadn't realized that his freedom meant quite so much to him. "You should not thank me; you have no more than your due, and what you could have had for asking if you'd gone to the Goths. And don't kill yourself, my friend, we have too much work to do."

Arbetio laughed, let go my hand, and gave the long rising whoop that Goths use as a victory shout. Everyone in hearing range turned and stared at him. He flung his arms in the air and shouted, "I'm free!"

"Will you buy a house?" Sebastianus asked him at dinner that evening.

"Yes," he said. "I want to, anyway. If I can borrow the money."

"You could have my house," I offered. "I mean to get rid of it. You can pay me when you have funds."

"I meant to borrow some money from you for something else," Arbetio said nervously.

Sebastianus eyed him carefully. "For what? Another slave? Ten to one it's a woman."

Arbetio grinned and blushed. "Yes."

"The best way to spend money," Sebastianus told him. He snapped his fingers and pointed for his slave to pour some more wine for Arbetio.

"I'll need someone to keep house for me," Arbetio said defensively.

"I'll lend you the money," I told him, smiling. "And the house as well. Really, I'll be just as pleased to have it off my hands. Valerius has found a bigger one for me; it just needs rethatching."

Sebastianus smiled at me. "So speaks the man of wealth. Athanaric says he's discovered something about you."

I couldn't stop the nervous start; I spilled my wine down my tunic. I sat up quickly and tried to mop it off.

"Lord God Eternal!" said Sebastianus, and laughed. "It can't be that bad!"

I sat still and tried to control myself. Even if Athanaric had guessed the truth, he had plainly not actually told Sebastianus anything; there was nothing in the duke's manner to indicate that he knew I was a woman. "Athanaric told me that he was digging into some matters that didn't concern him," I said at last, savagely. "Some of which touched on me. I regard the matters as strictly private, and if Athanaric has discovered anything, I hope he has the grace to keep his mouth shut."

Sebastianus stared at me in some surprise. "He simply wrote at the bottom of a letter that he had been thinking about some events in Asia and had discovered something about you, which he meant to tell me when next we met."

"I would thank Your Honor not to listen to him."

"Holy Christ, Chariton, it can't matter. I don't care if Festinus accused you of treason, or even if you're really a runaway slave. Whatever it is, I'm sure you're perfectly innocent, and Athanaric's sure as well. He gave no indication that whatever it was was discreditable to you, only that it was something I should be aware of. If he means to tell me anything, it will only be because he wants me to sort the trouble out."

I sat back on the couch, but was too tense and angry to recline properly. Something Sebastianus should be aware of. I couldn't think of anything but my secret — but if he had worked that out, why hadn't he just told Sebastianus in his letter? Was it that he feared that the letter might fall into the wrong hands? Or had he jumped to some false conclusion? I might yet escape. But still I was angry and frightened. "Doesn't Athanaric have enough to do with the present calamities, without chasing up stale old events in another diocese?" I asked bitterly. "Particularly ones that could hurt his friends."

"If I could help at all . . ." Arbetio said hesitantly, but I shook my head.

Sebastianus sighed. "Well, I'm sorry I spoke. I didn't think you'd take it this way." He snapped his fingers and pointed to my glass; the slave filled it. "I was surprised that Athanaric had time to think of anything but his work, now that you mention it. He's been to Antioch and back, he's been talking to Fritigern under a truce flag, and in his last letter he said that he was bound for Sirmium."

"What's the news?" I asked, recovering myself a little.

"The Goths have lifted the siege of Hadrianopolis. Apparently Fritigern realized that they didn't have the experience in siege warfare to accomplish anything, and were only losing men. They've left a small force guarding the city, but the rest have broken into smaller bands and are roaming about pillaging. We might meet some in Scythia soon after all."

"What about our troops?" asked Arbetio.

Sebastianus shrugged. "No one will come from the east before the spring. Lupicinus has been relieved of his command and Festinus of his governorship, and they've both been sent home in disgrace — but that just means that now nobody's in charge here. And His Sacred Majesty doesn't dare move anyone from the Persian frontier without first concluding a peace with the Great King. He's sent Count Victor to do that now. It's likely that they'll partition Armenia. And he's going to send Profuturus and Trajanus here with some of the Armenian legions. I imagine that Athanaric is taking a message to the West asking Gratianus Augustus for troops, though he didn't say so. Still, I think we'll have to manage on our own until the spring, and possibly even the summer." He raised his cup, eyeing us over the top of it. "Drink up. We won't have much time for drinking, soon."

Sebastianus was right in both his guesses: we did not receive any reinforcements until the summer, and we did see more of the Goths. The main body of the Theruingi moved back toward Scythia. On a wide plain near the boundary between Scythia and Moesia, where the Danube swings close to the foothills of the Haemus mountains, they built a permanent camp. They moved their wagons into a great circle to form a kind of city, where the women and children remained; the men went out in raiding parties which traveled widely through Thrace, looting and pillaging. Some of them passed within a few miles of Novidunum. They made no attempt to attack the camps or to lay siege to any of the fortified cities, but concentrated on getting hold of supplies and booty. In this they were very successful. Many Gothic slaves, particularly those enslaved recently by Lupicinus' practices, ran off from their masters and back to their own people; they then told their compatriots where to find the richest houses and the fattest cattle. The Goths amassed plunder more quickly than the most corrupt governor amasses bribes. They plundered the gold mines to the south, they plundered the farms, they plundered the towns and villas. They carried off all the Roman goods they had always valued — fine pottery, ironwork, silver, and glass; good imported clothing of linen and silk and wool; inlaid furniture, paintings, and curtains; books which they couldn't read. And they took Roman slaves. Men who had been slaves themselves a few months before carried off the wives and children of their former masters, and the Roman troops could do little to stop them. Sebastianus set up a few raiding parties of his own, to try to catch small groups of Goths on their expeditions and punish them, but he didn't have the troops to do much.

Most of the population of Scythia flooded into the fortified cities, into Tomis and Histria and, to a lesser extent, into the army camps such as Novidunum. Thanks to Thorion's grain hording there was enough in the cities to feed everyone, though Thorion quickly established a system of rationing. Or so we judged: communications were disrupted. It was not always safe to send messages by land, because of the Goths, but the Danube was now frozen, and no ships braved the Euxine in midwinter. Couriers rode with any troops who were going up or down the river, but for weeks at a stretch Novidunum might have been the only city in the world, standing alone on its bluff amid the snows. Occasionally an army party would come down the river and dump a load of wounded in the hospital, but no one came from the sea from December till the spring.

Despite the quietness of the camp, we were fairly busy at the hospital. Besides the wounded of our own legion, we had stragglers from Moesia who were deserting or escaping the Goths, and sick or injured peasant refugees. I worried about our supplies of drugs, quarreled with Valerius over money for more supplies, bullied him into authorizing some more attendants, and then argued with them.

Arbetio worked heroically and with wonderful good humor. I had moved into the new, larger house, leaving him the old one, and he borrowed fifteen *solidi* and bought his girlfriend to live in it with him. She was a short, plump young woman named Irene, one of Valerius' cooks, and Arbetio had apparently been in love with her for years. He manumitted her, and they settled down as man and wife, both of them seeming quite deliriously happy with the arrangement. "You don't know how wonderful it is," he told me, "to go back from the hospital to my own home, and find Irene there, just waiting and spinning. Nobody shouting at her to fetch anything, nobody telling me she's busy now — the whole evening to spend together, just the two of us, and the whole night, every night, our own. With that behind me, I don't care how crowded we get here!" And he dismissed the full ward with a wave of his hand.

"I'm glad of it," I said, smiling. "One of us has to stay calm." And then I noticed that one of the new attendants was trying to give a patient unmixed wine, "to make him sweat it out, doctor," and rushed off to put a stop to it.

At the end of February Sebastianus sent a letter asking me to come upriver to the camp called Ad Salices, "At the Willows," near the Moesian border. One of his counterraiding parties had been cut to pieces by the Goths, and it was easier to bring me up to treat the wounded than to send them all down to the hospital. I packed a good supply of drugs and set off with an escort of twenty cavalrymen. It had thawed the week before but frozen again; when we rode out the gates it was snowing hard, and the thaw had left a layer of ice to cut the horses' legs. I had to doctor the animals, and then one of the escort's horse fell on him and broke his collarbone, and I had to set it and send him back to Novidunum. It was the middle of my period when we set out, too, and I had a tricky job concealing this: it was a fearful nuisance to travel with.

After three days' hard riding in abominable conditions, we reached a crest of a hill and saw Salices below us, its walls etched black against the snow and the frozen river. My escort raised a ragged cheer and we started down. The tribune commanding them stood up in his saddle and waved at the fort — then leaned over to the side and fell off his horse. I wondered what he thought he was doing, when suddenly I was close enough to see the body. The side of his skull was broken in, cracked like a nut by a lead bullet from a sling.

The others saw it at the same time; they stopped cheering and started their horses into a gallop down the hill, dragging their shields off their backs and holding them over their heads; another man fell while doing this. I didn't have a shield. I laid my head flat against my horse's neck and kicked him hard. He was tired, but he'd caught the smell of blood, of fear: he galloped after the others. I heard something whizzing over my head and prayed desperately to God and His Christ to shield me. To my right a horse stumbled and fell; its rider jumped up screaming, waving his sword. I couldn't have stopped for him even if I had wanted to. I closed my eyes. My horse stumbled, reared; I opened my eyes again and tried to hold him. The escort had swung round in front of me, turning back toward the ambush. I held on to my mount's reins, wondering what was happening now. Surely the lunatics didn't mean to fight? But the men had stopped in line, their swords drawn, their shields raised. Down the hill ran a group of Goths, their fur cloaks flapping as they moved, the late evening light gleaming on their spears. The man who'd lost his horse gave a war cry, the shout that starts low and rises to a bellow, and the Goths set on him. More of the barbarians were pouring from among the trees. The Roman fell, and the enemy stabbed his body again and again, giving wild shouts and whoops of fury, and then advanced on us. Behind me I heard trumpets.

"Why can't we go to the fort?" I asked the men in front of me.

"Don't worry!" said the cavalryman nearest me. "They're coming from the fort to help us."

"Why can't we go back, then?" I asked desperately.

The man gave a snort. "The enemy would kill us as we fled. We can't protect our backs. This way we have a chance. *HaaaRAI!*"

I felt quite horribly unprotected. It was true that the others were in front of me now, but they had helmets and shields and mail coats; I had my fur cloak and my medical bag. I crouched low on the horse, clutching the bag beside my head and thinking about fractures, treatment of head injuries, compresses for wounds, methods of amputation, and doses of mandragora. Perhaps, I thought, I should take some now so I won't feel it when I'm hit.

The barbarians advanced closer, still shouting; my escort threw spears, and one of the enemy fell. Behind us the trumpet sounded again, closer now. My escort raised the war cry again, and charged at the enemy. I didn't move, just sat there clutching my medical bag. Some Goths fell; the rest ran back up the hill. The escort didn't pursue them, but turned and rode back. A hail of missiles followed them; another man fell, tried to get up, fell again. The escort turned and faced the enemy once more. Then hoofbeats thundered behind us; the cavalry from the fort was arriving at last. I turned my horse to join them, then gave a cry of dismay: there were more barbarians beyond the fort, and a mounted group of them were riding up behind the Roman cavalry.

The commander of the Roman force saw them too, and shouted for his men to form a circle, then a wedge. Horses and armed men were everywhere; my escort milled about with the newcomers, spears flashing in the sunset as they were leveled. More trumpets; more men set out from Salices, this time on foot. Shouting and confusion. "You're Chariton the doctor, aren't you?" asked the cavalry commander. "Go into the middle." I went, and the wedge started back toward the fort. The barbarian cavalry split into two groups, wheeling about on each side of us. Behind us the Goths who had ambushed my party were pouring down the hill. "By the Unconquered Sun!" said the commander. "Halt! Halt! Form a circle! Raise shields and hold!" And more quietly, to himself, "My God, this is a fix!"

The Gothic cavalry curled into a half-circle facing the Romans, firmly blocking the way back to the fort. Their horses danced, and they beat their shields with their swords and screamed. The Roman force was far outnumbered; even I could see that we didn't have much chance of getting to Salices through that. I pushed my way over to the commander. "Do we have to fight them?" I asked. "What do they want?"

"They want to kill us," the commander said grimly. "We killed some of their friends two days ago. Dear Lord, I didn't realize there were so many of them still here!"

"If we fight now, they'll lose a lot of men as well, won't they?" I asked. "And to no purpose. Listen, I'm a guest-friend of Lord Fritigern — I cured his wife before all this started. Let me go ask them for a truce. We go back to the fort, and they go off and do some plundering. Won't they agree to that?"

The commander looked at me in astonishment for a moment, then looked at the Goths. "If you're willing to talk to the devils, go, by all means!" he said. "Good luck! Here, Valentinus, give us some green branches: the doctor's going to go ask them for a truce."

The men all stared at me, then cheered. Valentinus, a tribune, cut down a roadside shrub and handed me the branches; the leaves were new and tiny, folded like clasped hands. I hoped the Goths could tell what they were supposed to mean. I held a branch in each hand, and the men let me through to the front rank. The Goths were drawn up opposite us, a few hundred yards away, waiting. I took a deep breath, lifted the branches in the air, and rode out.

A bullet from a sling crashed into the road to my left. I stopped and sat still, holding up the branches. "Truce!" I shouted. I could see the Goths pointing and talking to each other, noticing that I was unarmed and unarmored. I started riding toward them again, and this time there were no missiles.

When I was nearing the Gothic line, one man rode out from it and across to meet me; by the quantity of jewelry he wore, I judged him to be the commander. "Truce," I repeated, in Greek, then added "Friend!" in Gothic.

"Friend?" returned the Gothic commander in his own language, pulling his horse up opposite me and glaring. "No Roman is a friend to the Goths! Who are you, and what do you want?"

"I am Chariton of Ephesus, a doctor and a guest-friend of Lord Fritigern. I have come to ask for the Romans to ride back to Salices in peace. If you attack us, we die, and many of you die, and there is no gain." Fear improved my Gothic wonderfully.

"Chariton of Ephesus?" said the commander, and one of the other Goths, almost as importantly decorated and wearing a wolfskin cloak, gave a shout and rode over. He pulled the commander aside, and they talked briefly, whispering and glancing frequently at me. Then the commander turned back. "I welcome the guest-friend of Lord Fritigern," he said in a much gentler tone. "Stay here; give Triwane the tokens of the truce. Your people may ride to Salices."

Triwane, the one who had apparently told the commander about me, took the branches and, holding them in the air, rode slowly back toward the Romans. The commander shouted orders at his troops, and the Gothic line broke into two again and rode slowly back away from the river. The Romans started forward, led by Triwane, who held the green branches high. I swallowed hard. It was over, thank all the gods.

"I thank you, sir," I said, turning back to the commander. "May I join my people now?"

He looked at me thoughtfully, chewing on his mustache, then leaned over and caught my horse's bridle. "Lord Fritigern wishes to see you."

I stared at him stupidly for a minute. Fritigern wanted to see me. Then I realized: Fritigern undoubtedly needed doctors. "No," I said. "I am Fritigern's guest-friend, I saved his wife's life when she was ill after childbirth. I am not coming willingly. And Fritigern is a nobleman, and will not thank you if you kill his guest-friend trying to bring me by force." I gave my horse a violent kick, and, startled, it pulled loose from the Gothic commander; I turned it toward the Roman force, which was now passing, and galloped hard. Someone behind me threw something, but the commander shouted for him to stop; instead I heard other horses start after me. Ahead I could see the Roman tribune drawing rein, signaling to his men to stop. Then my tired horse stumbled and fell. I rolled off as it hit the ground, and lay there a moment, winded. The Goths galloped up beside me and jumped down. One of them caught my horse. I got up onto my hands and knees; the snow was wet, and the light was fading. For a moment I could not move. Caught between the two armies, I felt as though my very name had been stripped from me, and I was afraid. Afraid not so much of the violence all around me, though that had shaken me deeply, as of something more — of the darkness, of exposure, of being no one at all.

More hoofbeats, and then the Roman tribune rode up. I sat back on my heels, trying to control myself. The Goths were shouting, and one had drawn his sword.

"What's happening?" asked the Roman. "I thought we had a truce?"

The Gothic commander shouted to his man to put his sword away, then faced the Roman. "We have a truce," he said in perfectly good Latin. "But the physician comes with us."

The Roman commander looked down at me and touched the hilt of his own sword. "He is a Roman, and the duke values him highly," he said firmly. "You have no right to take him prisoner."

"Does the duke value him more than yourself and all your men?" asked the Goth. "There is time to call the truce off, still. Fight us, if you wish. Lord Fritigern has mentioned this physician as one whose services he wished to obtain. I will bring him to the king. If I have to kill some Romans to do it, so."

I climbed to my feet, feeling very small and cold. The tribune sat on his horse looking down at me. He looked at the Gothic commander, at the Gothic troops, then back at his own men. He sighed, shook his head. "I'm sorry," he told me. "You will have to go with him."

I looked at the Gothic line behind me. For a moment I thought I would disgrace myself by weeping. I knew that Fritigern would not harm me, but I desperately felt myself to be a Roman, to belong inside the fort with Sebastianus and the troops, not outside it with the barbarians and the snow. It was as though I would cease to exist if I were bereft of everyone who knew me — as though I would cease to exist as Chariton, anyway.

But weeping would do me no good, and Goths and Romans alike would consider it contemptible. "Very well," I told the tribune. The Gothic soldier was still holding my horse; I went over and grasped the saddle. The Goth kept hold of the reins. "Tell Sebastianus that I feel like Iphigenia at Aulis," I told the tribune, trying to keep my voice light. " 'I go, granting victorious salvation to the Greeks!' He'll like that."

The tribune looked blank, but nodded. "I am sorry," he repeated. "Perhaps someone will ransom you. Good luck. Farewell." He turned his horse and rode back to his own men, and the Roman troops trotted past through the dusk. Lamps shone from the gates of Salices; the infantry stood massed before the walls. I caught a glimpse of gold beneath the lamps: Sebastianus' gilded helmet, or perhaps his hair. "Lamp-bearing day and lightbeams of Zeus, I have been given another age, another fate. Dear light, farewell." Yes, I found Euripides' play apt, even if Sebastianus didn't.

The Goths turned their horses, pulling mine around. It couldn't be delayed any longer. I mounted, and we rode off into the night.

The Goths had their camp not far from the fort of Salices, so we did not have far to go. It was a large camp — there were about eight hundred Goths, and they had a hundred or so Roman prisoners among their plunder. The Gothic commander — his name was Walimir, which I couldn't pronounce — immediately set me to work treating the injured. He was polite about it, and phrased his order as a request, but it was nonetheless an order. The Goths had wounds, some of which were infected, largely because of their passion for tourniquets and magical charms; the Roman prisoners had wounds and various shackle galls. I enlisted the help of some of the Romans to prepare bandages and cleansing solutions, but it still took hours to treat all who needed it, and by that time I was too tired to try to escape. Walimir did not have me bound, because I was the king's guest-friend, but he did set a couple of cavalrymen to watch me. I doubt that I could have got away even if I'd been fresh. But my guards made my life very difficult. It was hard enough to keep my secret traveling with Romans, when I could enforce a little privacy: now I had no privacy, and I was at my wits' end within a day. I couldn't wash, and using a latrine was a trial on the rack — the Goths were very curious about what was actually done to a eunuch, and stared hard, though I kept my tunic down. I was glad that my period was out of the way for a month; I hoped to win, if not freedom, at least some space for myself before the next time.

The Goths broke camp next morning and set out for their wagon city and Fritigern. They had been raiding to the east, and had sent a smaller party northward, which Sebastianus' men had intercepted and wiped out; as the tribune had said, the raid on Salices had been punitive. They had camped out of sight and laid an ambush along the camp's supply route, hoping to kill a few Romans and then slip away again. But they had not been eager to do any more than that, and now they wanted to return with their booty to their wives and families. So we marched southwest, first a party of the cavalry, then the soldiers on foot, with the slaves and the wagons of plunder, then the cows, then the rest of the cavalry, riding slowly through a land white and emptied of all its people.

Even at our slow pace, it took only a day and a half to reach the wagon city — I hadn't realized it was so close. From a distance it looked like a real city, with wooden walls; only when you drew nearer did you see that the walls were wagons hitched end to end, with wooden palisades tied against them. When we approached, some of the Goths rode ahead, shouting and whooping and waving things they had plundered; and more Goths came streaming from the city, shouting back. Children pelted through the snow and ran alongside the columns, yelling questions, throwing snowballs and insults at the prisoners, running up to catch hold of a father or brother, uncle or cousin. The column stopped altogether long before we reached the gates. I sat on my horse with my shoulders hunched, feeling wretched. People stared at me and pointed, though no one threw anything.

After what seemed a long time, Walimir took his subordinates and me and rode into the city. There were more wagons inside, arranged in uneven concentric circles. Animals and people were everywhere. The smoke from cooking fires mingled with the smell of the latrines; chickens scratched on dungheaps where children were playing; women were stretching clothes out to dry on thorn hedges or over horse troughs by crude wells. I wondered how many Goths there were in Thrace now. From the look of it, this wagon city was far larger than any Roman one in the diocese.

At the center of the camp was a house. It was a Roman house, a large and splendid villa, with a columned front and a tiled roof and a bathhouse. A makeshift addition of wood, wattle, and thatch had been stuck at the back to enlarge it, and smoke from the center of this showed that it was heated only by a hearth fire — the villa had a hypocaust. Here Walimir dismounted and signaled for me to dismount as well. Guards in stolen Roman armor and bearskin cloaks stood before the house, and two of these came over and asked Walimir his business.

"I am returned from raiding," he announced. "I have taken much plunder and many prisoners; many Romans have I killed at Salices, and I have captured the famous physician and wizard Chariton, and brought him here to King Fritigern."

The guards looked at Walimir with respect, and at me with fascination. We were admitted to the hall of the villa, and one of them went to announce us to Fritigern. He came back and complimented Walimir on Fritigern's behalf, but begged him to wait a short time while the king settled some business. We waited. After about half an hour someone else came into the waiting room, a tall Goth in a cloak lined with ermine, and with a shock I recognized him as my former assistant Edico.

"Chariton, my dear master!" he exclaimed, beaming at me, and came up and seized my hand. "I am so glad to see you unharmed, and among my own people!"

I took my hand back. I was glad to see Edico — it was good to see any familiar face, and delicious to hear Greek spoken again — but I was angry. "I am not here of my own free will," I said flatly.

The smile stopped at once. "Yes, they told me you had been captured. But don't worry, you will come to no harm. You have many friends here, King Fritigern among them. You will be treated in every way as our guest."

"A guest is free to go when he pleases," I said. "Am I to assume that's true for me? If so, I'll leave at once."

He shook his head quickly. "I am sorry. We are very shorthanded here. There are not many doctors, and people are ill. I've tried to see that they use wells for drinking water, I've tried to do all the things you taught me, but we still are suffering greatly from disease. The people were badly weakened by those devils who held us at the river. And the wounded suffer very much since we don't have the supplies to treat them properly. I've run out of opium, and I've had boys combing the neighborhood for mandragora for weeks."

"Run out of the opium? What a pity. I'm afraid I don't have much: some thief stole half our supplies at Novidunum."

Edico had the grace to blush. "We needed it badly," he said earnestly. "I know you pitied us, Chariton; you tried to stop that business of Lupicinus'. But you never saw how much we suffered, and we weren't your own people."

"I can understand your taking the drugs," I admitted. "If you'd asked me before the revolt started, I would have given them to you, and sent you to help your people —"

"I would have gone before, but I was ordered to wait!" Edico put in eagerly.

"— but I don't know why you took that book of mine. It was my personal property, and valuable too."

Edico blushed harder. "I meant to copy it and send you back the original," he said. "But I haven't had time. We have so few doctors — even fewer that I can trust. I was overjoyed when they said we'd captured you. You will be able to save so many lives."

"I am not overjoyed! I can save lives among the Romans as well, and I'd far rather be with my own people. Edico, I taught you the art, and in your oath you would have sworn to regard me as your father. Intercede for me, try to persuade the king to send me home. Listen, if you're worried that I'm healing your enemies, I'll swear to go away from Thrace, back to Alexandria, or perhaps Constantinople. But I don't belong here. You know that."

Edico stood there, his face crimson above the ermine cloak. "I am sorry," he said at last. "We are shorthanded, and need help."

"Damn you," I said evenly. There hadn't been much hope of help from him, but that hadn't stopped my hoping. A door beyond us opened, the guards stood to attention, and another Gothic nobleman beckoned us to come in to see the king.

Walimir went in first, followed by his subordinates, then me and a guard; Edico trailed in behind, looking miserable. The room was large and magnificent. It had a mosaic of the zodiac on the floor, and glass windows; it was hung with curtains of green and gold brocade, and the green and yellow paneling of the walls was covered with paintings. At one side of the room the Goths had set a kind of platform covered in more brocades, and on top of this were several gilded couches. On the central of these sat Fritigern. He was wearing a purple cloak — God knows where he had got such a thing — and a gold diadem. Another chieftain, similarly dressed, sat on the edge of the couch beside him; I guessed that he was the other Gothic leader, Alavivus, or perhaps one of the Greuthungian nobles.

Walimir went down on one knee before the king, then rose again — a prostration that wouldn't have been nearly deep enough for a real emperor. "Greetings, Fritigern, king of the Goths!" he exclaimed. The other chieftain looked put out but made no comment. Fritigern rose from his couch and came down to shake Walimir's hand.

"Greetings, Walimir! And well done! The whole city is ringing with the news of your victories." Walimir looked pleased. "I hope the plunder is distributed according to your wishes and the customs of the people? Good. And well done, capturing Chariton. Lord Edico has been lamenting his absence for months."

"Leaving me to lament my presence," I put in. "Or am I to consider myself a slave now, and keep silent while others dispose of me?"

"You are our guest," said Fritigern in Greek, and offered me his hand.

After a minute I took it. "Lord Fritigern," I said, "I know that Your Honor's people have suffered a great injustice. I tried to stop it —"

"I heard of that, and thank you."

"— but I cannot serve you against my own people. Please let me go. I have helped Your Kindness in the past, and you owe me a better return than captivity."

Fritigern shook his head. "I am sorry. I do not ask you to fight against your own people. I think that as a doctor, you will not refuse to treat the sick. And we have very many who are sick or wounded — sick because they trusted the Romans and trusted me, and wounded because they were fighting for me. I cannot let you go."

"Then no matter what fine words you say about guests, you are making me a slave."

"If you choose to use that word, you may; I will call you my guest. You are welcome to my house. Have you eaten? Then perhaps you, and you, esteemed Walimir, would join me for dinner? Ah, Chariton, I suppose being a Greek you will want to bathe first. My own slaves will attend you."

"Thank you, no," I told him. I wondered how long I would have to stay among the Goths, treating their injured. I wondered if the Romans would regard me as a traitor when they eventually defeated the barbarians. Probably not; Sebastianus knew I had gone unwillingly.

"Well, a change of clothing, then?" Fritigern suggested, giving me an indecipherable look with his pale eyes. "You have ridden far, and it grieves me to see a guest so travel-worn."

I sighed. "If I may have a room to myself, I would like to be alone, to rest."

"My slaves will care for you."

"If Your Excellency does not object, I would prefer to be private."

The glassy eyes fixed on me, the look deepening slightly to a frown. "If Your Wisdom will excuse me, that is ill advised. It would be better if the slaves could look at you and report to their friends that you are indeed a man; it would set people's minds at rest. There have been some reports that you are a devil — I am sorry, many people here are exceedingly foolish and superstitious, and do nothing but

305

gossip. And then my wife and her women think that you are really a woman. We have no eunuchs among our people. Let the slaves attend you, as they do any person of rank, and they will stamp out silly rumors."

"I do not like to be stared at," I said at random, trying to think of a good excuse for my modesty. "Please, you have made me a slave; leave me my dignity."

Fritigern stared at me, frowning. Behind me Edico stirred. "How does it offend a gentleman's dignity to have slaves attend him?" he asked. "You're being too sensitive, Your Grace."

"I want people to know clearly what you are, now that you are serving me," said Fritigern. "My wife says you are really a woman. She says you adopt a disguise because the Romans do not permit women to study medicine. How can you serve me properly if people are saying things like that about you? You must yield to my judgment on this matter."

Edico gave a snort of amusement. "Women will say anything. If you don't want people to think a thing like that, forget this absurd modesty."

Damn Amalberga. She had seen too much, too quickly. And she had not even questioned me. She had suspected, discovered that I had a motive for disguising myself, and drawn her own conclusion. I tried to think of something more to say, but my tongue seemed frozen. I felt my cheeks grow hot. Fritigern kept watching me.

"I am used to privacy," I said when the silence grew unendurable. "I find this curiosity indecent."

Fritigern waved the objection away. "You almost make me think that my wife's suspicions are true."

"Your Majesty, I wouldn't worry about that," said Edico. "I worked with Chariton for almost two years. I know these rumors are false."

"Are they?" asked Fritigern, looking from Edico to me, then fixing the stare on me. "Swear it to me."

My heart was pounding in my ears. I looked away from the king, down at the mosaic on the floor: the Bull roared at the Celestial Twins. There was no way out. Once the question had been asked, there was only one answer. My whole disguise had depended on no one ever asking that question. Lying was of no use, once I was suspected. "They are true," I whispered. "I am a woman."

Edico stared as though he doubted my sanity. Walimir stared. Everyone stared. I put my hands behind my back and clenched them to keep them still.

"I never listen enough to my wife," said Fritigern thoughtfully. "She is usually right."

I looked back at him. "No one has ever questioned my skill at medicine."

"I do not question it," Fritigern returned. "It makes no difference to your skill what your sex is, and it is your skill that is needed. Only I cannot send you out of the camp. I couldn't protect you on a raid, and it would be a great dishonor to me if you suffered insult in my service. I will see to it that you are treated as a great lady."

I felt as I had in my dream when my father had turned into Festinus. If I was treated as a lady, the secret was out forever and ever. I would have to stay among the Goths all my life if I wanted to practice medicine — or I could go home and sit in solitary dishonor in my brother's house. Either way I had no power over what happened to me; I would be Fritigern's chattel or my brother's. My self-control abandoned me, and I cried out, "No! Please. I am utterly ruined if news of this gets out. I cannot go back to the Romans, I . . ."

Fritigern smiled. Of course. If I couldn't go back to the Romans, so much the better.

"No," I said again, numbly. "Please, I've done good to you and to your house. Don't return evil."

"You will be treated as a guest, and as a lady. I will see you lodged with my wife."

"If I had wanted to be treated as a lady, I would have stayed in my father's house in Ephesus!"

But Fritigern shook his head. "I cannot have you treated as a man and lodged among the common troops. You will stay with my wife. Then people will know who and what you are. I would be dishonored if any insult were offered to you."

"But you are ruining me, can't you see?" I shouted at him. "God in Heaven! I will lose my name, my career, everything; I will exist only as your servant! And if I try to go back home, I'll be nothing, no one — just a scandal. My friends and family will all be ashamed of me . . . No, please, I beg you . . ." I was starting to cry, and had to stop. I pressed my hands to my face. Fritigern watched me dispassionately.

"I will send you to my wife now," he said firmly. "You can rest."

And I was led out of the room in tears.

Amalberga managed me beautifully. I had never thought of myself as easily managed, and I think my family and friends would agree with that, but Amalberga handled me as easily as a nurse handles a fractious child or a skilled groom a stubborn horse, and I didn't even realize until afterward that she'd done it. I was led into the back part of the house, the women's quarters, quite blind with tears. Amalberga was sitting spinning by the hearth with some of the other noblewomen. She stared in astonishment while the guards explained what had happened, then jumped up, sent the men away, and led me to an empty bedroom. "Rest for a little," she told me, and left me alone. And I wept, hysterically I suppose, for about an hour, lying on the bed biting my sleeve and convulsing with sobs. I could have taken a knife to my own body; I was furious with it for being female, for betraying me.

When the violence of the sobs had eased somewhat, Amalberga came back into the room and stood by the door. "Esteemed Chariton," she said in Greek, "one of my women has a child that is ill; she is desperate for it to have attention. I know that Your Grace is tired, but could you perhaps just look at the baby?"

At that minute I hated her deeply, because her suspicions had led to my exposure. But how could I refuse to examine a baby? I got up, still swallowing sobs, and went to look at the sick child. It had earache and a fever. I dosed it for the fever, gave it nightshade and hot compresses to ease the pain in the ears, and reassured the mother that it wasn't terribly ill and would eventually recover. Amalberga then discovered another case that needed attention, but suggested that I might want to wash first: "I know that you Greek doctors set great store on hygiene in treating your patients. I've had the bathhouse readied, if you like." So I had my bath, with various slaves and some of Amalberga's women looking in to make sure I was really not a man or a devil.

When I got out of the bath, my old clothes were gone, and in their place was a long tunic with sleeves, some slippers, and a gold-studded belt. The slaves held the dress up for me expectantly, and I stared at it. But what was the point of protesting? I had a patient waiting, and the disguise wouldn't work any longer anyway. I put the thing on and fastened the belt around my waist. The dress was of wool, with a linen undertunic: good quality. It was a plain dark green, without fringes or pattern, and the sleeves stopped at the elbow, out of the way: good for working in. But I felt very strange without my corset, and the long skirt now felt unnatural.

When I came out of the bathhouse, Amalberga was back at her spinning, talking to another woman; some children were playing by their feet. She smiled, but made no comment on how I looked. I couldn't have endured it if she had. Instead she apologized for not having provided a cloak: "I thought you could use your old one, but it does need cleaning. Still, Frigda is just in another room, you won't need to go outside to treat her. Can I give you some earrings?"

"Thank you, no," I said.

Amalberga smiled apologetically. "It would be better if you had some jewelry. People would respect you more. They assume that someone with no jewels must be of low rank, and that a doctor of low rank must be incompetent. It would make your patients more confident if you wore some jewels. Here, take these." She handed me some pearl earrings — they were of Roman craftsmanship, plundered no doubt from some Thracian villa. I stared at them sullenly.

"I would rather not be your debtor," I declared, and tried to give them back.

"But it is I who am yours!" said the lady. "You saved my life, but I returned your kindness by destroying your name among your own people. I swear I never meant to. I had a suspicion, and I mentioned it to my husband — but that was before the war began, and I never meant him to expose you. For all that it's worth to you, I'm sorry. Let me at least help you to establish a new name among us. Your skill will do most of that, but it will help if you look like a noble-woman." She closed my hand about the earrings, her vivid blue eyes meeting mine with a look of earnest pleading.

After a minute I put on the earrings. My ears had been pierced as soon as I was born, and the six years I'd gone without earrings hadn't closed the holes.

Amalberga nodded approval. "Now you look more like a person of rank," she said. "May I ask you your real name?"

"Charis," I said, then stood there feeling naked and ridiculous in my new green dress.

"Of course," said Amalberga, smiling again. "You didn't really change it at all. Don't tell me any more than that, if you don't want to. Your patient is this way. She's pregnant, she's had a pain in her side for a week now, and we are all afraid for her. I hope you can help her."

Amalberga was a skilled ruler. I'd admired her self-possession at our previous meeting; few women with childbed fevers can give orders to their midwives. Now I saw that self-possession was the least of it. She was very adept at getting people to do what she wanted them to, far better at it than her husband was. She had a natural understanding of what others were feeling, and she could play on those feelings with great skill. It was not hypocrisy and play-acting: that was the strength of it. She was genuinely gentle, and interested in reconciling people — to each other, to her husband's edicts, to their lot. She understood perfectly how much the art of healing meant to me, and she used that to make me accept servitude. It was only when I went to bed that night that I realized that I had yielded quietly. I had patients needing attention, and I had to help Edico run a hospital: therefore I would submit to becoming a Gothic wisewoman.

I sat straight up in the bed, horrified. I was sharing the room, and indeed the bed, with a Gothic noblewoman whose husband was off raiding. The room had a stone floor spread with rushes, and walls of mud and wattle; it hadn't been cleaned for some time, and was smoky from the hearth fire in the main room of the women's quarters. My companion muttered and turned in her sleep. I remembered studying in Alexandria — the smell of Nile mud, the cries of the street vendors, the delicate pages of medical texts. I remembered my father's house in Ephesus. This barbarian city had nothing to do with me. If I left now, I thought, I might make it back to the Romans before the news got out. Salices wasn't far.

I climbed out of bed, picked up the green dress, and pulled it on. The stone floor was cold. I looked for my boots, then remembered that I had only the slippers, and that I didn't even have a cloak. How could I get out of the women's quarters, through the concentric rings of the camp, out the gate, and two days' ride through hostile country back to the Romans, without even a cloak? And could I ride a horse in a long skirt?

I stood there, clenching my fists helplessly. Then I went out into the main room. I had to do something; even if I couldn't escape tonight, I could at least get some idea of what I could do. The fire was low and the room was empty. My medical bag was sitting beside the door that led to the main part of the house. I went over and picked it up. The leather handle was black with use, and the sides were worn and dented where it had bumped against my side when I carried it. It was heavy, full of boxes and bottles of drugs, of knives, bandages, and my casebook. Its weight over my shoulder was so familiar now that I felt undressed if I left a house without it. If the news of what I am reaches the Romans, I thought, and if I do go back, I might just as well leave it behind forever.

Another of the doors opened, and Amalberga came in, her tunic undone and her long hair loose over her shoulders, shining in the dim light of the fire. She looked at me steadily a moment, then said, "It would be better if you rested. Whatever you do tomorrow, it will be better done if you sleep now."

"Whatever I do tomorrow?" I repeated bitterly. "I have no choice in the matter, do I? I thought it was determined that I would assist Edico with his patients."

"That is true," Amalberga said quietly. "I hope that you will help them."

"Do you know what you've done to me?" I asked her. "Perhaps you think I deserve slavery, for acting so indecently. But I never hurt you."

She shook her head. "I admire what you have done. Few women are able to determine so clearly what it is they wish to be, and fewer still can become it. It is cruel, I suppose, to take from you something you must have struggled hard to win, and I am sorry. But, you know, this is not slavery. Many of my people were enslaved last summer, and many of yours have been enslaved since. They would envy you your freedom even now."

I bit my lip. "Perhaps that's true," I said after a minute. "But it does not excuse you."

"Our people have suffered very much. We haven't been free either: we were forced into revolt. My husband still hopes to make peace with the emperor and become his client. What else do we have to hope for? No one can defeat the empire — it's too big. But his first duty, and mine, is to our people, to feed and protect them. I think you understand that, and understand why we wanted you here, even against your will and our honor." She came over and touched my hand, watching me earnestly. "But it doesn't have to be so dreadful. You can practice your art openly here, and be honored for it. That's something, isn't it?"

"I love my own people," I told her. "I don't belong here."

She dropped her hand and sighed. "I don't understand why people love the empire so dearly."

"We were born under it, and it shaped us."

She shrugged. "Very many Goths, born under our own kings, abandon their people and go to live under the dragons. My uncle Ermaneric did that, and his son, my cousin Athanaric, loves the empire as much as any Roman-born citizen could. But few Romans are willing to live among us, even if they are offered wealth and

311

honor. Even my husband still adores the dream of Rome, though he is at war with it."

"I don't love dreams. Only . . . the way of life that I have chosen is something that doesn't exist among your people. I am a doctor, a Hippocratic. Not a wizard or a wisewoman or an enchantress. I don't fit in here."

"A woman doctor is something that doesn't exist among your own people."

"But I wasn't one, was I?"

She smiled a little at that. "No. But you could be one, among us. You already have Edico half-trained in Hippocratic medicine. If we survive this war, you could teach others as well. Perhaps we are ignorant barbarians, but we want to be part of the empire, to learn Roman ways — particularly Roman skills and Roman arts, like yours. Why should you dismiss us so quickly? Among your own people you have to pretend to be something you're not, in order to be what you are. You have the chance here to create your own law, to be a Hippocratic and a woman."

I stared at her, stirred and excited against my will. Was that true? In Alexandria I had dreamed that I would one day be able to say openly that I was a woman and a doctor. But Alexandria is a city with as many different laws as the empire. The Goths have only one set of customs. And yet, they do have women healers. And they might survive the war, set up their client kingdom, and become a part of the empire. It was conceivable that I could (to use legal language) create a precedent.

And I didn't have much choice but to try.

Amalberga smiled at me, noting, no doubt, that her words had sunk in. She touched my arm again. "But rest. You will not do it without food or sleep."

So I went back to bed.

Of course I did as Amalberga said. I settled down very quickly to being a woman Hippocratic, imposing on my Gothic patients the full glories of the Alexandrian school of medicine. And they accepted it. It helped that the Goths were in quite desperate need of any kind of medicine from anyone who could give it. And it helped me, I suppose, that there was an enormous amount that needed to be done.

Edico had been put in charge of the health of the whole wagon city, and he had done quite well, considering the enormous difficulties. He had set up a hospital, modeled on the one in Novidunum. He had recruited all the skilled attendants he could — an assortment of ex-Roman army doctors, Gothic wisewomen and midwives, dubious-seeming wizards and sorcerers, and straightforward charlatans. He had lectured firmly on the need for hygiene, and insisted that the Goths dig wells for their drinking water. He kept infectious cases at the hospital and quarantined them and their attendants. His main fault was that he paid far more attention to the Goths wounded in fighting than to the diseased of the camp. This was owing partly to his own background — Gothic noblemen are always trained as warriors, and even though he had decided that he loved medicine, he could not shed the belief in the nobility of war — and partly to his training. Novidunum was, after all, a military hospital. It had not prepared him very well for becoming state physician for a great city, which was what the wagon settlement had undoubtedly grown into. Carragines, the Goths called it, using the Latin word: "the wagons." My first impression of it was not misleading. It was vast and it was crowded. It was also dirty and becoming increasingly dangerous.

The chief problem was sanitation. Edico had been clear on the need for wells, but he had known nothing about the need for drains. The arrangements were totally inadequate. The Goths had simply dug latrines, one for every ten families, scattering them about the settlement. That may be fine for a temporary camp or a small village. But for a city of many tens of thousands, it was impossible. Only the cold weather had prevented the latrines from contaminating all the water on the site. As it was, dysentery, diarrhea, dropsy, and enteritic fevers were abundant. Already far more people were dying of these than were being killed fighting the Romans, though of course most of those who died were children, which didn't affect the Goths' fighting strength. What the camp would become in the summer didn't bear thinking about.

But Goths aren't like Romans. They'd never had public drains, and they didn't understand the need for them. They think that worrying about such things is effeminate, menial, slavish. Edico simply looked confused when I told him that unless something was done at once, the camp would be a death trap come summer. Of course, he was very confused about me anyway. When I first appeared at the hospital dressed as a woman, he kept staring, then blushing and looking away. I was still wearing my cloak back from my shoulders, to keep it out of the way, and I'd tied the tunic around the top, crossing the cord between my breasts, because it was a bit too large and because I missed the corset's support. I suppose the change in my shape was startling. In the end I had to tell him to close his eyes and forget "Lady Charis"; I was his master in the art, and my knowledge hadn't changed. Even so, I couldn't get him to talk sensibly to me for a week. I didn't have time to wait for him to settle down: the weather was already beginning to turn warm, and as soon as the ground thawed the problem of the drains would be crucial. I abandoned the hospital on the first day and demanded an audience with Fritigern.

I was admitted to the audience room fairly promptly. Fritigern was alone today. He stared at me curiously and complimented me on my appearance. I ignored this and came directly to the point: I told him that dozens of his people were dying now, and hundreds more would die when the hot weather came, because of the latrines. He stared. I explained, quoting Hippocrates and Erasistratos and citing the example of Roman cities with their public sewers to avoid this problem. He looked uneasy, and asked what I thought he should do.

"Have a public sewerage system built at once," I replied. "Or an aqueduct. But a sewer would be simpler, and less subject to disruption by the Romans."

Fritigern frowned. He suggested that we wait and see whether the present system worked before we went about building a new one. I said it was already abundantly clear that the system didn't work. He said it was not a woman's place to decide such things.

"Your Excellency," I said, "you went to some trouble to acquire my services and to make certain I had no reason to return to the Romans. You might as well listen now you've got me. It may not be a woman's place to learn medicine, but I have learned it, and what I say is true."

"I expected you to work at healing the sick, not to tell me I need enormous public sewers!" Fritigern snapped back. "A system for the whole city will take hundreds of men to construct. That's expensive. And I don't even know how such things are built, nor does anyone else here — unless Your Wisdom learned that as well as medicine."

The construction of public drains had not been discussed in the Alexandrian medical school, but I knew that the Goths had taken plenty of Roman prisoners. I suggested that he find some of those who understood such things and offer them their freedom and a large sum of money for designing a sewer for Carragines. I said they were certain to jump at such an offer. It was not as though they were being asked to build fortifications or do anything that would be regarded as treachery by the Roman authorities. And the slaves were likely to suffer most in the event of plague.

"I can't free someone else's prisoners!" said Fritigern. "Half the quarrels I have to adjudicate already are over slaves; I can't uphold the law and then go seizing someone else's property. No, it's not worth it. You Greeks are simply fanatical about hygiene. Perhaps a lack of drains would make you sick. But we Goths are hardier. We don't bathe, and it's never hurt us, and nor will this."

I bit my tongue to stop myself calling him a stinking, ignorant barbarian. "Your Excellency, this is a question of contaminated water, not of baths. It is already killing people. There were several dead children at the hospital this morning. How many do there have to be before you admit there's a problem?"

"You're exaggerating," Fritigern said coldly. "Children die from many causes. I can't tell my men to stop raiding and dig drains because of the opinions of some Greek female doctor."

"It's not just my opinion! All the best medical authorities say that contaminated water causes disease! And a Roman state physician is supposed to safeguard the public's health."

"You are not a Roman state physician!" Fritigern snapped. "Now go back to the hospital and treat the sick!"

I glared at him for a minute, saw I'd get nowhere, and bowed stiffly. "If Your Prudence is unable to help me," I said bitterly. "Edico tells me he is out of a whole range of drugs; could Your Carefulness perhaps ask some of the raiding parties to look for them? I could draw pictures of the herbs we need most urgently."

"Edico has been begging for drugs since he came here. But my men aren't interested in digging up roots and picking berries when they're raiding. You will simply have to manage with what is available."

I set my teeth. "Very well. If Your Excellency is unable to control your men, and can't get them to dig and can't get them to look for drugs, I will have to ask for help from someone who is a bit more competent at ruling!"

He went red and jumped off his couch. "What do you mean by that?"

"I will go talk to your wife. Most noble Fritigern, much health!"

And I bowed and walked out, hoping that Amalberga would listen to me.

She did, bless her. I went straight to her and explained the need for the drains, and she understood at once. She had noticed that there were a lot of illnesses of the stomach around, but had not known what caused them. "And are they really caused by that?" she asked. "The latrines? I thought it was the air, or the water."

"It is the water," I told her, and quoted my medical authorities until she lifted her hand and begged me to stop.

"You haven't wasted any time brooding, have you?" she asked, smiling.

I shrugged. "The problem is very urgent." But it was only then that I realized that I was not acting in any way differently than I would have if everyone believed I was a eunuch. And of course I hadn't changed; only what others knew of me was different. But what others know is a powerful thing, and can change you; it might do so yet to me.

"Well then, we will have to build drains," said Amalberga. "Do you know how it's done?"

I told her the plan I had suggested to Fritigern, and then admitted all of Fritigern's objections. She looked at me ruefully. "And you've quarreled with him already? Oh, my dear! I hope you haven't offended him: it will make it much more difficult if he's angry."

"He kept saying he couldn't do things because of his men. I said I would talk to you because you were better at controlling them than he was."

She stared at me, then gave a soft, gurgling laugh. "Oh Christ! I hope no one else was there! It was. a private audience? It should be all right then. I can make it a private joke. Well, after that I have to do something, don't I? It should be possible. What do we need? Freedom and money for some Roman slaves who can design the system, workers to do the digging — I think the women and household slaves should be able to manage that. The men will never agree to dig drains. You should have come to me first. My husband is concerned first with the war, second with supplies, and third with administering justice. These little problems about the camp are the concern of women and slaves."

I pointed out that a serious epidemic would hardly be a "little problem about the camp."

Amalberga smiled. "Yes, but ordinarily . . . We are not used to such big camps, such great cities. We have never needed things like this before. I know, I will tell my husband that he is founding a great

316

city, like Constantine and Alexander did. That will make him take more interest in the problem."

"Fritigernopolis?" I asked sourly.

Amalberga laughed. "Is it really that much sillier a name than Hadrianopolis? But I suppose we'll still just call it Carragines; even with drains, we won't live here long. If we're lucky, we'll be allowed to settle on lands of our own. And if not . . ." She paused, her eyes involuntarily going to her little son, who was sitting in a corner of the room playing with a wooden horse. "If not, the city still won't last." She stared hungrily at the child for a moment, as though already the city were burning and he were dead; then she sighed. "But that isn't to the point. What else will we need for the drains?"

Amalberga spoke to her husband, spoke to her ladies and their husbands, and had the work on the drains started within the week. By that time warmer weather had arrived and we were in the middle of an epidemic, but we controlled this with hard work and strict quarantine, and by ordering everyone to boil their water, and so we limped on till the drains were completed a few weeks later. Then, predictably, the problem faded away, leaving the Goths greatly impressed by my wisdom and that of Hippocrates.

What's more, the queen cajoled several of the Gothic leaders into telling their men to search for medicinal herbs when they went raiding, and so we had a good, if erratic, supply of necessities like mandragora and hellebore — though we had to do without opium. Edico was astonished.

"I've been trying for months to get someone to look for them," he told me. We had grown back into a partnership during the epidemic. "I don't know how many times I've talked to Fritigern about it."

"For things like that, you can forget Fritigern," I said complacently. "Just let me talk to Amalberga. You can rely on the natural superiority of women."

Edico snorted. "I'm glad it isn't 'women,' but just you and Amalberga. Otherwise we men would be keeping house and minding babies, and the women would run the world."

"We couldn't let you do that," I said. "You make such a mess of running the world, we couldn't possibly trust you with the babies. It would be the end of the human race."

"I think I preferred you as a eunuch," Edico said, and I laughed.

All that spring I worked hard, attending to the sick of Carragines. I left most of the wounded to Edico. This was partly because he was now the senior doctor and so took the more prestigious patients, partly because women and children were felt to be more appropriate patients for a woman, and partly because I didn't want to attend the wounded. I did not like healing men who, when they were better, would go out and kill some of my own people. Women, children, slaves, the old and the weak — I didn't mind helping them, even if they were the enemy. I had settled into my new position now, and I no longer thought much about escaping. After the first couple of weeks my cloak and shoes stopped disappearing every night, and I might have slipped out of the camp — only, where could I go? Salices was not far away, but with Roman slaves escaping from the Goths and Gothic slaves from the Romans, news traveled quickly in Thrace. I assumed that by now all the troops in Scythia must know that Chariton of Ephesus was really a woman, and I'd have nothing but disgrace waiting for me among the Romans. They might even know more: that Chariton of Ephesus was really Charis daughter of Theodoros, something I had not told the Goths. It depended on what Athanaric had discovered and whom he had told. I hoped that he had either discovered or said nothing, because I did not want Fritigern to learn that the governor of Scythia was my brother. It was bad enough being a prisoner; I didn't want to be a hostage as well. I did not think the king would harm me, but he might tell Thorion that he would, and even if he didn't, nothing but trouble could come from it.

I grew comfortable with Amalberga and her ladies, and with the attendants at the hospital and a few of the patients — though there were too many of them for me to know any of them really well. I had to speak Gothic all the time, and got better at it; after a month or so I was speaking it even to Amalberga and Edico. I did miss my friends, and thought of them when I had the time, but I couldn't communicate with them, and I was sufficiently busy that the world outside Carragines began to seem unreal. I did hear some news of Sebastianus; the Goths were full of talk about what the Roman commanders were doing. Though none of them were doing much except waiting for reinforcements.

I thought often of Athanaric, wondering what he had discovered and where he was now. I couldn't help it: I wanted to see him now that I had been exposed as a woman. Though I feared that he would find me monstrous, or, worse, that he would try to treat me as some unknown gentlewoman, still I wanted to meet him and say, "Look. This is what I am, and perhaps you guessed it. Do you like me this way?" But there was no news of him. Amalberga and Fritigern were both eager to see him, eager for news of where he was. The first passion of plunder and revenge was passing, and the Goths wanted to negotiate a truce with the empire and expected Athanaric to come to talk with them. But it seemed that the empire was determined not to speak to the Goths until it had enough forces in the field to crush them. So we in Carragines waited for reinforcements too, and I was on the whole too busy to wonder much about myself or where it would all end.

Then one beautiful May morning, while I was examining new patients outside the hospital, Edico came up and said he needed to talk to me. I had a large group waiting for my attention, so I asked him whether it was urgent. He looked down and muttered that it wasn't. "Then we can discuss it at lunch," I said, and turned back to my patients. He stood staring at me for a minute or so longer, looking embarrassed, then went away.

At lunch in the drugs room of the hospital, I expected him to bring up whatever it was immediately, but no, he sat there munching his bread and sausage and avoiding my eyes until I asked him what he needed to talk to me about. Then he looked even more embarrassed.

"Are you a virgin?" he asked at last.

I stared in astonishment, wondering whether he had encountered some dreadful sexual disease. "Yes," I said at last. "But I've read Hippocrates on the subject of sex. Why?"

He did look up at this, met my eyes briefly, then looked down again. "Sorry," he said. "I just wasn't sure. King Fritigern wants me to marry you, and I agreed, provided that you were a virgin. I couldn't marry somebody else's woman, even if it is you."

I was left totally speechless, and I sat there gaping at Edico.

"You are freeborn?" he asked me hopefully, after a minute or so.

I could feel my face growing hot. "That is quite a lot for Fritigern to ask of you, isn't it?" I said, ignoring his question. "To marry a foreigner of dubious reputation and unknown parentage. And you're of good family, too — what will your family think of it?"

He shrugged. "My aunt won't mind, and my father is dead. My mother has no say in the matter. And you won't have to live with her anyway."

"Oh, well then! And I'm sure the king will provide the dowry? A big one, to compensate you for the sacrifice?"

"Well — yes." Edico took another bite of bread. "Quite a big one. But it's not a sacrifice, really. You're attractive, and an excellent doctor."

"I'm pleased you think so. But you can tell Fritigern that before he goes playing matchmaker again, he'd better check whether the bride will go along with the arrangements." Edico glanced at my face again, saw that I was furious, and looked astonished. "I will not marry you. There, is that a relief?"

He swallowed, then frowned. "Why not? I don't see that you have anything to object to in me."

I bit my lip to hold the words in. "You're a lot better than the last man I was supposed to marry," I said after a minute. "But I don't want to marry you, and you don't want to marry me, and I don't really see that Fritigern comes into it at all. Why did he suddenly suggest this?"

"He thinks you're a very clever doctor, and he wants to keep you here. What do you mean, the last man you were supposed to marry? You just said —"

"I didn't marry him. I ran off to Alexandria to avoid him. And I'll run off again if I have to. Why in the name of all your gods did you agree to such a stupid idea?"

He looked offended. "There's nothing stupid about it! We're colleagues, I'm a gentleman, the king wants to adopt you as one of our people. There's nothing more natural."

"Oh by Artemis the Great! We're colleagues, and we'd better leave it that way. Do you think I'm going to settle to being a good Gothic wife, keeping your house and bearing your children, with maybe a bit of midwifery on the side? I know twice as much medicine as you do!"

He waved this claim aside. "We'll have slaves to keep the house."

"Be honest: you can't look me in the eye and say you really want a woman who taught you your trade and gave you orders for two years, whom you believed to be a man. You want some pretty Gothic girl a few years younger than you, who'll keep your house running and admire your intelligence."

He didn't look me in the eye and say it. He looked at the ground and said nothing.

"Go back and tell the king that the match is off."

He looked up. "Very well. But what are your objections?"

"I don't want to get married. I like my independence. If that's not enough to satisfy him, lie. Tell him that I said I was a whore from a brothel on Market Street in Ephesus, or whatever you like, so long as you get out of it. This match would make us both miserable."

"I'll tell him the truth," said Edico, and got up. "You're quite right." And he went off looking relieved. I sat there for a minute or so, trying to calm myself. I was still holding my piece of bread and sausage, but I couldn't eat it. I was too frightened — and it was fear, now that Edico was gone, not just anger. Fritigern wouldn't trust me to Amalberga's management and love of the art; he wanted me shackled, firmly under the control of one of his men. Married, and no doubt soon pregnant with Gothic children. I'd had the name of Chariton stripped away, and he wanted to take Charis as well, to make me "Edico's wife." I might keep the art, but I'd lose myself that way, lose myself forever. Edico wouldn't oblige; would Fritigern try to find someone else?

"I won't have him," I said aloud, to reassure myself. And I went out of the ivy-scented pharmacy and threw my piece of bread and sausage to one of the camp's dogs. Another crowd of patients was waiting in front of the hospital for attention: tired old men and women sitting stiffly on the earth; a few wounded warriors off by themselves, looking superior; thin, worn-out women clutching sick babies or soothing tearful, feverish children. I wiped my hands on my dress and beckoned them over.

I don't know what Fritigern said to Edico, but that evening Amalberga called me over to her and discussed the matter. "My husband wants to establish you in your own house," she told me.

"You mean he wants to give me to a Gothic husband who can keep me under control and make sure I don't run off. What's happened? Have the Roman reinforcements arrived?"

She winced, then nodded unhappily. "Several legions brought from Armenia are marching from Constantinople. And it's rumored that troops are marching from Gaul as well."

"So Fritigern wants to tie me firmly to the Goths before they arrive. Well, tell him that I am more likely to want to stay if I am free than if I'm subjected to an unwelcome marriage."

Amalberga sighed. "I thought Edico would be a good match. You are both good doctors, and he respects your judgment and would not interfere in your practice."

I stared. "It was your idea, then?"

She nodded. "My husband said he wanted you to marry one of his men, so I suggested your colleague. My dear, you will have to marry someone. It might as well be Edico."

"I am not going to marry anyone! I swear by the most glorious Trinity that if you force me into some man's bed, I will take the first chance I get to run. You will not be able to trust me, and my usefulness to you will be at an end."

"You would not hurt your patients," Amalberga said flatly.

"I might refuse to take them," I replied. "You may get service out of a carthorse by blinkering and beating it, but a racehorse won't run if you crush its spirit."

She looked at me searchingly. "Why does it matter so much, if you mean to stay anyway? It isn't so dreadful, marriage. Or are you just afraid to marry a Goth?"

I started to tell Amalberga some lie, then decided to speak the truth: the truth was always the better course, with her. "I don't want to marry anyone, and I particularly don't want to marry a Goth. I am a Roman, an Ephesian, trained at the Museum in Alexandria! I'm nobody's slave. I didn't come here of my own free will; you had me taken prisoner. Well, I am here, I've made the best of it — and done you some service, as you know. You said you were sorry for the earlier injustice. Don't compound it by having me married against my will."

"Is there some other man?" she asked.

"Other men have nothing to do with it! I am not yours and Fritigern's to dispose of, and I won't be anyone else's property either."

Amalberga sighed and held up her hand for peace. "It is late," she said. "Leave it for now, then. I promise you, I will not force you into a marriage you detest. But I think still that you ought to marry, soon, someone who will respect you. Otherwise my husband will settle you with one of his companions, who might not understand or care anything about medicine."

"Then I will run away," I said. "Listen: I was resigned to staying here, before. I have nothing to go back to among the Romans. I would even be willing to swear an oath to stay, if Fritigern doesn't believe that being allowed to practice the art is tie enough. But I will not marry at your command. Whoever you choose will have to rape me, and I won't answer for what I do afterward."

Amalberga sighed again. "I will talk to my husband," she promised. "And we will see what the Romans do."

The Roman legions from Armenia came into the south of Thrace, marching from Constantinople. They had a number of sharp clashes with Gothic forces in the southern provinces, and forced the raiding parties to retreat back into the north. But they did not have nearly enough strength to fight the entire Gothic army, so they settled in Hadrianopolis and waited for reinforcements from the West. These were slow in coming. The whole Rhine–Danube frontier was unsettled: there was not a place along it where there hadn't been a war at some time in the past fifteen years, and it was difficult to draw troops away from any province without putting that province at risk. The Pannonian and transalpine auxiliaries arrived in early summer, but their commander was disabled by gout — or so he claimed — and on arriving they did nothing. Some Gaulish troops were supposed to be coming, but they were in no hurry, and half of them deserted rather than leave their home province unprotected. Fritigern called in the raiding parties and waited.

I stayed in Carragines. There was no more talk of marriage, and I was busy. Even with the drains, the dirty and crowded conditions of the camp bred disease. Many of the Roman slaves, in particular, were ill. They had suffered greatly from being captured, and were kept, often chained, in crowded and filthy huts where they contracted illnesses ranging from infected wounds to typhoid. They needed attention, and I was pleased to be able to give it to them, to do something for my own people, even among the barbarians.

Then, one day in July, I was summoned to see the king.

I was just about to start a very delicate operation, a Caesarean section. Philon had showed me a way of doing this used among the Alexandrian Jews, a way that about half the women survive, and I judged it to be the best chance this patient had. She'd been in labor for two days when I was called in, but the baby seemed to lie athwart the womb, and she could do nothing. So I had the attendants boil plenty of water, and boil some bandages as well, and I washed my hands, boiled my knives, washed the woman's stomach with a cleansing solution, and tied her down. Then Fritigern's damned messenger knocked on the door and said that the king wished to see me.

I went to the door and looked at him. "I'll come when I'm finished here," I told the man. He was one of Fritigern's "companions," a high-ranking warrior.

"The king wishes to see you at once," he replied reprovingly.

"This woman has been waiting nine months and two days," I said. "The king can wait an hour. Go away."

Behind me the woman had another contraction and screamed. I'd given her mandragora, but she'd lost it all. I would have sold the clothes off my back for some Indian hemp.

Fritigern's companion looked uncertain. "What are you doing?" he asked.

"Cutting a child out of her belly," I said, and closed the door. He didn't try to follow me. I washed my hands again and did the operation as quickly and cleanly as I could. I handed the baby to the midwife and stitched the woman up. She lay there with tears of anguish running down her face, groaning — a fairly good sign, actually. She was alive, and strong enough to groan. The baby had seemed dead when I took it out, but just as I was bandaging the woman's stomach I heard it start to cry. The woman heard too, and stopped groaning, her eyes opening with astonishment.

The midwife gave a chortle, and brought the child over to her. "You have a son!" she told the woman, and the woman said "Oh!" and reached out her arms for him. Sure enough, the baby was red and bruised-looking, but alive. He clung to his mother, and she to him, in terrible pain still but crying now with exhaustion and relief. It was more likely that the woman would live now that she knew she had not suffered for nothing. I had the sense one has sometimes, in the art, that God had granted me the gift of working a miracle.

I took off my apron and washed my hands, meanwhile giving the woman's family strict instructions about hygiene and threatening them with dire consequences if they used unboiled water or shoved any filthy magic charms into the wound. Then I picked up my skirts and ran to Fritigern's house. Kings don't like to be kept waiting.

I arrived disheveled and out of breath, and the guards admitted me to the audience room at once. The room was full of people. Fritigern, his colleague Alavivus, and Colias, the former commander of the federate troops at Hadrianopolis, were all sitting on their couches on the dais, and their attendants ringed the room; Colias was saying something about Roman legions. Amalberga was standing behind the dais; she looked up and nodded to me as I came in. Another man was standing in the center of the room, his feet on the mosaic sun in the center of the zodiac pattern. His back was to me, but even so the brown hair and the arrogant angle of the head were instantly familiar. I hadn't placed a name to them, though, when the attendants struck the butts of their spears against the floor to signal my entrance. The man turned, and I saw that he was Athanaric.

I stopped short, staring at him. It had been nearly a year since I had seen him, and I had hoped that time and the calamities of the state had killed my passion, but when his eyes met mine I could neither move nor speak, and it was as though the rest of the room disappeared. Then I thought, stupidly and irrelevantly, that I must look a sight, with my half-grown-out hair coming loose from its pins, my cloak pulled off my shoulder by my medical bag, and blood on my arms and probably my face as well. Athanaric stared at me with a strange expression — pleasure, relief, satisfied curiosity. I became aware that Colias had stopped talking.

"Here is the lady, then," said Fritigern. "As you can see, she is unharmed. Now will you discuss what terms your masters would accept for a truce?"

Athanaric turned back to the dais. "I have told you that I am not authorized to discuss anything, that I have been posted elsewhere, that I have taken leave from my duties to come here, and that no one at the court will listen to me anyway. You can forget the truce: you won't get one, and everything you've insisted on telling me since I arrived doesn't count for anything. I came here, as I said, to discuss a ransom for this lady on behalf of her friends."

"Which friends?" asked Alavivus.

"Duke Sebastianus and the lady's family," Athanaric said promptly. "The sum is a hundred pounds in gold."

"Who are the lady's family?" asked Fritigern, surveying me.

"I am not at liberty to say," Athanaric returned. "Ephesians, and persons of distinction."

"A hundred pounds of gold is fairly distinguished," Colias said, grinning. "I'd sell any of my prisoners for that, Fritigern."

Fritigern shook his head. "She's worth more than that. She's saved more than that number of lives since she came here. No."

"Two hundred pounds," said Athanaric.

Fritigern's eyes narrowed. He shook his head. "I need doctors more than I need gold. We've taken plenty of gold, but no doctors."

"Four hundred pounds."

Murmurs. Colias whistled. I stood there like a slave on the block, wondering how far Athanaric would have to go, not sure whether I was pleased or dismayed.

"Why is Duke Sebastianus interested?" asked Fritigern suspiciously.

Athanaric glanced at me, shrugged a kind of apology. "He was this woman's commanding officer when it was thought she was a man, and he feels responsible for her captivity."

Laughter around the room. "He was a fool not to realize what he was commanding," said Alavivus.

"It is easier to tell the sex of a prisoner whom you can force into what you want than of a free person who is trying to conceal it," Athanaric said sharply. "And Lady Charis was a free person among the Romans. She was free when she cured Lord Fritigern's wife, and when she tried to help your people against Lupicinus. Now we're discussing what ransom you'll take for a woman who was your guest-friend, whom you ought to set free without wanting money for it. Her friends are offering four hundred pounds in gold."

Fritigern gave me that indecipherable look that I had come to hate and fear. "She is obviously of high rank, for her family and the duke to offer four hundred pounds in gold for her release. Lady Charis, who are your family?"

I pressed my hands together. "If they do not want to give you their names, who am I to betray them?"

The pale eyes fixed on me a moment longer, then moved to Athanaric, paused. Then Fritigern shook his head. "It is not enough."

"Four hundred pounds isn't enough for one woman?" asked Colias incredulously. "We could use that money. Take it, for the gods' sake!"

"What do we need money for?" Fritigern demanded. "None of the Romans will trade with us, and gold buys us nothing. Our only currency is the sword. And she's my prisoner, not yours. No. It is not enough."

"Six hundred pounds in gold," Athanaric offered, but I could see that he was sweating.

"They must *own* Ephesus!" said Colias.

Fritigern frowned suddenly. "Theodoros," he said. "The governor. He had a sister —"

"— who was supposed to marry Festinus!" Colias finished, and everyone in the room began talking at once.

"There are many wealthy families in Asia!" Athanaric protested, but the uproar drowned his words. Ours was the only really wealthy Asian family the Goths had heard of, and that a daughter of the house was known to be missing was, in their eyes, incontrovertible proof. They craned their necks to see me, the notorious sister of Theodoros who had left Festinus brideless in his marriage garlands.

Fritigern looked at Athanaric and smiled. "I will not release her."

I knew then that it had been pleasure, not dismay, that I felt before: I felt dismay now.

"A thousand pounds in gold!" Athanaric shouted. "I cannot offer more."

I was sure he couldn't. Thorion would have to borrow heavily to get that.

"The most excellent Theodoros can keep it," said Fritigern. "That devil Festinus lost his bride, and one of my own men will get her."

"No!" I protested sharply.

"Don't be ridiculous!" Athanaric said. "Do you think Theodoros will marry her to Festinus? He hates him as much as you do!" Then he stopped, biting his tongue; he had admitted that Fritigern was right.

Fritigern took no notice: he'd been certain that he was right anyway. "Then who does he wish to marry her to?" Fritigern demanded. "Duke Sebastianus?" He watched Athanaric carefully, then nodded. "I will not hand the woman over to any of my enemies."

"That's even more ridiculous," I said, interrupting again. "Sebastianus is a gentleman of the highest rank. He can do much better for himself than an army doctor whose dowry's already spent on her ransom."

Athanaric gave me a quick straight look, then looked away again. Fritigern grinned. "It doesn't matter, Sebastianus or Festinus or another. The lady will not marry a Roman now. Festinus' bride will marry one of my men and grow old among our people, a reproach to the Romans. That is worth losing a thousand pounds in gold for."

The Goths cheered, even Colias. Athanaric went white and stood there clutching the hilt of his sword. I felt that I must do something, say something, or it would all be decided: I would be packed off to the house of some Gothic nobleman to spite Festinus, Thorion, and Sebastianus, and no one would even consider that they had done me any injury.

"Lord King!" I said, and stepped forward. Everyone looked at me, the Goths grinning as though I were some second-rate actor in a theater, come out to speak his piece. "Lord King," I repeated, and then for a moment could think of nothing more; I felt sick. "I have done you some service," I said at last. "I helped you and your house before this war started. You repaid me by making me a prisoner. I told you how to avoid a great epidemic, which would have cost you hundreds, even thousands, of your people, and you want to sell me off like a slave. Lord Christ Eternal! It would fit Your Honor better to return me to my home without asking any ransom."

"I am not selling you off like a slave," said Fritigern. "I will establish you honorably in a marriage to a nobleman."

"I will not have him," I said flatly, and then, perhaps because everyone was watching and I felt like an actor in a play, I went on. "There was a doctor at Novidunum who wanted to take me against my will. I killed him with his own knife. I'll do the same to any other man who tries it, and if he hasn't got a knife, I know a few hundred drugs that will work just as well. I can't deny any longer that I am the daughter of Theodoros of Ephesus, but I don't see why that makes your obligations of guest-friendship, or your debt to me, less heavy. And I don't see why that means I no longer own myself and can be disposed of as you please, just to spite your enemy, as though my own wishes were completely insignificant."

Athanaric gave me a look of pure admiration and pride; it made me dizzy to see it. The Goths regarded me with a kind of grudging respect. Fritigern and his colleagues looked angry; behind them, Amalberga looked appalled. I saw her trying to signal her husband. I knew what she wanted to tell him: "Let it be for now, I'll talk to Charis, you'll never manage her by shouting at her." She was the danger to me, not Fritigern. But on the question of marriage I didn't think she'd manage any better than her husband.

"You brazen, arrogant woman!" said Fritigern, and then Amalberga caught his eye. He hesitated, and she hurried forward and whispered to him. He looked back at me, chewing on his mustache. Amalberga whispered some more. Then Fritigern slapped the arm of his couch. "There is no reasoning with a woman in her pride, unless another woman does the reasoning. I declare this audience to be recessed, if my colleagues agree. Cousin Athanaric, I will take no ransom for my prisoner. If you wish to discuss a truce with us, you are welcome to stay. Otherwise, I ask you to leave the camp by sunset tomorrow."

Everyone started talking again, around me and about me but not to me. Colias jumped off the dais and ran over to Athanaric. The Gothic attendants milled about. I stood there stupidly. Then Amalberga came over and caught my arm. "You had better come with me," she said, glancing nervously at Athanaric, who was already being escorted out. I glanced at him too; his eyes met mine, and he shrugged. I went with Amalberga.

As I expected, and as Fritigern had promised, she talked at me hard. Of course, she said, she understood my feelings, but really, what was wrong with marrying some Gothic nobleman? She understood now why I'd objected to Edico, she said; of course, he was of much lower rank than I was — but now they'd find someone really noble for me, someone Romanized. There was Munderich, her cousin, who'd traveled widely before the war started and had spent a year in Constantinople; he was thinking of marriage. He would have been considered a good match even when I lived in my father's house. Didn't I see how delighted the people were at the idea of my becoming one of them?

"But I'm not delighted," I said. "I don't want to marry into a people who are at war with my own. Why don't you go talk to Fritigern? Don't you see that you owe me my freedom? Why don't you seize the chance to show your nobility by giving it to me?"

She looked down, blushing, and I saw that she did believe that I was owed my freedom but that she would never say so, even to me, because she knew that her husband wouldn't give it to me.

"You wouldn't kill any man who married you, would you?" she asked instead.

"Any man that took me against my will. I said it and I meant it." I wasn't at all sure that this was true. It is one thing to make fine speeches, but quite another to stab or poison a real young man whose worst fault is being too stupid to take no for an answer. And to use my knowledge of the art to harm someone was flatly contrary to my Hippocratic oath. But I had said it, and there was no point in having done so unless I made the Goths believe that I might keep my word. So I looked resolute and said, "It's true what I said about the man at Novidunum, too. His name was Xanthos; you can ask Edico about him."

Amalberga looked at me searchingly, then sighed. "My dear," she said, "you must see that we cannot let you go now. Even if you do not marry into our people, we cannot afford to release you. We may need help from your brother."

I looked back, equally searchingly. "You think I should marry so that I cannot be used as a hostage," I said. "You think that I need that protection. Would you really have me killed or tortured to get some concession from Theodoros?"

She looked away. "We might need to sell you for grain rather than gold," she said after a moment. "There is not much food to be had north of the Haemus mountains, and if the riding parties are kept in much longer, we will start to run out of supplies. There is plenty of grain in Tomis, and the governor could give it to us."

"And if my brother didn't buy me at first, you would injure me, or threaten to, to force him? Although you owe me hospitality and a blood debt for healing you?"

"If the people are starved again, we will do anything," she returned, meeting my eyes. "Unless you are married, and one of us."

I got up; I needed to move to calm myself. Was Amalberga telling the truth? Or was she only trying to frighten me into obeying her husbnd? I couldn't believe that Fritigern would actually have me harmed. I was his guest. Besides, I was useful to them, worth a couple of hundred pounds in gold for my skill alone.

On the other hand, hunger is a terrible thing. No one can say what they will or will not do when they're really hungry.

But the day of hunger was a long way off, if it came at all. The Goths might be soundly defeated by the winter, and I might be dead or free. Or the Romans might lose the next battle, and the raiding parties would be able to provide plenty of food. And Thorion would not be governor much longer, and it would be pointless to hold me hostage if a stranger ruled Scythia. No, I could not take the threat seriously.

"I am not going to be married off against my will," I declared, turning back to Amalberga. "If you won't let me go home, then leave things as they are. I will continue to treat the sick faithfully and harm no one — so long as you leave me free."

"The one thing we cannot do is leave you free," she said sadly. "But leave the matter for now. We can still afford to wait."

I wanted desperately to speak with Athanaric, to find out what was happening among the Romans and how my family and friends were. But when I asked Amalberga to arrange a meeting, she refused, and I saw that I was to be isolated, cut off from anyone who might support me in my resolve. That night my shoes and clothes were taken away so that I couldn't slip out after dark, and next morning I was led to the hospital by an escort and handed over to Edico's supervision like a prisoner. Edico looked embarrassed.

"I didn't realize you were a noblewoman," he told me. "I'm sorry if I've offended Your Grace."

"Oh, be quiet!" I told him irritably. "My family isn't nearly as important as everyone seems to think; they just have money. The only thing that will offend me is if you insist on having me guarded all the time."

"The king has said that you are not to be allowed to escape," Edico said unhappily. "I'm sorry, but I have to make sure that someone is with you constantly now."

I swore and went off to prepare some medicines. It was pretty much what I expected, but I didn't like it. One of the assistants came in to watch me, so I made him work at grating the mandragora, and wondered where it would end.

Around the middle of the morning I went to check on my Caesarean patient, whom I had treated in her own home; the midwife came with me. I walked very quickly, glaring at the camp, and the midwife had to run to keep up. Just in front of the woman's wagon I almost fell over Athanaric. He was sitting calmly by the nearest well, sharpening his sword, looking Gothic to his back teeth. I stopped short, staring at him; he looked quickly at the wagon and shook his head. I caught his meaning and pretended that I was just waiting for the midwife to catch up, and then went into the wagon.

The woman seemed to be recovering. The wound was inflamed, but not excessively so. If it was kept clean, she would probably live. I dressed it myself, lectured her family on hygiene again, then sent the midwife off to fetch some drug I said I'd forgotten. She went, and I pretended to find that I had the drug after all. I dosed the woman, then went out, alone. Athanaric was waiting.

I ran over to him, and he caught my arm and pulled me aside. "Here!" he said, and indicated a crawl space under the nearest wagon. I crept under, and he followed. We were out of sight, and as private as anyone could be in this crowded city. "Will the woman come back?" asked Athanaric.

"I sent her to fetch a drug," I said. "She'll probably assume she just missed me on the way, and go back to the hospital. We have about half an hour before they start looking for me."

Athanaric sighed and rubbed his face. "And they will look for you?"

"They've just received orders to watch me so that I can't escape."

"They didn't need to have you watched for that," he said bitterly. "You can't escape anyway. Not now, that is. All the raiding parties are in, half of them know me, and all of them seem to know you; I could never get you out of here. But I had to talk to you."

His eyes were sharp and earnest in the shadow under the wagon. He was speaking in a whisper, in his quick, staccato Greek, so as not to attract attention. I felt a lump in my throat, and swallowed hard. "I'm glad," I whispered. "I need . . . I am very alone here. How did you know where to wait for me?"

He smiled. "The king sent for you when I arrived yesterday. His messenger came back saying that you wouldn't come because you were cutting a child out of a living woman. People talk about something like that, so I just listened until I heard where it was, then waited for you to check on your patient. I gather she's actually still alive?"

I nodded. "It's a question of where you make the incision. Amalberga says I should marry someone so that they can't use me as a hostage."

"Don't," said Athanaric. "They wouldn't dare hurt you. And your brother is to leave Tomis this autumn: he's been offered another governorship immediately, in Bithynia. You'd be no good to them as a hostage anyway. Would you really kill any Goth who tried to marry you?"

"Probably not," I told him. "But I want them to think so. I don't want anyone to try it."

"If you can get them to believe you, you should be safe. They won't worry about knives, but they're afraid of poison. This war can't last forever, and we'll get you out somehow."

I had told myself, and others, that there was nothing for me to return to among the Romans; I hadn't expected my heart to race so at the thought of escape. But perhaps it was just Athanaric.

"What will happen?" I asked him. "Do you think the war will end soon? Can you negotiate a truce?"

He shook his head. "Ever since I arrived, everyone has been telling me the sort of truce I should negotiate. But I'm not officially here.

I've been posted to Egypt. I only came because somebody needed to ransom you."

"To Egypt? But —"

"They don't trust me at court," Athanaric explained, giving an uneven smile. "I pleaded too hard on Fritigern's behalf before. And they're starting to distrust all Goths. My father is virtually under arrest. But the master of the offices values me, and so I keep my job and my rank but get moved elsewhere. I'll be safe in Egypt, they think at court, spying on the followers of your old friend Athanasios. Is this what he discovered about you? That you're a woman?"

I nodded. "Won't this trip make trouble for you, though?"

"Not too much, if I go straight to Egypt when I leave. Sebastianus and your brother can vouch for me. And they needed me to come; there was no one else they dared send into the Gothic camp."

"Will the Goths let you go?"

"Oh, no fear about that. Colias is my cousin, and his men used to take orders from my father. They won't interfere with me. But I can't get you out. I've been up all night trying to think of some way, but with all the troops back here it's no use; the fortifications are crawling with guards, and I'm supposed to be gone by this evening. Fritigern doesn't trust me to stay longer. You will simply have to be strong, and wait. I've talked to some of Colias' men, and they'll try to protect you if the camp's invaded. I only wish I could do more."

"I will wait, then," I said, trying to resign myself. "At least I have work to keep me busy. How is Arbetio managing at Novidunum?"

Athanaric stared at me a moment, then shrugged. "Fairly well. He's hired another assistant. The troops all say you're a better doctor, though. What's this about saving the Theruingi from an epidemic?"

"I had them build drains."

"And that stops an epidemic? An epidemic might have been useful to us."

"It would have killed mostly the old and the children, not the warriors. I've been trying not to treat the men — don't worry about that. What about my slaves at Novidunum? Do you know how they are?"

"Arbetio has been supervising them for you. He's married that girl he bought from Valerius, and they're all living in that new house you bought, with Arbetio putting aside some money for the rent for you. You can trust him. He wanted to offer to exchange himself for you, but Sebastianus thought that a fat ransom was more likely to succeed."

"Did we get some more drugs from Philon in Egypt?"

Athanaric didn't answer. "Lord God, Charis!" he exclaimed instead. "Why on earth didn't you tell someone who you were? Sebastianus would have sent you home in a flash, and then you wouldn't be in this mess. This is no place for you."

"And what do you think is a good place for me, then?" I demanded. "Festinus' house, where my father would have sent me?"

"Of course not. But I've talked to your brother, I know he's been trying to persuade you to come back for years now."

"Come back to what? To sit in his house in disgrace, or to marry some clod and spend my time reading Homer and staring at the floor? I'm a doctor, and good at it."

"Sebastianus isn't a clod, and wouldn't expect you to spend your time staring at the floor."

"Don't be absurd. Sebastianus wouldn't marry me."

"He's asked your brother to draw up the contract, and your brother's agreed."

I stared.

"For God's sake! You were there in Marcianopolis when he described his idea of the perfect woman; you must have realized you fit the description. The day after I told him who you really are, he told me that he wanted to marry you. 'I won't get another chance at a woman like that,' he said."

"But . . . but his family certainly outranks mine. And I wouldn't have thought my dowry was up to scratch."

"A thousand pounds in gold would be enough. But in fact Sebastianus is willing to spend the dowry on the ransom and draw up the contract without his father's approval. And your family is as good as his — consular rank."

"Only consul in Constantinople. His father's been consul in Rome."

"Consular rank is consular rank. And he wants to marry you."

"But why? I must be the scandal of half the empire."

"Oh, for God's sake! What do you want me to say? That he wants you because you're brilliant, accomplished, noble, rich, courageous, virtuous, and rather beautiful? That he's said all that to me? You made all that clear to him, you must know he thinks that; why do you have to hear it from me?"

I sat there in the shadow under the wagon and gaped at Athanaric for a minute, and then I shook my head. I suddenly wanted very badly to cry, and put my arm to my mouth to stop myself. "I know I'm clever," I said after a pause. "But I didn't . . . that is . . . oh, Holy Christ!" I bit my sleeve, but it didn't work: the tears were coming anyway. I was very tired, from the hard work and the trouble and the waiting, and it suddenly seemed too much to bear, that Athanaric was angry and was accusing me indirectly of having entrapped Sebastianus.

He stared at me in surprise. "I thought . . ." he began; then: "You are pleased about it, aren't you? You are in love with him?"

I shook my head.

"But . . . but then who did you mean, that time in Tomis? You said you were in love with someone. I assumed —"

"Never mind," I said. If he couldn't guess, I shouldn't tell him; I'd only make myself ridiculous. If he felt half of what I did, I told myself, he'd know. "I like Sebastianus. I'm just not in love with him. And I'm not sure he's wise, deciding to marry me. But then, I can't really see myself settling down as a respectable matron with anyone."

"I would have thought you could use your dowry to found a private hospital," said Athanaric — a startlingly practical suggestion that took my breath away.

"Would Sebastianus approve of that?"

"I don't know," he said honestly. "But who did you mean, then? Someone in Egypt — that fellow Philon?"

"Never mind! No, of course not Philon. The trouble with you is, you want to know everything, and you won't leave anything alone. How did you manage to guess about me? I gather you did guess, even before I was captured."

Two of Fritigern's companions came hurrying past the well and banged on the door of my patient's wagon. Athanaric pulled me further back into the shadow. "The search is on," he said. "I think we'd better leave discussions of why I didn't spot the obvious sooner, until the next time."

"Will there be one?"

"Dear God, I hope so. Though I don't know when I'll be allowed away from Egypt. Perhaps Sebastianus will manage to get you out before then. Whatever you do, though, don't let them marry you to anyone. It will make it much more difficult to get you out, and it would hurt Sebastianus as much as anything on earth. Can you send him any message, even if you're not in love with him?"

"Tell him I am honored by and grateful for his offer, but doubt its wisdom. And tell him I'm all right. And tell Thorion that too, and tell him not to worry, at least no one's accusing me of sorcery. I must go; I can't have those men disturbing my patient. Dearest friend, much health!"

He caught my hand and stared into my face, frowning. I heard people start shouting inside my patient's wagon, and the baby began to cry. Because I had to, I leaned over and kissed Athanaric quickly — stolen pleasure! — then pulled my hand loose, slid out from under the wagon, and ran to rescue my patient. Athanaric said nothing, and I didn't dare look back at him. When I came out with the companions (I told them that I'd gone to check on another patient and rebuked them soundly for disturbing the sick woman), I looked under the wagon, but Athanaric was gone.

The year that followed was the worst of my life.

Even after Athanaric was gone I was watched constantly. Every night my clothes were taken away and not given back until the next morning. I was escorted directly to the hospital and constantly supervised and spied upon until I was escorted home. I was forbidden to treat Roman patients. In protest at this I flatly refused to treat any Gothic warriors, but this didn't have much effect, as others were willing to do that and no one but me had been attending to the Roman slaves. It broke my heart to see them sick and suffering about the camp, and to be unable to help. I would almost have agreed to marry some Goth, if they'd have promised to let me treat Romans — but Amalberga would only say that such a promise would have to be up to my husband.

And everyone went on and on at me about marriage. After my bloodthirsty declarations no one wanted to marry me against my will, but a number of Gothic chieftains thought they might be able to convince me to change my mind. I was at first surprised that they bothered; after all, few Romans would want me, a runaway with no dowry. But I discovered that there is nothing like notoriety for attracting attention. For a young Gothic nobleman who wanted to make a name for himself I was a golden opportunity: marry the woman who had shamed Festinus and he'd have fame on a platter. Besides, they mostly expected that once I was married, my family would give in and provide a dowry as well, making the best of a bad deal. So at regular intervals I was left alone with one or another of these notables, and they endeavored to make conversation or love or both, while I fended them off as politely as I could. I had to be polite, as I didn't dare seriously offend such powerful men. But they were under no such obligation; they were honoring me enough by offering marriage, they thought. Some of them preserved the social decencies, but some didn't, and I needed quick wits and a stiff arm. It would have been funny if it hadn't been so frightening, and if I hadn't felt so mauled every time I got away. And of course they *were* offended. I developed considerable sympathy for Penelope of Ithaca, who had stood ten years of that sort of thing — but none of the Goths had heard of her, and no one would help me laugh. All the noble ladies told me again and again about the courage and hardihood and manly virtue of Munderich or Levila or Lagriman or whichever of those ignorant, sword-toting barbarians I was then being considered by, until I was quite sick of the sound of Gothic and wished I'd married Festinus and had done with it.

But all these weren't serious difficulties; those started that winter. In early autumn the combined Roman forces marched north and met the Goths at Salices, where they fought a pitched battle. There was very great slaughter on both sides, and no clear victor. The Gothic troops retreated to Carragines, the Romans to Marcianopolis. The Goths treated their wounded and argued what to do next. The Romans, more practical and industrious, built barricades across the passes in the Haemus mountains. By the time the Goths realized this, they were trapped in the north of the diocese, where, as Amalberga had said, there was nothing to eat.

The Goths made a few attempts to break through the Roman line into the more populous and well-supplied south, but achieved nothing but loss of life. Fritigern sent envoys to the Romans in Marcianopolis, but they were driven away from the gates and not even allowed into the city. The Romans were not ready to negotiate. Fritigern sent to Tomis, offering to ransom me for grain supplies, but it was late autumn by the time he did this, and Thorion had apparently already gone to Bithynia, and the new governor didn't listen to Fritigern's threats. I was held prisoner in the house while this was going on, but in the end the king realized that no one would pay any attention to what happened to me, except perhaps to revenge it, and sent me back to treat the sick. My skill was more necessary than ever.

People fall ill easily when they are cold and hungry. They die easily too. Medicine at its best has been called "a meditation on death," and that winter in Carragines death sometimes seemed the only topic I could think of. The days were indistinguishable with hunger and cold, disease and hard work; emaciated bodies, fever-stricken, shivering under flea-infested blankets; gray-skinned corpses piled in carts, awaiting burial, their eyes glazed with ice; the thin crying of starving children, the quiet deaths of old women; wood smoke and the sharp scent of gentian. My Caesarean patient lost her baby, then died herself; the Roman slaves I had stitched up that summer were thrown in ragged heaps under a thin scraping of frozen earth. For me, it was worse than the Goths' attempts at marriage, worse than being a prisoner, worse even than being forbidden to treat Romans. I was surrounded by death, and all my art was useless.

The Goths began to say that the Romans would never negotiate, that they meant to wipe out the Gothic race. I don't think it was true — the Romans would have concluded a peace treaty once the Goths were completely broken and were willing to accept any terms. Fritigern's client kingdom would have been out of the question, but the Romans still cherished the idea of Gothic settlers for the wastelands. But the Goths didn't break. Instead they looked back across the Danube at the enemy they had come to Thrace to escape, and in their desperation they made an alliance with the Huns.

I didn't see much of these savages in Carragines. They don't like towns, and avoid houses as we do tombs; Fritigern always spoke to them far from the camp, sitting on his horse as they sat on their shaggy ponies. He hated and feared them — all the Goths did — and Amalberga's women told monstrous stories of their savagery and cruelty, until I felt quite sick for my people. Fritigern had persuaded the Huns into the alliance by promising them rich plunder, of course — Roman cities stuffed with gold and silk and treasures; Roman slaves. The Goths provided a bridge of boats, and the Huns came swarming across the river, thousands upon thousands of them, a fast-moving, savage, and fearful army.

When the Romans discovered what had happened, very early in the spring, they withdrew the troops from the fortifications in the mountains. They did not have the numbers to hold out against the Goths, Huns, and Halani all together, and the Roman commander judged that his men would be better employed protecting the neighboring regions of Dacia and Asia. So Thrace was surrendered for

338

pillage. The barbarians still did not attack the fortified cities — the Huns had even less experience than the Goths of siege warfare — but they poured down into the south as far as the Middle Sea, plundering, murdering, burning, and raping as they went. There was food again in Carragines, but I scarcely wanted to eat it, knowing how it had been taken.

About the middle of May I fell ill. Fevers were common in the camp, but no longer epidemic; I think normally I would have shrugged the disease off, but I was weak after the long hunger and exhausted by work and the problems of Marriage. It began with a headache and fever. I stopped work, afraid of transmitting whatever it was, and I went to bed. I very nearly never got up again.

Amalberga tried to attend me, at first, and then in the second week of the illness Edico returned from accompanying Fritigern and the army, and she sent for him. By that time the fever was high and accompanied by vomiting and diarrhea. I felt dull and stupid, and wouldn't answer Edico's questions or cooperate in the treatment he prescribed; I just told him to leave me alone. He didn't; he gave me hemlock on a sponge, to lower the fever, and then honeywater and wine and some barley broth — all the things I would have prescribed myself. I wept, accused him of stealing my learning, called him a traitor, and told him to let me die in peace. And I really did wish to die, then. I was so tired of it all. I remembered how Athanasios once said that exchanging this world for Heaven is like exchanging a copper *drachma* for a hundred gold *solidi*; I didn't know about Heaven, but I certainly felt that my life wasn't worth a copper *drachma*. Carragines was unbearable, but where else could I go? There was nowhere on earth I could be whole: a Roman, a doctor, and a woman. In Heaven, I thought, everyone must be themselves, and complete; slave or free, male or female, it makes no difference there. I thought death would be like staring into water: the surface is troubled, the depths churn for a moment, but then when it grows still you can see clear to the bottom of everything.

I also thought that in Heaven they would certainly speak Greek; if I had to listen to more Gothic, it couldn't be Paradise.

One night, after I'd been ill for a couple of weeks without responding to treatment, I woke up and saw Athanasios standing over me. He was dressed as he had been at his death, in a linen tunic with an old sheepskin cloak. After he died the attendants changed him into his best clothing, all brocade and cloth of gold, but he'd always preferred simplicity. I sat up. My dulled head felt quite clear. "Your Holiness," I said, "have you come all the way from Egypt?"

He smiled and jerked his head back: no. "Not from Egypt." It was good to hear his voice, the singsong accent and the careful Greek words. "Charis, my dear, I told you that you would marry, and you seem determined to prove me wrong."

"Don't you start on me," I said. "I'm sick of that song. I thought you didn't like marriage."

He smiled again. "I have been known to make mistakes. Though the world has made greater ones. Marriage should not be a means of getting property, nor of gaining power, nor of subjecting women. That's the song you're sick of hearing, and I can't blame you."

"I thought you didn't like it because it involved lust."

He laughed. "From where I am, lust looks completely different. The world is a dark place, and nothing is pure in it, for good or evil. Not lust, not the empire, not the Goths. But none of them will endure."

"Not even the empire?" I asked.

"Because something has lasted a long time does not mean it is eternal," he replied gently.

"I'm tired of the world," I said, despairing now.

"You, who have kept so many people in it?"

That still had power to move me. "It isn't wrong to heal!"

He smiled again, and touched my forehead. "I wish you loved God as much as you love Hippocrates. But 'every good gift, and every perfect gift, proceeds from the Father of Light,' and if you follow it back far enough, perhaps it will lead you to its source. God made the world, and printed his image on us, and we have never been able to efface that totally. Yes, it is good to heal. God heals. And you have more healing to do yet, before you go."

"But I'm tired!" I protested.

"Then rest." The brilliant dark eyes rested on mine, deep, affectionate, commanding. His hand felt cool, pressing me gently back. I lay down, and the coolness spread; I closed my eyes and felt the earth sway under me like water, like a cradle rocking to the beating of my heart.

I slept, and when I woke up it was morning, with the light coming in slantwise through the shutters and laying bars of gold across the foot of the bed. My head and stomach still hurt and I felt very weak, but I knew that my fever was lower and that I would live. I lay on my side, staring at the place where Athanasios had stood. After a minute the door opened and Edico and Amalberga came in.

"She's awake!" Edico exclaimed excitedly. He hurried over and checked my pulse, touched my forehead.

"The fever's down," I told him. "Did you see him?"

Edico looked blank. "Who?"

"Bishop Athanasios. He was here last night; he stood exactly where you are now."

Edico moved uneasily away. "You have been very ill," he told me. "You haven't been conscious for days."

I sighed and put my hand to my eyes; the hand felt very heavy, and my eyes ached. It was too much effort to try to determine whether I had had a vision, a visitation, or a dream. But I was comforted. Whether he had been there or not, I was glad to have seen someone from the good days in Alexandria, when I had been happy. I realized suddenly that I had spoken in Greek, and that Edico had replied in the same language, for the first time in months.

"Will you have something to drink?" Edico asked eagerly. "Some barley broth?"

I looked at him, and then at Amalberga. "If I recover, may I treat Romans again?" I asked her.

She went pale, and sat down on the bed. "If only we were all free!" she said suddenly, and clasped her hands together. "I swear I never hated the Romans, even after they injured us. And yet now they are enemies, and the Huns, whom I did hate, are our allies, and we are tied to this war like a slave to a rack!"

"I have never hated the Goths," I returned levelly. "But you have used me very cruelly, for whatever reasons. I wish I were very far away from here. I would rather die than go on as I have." And, I realized, I wished I were married, to Athanaric, and running a private hospital of my own. It was the first time I had shaped such an ambition, clear and precise as that, and in the surprise I forgot what else I had meant to say.

"I cannot let you go," Amalberga said wretchedly. "The war is going badly, and we may need . . ." She stopped, staring at me miserably. They might need to sell me to save their own lives, she meant. And even if they didn't, I had no hope of freedom from them. Fritigern was proud of such a notorious prisoner, and I was still very useful as a doctor.

"I am sorry," Amalberga went on, after a pause. "I do not want us to be enemies. I will try to see that you are allowed to treat Romans. And I can protect you from any more suitors — they're all going into the south now anyway. But I can't do more for you than that."

"If you'll let me do something for my own people, it will be enough," I said. "Yes, I would like some barley broth. And maybe a little honeyed wine."

It was a couple more weeks before I was well enough to treat anyone, and when I was on my feet again, no one seemed to mind much what I did: there was too much else to worry about. Fritigern had gone south with nearly all the men, leaving Carragines under a light guard with Amalberga in command. Edico went with him, and most of the hospital attendants. I was left unofficially in charge of the health of the camp, with a few midwives and wisewomen. I was not really trusted and was still kept under a constant watch, but there wasn't really anyone else to put in charge.

The emperor Lord Valens the Augustus had concluded a peace treaty with Persia and was said to be hurrying to Constantinople, gathering troops along the way. The western Augustus, Gratianus, was reported to have defeated the Alamanni in Gaul, and was coming east with the Gaulish legions, ready to attack the Goths. The troops already in Thrace had a new commander: Sebastianus' father, the former count of Illyria. He was a very active and skillful general, with a formidable reputation he had no trouble living up to. He had scarcely arrived when he succeeded in ambushing and annihilating a particularly large raiding party, and so alarming Fritigern that the other raiding parties were called in — not to Carragines, but to a town in the south called Kabyle. The men were not eager to be trapped north of the mountains again. They gathered together — the Theruingi, the Greuthungi, the Halani, and the Huns — and they waited for the Romans to arrive.

It was a hot summer that year, hot and wet. The camp was old and stinking now, full of flies and disease. Even when I was back on my feet, I found that I tired very easily, and didn't have the energy to fight for the things I should have — aqueducts to bring in fresh water, rubbish dumps outside the walls. I had seen so many patients die over the winter, it scarcely moved me anymore. I was allowed to treat the Roman prisoners again, but after all I had been through for that, I couldn't seem to help them much. Edico had taken nearly all the drugs with him, and I couldn't get the prisoners better conditions to live in. My barbarian suitors were all gone now, but it didn't make the difference I had expected. I couldn't think straight, and my feelings seemed blunted, thick and heavy like the air. One evening I realized that the camp was lightly enough guarded that it should be easy to slip out of it; but wretched as I was, I could do nothing about it. I was too tired to plan an escape, too tired for anything but a mechanical, helpless imitation of work. Even news of the war could not make much impression on me. Valens had left Constantinople with a great force; the Goths were retreating toward Hadrianopolis; the emperor and Count Sebastianus were considering attacking them without waiting for the additional troops from the West — great events, and my own fate depended on their outcome, but they seemed somehow tedious, as though they had happened many times before.

And then, one sticky afternoon in early August, I came into the hospital after visiting some convalescents and found Athanaric sitting quietly among a group of new patients waiting to be examined.

He was dressed in a rough woolen tunic, like a common soldier, and he had his arm in a sling. For a moment I doubted my eyes, but then I saw the recognition in his face, and a look of shock. He quickly looked away again and scratched his beard with his unbandaged hand, and I managed to understand. I changed my stare into a sneeze, wiped my face, and began examining the patients.

I had a midwife to help me with this task, luckily a woman who had never met Athanaric. When she tried to see to his arm, he protested. "I want the Roman doctor," he said in Gothic, "not some old witch who only knows about babies."

"The Roman doctor will not treat men injured in the war," said the midwife, pulling at the sling. Athanaric winced and clutched his arm as though it pained him.

"Oh, leave it!" I told her. "I'll look at this one. Can you fetch some more cleansing solution?"

She left to fetch it, and I went to look at Athanaric's arm. I still did not dare to talk, not in front of the other patients. I felt dizzy, and my blood roared in my ears. "What happened?" I asked Athanaric, undoing the sling.

"Sword wound," he replied in a sullen tone. "It's broken. The doctor in the south set it. But now it's infected."

I took off the bandage carefully. The arm was perfectly whole and uninjured, to my relief, but there was a note folded up inside the bandage. I hesitated, then palmed it, looked up, and raised my eyebrows, and he said, still in the sullen tone, "See?"

343

"Very bad," I said. "You should not go shoving magical charms into it. But you're lucky; it doesn't need cauterizing yet."

The midwife came back with the cleansing solution, and I directed her to one of the other patients, a sick child. I pretended to clean and rebandage the arm. I told him to wait while I fetched another drug, and went into the pharmacy. It was empty, thank God. I unfolded the note. It was very brief: "Treat me and send me off. Then go as soon as you can to the wall behind the hospital."

I thought I would faint, from excitement and from the suddenness of hope. I tore the note up and ate it, then went back into the examining room; I had to stop, go back, and fetch the drug I had ostensibly gone for. I gave it to Athanaric and ordered him to go home to his family and rest, and to come have the wound cleaned and rebandaged next morning. He went.

I had no opportunity to follow him immediately. I treated a few more patients and prepared some drugs. By then it was late afternoon, and my usual escort showed up, prepared to take me back to the women's quarters of Fritigern's house. Fritigern's companions, who'd originally performed this task, had all gone south. My escort now consisted of two of Amalberga's ladies who liked to take a walk about the camp every afternoon and picked me up on their way back to the house. I went with them quietly almost all the way back, and then exclaimed that I had forgotten my medical bag.

"Well, leave it," said one of the ladies. "It will be there tomorrow."

"Oh no!" I said. "The drugs in it are dangerous; I can't just leave them lying about. I'll run back and fetch it. You go on to the house. It's not worth your while going all the way back to the hospital."

They were tired, it was hot, and no one expected me to try to escape now. They agreed. I started back toward the hospital, forcing myself to walk calmly as though there were no hurry and no excitement. It was the first time in months that I was alone, and my thoughts seemed to run circles around my head, like a troop of cavalry at full gallop: Athanaric, escape, freedom, release, the great world. I stopped and looked up into the deep sky, which was overcast with a damp haze, and I thought I could fly into it, right up to the sun itself. I was abandoning my patients and probably my career as well, but I no longer cared. I was sick of death. I wanted to live, to be free. I made myself keep walking.

The hospital backed directly onto the camp walls, and it was set a little apart from the other wagons and shelters, to keep infectious diseases isolated. I walked straight past it, trying to look confident, as though I had some business. When I had almost reached the palisade, I heard a soft hiss off to my right; I looked, and there was Athanaric, waiting under one of the wagons. I ran over as though my feet were winged.

Athanaric wasted no time in greetings or explanations. He caught my arm, pulled me under the wagon, and pushed me toward the palisade; a hole had been scooped out underneath it. I slid down, under, and out, and Athanaric followed. He jerked his head toward a clump of trees a bit further on, and we ran for it.

"A guard comes along about every ten minutes," he explained when we reached the trees. "He's just gone. Now we wait for him to go past again, and then we head out. I have some horses waiting about three miles from here; can you walk that far?"

"Of course." I sat down and leaned my head against a tree trunk, staring at the walls of the wagon city.

"You don't look well." He stooped over me, looking concerned.

"I've been ill," I told him, "and it's very sudden. But I can walk three miles. Eternal Christ, I'd be ready to crawl them. Thank you. I don't have any words for it. Thank you."

He touched my shoulder, frowning, then crouched down beside me as the guard came into sight, walking slowly along the outside of the wall, his spear over his shoulder. He paused, took his spear down and shoved it idly into a rabbit hole, then shrugged and walked on. Athanaric touched my shoulder again, and we slipped out of the wood and walked briskly across the open field that ringed the camp.

Across the field, down into a ditch, along the ditch ("Can you run? Then do it!"), along another ditch, across other fields and ditches, striding and running, then up into a patch of woodland. Late afternoon sun slanting through the leaves; the smell of leaf mold and damp moss, strange and delicious after nothing but camp stink, medicine, and wood smoke for so many months. Athanaric indicated a direction and strode off in it, and I stumbled after. Birdsong, the crunch of leaves underfoot, my breath panting harshly after the run. Then the jingle of harness and the soft snort of a horse; the slanting light picked out the rich brown and light gray of horses. "Athanaric!" someone said in relief, and then, "Chariton!" And Arbetio ran up and embraced me.

"You?" I said stupidly. "But what are you doing here?"

"Athanaric needed someone to hold the horses," Arbetio said, smiling. Then the smile faded, and he stepped back, looking at me.

He didn't make any stupid comments about my apparent change of sex; he just said, "But you've been ill."

"A couple of months ago now. I can ride — oh, damnation!" I'd forgotten about the long skirts, impossible for riding. I stared at them, mortified.

"Just pull them up," ordered Athanaric, untying one of the horses and leading it over. "There's no time to do anything about them now. They must know in the camp that you're missing."

"They'll search inside first," I said, but I tried to climb into the saddle. My foot caught in the skirts. Arbetio bent and offered me his shoulder, and I clambered up, trying to keep the skirts out of my way. Athanaric was already mounting his own horse, and Arbetio ran over to the third animal and leapt into the saddle, smiling again. Athanaric set off at a gallop, riding northeast across country, splashing through streams and over stone to confuse the scent if the Goths tried to track us with dogs. I was soon too busy trying to stay in the saddle to think.

We rode for hours, until it was dark and the horses were too tired to continue, and then Athanaric found a place in another wood and we stopped. By then I was too exhausted to ask questions. I hadn't ridden for more than a year, and had had a full day's work before the escape. I simply lay down in a hollow in the ground and pulled my cloak over me. In a little while Arbetio woke me up and pointed to a bed of bracken he'd made for me, so I moved over on to that and went back to sleep.

I woke at dawn next morning. The wood smelled alive, and the birds were singing. I was covered with mosquito bites, ached from the riding, and felt wonderful. I sat up. The other two were already up: Athanaric was feeding the horses, and Arbetio was unpacking some breakfast. Arbetio smiled. "Sleep well?" he asked.

"Better than I have for months," I said honestly, and got up — very stiffly, since my muscles ached and I had two or three raw patches from riding with my skirts pulled up. I hobbled over to help the others, but Arbetio handed me some bread and a cup of watered wine and told me to rest. "You don't look well," he said again. "What did they do to you in that camp?"

I shrugged. "Tried to marry me, mostly. But as I said, I've been ill. Dear God, it's good to see you. But why are you here? I wouldn't have thought Novidunum could spare you."

"I'm absent without leave," Arbetio said cheerfully.

"I needed help from someone I could trust," Athanaric put in, coming over. "So I wrote and asked Arbetio."

"And why are you here, too? I thought you were in Egypt," I said. He stood there holding a bridle and looking down at me with a frown, the early sun dappling his face with light.

"I'm absent without leave as well," he told me, and sat down. Arbetio handed him his own chunk of bread.

"Won't that be dangerous for you? You said before that the authorities no longer trust any Goths, and if you abandoned your post in Egypt to come to Thrace . . ."

"It's all right if I come back with you. You can vouch for me. If I came back without you, I suppose I might be accused of treason. But I haven't come directly from Egypt, only from Constantinople. I had to take a message there. The Master of the Offices was going to send me to Armenia, but I didn't wait for him to arrange it. His Sacred Majesty was marching into Thrace, and I thought Carragines might have been left unguarded. So I sent Arbetio a letter asking him to meet me in Tomis."

I looked from one to the other of them. "You were taking a horrible risk."

"You are my master in the art," said Arbetio. "And I owe you my freedom. But Athanaric wouldn't let me go into the camp."

"It wasn't dangerous for me there, and it would have been for him," said Athanaric apologetically. "The Goths wouldn't have harmed me, even if I was caught."

"Oh," I said, looking from one to the other again. "I thank you both, more than I can say. I think I would have died if I had had to spend another winter in Carragines."

"You look like you half died already," Athanaric said harshly. "You're nothing but bones and eyes. You said they kept trying to marry you. They didn't . . . that is —"

I was a bit surprised at this delicacy. "Rape me? No. But . . . well, my brother once said that no one would want to marry a female doctor. I began to feel that absolutely everybody I disliked did want to. I felt like Penelope of Ithaca."

Athanaric smiled hesitantly. "Circumspect Penelope?"

"And circumscribed, too!" I said, smiling back. "Spied on all the time. And then there wasn't much to eat last winter, and people kept dying, until I wanted to die myself. But now . . . 'Oh radiance, oh light of the four-horse chariot of the Sun, oh Earth and Night which filled my gaze before, now I behold you with free eyes!' " I leaned back and looked up at the sun with free eyes; I felt as though the whole year of wretchedness and confinement had dropped away like the muddy shell of the caddis fly, swept off downstream when the fly grows its wings.

Athanaric snorted. "Sebastianus said you went into captivity quoting Euripides. I suppose it makes sense that you come out the same way." He bit off a mouthful of the bread and chewed it hard.

"And how is Sebastianus?" I asked.

Athanaric swallowed quickly, and he and Arbetio looked at each other uneasily.

"He's well," Arbetio said after a moment. "He's with the army. With his father, the count."

"His father had the marriage contract annulled," Athanaric said bluntly. "He said it was invalid because it lacked his consent, and he tore it up and burned it. He . . . disapproved of you."

"Oh," I said, rather feebly. "What did Sebastianus say?"

"He swore that if his father wouldn't let him marry the woman of his choice, he wouldn't marry the woman of his father's," said Arbetio.

"But he won't run off and marry you anyway," said Athanaric. "He would risk his career."

"Oh," I said again. "Well, I never believed in that marriage. I suppose Sebastianus still has Daphne?"

"You don't have to be jealous of her!" said Athanaric.

"Jealous? I'm not jealous. I'm relieved: I'm just as glad that marriage is out of the way again. But when I saw you before, you swore that Sebastianus had his heart set on this scheme, and I thought Daphne could console him."

Athanaric watched me with a frown. I ate some of the bread. It was journeybread, full of rough grain and hard; I had to gnaw on it like a mouse. But it tasted good.

"He still has Daphne," Athanaric admitted. "That is, she's in Tomis, waiting for him to get back from the war. I thought you'd be disappointed."

I shook my head. "I never expected Sebastianus to want to do something like that, I never really believed it would happen, and I don't think it would have worked very well if it had. But I'm surprised. You . . . that is, I thought you'd come to fetch me for Sebastianus, as a favor to your friend."

"You're a friend too," Arbetio said. "That you're a woman doesn't change that."

Athanaric nodded. "We couldn't leave you in there. I promised to get you out, and now I have."

We sat in silence for a moment, and then Arbetio asked, "What will you do now? Do you have somewhere to go?"

"I'll find something to do with myself," I replied, trying to think of what. I was not used to having a future. Perhaps I didn't have one, really; perhaps I was fated to grow old in my brother's house. But perhaps I could persuade Thorion to let me go. I decided, suddenly and recklessly, that I would assume that I could choose for myself, order my life as I pleased; and I thought about what I would do. After a minute I added, "Maybe I'll go back to Alexandria. I presume my army contract's been torn up."

Arbetio laughed. "Could you teach in Alexandria?"

"I suppose not. But my old master, Philon, would probably take me on as a partner. That is, unless I'm still under suspicion for my part in Bishop Peter's escape."

Athanaric stared again, then looked at his half-eaten bread. "Bishop Peter is back on the throne of St. Mark," he stated. "That was the message I took to Constantinople."

"What!" I exclaimed. A week before, even news from Thrace had seemed stale and uninteresting; this morning I was thrilled with everything. "What happened to Lucius?"

"His troop of guards was recalled, and he thought it wise to leave Alexandria. His Sacred Majesty didn't have time or troops to waste on Alexandrian riots, and he's leaving Peter the episcopal throne so as to have some peace."

"Then I'll go to Alexandria!" I said, and finished my wine in a gulp.

"The hell you will!" said Athanaric. "Peter will be back in exile as soon as the emperor has settled the Goths — unless he's dead. They say he's ill."

"Then he'll need a doctor. He may not even mind that I'm a woman, if I tell him that Athanasios didn't mind."

"You barely escaped the rack when you left Alexandria last time!"

"This time I'll be more careful. I'll try to put a bit of distance between me and the church. I'll stay with Philon."

"He won't mind that you're a woman?" Athanaric asked sarcastically.

"He knew that before I left. He treated me during an illness. And he was like Arbetio — we were colleagues; it was a shock at first but made very little difference." Arbetio grinned and nodded. "I suppose you think I should go to Bithynia and sit in my brother's house looking ladylike?"

Athanaric opened his mouth and closed it again. Then he said, "Your brother is very anxious to see you again."

"Well, I'd like to see him too. If he'll agree to let me go when I want to, I'll go to Bithynia first. But then I will go to Alexandria. It's a wonderful city, Arbetio, the best place in the world for medicine. Come on! Let's get away before the Goths come looking for us. Who would've thought I'd have to urge haste on a courier?"

Athanaric scowled, shoved the rest of his bread into his mouth, and went over to the horses. Arbetio grinned at me. "That's more like the man I remember," he told me. "You look better already."

I laughed and stood up, then looked at my skirts again. "You don't have any spare trousers?" I asked Arbetio.

"We didn't think of that," he replied. "And we wanted to travel light. Sorry."

"Ouch," I replied. "Lend me your knife, then."

Arbetio handed me his belt knife, and I cut some strips off the bottom of my undertunic and began to bandage my knees, which had been scraped raw against the saddle on the previous day. Athanaric brought my horse over, then stopped, staring at my legs. I stared too. They were not a pretty sight: very thin, and besides the raw knees they had scratches over the shins from the day before. "You should have brought trousers," I told him.

Strangely, he went quite red, and looked away. I felt embarrassed as well. I threaded some of the skirts through my belt to make them more trouserlike, then scrambled into the saddle. Arbetio handed me the rest of my bread.

We started off. "We're going to Novidunum," Athanaric explained. "Salices is closer, but I judged that the Goths might send a party out in that direction to look for you. This way we should be safe — they don't have the men in Carragines to search all directions, and the countryside should be deserted."

It was. Much was waste as well, wild forest and open heath, but we crossed abandoned farmland too, and passed some houses and a village, all deserted by their inhabitants and burned down by the invaders. We rode at a walk, because the horses couldn't stand another long gallop, and for a while we rode in silence as well. Then, partly to ease the awkwardness between us and partly because I was genuinely curious, I asked Athanaric when and how he had guessed my secret.

Athanaric snorted. "A long time after I should have done," he said. "I'm supposed to notice things, too; it's my job. But I didn't spot something that a seventy-year-old clergyman saw at once. When I did realize, I was thoroughly ashamed of myself."

"Athanasios said that God revealed it to him," I said. "And he was the only one that ever did guess. People believe what you tell them — particularly when the alternative is more preposterous than the story itself."

Athanaric snorted again, then smiled apologetically. "That was it: the idea was too preposterous. But I should have guessed. I knew a fair bit about you — I asked around about you in Egypt, when we first met and you turned down the bribe I offered you. Everyone agreed that you were a very clever doctor and not interested in money. I went and asked the chief physician at the Museum about you; he said the same, and added that you'd turned up quite suddenly one spring, practically without references and practically without money, claiming to be connected with the household of a certain Theodoros of Ephesus and begging to be taught the Hippocratic art. He said that he had thought a eunuch wouldn't be able to stand the hard work involved in the study of medicine, and that he thought you might be a runaway slave, and that he had advised you to go away. He said that Philon had only taken you out of charity, but that you'd done brilliantly since then and were very gifted. When I pressed him, he admitted that he still thought you were a runaway slave, and a few others suspected the same. But I agreed with him that a eunuch was better employed treating the sick than taking bribes in some rich man's house, and I left the matter at that.

"I already knew the story of how Festinus was jilted in his marriage garlands — it caused a stir in Asia when it happened — and when your brother and Festinus were both governing in Thrace I checked up on it, because I thought a private enmity like that might cause problems. And I learned that the sister of the most excellent Theodoros had simply vanished one spring, vanished without a trace. Her brother was still under their father's authority at the time and didn't have a separate household in which to conceal her, and all the searching by her father and Festinus couldn't uncover any sign of her. I did wonder then whether you might be connected with the disappearance, and whether you had gone to Alexandria in a hurry to get away from Festinus, but I didn't suspect the truth. You said you were a eunuch, and everyone else agreed; I never doubted it. Though I should have realized you weren't. I suppose in my heart I did realize, but what my heart saw, my brain dismissed very quickly. I suppose I was even offended with myself for thinking such a thing of another male.

"And then you were accused of sorcery. Your own slaves thought you were a sorcerer, and one of their reasons was that you always bathed and dressed yourself in private. But I didn't think anything of that. Eunuchs have reason to be modest. Then the governor of Scythia treated you like a brother. Well, I reasoned, he's the Theodoros you knew before, he may owe you some great favor. He referred to you once or twice as 'she' — a slip of the tongue, or a private joke? I wondered if, despite what you said, you'd been lovers — only he didn't seem the type. I was puzzled by it, but I still didn't connect Chariton the doctor with Theodoros' sister — and I'd never heard your name, either; people don't mention a young lady's name.

"And then, that night in Marcianopolis — Festinus was still brooding over his injury and accusing Theodoros, and I thought, 'Here is a very powerful, vindictive, and cruel man, and he couldn't find any trace of the girl; where could she have hidden?' And he didn't remember you, though you were afraid of him. I still didn't suspect, not with my mind, but I started to feel that I knew something I hadn't realized yet. And you quoted a bit of poetry you said you'd heard Festinus quote, but you quoted it wrong, saying 'Charis' where the poem reads 'Chloe.' The natural assumption was that Festinus had quoted it to a girl called Charis, but would he have done that with one of Theodoros' eunuchs looking on? So I asked you for help, and you told me very firmly to let the matter be — and still I didn't guess. Or rather, I couldn't admit to myself what I had guessed.

"Well, I was kept busy. I talked to Fritigern, went back and talked to Lupicinus, and then rode back and forth between Antioch and Hadrianopolis, too busy to think about anything but Gothic problems. Then I was kept for a couple of weeks in Antioch, reporting and discussing with various officials and not getting them to see sense. And one night I got drunk with a friend, and when I got back to my rooms I fell asleep and had a dream about you. Never mind what; you were a woman in the dream. And when I woke up, with a splitting headache, I thought, 'Christ Eternal, what a crazy dream!' and then I thought, 'Is it really?' And everything came together. But I still wasn't certain, not certain enough to write to anyone about it. Instead I asked around for someone who knew Theodoros of Ephesus, and I found an assessor at the governor's office, a fellow by the name of Kyrillos."

"Kyrillos? He studied law with my brother; Thorion wanted me to run off with him instead of going to Alexandria."

"That weedy logic-chopper?" Athanaric said in disgust. "Your plan was bad, but that would have been worse. You, marry some wordy lawyer?"

"I don't think he'd want me now," I conceded.

Athanaric gave me an odd look, then shrugged. "I told him that I was a friend of Theodoros' and took him out for a drink, and we talked about your brother until I could ask him about you. 'Do you know what happened to his sister?' I asked. 'What was her name — Charis?' 'I don't know, but he must,' he replied at once. 'He tells me she's well. I hope it's true; she was a splendid girl, as clever as any man. She would've been wasted on an ignorant money-grubber like Festinus.' And he told me how you learned Latin to help your brother out and were better at it than he was, but that this wasn't your real interest; really you liked medicine. I felt as though he'd kicked me — and I could have kicked myself, for having been so stupid. So I said that I thought I might have seen you in your brother's house in Thrace, and I gave him a description, and he agreed to it, and hoped that your brother would bring you out of concealment soon. We drank to that, and I went home and . . . never mind that. I wrote to Sebastianus."

"He told me," I said.

"She was furious," put in Arbetio.

"I didn't see why you should expose me," I said. "It would have ruined me. Though I suppose now I'm ruined anyway."

"I wouldn't have exposed you," Athanaric said wearily. "But Sebastianus had to know, and do something. A noblewoman of high rank and fortune is not someone to be hazarded in some rough campaign. And I was responsible; I'd sent you to him. I thought he would probably fall in love with you, once he knew. As I thought you were in love with him. But I was cautious; I didn't want the letter to fall into the wrong hands. I was due back in Thrace soon, I thought I could wait until I saw Sebastianus personally. But war started, and I was kept dashing about carrying messages and trying to reorganize the posts, and I couldn't get to Scythia until the week after you'd been captured. Sebastianus was still angry with his tribunes about that. But he told me that there were rumors from the Goths that you'd been unmasked as a woman, and he asked me what I made of them. I tore my hair and cursed both of us, and after a while Sebastianus did the same."

"I didn't know what to think when I first heard the rumors," Arbetio said. "I didn't believe them, until I treated some escaped slaves who'd met you and who confirmed it. And they said you were going to marry Edico."

"That was Fritigern's first idea. Before he knew who I was. Edico was very much relieved when I said I wouldn't."

Arbetio thought for a minute, then laughed; Athanaric scowled. "Edico always was a bit afraid of you," said Arbetio. "And I don't suppose he finds it any easier to think of you as a woman than I do."

"We are friends, you and I," I said. "And colleagues. How is everyone at Novidunum?"

Well, it seemed. Arbetio and his wife had been living in my new big house, with all my slaves. "I hoped you wouldn't object," he told me. "I was trying to look after all your household as well as mine, and needed the space."

"Keep it," I said, "as a gift from me. I won't need it; I'm leaving Thrace."

"I hope not forever," Arbetio said, smiling earnestly. "We would like to see you again."

"You can come visit me in Alexandria. You ought to go anyway; they can still do dissections there sometimes, and it's wonderful what you can learn from a cadaver."

Athanaric winced. "I hope your brother keeps you in Bithynia," he said harshly. "He should never have allowed you to go to Alexandria in the first place, and he's doubly a fool if he lets you go back. A woman has no place practicing medicine on her own in such a dangerous city."

I stared in surprise, then in anger. "You always talk in generalities," I told him. " 'There are no honest eunuchs,' 'women shouldn't practice medicine.' One thing I learned in Alexandria is that every case must be treated on its own merits. You can't say something like 'women should have half a man's dose of opium' — it would be too small an amount for a large, strong woman in good health, and too large for some sickly maiden, and in some cases you might not want to use opium at all, but mandragora or Indian hemp or hellebore, depending on the patient and the disease. If you can't prescribe drugs for a whole sex, why should you prescribe behavior? I am an Ephesian of good family, a Roman, and a Hippocratic as well as a woman, and the first three are at least as important as the last one. And if you consider the first three, there's no reason that I shouldn't go to Alexandria."

"I didn't say that women shouldn't practice medicine!" Athanaric said irritably. "And I certainly didn't say that you shouldn't; I can't imagine you stopping for any reason short of death. But you've managed to get yourself into trouble in four provinces already, and saying that you'll be more careful this time isn't good enough. If you go sailing into Alexandria to treat Bishop Peter, you'll probably end up accused of sedition and heresy. And knowing you, I'll bet there'll be some oaf waiting to marry you as well. You must already be the most un-married woman in the Roman Empire — Festinus, and Kyrillos, and Edico, and half the Gothic nobility, to say nothing of Sebastianus."

"No one will want to marry me now," I replied. "No one important, that is. I'm disgraced."

"Oh, is Your Grace going to change her name again?" Athanaric said sourly. "For God's sake, be sensible for once in your life! Wait and see what happens in Alexandria, and what happens here in Thrace, before you go anywhere. You're lucky to be alive at all! Next time you may not be lucky. And you could use a rest anyway, from the look of you."

I bit my lip. It was good sense, though I hated to admit it. The thought of Alexandria was so tempting, after Carragines. Though perhaps if I went back there as Charis daughter of Theodoros, I would find it completely different from what I remembered as Chariton. And most likely I wouldn't be allowed back at all. But I didn't see why Athanaric should presume to tell me what to do.

Except that he had just risked himself and his career to restore me to freedom. Considering it objectively, I admitted that that did give him some right to advise me.

"Very well," I said. "I will stay with my brother in Bithynia for a while, and see what happens." And I smiled at Athanaric, trying to apologize for my anger.

He looked away and frowned again. I couldn't understand the frowns; I remembered how easy and cheerful he used to be. Perhaps he just didn't know how to treat me as a woman. Or perhaps he felt that I had caused him more trouble than I was worth. I sighed, and we rode on in silence.

I was once again very tired by that afternoon, and exhausted by evening. If I had escaped from Carragines on my own, I thought, I wouldn't have got very far, walking across country in my present state. Thank God for horses! Ours were sturdy animals, and though we traveled some thirty-five miles that day and had galloped fifteen or twenty the day before, they were enduring well. But Athanaric was impatient because we had to proceed at a walk. Still, he judged that we should reach Novidunum during the next day.

We camped in a deserted farmhouse that night; we hadn't seen a human form all day, and Athanaric judged that it was safe. It was certainly more comfortable than the woods: though everything was in one room, there were beds, with mattresses, to lie on, and firewood stacked beside the hearth, dry enough for Athanaric to agree to light a fire. My muscles ached savagely from the riding, and I lay down as soon as we arrived, leaving the others to tend the horses and prepare the food. I feel asleep instantly.

I woke up when I felt someone watching me. I opened my eyes just a fraction, cautiously, and peered into the darkness. There was a fire burning on the hearth, and that gave enough light for me to recognize the shape of Athanaric. He was standing over my bed and looking at me; I couldn't see his face, since his back was to the fire. I didn't move. I was feeling tired and, in the tiredness, once again depressed. He had treated me with such anger, suppressed but clear. I felt ashamed, a fool for dragging him to Carragines to rescue me from what he clearly viewed as a situation of my own making.

"She's still asleep," he told Arbetio, turning away.

"Well, wake her up," said Arbetio. "She needs to eat just as much as she needs to sleep."

Athanaric turned back, put out a hand to shake me awake, then stopped, just before I worked up the energy to get up on my own. Instead he pulled my cloak over me, then touched my hair very lightly. I thought my heart would stop. "Let her sleep a little longer," he said in an unfamiliar, gentle voice.

Arbetio made a noise of disgust. "So you can look at her?"

"She's tired."

"She's tired because she's half-starved and hasn't ridden for a year. Food will make her feel better. If Your Excellency can give it to her without reminding her what a fool she's been to let herself get into this state in the first place."

"Have I been doing that?"

"Yes. She probably thinks you despise her."

"Oh Lord God! I can't help it; it's all this talk about Alexandria, and being disgraced. She's so reckless. She'll get herself killed. And I'm bound to go to Armenia."

"Why don't you just *tell* her?"

"The last thing she needs is another Goth proposing marriage. Particularly not in the middle of the journey, in the wilds of Thrace. It would certainly make it very awkward for her to turn me down."

I sat up. Athanaric jumped back in a hurry. I didn't know what to say, whether he could possibly mean what he seemed to.

"*Sacra maiestas!*" Athanaric said. "You're awake."

"I . . . I just didn't want to get up. What did you mean by that?"

"Nothing," said Athanaric. Even in the firelight I could tell that he was going red.

"But you said —"

"I don't mean anything by it. I know you don't want to hear anything about it, and you can forget I said it. We are friends, and I would have done as much for any man I valued."

"But what did you say? Arbetio, what did he say?"

Arbetio hesitated, looked at Athanaric, and then said slowly, "He meant to ask your permission to arrange a marriage with you, when you are back safely in Roman lands."

I pressed my hands together to stop them from shaking. "Did you?"

"You can forget the idea for now!" Athanaric said hurriedly. "I know you don't want to hear anything more about marriage now — maybe in a year, if you could bear to think about it . . . If you don't dislike me, that is."

I stared at him with my mouth open. "But why? You don't have to do a thing like that to protect me, you know: I can manage for myself. And I thought you wanted someone like Amalberga."

"You can manage yourself into trouble," Athanaric said, recovering himself a little. "But that has nothing to do with it. Amalberga isn't worth mentioning beside you; she's a swan, perhaps, but you're a phoenix. One of a kind, and a kind unto itself."

I closed my eyes. I couldn't bear it; I thought that like the phoenix I would be consumed by fire, a fire of delighted love.

"You don't need to say anything!" Athanaric cried, alarmed by the gesture. "I shouldn't have spoken; I wouldn't have, but I thought you were asleep. Forget it all."

"Not in a thousand years," I said firmly, and I opened my eyes and looked up at him. And that was a sight to remember a thousand years, too: his face, half turned to the fire, with the light snared in his hair, and his eyes alarmed, puzzled, unsure. "Do *you* really love *me?*" I demanded, not daring to believe it.

"Of course. Isn't it obvious? But you don't need to worry that I'll force myself on you. I know that you've heard far too much of this sort of thing already. And you told me once that there was a man you were in love with. If you still want to go looking for him, I won't try to ruin it."

I jumped up. "Oh ye gods! Athanaric, that was you! There was never anyone but you! Isn't *that* obvious?"

He gaped for a moment. Then he touched the side of my face, very hesitantly, and then kissed me. I put my arms around him. I wished I could die in that instant. Nothing in my life, I thought, will ever be this wonderful again.

Arbetio gave an embarrassed cough, and Athanaric drew back and stared at me in bemusement. I didn't let him go; I'd waited too long to let go quickly. He started to say something, but I kissed him, and his arms came round me and he forgot whatever it was he'd meant to say.

"You really mean it," he said in a surprised voice when we eventually separated.

"My life and my soul!" I said, and put my head down against his shoulder. I could feel the hardness of muscle and bone under the cloak which smelled of sweat and horses, and the ring of his arms against my back, and the beat of his heart. Hippocrates says that the body is wise. It understands, certainly, how to give happiness.

Arbetio gave another embarrassed cough and shuffled his feet. Poor man, he had nowhere to go to avoid intruding, except outside with the horses. If he hadn't been there, I suppose Athanaric and I would have dropped into bed in an instant. But it wasn't fair to Arbetio, who had, after all, risked everything to help us. I remembered a few manners, let go of Athanaric, and stood back. Then I had to sit down in a hurry: my knees were shaking, from the shock and from all the riding. Athanaric caught my hands. "Are you all right?" he asked.

"I've done too much riding," I said, "but I've never been so well in my life." And I sat there smiling at Athanaric, and he stood there holding my hands and smiling back with a stunned expression.

"You ought to have something to eat," Arbetio said, resolutely trying to impose normality. At once Athanaric helped me up and led me over to the fire. They had made a stew with some dried meat and a few onions and pot herbs that had survived in the abandoned kitchen garden. I sat there smiling stupidly while Arbetio broke another loaf of journeybread. There were no serving dishes, so we huddled about the stew pot and dipped our bread into it. Athanaric dipped his bread and sat staring at me, but now that the stew was in front of me I was ravenously hungry, and I dipped mine and ate it, though I had to keep looking at Athanaric to make sure he wasn't a dream. Arbetio looked at each of us, then laughed.

"I never would have thought it of you, Chariton," he said. "You, in love?"

I swallowed my mouthful of stew. "What's wrong with that?"

"Oh, nothing. But you always seemed so . . . professional, as though personal feelings didn't exist."

"I thought I must have been obvious. Always being sure to be in Novidunum if Athanaric was going to be there, all those invitations to dinner . . ."

"You always forgot them," Athanaric said.

I shook my head. "Not ever. But I couldn't let you guess, could I?"

"Why not?"

"Because it would have been the end of me. Exposure, disgrace, a quick trip home, and a long death sitting there with nothing to do. That's what I thought, anyway. I never thought you'd want to marry me, and I didn't think you'd agree to a clandestine affair either."

He looked even more stunned. "And you would have?"

I looked down; it had been a shameless thing to say. "You said yourself that desire is a torment."

"But . . . me? Sebastianus —"

"I like Sebastianus. But not that way."

"He's better-looking than I am, of pure Roman birth, better educated, wealthier, and cleverer. Why should you, who could have anybody, prefer me?"

"He's not cleverer. Better read, but not cleverer. And I don't know why. I thought in Egypt that you were good-looking, but it wasn't until I saw you here in Thrace that I realized that I loved you. I suppose it is because you are yourself, and Sebastianus is always a duke and a gentleman as well. He will fight for the empire and enjoy its culture, but he never looks at it from the outside. He doesn't love it. And he doesn't love virtue either; he just admires it. You are like Odysseus, who could go out onto the great sea, lose all his goods and his friends, come to the boundaries of death, and return still himself. And what do you mean, I could have anybody? Very well, Sebastianus thinks I resemble some girl a Latin poet fell for centuries ago — but his father put a stop to that nonsense pretty quickly. I must be one of the most notorious women in the empire, what with running away from home, jilting a governor, working in the army, and being offered in marriage to half a dozen different Goths. I never was more than tolerably well-born, rich, or pretty to begin with, and now I'm getting old — old for marriage, that is. I shouldn't think your father will like me any more than Count Sebastianus does."

"I expect my father will have more sense, and I don't care if he doesn't. And you're not old. You're what, twenty-eight?"

"Twenty-five," I confessed.

"No more than that? Immortal God, how old were you when you left Ephesus?"

"Seventeen. Marriageable age."

"So is twenty-five. And do you really think that people will see you as scandalous?"

"How else?"

"As a cross between Medea and your Penelope of Ithaca. And for every traditionalist who thinks you're shameless and brazen, there's another gentleman who thinks you're splendid. It's only stupid or conventional men who like stupid, conventional women. As for your 'tolerablys,' don't be ridiculous. You're of consular rank, of one of the wealthiest families in the province of Asia, and beautiful."

"Beautiful! You must be in love *and* blind. I was pretty once, but never beautiful. Daphne and Amalberga are beautiful."

"So are you."

I laughed and shook my head, pleased that he thought so. "So are you. Dearest."

His lips repeated the endearment without sound, his eyes fixed on mine.

"Well," said Arbetio. "Love is certainly a great god, to make two intelligent people look so foolish." We both glanced at him in irritation, and he grinned. "Esteemed Chariton — Charis — I advise that you finish your dinner and go to sleep. You need food and rest, and we still have a day's riding ahead of us."

The torments of desire did not keep me awake that night: I was too exhausted. I woke up feeling even happier, and even sorer, than I had the morning before. We had a very cheerful breakfast and set off. Athanaric looked as though he had not slept as well as I, but he was in high spirits, and almost at once began talking of our marriage.

"It will have to wait until we have made the arrangements with your brother," he said.

"Will it?" I said, not thinking much of this idea. In fact I felt happier about loving Athanaric than I did about marrying him, but I suspected that he would insist on everything's being respectable until we were married. It's one thing to consummate a passion, and quite another to consummate a marriage, with all that that entails in financial arrangements and legal settlements. Legal subordination, too. A married woman has more freedom than an unmarried girl in many ways, but she is required to obey her husband. I thought I could trust Athanaric not to abuse his power, but even so, the idea frightened me.

"It needs to be official, well testified, and respectable," Athanaric declared firmly. "After starting off as unconventionally as this, we need all the legality we can get."

"Damn respectability."

" 'Rumoresque senum severiorum, Omnes unius aestimemus assis! Da mi basia mille!' "

"Damn respectability, and give you a thousand kisses? Gladly. What's that?"

"Sebastianus' favorite. Catullus."

"Perhaps I should read Latin poetry after all."

"Ah, but in the end she lost respectability and he lost her. We need to be official. I don't want anyone questioning it afterward, not even my own father, if he does decide to be an idiot. Besides, you'll need your dowry in full if you want to found a hospital."

My fear vanished. I would have control of my dowry, and he was the one who had suggested founding a hospital with it in the first place. I laughed, trying to picture a hospital of my own. "Very well."

"We will have a thoroughly respectable wedding, blessed in a church, with none of this pagan business of carting the bride off like a captive. We will go up to the altar, very solemn, and swear in the name of the most sacred and glorious Trinity, and of Divine Healing, and of St. Hippocrates, to love one another forever, and then I will have to swear the oath of Hippocrates."

"And why will you have to swear that?"

"So as not to be outdone by you. How does it go? 'I will use my art to heal and not to harm, I will be chaste . . .' "

"I hope not excessively so."

"No fear of that. Then we will go home. I will get a permanent position somewhere, with a fixed base, and you will have your hospital. We will have a big house, and both leave it every morning for work."

"We will make my Maia the housekeeper," I said, beginning to look forward to it.

"Your Maia? You have an old nursemaid somewhere?"

"She's housekeeping for my brother and his concubine at the moment. But I was the one she nursed; it cut her to the heart to see me run off, though she helped me do it. Festinus had her tortured when my father was accused of treason; I suppose she's the real reason I did run away. But what she's always wanted is to manage my house for me and play grandmother to my children. She'll be enchanted to see me respectable again." I tried to picture her excitement, and her inevitable boasting about Athanaric's title, mutilating the Latin words as she always did. Would she and Athanaric get on? Yes; they would want to, and there was no reason they shouldn't.

Athanaric laughed. "We will have children!" he exclaimed enthusiastically. "The boys can go into the civil service, and the girls can learn medicine from their mother."

"What if the boys want to learn medicine?"

"I suppose I might allow it."

"What if the girls want to go into the civil service?"

"I will tell them to cut their hair and pretend to be eunuchs, but not to expect any bribes from me."

I laughed. "And where will we go, to raise a family like that?"

"Armenia? Alexandria? Ephesus? Rome? We have the whole empire waiting for us." He swept an arm east and south and west, as though he were brushing away the wild and deserted land of Thrace and promising the great bright glittering world. I laughed again, for sheer joy, and Athanaric and Arbetio both laughed too. We do have the world, I thought, we do have the whole world to choose from.

We reached Novidunum late that afternoon.

I was once again very tired, and the sky was darkening for a storm. The countryside around us was still and deserted: flat green and yellow grasses, unsown fields and empty houses, the song of cicadas in the hot, thick air. But in the northeast the thunderclouds were already black. Then Arbetio reined his horse in and pointed, and there in the distance rose the walls of Novidunum, the bluff towering over the flat country, outlined against the darkening sky. Despite my exhaustion I gave a shout of happiness, and we kicked our tired horses into a trot.

"With luck," said Arbetio, "we'll be indoors when the storm breaks."

Since early afternoon we had been traveling along the main road north; the countryside around it was flat and open, so we didn't have to fear an ambush. Now for the first time since we left Carragines we saw cows and horses grazing in the fields, and houses that looked inhabited; their owners could shelter safely in the fortress if the Goths attacked.

"Are there many men in Novidunum?" I asked.

"Plenty," said Arbetio. "We've been made the main convalescent hospital for the whole of Thrace."

"And you went absent without leave?"

He grinned and shrugged. "I have plenty of assistants. And it was your fault we were chosen — we had the best record of recoveries. At any rate, the fortress is full, though mostly with convalescents, and Valerius is still in charge of it. When the injured are well enough to hold a spear, though not to travel, they're supposed to guard the walls and prevent any more barbarians from crossing the river." The smile disappeared, and he went on quietly but grimly. "What they'd do if another barbarian horde actually appeared, I don't know. They certainly couldn't stop it. But I think all the barbarians are down in the south, killing our people."

There was a rumble of thunder far away over the delta. The horses' hooves clattered on the road. A man and a woman ran from a house nearby and started driving their cows into their shed. They glanced at us curiously, fearfully, but when we didn't stop went on with their business. We urged our horses more quickly toward shelter.

When we were just near enough to see figures on those towering walls, Athanaric turned his horse off the road, over to an apple tree in an orchard. He cut off some green branches and handed one to each of us. "So they understand at the fort that we're peaceful," he said. "We don't want to end up killed by our own people."

So, holding my green branch high in token of peace, I rode back to the fortress I had left so carelessly a year and a half before. The figures on the wall pointed and shouted but didn't throw anything, and we rode together up to the locked gates.

The guards stood on the watchtower, shields raised and spears at the ready, and one of them asked us loudly to give the password.

"We don't know it," Athanaric said clearly, holding his hands well away from his sword. "We are escaping from the Goths at Carragines. I am Athanaricus of Sardica, *curiosus* of the *agentes in rebus*."

He held up his license on its chain. "This is Arbetio, the chief physician of this fortress. And this is the lady Charis, daughter of Theodoros of Ephesus."

They had all stared at, and recognized, Arbetio, but as soon as Athanaric named me all attention switched to me. There were muttered exclamations, then a ragged cheer. Someone ran to open the gate; the great ironbound doors swung open, and we rode through into the fort. A gust of wind caught at the doors as the guards closed them behind us, and the first drops of rain splashed fat and heavy against the secure protection of the walls. And a long farewell to you, Thrace, I thought to myself. From here I go down the river by boat and so out into the Euxine, where there are no barbarians.

The soldiers of the fort crowded round. I could see now that they were indeed convalescents, limping or gaunt with illness, with arms in slings, their chests or heads or thighs bandaged. But they were grinning and shouting joyfully. I recognized one or two faces from my time at the camp, but most were strangers — men from other legions, from other provinces, brought here by injury or disease. But they had evidently heard of me. "Charis of Ephesus!" they shouted. "Snatched from the Goths!" "*That* for Fritigern!" one shouted, making an obscene gesture; his neighbor cuffed him: "Mind the lady!" Several of them caught my horse's bridle, and I quickly slid off and pulled my skirts down. No use displaying my ruined legs to the entire fort. The men crowded round me, grinning, and I felt a bit dizzy; my legs were trembling with fatigue. I hung on to my horse's saddle and smiled feebly back. Athanaric rode his horse into the crowd around me; I was vaguely aware of Arbetio arguing with a man about a sling and pulling it off to look at an arm.

"Stand back!" Athanaric shouted. "The lady needs some rest. Let her go to her own house — out of the way, you!"

They milled about a bit, uncertainly, and then someone shouted, "Attention! Fall in!" and they snapped into line like a bent branch snapping straight again. The tribune Valerius hurried through them. His eyes, skimming the crowd, missed me and fixed on Athanaric. "Most excellent Athanaric!" he shouted eagerly. "Do you have news? Has the emperor been found? Are our people safe? Is Duke Sebastianus still alive?"

Athanaric looked at him blankly. "I came here on a private mission. What do you mean, has the emperor been found?"

Valerius stopped, looking at him in confusion. A gust of wind pulled at his scarlet cloak, fluttered the crests of the soldiers' helmets, splattered a few more drops of rain. "Haven't you heard?" he asked.

"Heard what?" Athanaric asked; then, more urgently: "What has happened?"

"The barbarians have won a great victory at Hadrianopolis," Valerius said slowly, the hope going out of his eyes. "And the emperor is missing, probably dead, and most of the army with him, and the rest under siege in Hadrianopolis. I hoped that you were bringing better news."

Athanaric gave a wordless cry of pain and horror. My battered legs refused to support me any longer, and crumpled; I sat down on the bare ground, feeling sick and faint, and bent over, holding my head. Athanaric jumped off his horse; the soldiers broke ranks and crowded round, but he shoved them aside. I lifted my head just as he knelt beside me. "I'm all right," I told him. "It's just my legs, with the riding."

Valerius appeared in front of me and stared down at me in astonishment. "Chariton!" he exclaimed. "How on earth —"

"Athanaric and Arbetio rescued me from the Goths," I said.

"Arbetio? He went missing; I thought he'd deserted."

"No. He was just busy saving Roman maidens from barbarians. Well, saving one Roman maiden, anyway. He has earned my gratitude, and I am sure that of my brother Theodoros the governor and my friend Duke Sebastianus as well. I trust Your Carefulness will overlook a week's absence without leave. Your Honor, I am very tired. With your permission, I will go to my house and rest."

Valerius gaped at me, then backed off, nodding helplessly.

Athanaric helped me to my feet and I hobbled off, clutching his arm. Arbetio broke off from his patient and followed us. I presume somebody else saw to the horses, because none of us did. There was a violent crack of lightning, and it began to rain.

By the time we reached my house news of our arrival had spread through the camp, and half the inhabitants were following us, even through the downpour. I was very glad to reach the house. It was the new house that I had bought just before my capture, and the entire household was waiting outside the door for us: my slaves, Raedagunda and Sueridus, Gudrun holding the baby (a big baby now) and Alaric (also bigger than when I left), and a small, plump, fair woman who wore the keys at her belt. I'd only met her a few times, but I recognized Arbetio's wife. She hugged her husband, let us all in, and closed the door behind us. I sat down on the bench beside the door and leaned back against the wall. The water ran from my hair down my face into my eyes, so I closed my eyes. In the darkness behind the lids I saw the unknown country around Hadrianopolis, and the dragons and eagles of the standards falling, and the imperial purple stained with blood. I opened my eyes. Arbetio's wife was standing in front of me, looking worried.

I tried to smile. "Very many greetings, Irene. It's good to be home."

She bowed. "Yes, Your Kindness. Is Your Wisdom . . . well?"

"I am very tired. You must have rearranged the rooms since I left; can you tell me which one I could use? I must rest."

"We prepared your own room for Your Grace. I hope Your Kindness doesn't mind that we used it ourselves for a while, only we didn't want it to stand empty, and —"

"I am greatly in your debt for your care for my property in my absence." I picked myself up and stood dripping onto the stone-flagged kitchen floor. Athanaric stood watching me, very pale. "Dearest," I said, "please be my guest here tonight. Don't go up to the presidium yet."

He shook his head. "I must hear the news. And I should stay in the presidium; it wouldn't be proper to stay here."

I sighed and looked at the floor. "Come back here for dinner then."

"I will do that." He pulled the end of his cloak over his head and walked back out into the rain. I stared after him, biting my lip, then stumbled off to bed.

I fell asleep with the thunder rumbling about the eaves, and woke up to hear only the rain, beating down steadily and hissing in the thatch. It was quite dark now, and I lay motionless, staring into the blackness. I'd pulled my wet cloak and tunic off before collapsing; the sheets were smooth against my skin. The emperor was missing, presumed dead. His Sacred Majesty, our Lord Valens the Augustus, master of the world, dead, fighting the Goths. I had hated many of his servants and favorites, hated some of his policies; I had thought that I hated him. But I felt only pain in response to his death. The man didn't matter: he was emperor, he had worn the sacred purple and ruled the world I lived in, and his death left the state blind and headless.

He wasn't the first emperor to die fighting the barbarians, even in my own lifetime, though he was the first in my memory. Julian had been killed in the middle of his campaign against the Persians, when I was a little girl. But he hadn't left a whole Roman diocese overrun by barbarian hordes, and an army either slaughtered or scattered about the provinces. Of course there remained the western Augustus, Gratianus, even now on his way with the Gaulish legions; and there were other troops in the East — on the Persian frontier, in Egypt and Palestine. It was unlikely that the barbarians would conquer more than just Thrace. Though they might invade more. Constantinople, the radiant queen of the Bosphorus, richest city in the East, lay in the extreme southeast of the diocese. Whether the barbarians could take it was uncertain, but it was certain that they would try.

The war would go on, probably for years. And it would not be confined to Thrace; other provinces would suffer too. We couldn't leave it behind.

I sighed again and sat up, realizing that I did not know where the lamp was. "Raedagunda!" I called, pulling up the sheets.

She came in a moment, carrying a lamp. "Yes, master?" she said, smiling nervously. Then, still more nervously, and not smiling: "Mistress."

I smiled at that. "Don't worry about the title," I told her. "How long have I been asleep?"

"Only a couple of hours."

"Is the most noble Athanaric back from the presidium yet?"

"No, not yet. I heard you invite him to dinner; I've been preparing something, but he hasn't arrived yet. But I've also put some water on to heat for a bath, if you'd like one."

"Bless you," I said fervently. I held the sheets against me and looked around. "Where are my clothes?"

She put down the lamp and went over to the clothes chest in the corner. "I took the wet ones away to wash," she said apologetically. "But Mistress Irene and I fixed some long tunics for you to wear. We couldn't buy new ones because we weren't to tell anyone that you were coming, but Mistress Irene said that you would need something and these would do." She took out two long tunics, which must have been altered from Irene's own: they had a border stitched around the bottom to make up about two hands' width of difference in height.

"That was very kind of Mistress Irene," I said, touched by it. I had come to turn her out of her house after risking her husband's life for her, and she had busied herself making clothes for me. "Where is she?"

"She and the master — that is, she and Arbetio have gone back to the old house, since that's theirs, and you're home now."

"Have they? I suppose I had better invite them to dinner as well."

Athanaric plainly wanted the dinner to be respectable. "Send Sueridus over to invite them — and thank Irene for the tunics."

Raedagunda hesitated. "We usually send Alaric with messages."

"Well, send him then. Is the bath ready?"

"I'll get it ready for you now." She started out; I called her back and told her to light the lamp in the room. She did that, then hesitated, clutching her own lamp nervously. "Welcome home, master," she said.

I smiled wearily. "Thank you, Raedagunda. But you must know that I'm not going to stay here."

She nodded, speechless with tension; it was, of course, the point of her unease. I was plainly not going to remain an army physician, so I would leave, and my slaves would be sold.

"I intend to free all of my household when I go," I told her. "You and the others must think about what you mean to do with your freedom, and I will try to help you arrange it. I meant to send Gudrun and Alaric back to their families, but I intend to stay as far away from the Theruingi as I can now, and they will have to think of something else to do with themselves until the war is over."

Raedagunda stared, then beamed, then knelt and kissed my hand. "Oh, thank you, sir!"

" 'My lady,' " I corrected her, smiling. "So, think about it. And do fix that bath; I've had three days' hard riding and I ache all over."

When I went through the kitchen to reach the bath, wearing only a cloak and holding that closed with one hand, my slaves were all standing about laughing and talking eagerly. They rushed over at once to kiss my hand, even the boy Alaric. "You'll really set us all free?" Sueridus demanded, aflame with excitement. I nodded, and he immediately went on. "Most noble and generous master! Could I borrow some money from you? Valentinus at the stables wants to start a stud farm, and if I had twenty *solidi* I could buy a couple of brood mares. Then I could work for him, for a salary, and sell the mares' foals, and it would make a lot of money; we'd pay you back within ten years, I'm sure!"

I laughed. "Very well. Twenty *solidi* for you to spend on horses. And Raedagunda, I'll give you seven, to set yourselves up in a house. Gudrun, do you know what you want to do with your freedom?"

She blushed. She had changed too in my absence, grown and filled out. I realized with a shock that she was as old as I had been when it had been arranged for me to marry Festinus. When she spoke, it was in good Greek. "If you please, sir — my lady, I mean — I'd like to stay here in Novidunum until there is peace. Mistress Irene has said that she will pay me wages, as a servant, to stay on with her. But I don't mind the wages. I'd like to learn how to be a midwife, if Arbetio will teach me. I like babies, and I like healing. And Alaric will stay with me, at least for now."

I couldn't believe it for a moment, and then I smiled. "Of course. I'll ask Arbetio on your behalf tomorrow. And I will give you ten *solidi* as well, to use as your dowry or for whatever end you choose."

"You paid less than that for me in the first place!" said Gudrun, blinking.

"But I would pay more, for another woman to study medicine. Now let me go take my bath."

When Athanaric arrived I was back in my room, looking through my books. I had missed them as much as I had missed any of the people in Novidunum — my well-worn texts of Hippocrates; the good, clear Alexandrian editions of Herophilos and Erasistratos, their papyrus page edges soft from use; and my beautiful parchment codex of Galen. Edico still had my Dioskourides, damn him, but I supposed I could buy another copy; it's a standard work.

I was leafing through the Galen when I heard Athanaric's knock on the house door. I stopped worrying about the function of the gall bladder at once and wished I had a mirror. I had put on the finer of the two tunics and my best cloak, stupidly wanting to look beautiful for Athanaric. I'd given my disease-thinned hair a rinse of cedar and rosemary and tied it up with a pearl-studded gold rope that had been my mother's. I'd never needed to sell that particular piece, and it went well with the pearl earrings Amalberga had given me. I suspected, though, that the jewels only made me look thinner and sicker. Well, too late to take them off now. Raedagunda knocked on my bedroom door and announced "the most excellent Athanaric"; I thanked her and came out.

This house had quite a pleasant dining room, small but attractive, with a red-and-white tiled floor and red curtains. During the day it was well lit by a large window onto the garden, and at night the opposite wall held a rack of lamps. Athanaric was standing with his back to the lamps, looking out the window at the rain, but he turned when I came in.

"Oh!" he said. "You managed to get another gown. I wondered what you'd do about that."

So much for my beauty. "Arbetio's wife altered two of hers for me. She and her husband should be here soon; I invited them."

Gudrun, who was setting up the wine bowl under the lamp rack, immediately shook her head. "No, my lady: Alaric says that the master said that he wants to stay home with his wife tonight. He invites you to dinner with them tomorrow."

"Oh," I said in turn, and looked at Athanaric. I silently prayed that Arbetio and Irene would have all the joy and prosperity their tact, kindness, consideration, and generosity so richly deserved. An evening alone with Athanaric, a chance to talk, with the respectable excuse that an invited guest had not showed up.

Athanaric smiled faintly. He looked tired, and had obviously come straight from talking to Valerius, without taking time to bathe or change into clean clothes. "By 'the master' you mean Arbetio?" he asked Gudrun.

She blushed. "Excuse me, my lady," she said humbly.

"Never mind," I told her. "Do we have any honeyed white wine? Good. Athanaric, please sit down and try to relax."

Athanaric reclined on one of the couches in the room, and I reclined on the other, with the table between us. Gudrun brought us the white wine and some white cumin-seed rolls. "So," I said, "how bad is the news?"

He stared blindly past me for a moment. "About as bad as it can be," he said at last. "They say that two-thirds of the army was wiped out, that the emperor is presumed dead, and that many of the chief generals are certainly dead. Sebastianus' father is, and Trajanus, Valerianus, Aequitius the master of the palace, Barzimeres, and dozens of the tribunes. It is the worst defeat in the history of the empire. And it seems that up to the last minute Fritigern was still suing for peace and offering to break with his allies and fight against them if the emperor would grant him a client state in Thrace. There never was such a stupid, ruinous, and unnecessary war."

"What about our Sebastianus?" I asked after a minute.

"Nobody knows. His name wasn't included among the dead. But he would have been fighting beside his father. It may have been an oversight."

I sat clutching my hands together, trying to understand what it meant. I had known all along, of course, that it was possible that the Romans might be defeated. But I would have reckoned defeat to be another drawn battle, or perhaps a forced retreat. Not a wholesale slaughter.

Athanaric sighed and began to rub the back of his neck, as though his head hurt. "They say that the western Augustus, Gratianus, has already been informed of the disaster. He's sending letters to the troops in Syria, to the duke of the East and the duke of Egypt, trying to collect more men. And he's appointing a new master of arms, who'll probably end up as his colleague and eastern Augustus — Sebastianus' friend Theodosius the younger. He's Gratianus' age, and it seems they're friends, despite what happened to Theodosius' father. It wouldn't be a bad choice. Theodosius is a very strong and energetic general, and did very well against the Sarmatians when he was duke of Dacian Moesia. He may be able to stop the flood from overwhelming the state."

I remembered the ruinous oracle and shivered. "So 'THEOD—' will succeed Valens after all."

Athanaric stopped rubbing his neck and smiled bitterly. "So he will. And it seems that the plain to the south of Hadrianopolis is called Mimas' Plain, after some ancient hero who was buried there. The demons tell the truth sometimes, though not to help us. Charis, it's the end of us. I don't think the empire will ever completely recover from this blow."

"You're tired," I told him. "And it is dark, and raining, and your cloak is wet. The empire is a very great thing, and it takes more than one defeat, even one like Hadrianopolis, to destroy it. Drink your wine, my dearest, and rest. You'll feel better tomorrow. The enemy still don't know anything about siegecraft." That was one of Fritigern's favorite themes; he was always advising his colleagues against "throwing away our lives on stone walls."

"That's true," said Athanaric, but he didn't look any more hopeful. "And they're laying siege to Hadrianopolis now. That will get a few of them killed. It may delay the ruin. But it won't stop it."

We were both silent for a few minutes. Gudrun brought in the first course, leeks in wine sauce.

"You're tired tonight," I repeated. "You'll feel better in the morning."

He drank some wine, looking at me as he did so. "Sitting here with you I can almost believe that. And yet — the empire is too large. I've seen more of it than most. I've been west as far as Mediolanum, and east as far as Amida, and south into Egypt. Everywhere there's trouble: barbarians in the north, Persians in the east, in the south the Saracens and the Africans. And we don't have the strength to keep them out. Too many lands are deserted, and the church quarrels with the state; bureaucrats and governors line their own pockets, often to the ruin of the public good, and the men who are distant from the frontiers despise the soldiers who protect them. It has started to crumble. It won't fall quickly — it may even last longer than our own lives — but fall it will, and we will see it go. 'Desinas ineptire, et quod vides perisse, perditum ducas. Fulsere quondam candidi tibi soles . . .' " He stopped, looking at me longingly.

Stop playing the fool — I translated to myself — and what you've seen die, call dead. Bright suns shone on you once . . . Some Latin poets *did* write odd verses.

And now Athanaric was going on. " 'Nobis cum semel occidit brevis lux, nox est perpetua una dormienda.' 'Once the brief light has gone for us, we sleep for one eternal night.' "

I stirred. "Athanasios told me that nothing human lasts forever, not even the empire. But he said that when what is human has worn away, the eternal remains, and that human life is shot through with eternity."

"When did he say that?"

"It was in Carragines. When I was sick. Maybe it was a dream. But however I heard it, I think it is true. Even if the empire is ending now, something of what was best in it may survive. And it may not be the end yet. The most desperate cases sometimes recover, and survive for many years more."

"But you think it is old, and likely to die soon."

I looked down at my wine cup, then looked up at him again. He was watching me intently. "Death is sad," I said. "Even the death of an animal. And we're talking about a great empire. But it may yet live, and even if it doesn't, all things on earth must die, and we must resign ourselves to it and make the best of life while we have it."

Gudrun came in, took away the almost untouched first course, and brought in the second one: wild boar in pepper sauce.

"What do we do now?" I asked as we started eating.

He shrugged. "The same, I suppose. We go to Bithynia. We make the arrangements for the wedding, in a hurry, and we decide where we want to live. I will have to leave you there, though; I will have work to do. I can't abandon my duties in an emergency like this. The court will be short of couriers, and we must not lose contact with the West. You can go off to wherever we decide on and start founding your hospital."

I knew, and understood, but I would not agree. Not to being left unmarried in my brother's house, that is. "Athanaric," I said earnestly, "don't go back to the presidium tonight."

He looked at me, his eyes wonderfully deep in the lamplight, his mouth slightly open. He knew what I meant. "We need to be official," he said uncertainly.

"I need you," I replied. "And I don't want to marry anyone else, or have anyone ask me stupid and insulting questions about whether I'm a virgin and his for the taking. The law on marriage isn't that formal; we are married if we live together. And my brother won't try to cheat me out of my dowry."

"Live together? We're not either of us living anywhere at the moment. Halcyons skimming the waves before the storm, that's what we are. You can't establish a contract on the strength of that." But he kept watching me, intensely, hungrily.

"Then establish the contract when we get to Bithynia. I promise you, Thorion won't make trouble — at least, not after I've talked to him. But you must settle with me before you go anywhere else."

He stood up suddenly, and came round the table to sit on the couch beside me. "You're right," he said, and kissed me.

We did in fact finish the meal, but largely because I insisted that we both needed the food. Then I called my slaves together and told them that Athanaric was my husband and was staying the night. They cheered and congratulated us — they were half-drunk anyway, celebrating their impending freedom, and were past being surprised at anything their eccentric owner chose to do.

Then we went to bed. Love is the sweetest of all things, as the poets say: sweet enough to make honey seem bitter in comparison; sweet enough to wipe out the image of Romans dying on the battlefield and the imperial purple crumpled in blood. I had always praised the body's wisdom, but I felt now that I had never understood it or appreciated its mystery, which can make a simple act become somehow an image of eternity.

And when we had finished we lay very quietly in each other's arms, listening to the rain hissing in the thatch. "What did you say we were?" I asked Athanaric, after a long while of complete contentment. "Halcyons?"

"Because they lay their eggs on the surface of the sea, in the calm of the midwinter solstice. All around them is the storm, and they breed in peace."

"Yes." I kissed him.

"But I love the empire," he said, the note of raw pain coming back into his voice.

"I know. You love it as much as I love medicine. But it isn't finished yet, my dearest; it won't sink easily. Only leave the storms until tomorrow: tonight is the solstice, and the winter calm."

He kissed me again. Outside the rain beat against the thatch, and away over the river came the distant rumble of the thunder.

EPILOGUE

O F COURSE the Roman Empire did not fall immediately after the Battle of Hadrianopolis (or Adrianople, as it is sometimes called) in A.D. 378. Indeed, the Eastern Empire continued for another millennium. The emperor Theodosius "the Great," who was proclaimed Augustus in January 379, agreed in October 382, after years of bitter fighting, to assign the Visigoths a client state in Thrace. The Huns and Halani were pushed back outside the empire — for the time being.

Theodosius was an adherent of the Nicene theology, and Arianism was branded as a heresy by the bishops of East and West alike. Unfortunately, the Goths had been converted during the period of Arian dominance. (Ulfila, "The Apostle of the Goths," was a friend of Fritigern; I wanted to introduce him into this book, but there really wasn't space.) That the Goths were heretics as well as barbarians did not help their peaceful inclusion in Roman society; moreover, they and the region were still plagued with severe shortages of food. After the death of Theodosius in 395 the Visigoths were on the move again, invading and devastating Greece before migrating to Italy; they were the ones who sacked Rome in 410. But it was left to their cousins, the Ostrogoths, to give the death blow to the Western Empire after the deposition of the last western emperor in 476.

Although the Eastern Empire was spared invasion, the prolonged wars were a devastating drain on its resources and must have exacerbated its already formidable political and economic difficulties. It too suffered a decline; trade dropped, lands were lost, and cultural horizons closed in. The Byzantine civilization that eventually emerged was something different from its late Roman parent: narrower, more intolerant, and less flexible.

Much of the intolerance of a desperate society was canalized by the Christian church. In the century following the Battle of Hadrianopolis, pagan worship was banned, and fierce edicts were published against heretics; the civil rights of minorities such as the Jews became increasingly circumscribed. In 391, for example, Theophilos, archbishop of Alexandria ("a bold, bad man," according to Gibbon, "whose hands were alternately polluted with gold and with blood"), managed after a period of riot and siege to destroy and dismantle the Temple of Serapis; what happened to the remnants of the great library there is unknown. Medicine in the West fell steadily into a horrific state of superstitious brutality, and it may be said that it was not until well into the Renaissance, and perhaps even the eighteenth century, that it recovered the ground it lost at the Fall of Rome. The same might be said of a lot of other things — science, trade, even population. The Dark Ages were not as pitch-black as Gibbon paints them, and Byzantium and medieval Europe certainly had their splendors, but students of the period can still feel that the Fall of Rome was, for the West anyway, "the greatest, perhaps, and most awful scene in the history of mankind."